THE MANUAL OF
DARKNESS

Enrique de Hériz was born in Barcelona in 1964. He has worked as an editor and translator, including translations to Spanish of the work of Annie Proulx, Nadine Gordimer, Stephen King, Peter Carey, and John Fowles. His first novel, *Lies*, won the Llibreter prize in Spain.

Also by Enrique de Hériz
Lies

THE MANUAL OF
DARKNESS

Enrique de Hériz

Translated from the Spanish by Frank Wynne

Weidenfeld & Nicolson
LONDON

First published in Great Britain in 2011
by Weidenfeld & Nicolson
An imprint of the Orion Publishing Group Ltd
Orion House, 5 Upper St Martin's Lane
London WC2H 9EA

An Hachette UK Company

First published in Spain as *Manual de la oscuridad* in 2009

1 3 5 7 9 8 6 4 2

This work has been published with a subsidy from
the Directorate General of Books, Archives and
Libraries of the Spanish Ministry of Culture.

A CIP catalogue for this book
is available from the British Library.

ISBN 978 0 297 86052 5 (cased)
ISBN 978 0 297 86053 2 (trade paperback)

Typeset by Input Data Services Ltd, Bridgwater, Somerset

Printed and bound in Great Britain
by Clays Ltd, St Ives plc

www.orionbooks.co.uk

To Pere, up and down

'We must conclude that man is this: someone who looks upon things and knows the names of them.'

Carmen Gándara, from the story 'The Ball of Paper'

'It is just in this way that otherwise sensible people allow their senses to be deceived, and their imaginations preyed upon'

Harry Kellar, in *A Magician's Tour*

'These grosser physical manifestations can be but the mere ooze and scum cast up by the waves on the idle pebble, the waters of a heaven-lit sea, if it exist, must lie far out beyond.'

Horace Howard Furness 'Preliminary report of the Seybert Commission for Investigating Modern Spiritualism', University of Pennsylvania, 1887

part
one

The Green Door

There are only a few steps between him and the green door – eleven, twelve, maybe. It is too dark to count them. Víctor Losa stops, takes a deep breath; this, he thinks, is the happiest moment of his life. He did not feel like this a week ago in Lisbon when he was named World's Best Magician at the FISM World Championship. Nor will he still feel this way a moment from now when he reaches the landing, opens the green door and steps into the room to receive an ovation from the professional magicians of Barcelona, gathered at the behest of his former teacher Mario Galván to pay tribute to him. He knows that this is a haven, a hiatus in life, a vantage point offered to him by time.

He does not want to jump for joy, to rush up the stairs and revel in the applause that awaits him. No, he wants to stay here, to float, to hover above this moment. He has his reasons, for this is where it all began. It was here, twenty-two years ago, after his first lesson with Galván, that he overheard the curious prediction from the master's lips: 'That little wretch is going to be one hell of a magician.' He was standing on these stairs, who knows, perhaps on this very step, petrified, listening to the voice behind the door, muttering words the maestro could not have known he might overhear. So it is hardly surprising that Víctor should want to stop here, halfway up the stairs, to relive that moment when he heard the maestro make his prediction through gritted teeth, and revel in the long series of triumphs that have led from that moment to this.

As he is about to climb the last remaining steps, Víctor looks up and gets the fright of his life: the green door has vanished. It is still there, of course, it has to be; but he cannot see it. Instead he sees a milky stain, a whitish halo as though he were looking at the

3

world through a veil. He takes off his glasses, rubs his eyes. When he looks again, the door is there in front of him, scruffy, the paint peeling, just as it has always been. Things disappear and reappear in unexpected ways. No one knows that more than he does.

It was an optical illusion, one he can easily put down to lack of sleep, due to some rather extravagant celebrating of late. Besides, it lasted only a second or two. It can't be anything serious; it cannot account for the fear that suddenly grips Víctor, rooting him to this spot as though the air on which only a moment before he felt he could float has suddenly turned to cement.

By rights, he should feel exhilarated. He should take the stairs two at a time, fling the door open wide, stride into the room, throw his arms around Mario Galván and hug him hard. This, after all, is the moment they have both been waiting for, the moment they both – though they never dared say as much – feared might never come. Or might come too late; too late for Galván, who must be over eighty by now. Víctor has never known precisely how old the maestro is, but he was already an old man when they first met. And he has been ill for a long time.

What is stopping him? Not fear of what awaits him. He only has to perform one trick. He has been performing on bigger and more daunting stages than this for years, often before audiences who were much less receptive. He no longer remembers all the countries he has visited, the television studios where he was hailed as the star of the moment – a moment that has now lasted long enough to warrant another name – the festivals at which fellow magicians jostled to be in the front row so they could watch his work close up. So what exactly is this fear? Stage fright? The fear that some pathetic cliché is about to come true, that having reached this dizzy height, it will be all downhill from now on? Rubbish.

It is something else. A sense of foreboding. He wishes he could bring time to a standstill, he concentrates on this thought, like someone who has cut themselves staring at the wound as if to cauterise it before the blood wells up.

He reaches out his left hand and places his palm against the wall to steady himself. He will soon learn that this is not how it should be done, not with the palm of the hand. Soon, someone will teach him that the best way is to brush things with the back of the hand. Soon? That's just a word. At this moment, the future is beyond reach, as unattainable as the stair he cannot climb. Or maybe does not want to climb, since he seems to be making no attempt to do so. It should be easy. This is a man who has made bodies levitate onstage. Come on, Víctor. It's only one step. Grab hold of the banister and push. Give me a place to stand, and I will move the whole world.

Take one step. *Hup!* Then another. Then the rest of the stairs, two at a time: eleven or twelve of them; it is dim, there is barely any light, but Víctor is no fool, he knows that now that he has reached the top, he must penetrate his lowest, darkest self. Magic? He strides across the landing, reaches out and grasps the handle. In the moment before he opens the door, he can hear the excited murmur of the crowd. On this side of the green door is the past, so many memories that they are forced to huddle together simply to carve out a small space for the present, even if that means blending into it. That little wretch is going to be one hell of a magician. That little wretch. That ... On the far side of the door, he imagines, is the future; a cavernous room he would like to imagine is empty, almost dark, with just a faint glimmer of light from a small window at the far end of the hall. That is how he remembers it. But he knows there are ninety-two people inside now, Galván's daughter phoned this morning to tell him. Ninety-two: seventy-four seated, the rest standing, some leaning against the walls, some crowding the aisle, who step aside now to let him pass. Víctor glances around him in astonishment at the winks, the whistles, the thunderous stamping of feet, the slaps on the back, urged on by hands warm from clapping so hard. He reaches the small platform that serves as a stage, steps up and melts into Mario Galván's arms; Mario, who is standing, waiting as though he never left, as though through all the years that have passed since he uttered his prediction, his curse, he has been standing here, rooted to the spot, waiting for the moment when he might see his prediction come to pass. This moment.

Víctor's arms squeeze Galván tighter and tighter, as though he is his salvation, the one thing that might prevent him from falling. The maestro is astonished. He finds it hard to believe that Víctor could be nervous or afraid, but he cannot think of any other reason for his behaviour, for Víctor's convulsive hug, for the rigid tension of his body, which slackens only at the neck as Víctor presses his face into Galván's shoulder and, not relaxing his pincer grip even for a moment, bursts into tears. He could snap Galván in two. Galván is tall and thin. He is eighty years old or more. He smiles, strokes Víctor's back. Up and down, with one hand. Twice, three times, four times. With his other hand he pats him on the shoulder. It's OK, he says, it's OK.

The master leads the student to one of the two chairs and sits him down. It is as though their ages have been reversed. Galván stands and turns to the audience. Only now does the applause fade, as though those present had made the most of Víctor's lateness to rehearse their part in this tribute.

Mario Galván declares that this is a day not for speeches but for celebration. He promises to be brief and he keeps his promise. He finds precisely the right words to retell the story everyone in the room already knows yet wants to hear again: how when he first set eyes on Víctor, he knew this happy day would come; how his intuition was rewarded by the unstinting efforts of the best student it had ever been his pleasure to teach. He apologises, knowing that some of his other students are present, and insists that he follows their careers with pride and admiration, too. 'But,' he concludes, 'this is not my opinion. It is that of the FISM, the International Federation of Magic Societies, which last week officially declared something I have always taken for granted: that Víctor, Víctor Losa, is the finest magician in the world. I give you Víctor Losa.'

There is another ovation, briefer but no less fervent than the first. This one is clearly for Galván, not so much for his speech but to acknowledge his part in the achievements of his student. This, at least, is clearly what Víctor thinks, because he throws out his hand, gesturing to the maestro, and joins in the applause. Galván thanks everyone with a shy nod and goes to leave the stage.

'Wait, Mario,' Víctor says. 'Could you blindfold me, please?'

He takes a black scarf from his pocket and hands it to Galván, who blindfolds him, tying the scarf in a knot at the nape of his neck. The maestro then leaves the stage and takes the only empty seat in the audience.

Víctor allows the silence to hang in the air for a few seconds longer than expected. It is not a calculated move, but an instinctive understanding of drama, of magic as theatre, a skill he incorporated into his act from the beginning. He knows from experience that at this moment, any word, any movement on his part, even a slight wave of his hand, takes on great significance.

'Unaccustomed as I am to public speaking,' he says eventually. Scattered laughter. All those present know that Víctor's success has been based on his way with words, but only the few who know him well know that his reticence in public is genuine. 'I would like to thank Mario Galván. If only for pointing out to me the difference between a pianist and a typist. You know what I mean, Mario.'

Over the past few days, he has thought long and hard about this moment. If it were up to him, he would skip the performance, thank everyone for coming and suggest someone open the bottles of champagne that are sitting at the back of the room on a folding table that looks suspiciously like the one at which he had his first lesson in magic. But many of those present were not in Lisbon and missed the grand final. Víctor, they have heard, won with a single trick. While every other contestant performed tricks that were spectacular or showcased important technical innovations, Víctor had walked onstage with just a pack of cards and mesmerised the judges. They are hoping he will do the same trick now. It is only fair: there could be no better moment to share a success that even he does not believe is entirely his. He wants everyone to feel as though they are sharing in this chance blessing, and not simply out of generosity, but because all those present are links in a single chain of knowledge. He gets to his feet and takes three paces forward to the edge of the stage. Casually, as though he were not wearing a blindfold. Just as he is about to open his mouth to speak, someone in the front row pre-empts him and shouts:

'My father died . . .'

The audience laughs at this joke. Víctor can hardly be irritated by it; for years now, every show has opened with these words. It is the one sure thing the dedicated fans know about a particular

7

show before they see it. This prelude, this opening, these talismanic words: 'My father died when I was seven years old.' In fact, part of the anticipation generated by each new show is the way these words will veer off in unexpected twists and meanders, to arrive, every time, at a different yet plausible conclusion.

Víctor enjoys the laughter and the sibilant *shh* that follows.

'Of course,' he concedes finally, 'you all know that my father died, but what I've never told anyone is that his legacy to me was a wooden trunk full of his belongings. And in that trunk was a pack of cards. This pack of cards.' He holds up the deck for the audience to see. 'New, unopened, the seal still intact. For years I've been waiting for the right moment to use this deck. I was planning to perform a trick with them tonight, but now the moment has come, I can't bring myself to use them. They scare me. So I'm going to ask you all to do me a favour: I want you to perform the trick for me. I'm hoping that together we can overcome the curse I suspect has been placed on these cards.'

He tosses the pack into the front row. Someone leaps to their feet and catches it.

'Please, don't sit down,' Víctor says quickly. 'Turn around so everyone can see what you're doing. Everyone except me, obviously. I can't see anything. Now, I want you to break the seal that has been on that pack of cards for thirty years. Take out the cards and hand them to a person in the second row. Anyone you like.'

As if the blindfold were not sufficient guarantee, Víctor now turns his back on the audience and stays that way for the rest of the trick. Yet he continues to give precise, perfectly timed instructions, as though he can see exactly what is happening in the stalls. He instructs the second person to pass the cards to a third, to whom he offers the opportunity to shuffle the cards. Since this person chooses an American shuffle – immediately recognisable by the sound of the cards as they cascade – Víctor asks the next person to do a traditional overhand shuffle. Lest there be any doubt that this has been a clean shuffle, he offers a fifth person the opportunity to cut the pack and pass it on. By now, most of the audience is on its feet, staring towards the middle of the sixth row so as not to lose sight of the cards.

'Maestro Mario,' says Víctor, as the man who has just cut the cards hands the pack to the maestro, 'I want you to pick a card. Take your time, then show it to anyone you like.'

Before picking a card, Galván fans out the deck and looks at them to make sure the cards are not in an order that could easily be memorised. He checks the backs of the cards, then snaps the pack together, checks the cards again to make sure they're not marked, shrugs, then takes out the three of diamonds. He holds it up for everyone to see, then says:

'OK.'

Víctor asks Mario to put his card back in the deck anywhere he likes and hand the pack to someone in the next row. The seventh person is instructed to shuffle the cards and keep passing them on. And so the cards reach the back row and slowly begin their return journey towards the stage. Víctor now asks that, on each row, someone cut the pack, keep one pile and pass on the rest. The shrinking pack moves forward until, when it reaches the second row, there are only two cards left.

'I don't know who you are,' Víctor says at this point, 'but you are holding two cards. The person who took the deck out of the box is sitting in the front row. Could you please find that person and give him the cards.'

The murmur that has grown louder as the pack of cards shrinks is now overwhelming.

'Please, don't look at them. Take out the box you put in your pocket earlier, then place one of the two cards inside. You can keep the other one. Hand the box to Mario Galván. I think there's something in there that belongs to him.'

Some of the audience break into applause even before Galván takes the box. Others laugh or shout or whistle. But many of them stand silently, waiting for the conclusion of the trick, unable to believe what they are seeing or, worse still, alarmed precisely because they can see it and cannot help believing. Someone shouts:

'It's not possible!'

Víctor has just performed the trick that won him the Grand Prix a week ago: a new trick devised by him in which magic truly seems to happen all by itself, without the intervention of the magician. His back is turned. He's wearing a blindfold. In front of an audience of professionals. The most sceptical members of the audience, instead of looking at Galván, glance around the room, at the ceiling, in the corners, looking for cameras, cables, mirrors, any gadget which, in conjunction with some illusion involving Víctor's blindfold, might explain the trick. Everyone here knows what can be done with a single mirror. A number of people are still holding the cards they kept as the deck was being passed back. Some check their cards for the most obvious explanation, that they are all identical. Others slip cards into their pockets, happy to have a memento of this unforgettable moment; more than one does so convinced that, once he gets home, he will be able to work out how the trick was done. As Galván takes the box, there is a tense silence which lasts three full seconds before he opens it and shows the three of diamonds to the audience, not bothering to look at it before he does so, as though even to think about checking that the trick has worked would be an insult to his student. Víctor still stands, his back to the audience.

'What is the card?'

Nobody answers. Maybe because they know that the question is simply a formality, or maybe because, in the thunderous rumble of applause, they have not heard the question. A fleeting smile plays on Víctor's lips and, in a whisper his audience cannot hear, he says: 'It doesn't matter. They are all God's children.'

He turns. Acknowledges their applause with a slow bow. He smiles and removes the blindfold. Opens his eyes gradually as though the light were a lance. And it is; he quickly closes his left eye again and covers it with one hand. Then opens it, his hand still cupped to his face to protect his eye from the dazzling spotlight. Has he got something in it? He lightly touches his eyelid with one finger, applying no pressure, unable to resist rubbing it but terrified that he will find a piece of glass or grit, something abrasive. A moon. That is what is in his left eye. A diminutive full moon. A capsule. A small white wafer.

The applause does not stop. Víctor blinks. First once, slowly and deliberately, then rapidly, repeatedly, almost like a nervous tic. He scans the front row from right to left and notices that the white halo moves too. It is a strange sensation. Anyone else in his position would run to the bathroom and bathe his eyes under the tap. Víctor senses that this would not do any good, perhaps because he cannot help connecting this strange episode with the powder flash that briefly eclipsed the green door barely half an hour ago.

Above the racket, a voice shouts:

'Víctor! Here!'

It's Galván. Seeing Víctor has heard him, with a flick of his wrist, he sends the three of diamonds leaping into the air, where it spirals across the room. This is something they have practised a thousand times. Galván could flick every card in the deck to him from much farther away, with his back turned; he could even walk around as he flicks one card after another, and every one of them would come to rest in the half-open hand Víctor now extends to catch the three of diamonds. Only the poise that comes from years of practice makes it possible for him to wait patiently, pretending to follow the card as it flies. Because he cannot see the card. The wait seems endless, as though some cog in the machinery of time has suddenly broken. Nothing outlandish, nothing that would make the earth shake, nothing that would deflect a planet from its orbit: it is a pitiful rattle, a turn of the screw. In a few months, when he tries to recall this moment, it will seem to him that he can only reach it by crossing a desert of empty days. He closes his hand just in time to pluck the card out of the air. He looks at it. At first, he can see no three, no diamonds, nothing but a blank card. Only if he closes his left eye can he see the blurred shapes printed on the card.

Confused, he steps down from the stage and mingles with the crowd. There is more back-slapping, more gentle nudging. They say things, whisper congratulations into his ear. And he can also hear, though they seem to come from another planet, the comments they make to one another. He's the best, they say, the very best. He manages to smile, if his grimace could be called a smile, but he does not stop to speak to anyone. The inertia of the crowd has allowed him to reach the back of the room, where Mario and a number of volunteers are opening the first bottles and filling little plastic glasses. Víctor is next to the door. Before he leaves, he looks around the room one last time. Here, he believed he was reborn twenty-two years ago. Here he suffered, struggled, wept with rage at the impossible, wept with joy at the unexpected. His whole life has been here, a life which, barely half an hour ago, seemed so happy. Hiding under these seats, melting into the shadows, all the men he has ever been since he first walked through the green door are watching him.

Before he realises it, he is two blocks away. He is walking quickly, fingering his house keys in his trouser pocket, clinging to the faint hope that he will be able to sleep and tomorrow will bring the miracle of recovery. He is still blinking, still jerking his head quickly as though there is a parasite in his eye, a bug attached to his cornea. It will be some time before his guests notice his absence and begin to ask who saw him last and where can he have got to. They will miss you, Víctor.

Populus Vult Decipi

He arrived a few minutes early and, although the front door was open, he buzzed the intercom. No one answered. Víctor took a piece of paper from his pocket, smoothed it out and checked the address: 1st Floor, 6, Carrer de l'Oli. He stepped into the tiny hallway, rubbed his hands together and pulled up the collar of his cloak. It was colder in here than it was outside. He reached out to touch the wall, searching for a light switch, then pulled his hand away, revolted by the feel of the dank, spongy plaster. He climbed the stairs to the green door on the first landing. He pressed the doorbell, but it did not even seem to ring. He rested his hand on the handle and pushed gently, expecting the hinges to screech dramatically, but the door opened in well-oiled silence as though on to nothingness. At the far end of the room, a small window let in just enough light to emphasise the accumulated grime on its glass.

With one foot inside, but without crossing the threshold, Víctor called out:

'Hello? Anyone there?'

He would have sworn he saw his breath misting in the air. He stood completely still, listening for the slightest sound, an intake of breath, any clue that might reveal the presence of another being in the room. In spite of the silence, he had the sensation of eyes crawling over him, like a persistent insect. All he could offer in return was his gangling adolescent body, his clumsy, short-sighted tics, his hesitant stance. However, the eyes that did move slowly in the darkness quickly noticed the artless way that Víctor moved, the gracefulness of his gestures, the natural candour of his smile, the way he refused to lean against the wall or put his hands in his pockets; all of which could be summed up with the simple word

13

elegance. Let us give Galván his due, it took him only a moment to recognise in this seventeen-year-old both the frozen image of the lonely boy he had been and the charming, charismatic man that time would make of him. He must have seen all this at first glance, since otherwise Víctor would have left the room thinking there was no one there. Galván was not prepared to settle for yet another mediocre student. Nor even a good one.

Víctor was about to leave when he heard the quick, rasping, instantly recognisable sound of a lighter being struck. He turned just in time to see the flame, a yellow quivering that disappeared immediately, leaving only a spark hovering in the air. Then, suddenly, a spotlight on the ceiling sliced through the darkness, a powerful beam, but one so narrow that, even when his eyes had adjusted to the semi-darkness, he could not make out the size of the room. In the centre, his faced shrouded by the first puff of smoke, was a man, sitting at a small table. He must have been dressed entirely in black because Víctor could see only a shock of stiff hair, the pale straw colour blond hair takes on with age, and the cloudy reflection of a pair of smudged spectacles. The man's eyes peered out at him as though through a murky fishbowl.

On the table were a green baize cloth and two decks of cards. On the other side, an empty chair. With an impatient wave, the man gestured for him to take a seat. As he drew closer, Víctor could see the area around the table more clearly. The spotlight lent the green baize a dull sheen. Only the decks of cards were new. Everything else looked old, antiquated, shabby. Or fake: he had the feeling that if he moved to the other side of the table, beneath that floating head he would find the body of a robot, its back a tangle of plugs and wires. He concentrated on the man's features: the harsh nicotine stains on his teeth, his clean-shaven face and, most of all, the pallor of his skin, so pale that it seemed to justify the darkness of the room.

As though bothered by this scrutiny, the man drew back his head a little, out of the spotlight, so that it merged into the darkness. It was almost a minute before he reappeared, the cigarette still clenched between his lips, his eyes fixed on Víctor.

'Mario Galván,' he introduced himself, stretching out a hand.

14

Víctor shook it, and said his name, his voice thin and barely audible.

'Pleased to meet you, Víctor. Before we begin, I should warn you that if you arrive late again, I will cancel the classes.'

'Late?' Víctor said, surprised.

Only when he brought his hand up to his face to look at his watch did he remember that their handshake had lasted a fraction of a second too long. His watch was now swaying like a pendulum from Galván's index finger.

'Great trick,' he conceded.

'We're getting off to a bad start,' Galván said, peevishly. 'Magicians don't play tricks on each other. Clowns, yes. And thimbleriggers. Magicians perform magic.' His voice was hoarse and thick phlegm rattled in his chest. 'Let's start at the beginning,' he announced. He took a pack of cards, broke the seal on the box, removed the cards with his left hand then turned his wrist slowly to show them face up and said: 'This is a deck of cards.'

'OK.'

'Let me stub this thing out first, they'll be the death of me.'

Galván took the cigarette from his mouth with his right hand, brought it down to his waist, let it fall to the floor. Then he stamped on it. When Víctor looked up at his face again, he saw that Galván was still holding the cigarette, trailing smoke, as though it had never left the maestro's lips.

'The first thing we're going to learn ...' he said, as though nothing had happened.

'Hang on,' Víctor interrupted. 'How did you do that?'

'Never ask a magician that question.'

'It's not that, it's just ...'

'... just nothing. You did come here to learn magic, didn't you? Lesson one: asking how something works is distasteful.'

'But I saw the cigarette fall. I saw you stamp it out.'

'So what? What's important is what you *didn't* see.'

'Do it again.'

'I can't.'

Víctor smiled as though Galván had admitted defeat. If he were to do it again, Víctor might work out how the trick was done.

'Make no mistake.' The maestro's eyes never left his. 'I could do it a thousand times and you still wouldn't work it out. But that's not the point. Magic is not a game, Víctor. It is an art. A typist can repeat something as many times as necessary, a pianist cannot; the art is lost.'

Víctor looked as if he was about to leap to his feet and run out the door; his back stubbornly refusing to relax, his body half-turned, his legs to one side. He was irritated by the cold, and the damp. but most of all by Galván's self-important tone.

'Let's start again. I brought my right hand up to my mouth and took the cigarette. Like this.' He repeated the gesture, though this time his fingers held only a cigarette butt. The filter smelled as though it was burning and the green baize was covered in ash. Víctor noticed all this, and thought that the maestro was about to burn himself. 'Then, I brought it down to my waist and dropped it. All the while it never left your sight, did it? Then I moved my right foot to stub it out. And when I brought my hand back to my lips ...'

'Hey!' Víctor thumped the table. 'You've just done the same trick twice. You told me ...'

'I told you that I don't do tricks,' Galván corrected him.

At that moment, with a sudden burst of speed, he took his hand away. Between his lips was a perfect short-stemmed rose.

'Besides, as you know, nothing is what it seems,' he concluded before taking a deep breath. The rose, wreathed in smoke, hung from his mouth for only a moment before it wilted and crumbled to dust. 'I smoke too much,' said Galván.

With his right hand, he placed the remains of the flower on the table. Víctor leaned forward to touch it and, realising that it was not an artificial flower, he stared at the magician, incredulous. He ran through the sequence again, determined to find the missing link, the moment when, unbeknown to him, his eyes had been misdirected. Despite the maestro's bluster, it had to be a trick, or a sequence of tricks, and he was here to learn. Sooner or later. With Galván's help, or without it. Though he did not realise it, his fingers were still tracing anxious spirals in the air.

'OK, let's get to work,' said the maestro.

He moved the decks of cards to one side of the table, smoothed out the green baize with his palm, and as his hand moved over the remnants of the flower, it closed into a fist. Then he opened it, as if setting free a fly he had caught. Nothing – not the least trace of the flower. Víctor's bewilderment crystallised into three simple words:

'It's not possible!'

'At last,' cried Mario Galván. 'It's not possible, it's *not* possible. Say it again.'

'It's not possible,' Víctor whispered.

'Louder, damn it! Shout with me: IT'S ...'

'... NOT POSSIBLE!' Víctor shouted, caught up in the maestro's excitement although he did feel slightly embarrassed and faintly ridiculous.

Abruptly, Galván got to his feet, came round the table and crouched down next to Víctor. Barely a palm's breadth separated their faces.

'Listen to me, Víctor Losa. When you ask me how it works, you insult me. When you refer to it as a trick, you insult me. When you ask me to do it again, you insult me. But when your mouth drops open and you tell me it's not possible, it's like a breath of life. Because that is what magic is about, do you understand? Hearing someone say "it's not possible", but making it possible all the same. Now, let's see if you're any good.'

Perhaps intimidated by Galván's proximity, but certainly exasperated by the feeling that he had stumbled upon some secret he could find no way to unravel, Víctor pursed his lips and snorted. Galván got to his feet and went back to his side of the table.

'Do you mind if I ask you a question? Why do you want to be a magician?'

'Because, when my father died ...' Víctor said after a pause, but he did not finish his sentence. His voice did not crack and there was no trace of grief in his tone, in the steady way he held Galván's gaze, nothing that might signal that he was picking at the scab of a recent and still painful wound. On the contrary, the reticence of his answer and the sigh with which he trailed off sounded like signs of weariness. Or a profound mistrust of words.

'Go on ...'

Víctor shrugged.

'Don't worry,' Galván reassured him. 'You can tell me some

other time. Now, let me ask you something else. Let's suppose I agree to take you on only for us to discover you don't have the gift. It wouldn't be the first time I was mistaken about a student. What would you like to be?'

'A myrmecologist.'

'I'm sorry, I don't know what that is.'

'Someone who studies the behaviour of ants.'

'Oh. So your father was a myrmecologist?' Galván deduced.

'Yes.'

'You don't say very much.'

Although this was not a question, Víctor nodded.

'OK, that's enough,' Galván said. 'Do you have a girlfriend?'

'No.'

'Here.' He handed Víctor the other deck of cards. The boy was about to break the seal and take out the cards. 'From now on, that's your girlfriend. You eat with her, sleep with her, you take her everywhere with you, got it?'

'Got it.'

They spent a long time on something as simple as the perfect way to hold the cards. Then they moved on to practising the various standard shuffles. Little by little. There were no tricks yet. Galván explained that before you could be a magician, you had to be a croupier. The hour the lesson was supposed to last had long since passed, but the maestro did not even look at his watch. With infinite patience, he answered the torrent of questions Víctor asked, gently corrected the position of his hands and offered him practical advice so that he made quick progress. Until Víctor asked:

'OK, so what can I do with all that?'

Galván gave a heavy sigh and then said, 'I give up. Look, I'm not going to teach you a little sleight of hand so you can show off at school. Not today, not ever. What you'll learn from me are the fundamentals of the art, and a little of its history. You'll learn everything I know. Or most of it, at least. And what you can do with that. The rest is up to you. That doesn't mean I don't understand why you're so eager to put what you've just learned into practice.'

He got up, took two or three steps and vanished into the darkness.

'Can you read English?'

'A bit.'

Galván stepped back into the light carrying a thick sheaf of photocopies ring-bound along the spine. He pointed to the cover, to the title in huge capital letters: MODERN MAGIC. Underneath were a number of short sentences, each on a separate line.

'Not very modern. The book dates from 1876.'

'A practical treatise on the art of conjuring,' Víctor translated. 'By Professor Hoffmann. With three hundred and eighteen illustrations. And an appendix ... do you want me to go on?'

'Please. Some other day I'll tell you who Hoffmann was.'

'... Containing Explanations Of Some Of The Best Known Specialities Of Messrs Mask ...' He stumbled.

'Maskelyne And Cooke,' Galván corrected.

'Populus ... this bit is in Latin.'

'*Populus vult decipi: decipiatur.*'

'No idea what that means.'

'People want to be deceived: let them be deceived. A good motto for a magician, don't you think? The quotation is apparently from a cardinal in the sixteenth century. Skip the introduction and start on page forty-five. The trick is called "The Turning Card". There are various methods of doing it. Concentrate on the third.'

Without putting down the deck of cards he was holding, Víctor tried to find the page and began translating quickly in a low voice, but Galván, once again plunged into darkness, announced that the lesson was over.

'No. Practise it at home, it's getting late.' The room was clearly much larger than Víctor had realised, because the maestro's voice seemed to come from far away. 'Take the deck of cards. My gift to you. Remember that today, I am the only person watching you, but one day you will have an audience. Practise in front of a mirror whenever you can. Buy a green mat. Next Tuesday, same time. On the dot.'

Víctor slipped the deck of cards into his pocket, picked up the photocopy of *Modern Magic*, slung his knapsack over his shoulder and headed towards the door.

'Oh, one more thing.' Galván's voice stopped him. 'Seeing as you're in such a hurry, next time I'll ask you to demonstrate what you've learned. If you can't get it quite right, it doesn't matter. Don't get too obsessed with your hands. You'll perfect the movements in time. What is important is that you can tell a story.'

'Tell a story?' It felt strange, as if he were talking to a shadow. 'But if you already know ...'

'No. What I know is that if you do certain things to a card, it will land face up when the rest of the pack fall. What I don't know is what sort of story you want to tell me with that card. And for the moment, that's all I care about. I'll see you on Tuesday.'

Galván's dismissal was final. As he went, Víctor left the door ajar and stopped on the landing. A story? He didn't have the courage to go back inside and ask again. He slowly started down the stairs. If Galván had made himself disappear, if – rather than through sleight of hand and a way with words in the darkness – the magician, the room, even the whole building had vanished in a puff of smoke, Víctor would have believed it.

The maestro, on the other hand, was worried about more practical matters. With the haste of someone afraid to trust vital information simply to memory, he took a pen from the inside pocket of his jacket and fumbled vainly in his other pockets for a piece of paper. He tried to scribble something on a card, but the pen kept slipping. In the end, he opened his left hand, and on the palm, beneath the initials 'V. L.', he wrote: 'cuffs and eyebrows'.

We all have nervous gestures which appear when we are under pressure: there are those who pat their pockets, who stick out the tip of their tongue, or rub their fingertips together in a particular way. Good magicians shun such tics and make superhuman, often fruitless, attempts to overcome them. Every time you palm a card, you raise the opposite shoulder slightly. You are about to pick up the thimble that contains the hidden pea and you wink involuntarily. Galván had noticed that, each time before beginning a new exercise, Víctor tugged at the cuffs of his shirt. Also, whenever he made a mistake, his eyebrows immediately shot up in a look of bewilderment which was emphasised by his glasses giving a little jump on the bridge of his nose. It was vital to correct these reflex gestures quickly, though neither was serious. If Víctor turned out to be as talented as Galván suspected, he would soon be segueing from one trick into another so quickly he would not have time to think about fiddling with his cuffs. The thing with the eyebrows would resolve itself: all he had to do was not make any mistakes.

Galván stood for a moment, the pen hovering in the air, his left hand open, searching for the right word to describe the third tic, which was much more worrying. He dismissed 'coughing' and 'humming' and finally wrote 'singing', though he was not entirely sure that the almost inaudible vibration that emerged from Víctor's throat when he was tense was a melody. He had heard it seven or eight times during the lesson and at first he had thought the boy was just clearing his throat. He took it for granted that Víctor was completely unaware that he was doing it, but since he did not know what triggered it, Galván knew from experience that drastic measures would be required to stamp it out. As soon as possible.

When he reached the door to the street, Víctor realised that he had not paid for the lesson and started back up the stairs. He was a few steps from the landing when he heard sounds coming from the other side of the green door: first, feet shuffling across the floor and the maestro folding the chairs and propping them against the wall. He could make out each sound with perfect clarity. He could even hear the rasping breaths of bellow-like lungs abused by years of smoking, then a heavy sigh and finally a whisper:

'That little wretch is going to be one hell of a magician.'

Víctor climbed the few remaining steps, bent down and slipped the envelope with the money under the crack of the door. As he straightened up, he felt a shiver run down his back that had nothing to do with the cold. He hated predictions. Even favourable ones. He had watched a terrible prediction come true. He knew only too well the magnetism of predictions, their ability to draw reality to themselves. 'That little wretch is me,' he thought, though this first part of the prediction did not fit with his personality. 'I'm going to be one hell of a magician.'

Though the light was too poor for him to be able to read, he still held Hoffmann's book open as he went back down the stairs, as though he must immediately read it if Galván's prediction were to come true. With his other hand, he patted his left pocket to make sure the deck of cards was still there. Even he could not have explained his excitement. After all, aside from Galván's prophetic words, he had learned very few things during that first lesson: this is a deck of cards, you hold it like this, and this is how you shuffle. If you want to know more, read this book.

Upstairs, with a brush in his right hand and a dustpan in his left, Galván was standing next to the small window. He saw Víctor leave and, over the boy's shoulder, he could glimpse the illustration on page two of *Modern Magic*, of a head appearing from inside a box that sat on a table. Under the table, a dotted line indicated the space where the body was hidden.

'Hoffmann,' said the maestro aloud, smiling to himself. 'Lucky bastard.'

When Víctor disappeared from view, Galván set about sweeping the floor. When he came to the table, he pushed it aside with his hip and picked up the three cigarette butts, the remains of the flower and the little piles of ash on the floor. With each sweep of the brush he said a name aloud in a theatrical voice, drawing out the vowels as though announcing the winner of a raffle.

'Harry Kellar! Pete Grouse!' He continued on towards the door. Each sweep of the brush more powerful, each name he uttered louder. 'John Nevil Maskelyne! Auzinger.' He stopped and picked up the envelope, and as he stood up again, he flung his arms wide, scattering everything he had just swept up. 'And Víctor Losa!'

As If By Magic

He lashes out with his foot in sheer frustration, bringing a flutter of objects – cards, thimbles, balls, small garishly coloured scarves – tumbling down; all except the scarves, which hang in the air for a few seconds. Víctor does not dare look up, afraid to discover that, after the hours, the days, the months of effort, he is back where he had started, up to his knees in a jumble of preposterous bits and pieces. Most of them are small and light, but they have accumulated so quickly that any attempt to forge a path through them is a heroic feat.

He takes a deep breath and throws himself forward as though he is about to lie down on, or perhaps dive into, this sea of clutter, swim through the scattered objects at his feet in order to find somewhere to lay his head. But the layer of objects is so thick that Víctor lands face down, on top of everything, rocked by the solid wave created as the weight of his body forces the objects to spread out beneath him. With a look of disgust, he flings one arm out and swipes at the nearest thing to hand, propelling himself forward another two feet. With his other arm, he repeats the exercise and realises that it is not an optical illusion. Not only has he advanced; everything else seems to have moved too, as though, beneath the apparently tranquil surface of this clutter there is a current, a direction, a purpose. He finally lifts his head and sees, so far away that the distance would have to be calculated as days of walking, the outline of a wardrobe, a cabinet. Everything is flowing towards it, as though the objects know that only inside it will they find the order that justifies their existence.

Though it seems completely contradictory, the sudden appearance of this large, solid piece of furniture among so many tiny objects brings a logic to the scene that it lacked. It is a Proteus

Cabinet, patented in London in 1865, though probably in private use for decades before that. For thirty or forty years, anyone who considered himself a magician or spiritualist would have had such a cabinet, or one like it, and attempted to improve on it, to make a more sophisticated version, to adapt it using some new technology. Inside this cabinet, men and women would disappear, spirits materialise, impossible noises occur. Víctor smiles with relief. Although he still does not know where he is, nor how long he has been here, at least he knows where he is headed. His only regret is that it has taken him so long to discover the thread common to all the objects he can see before him. Magic has made all of them disappear at some point. It would have made Víctor calmer had he known this earlier. Thanks to the cabinet, he finally realises that the nine of clubs floating on the surface next to his left elbow, its corners almost imperceptibly shaven, once belonged to the great Maskelyne. And the ridiculous wig half buried must be the Egyptian headdress which Stodare used for his Sphinx Illusion, a trick involving a decapitated head. And something over there . . .

He cannot linger over such trivial details. To identify each of these objects would take him centuries. Besides, if he goes on thinking like this, he might succumb to the temptation of wondering about the one vital piece of information he still does not have: what is *he* doing here? Because he has never disappeared by magic. Or he doesn't believe he has.

He does another few clumsy strokes, pulling himself forward with the instinctive doggedness of a long-distance swimmer. When he tilts his head from time to time to breathe, the subtle changes in the light around him lead him to think that days and nights are passing and nothing is happening. The suspicion that it may take years before he arrives at his goal does not discourage him. On the contrary, it confirms that he is floating on the sea of the past, drawn by a current of dates that have elapsed and which he will only be able to explain when he finally gets close enough to make out the details of the cabinet and work out which version it is. Because he has owned a number of cabinets. Just as he decides to throw out his arms and allow the current to take him where it will, a great wave knocks the breath out of his lungs, tosses him in the air like a puppet and deposits him, dazed, on a smooth, hard surface. He rolls over half a dozen times before he manages to stand up. He touches his neck, his ribs, unable to believe that no bones have been broken.

He walks around the cabinet, estimating its size with an expert eye, runs his fingers over the wood. He notes that at head height on both doors there are holes roughly the size of a fist. It could be the work of the Davenport Brothers or one of their many imitators. But then he notices that there is a small lock with a key sticking out of it. Perfect, there can be no doubt now. This is Harry Kellar's cabinet.

'Peter Grouse?' he asks.

He knows Grouse is inside. He wants to throw himself at the cabinet, fling the doors open and welcome him with a hug, but a nagging doubt prevents him. During his years as an apprentice, Grouse was a role model for him. His legend illuminated every difficult moment, and in times of success, when he wanted to pay homage to the greats, Grouse was always the first name that came to him. And he realises that, having spent so much time watching himself in this symbolic mirror over the years, his mind has created an impossible photograph in which Grouse is the spitting image of him. A little older, perhaps. He does not want to open the doors now to discover some fat, bald man with bad breath. Or the reverse, someone unbearably handsome.

'Mario?' a dull voice finally asks from inside the cabinet. 'Is that Mario Galván?'

'Yes,' Víctor answers. 'It's Mario.'

'I've been waiting for you for over a hundred years.' The voice is not in the least reproachful. It is a little difficult to understand because it is almost drowned out by a maddening peal of bells. 'Did you bring mine?'

'Of course,' Víctor says.

He half-turns the key and opens the doors but the mirror inside simply reflects his own image, barely lit by the tiny flame of a match, an oil lamp, perhaps a gas lamp that someone is holding up. Víctor squints and discovers that in his left hand he is holding the cap of a pen. Well, he has to call it something. It looks like a finger, or to be precise, half a finger. Half a thumb neatly severed at the phalange. But it is made of plastic or some thin, flexible material and hollow inside. In fact, he is wearing it over his own thumb like a cap. He holds it up, pronounces Grouse's name twice, or three times, and, confused when there is no reply, closes the cabinet again. Immediately, there are three loud knocks from inside. It is the sound of flesh on wood, but to Víctor it sounds like bass chords from some instrument and he rushes to open the cabinet again. Even he does not know why he is in such a hurry, but he has the feeling that if he waits even a second longer, if he allows the fourth chord to sound, the swell of time will burst its banks again and sweep him far away from here, from the cabinet, from any possibility of finding some purpose to this moment and giving it meaning.

'Idiot!' he mutters to himself, shaking his head as he turns the key again. 'You'd think I'd never seen this cabinet before. Grouse must be hiding behind the mirror.'

He opens the doors, pushes the mirror gently; it swings back on a large hinge.

'Who said more than a hundred years?' The voice coming out of the darkness now is a male voice speaking with irrefutable authority. 'It's only been thirty-two.'

'It's not possible,' Víctor says.

'What do you mean it's not possible?'

'It's impossible, *Papá*,' Víctor insists. 'There's no such thing as spirits. And don't take my word for it, it's been proven. You only have to read the Seybert Commission Report. It was published in 1887.'

'A worthless piece of drivel,' his father answers.

'Not at all. It's pure science. It's in the library of the University of Pennsylvania. And it concludes that ...'

'Don't talk to me about science, son. You want proof?' The sound of footsteps, the cabinet shakes slightly and Martín Losa, Víctor's father, appears before him. 'Look at this,' he says, holding out his left hand.

Víctor hesitates for a moment. He stares into his face and, although this confirms beyond a shadow of a doubt that it is indeed his father, he finds it hard to accept the flagrant temporal incongruity, since this man is the same age as he is. However, he is not surprised to see the line of ants marching across the ghost's forehead.

'I'm telling you, it's not possible,' he insists.

But, in the end, he looks down and sees that there is a dark mark on the outstretched hand, what seems at first to be a dry, amber stain like nicotine, but as he examines it more closely it turns out to be wet, bubbling, and though he cannot bring himself to touch it, he would swear that it is blood, and that it extends far beyond the fingers, that it starts at the thumb, which has been severed right in the middle, runs down to the wrist, to the elbow from which it trickles, almost gushes, to the floor. A puddle is forming.

'Cockroaches don't have blood, *Papá*, or at least not much,' says Víctor, trying to keep his voice calm.

He scans the darkness in the hope of finding a cloth, a piece of string, something he could use to make a tourniquet and staunch the flow. He puts his hand to the wound and applies pressure, he is soaked too now, but still the blood spurts.

'You always turn up too late, *hijo*,' his father says. And seeing that Víctor, preoccupied by trying to stop the blood, does not answer or apologise, he insists: 'You treat everything in life as if it's a game, and you always turn up too late.'

The wound does not seem to hurt, though Víctor would swear he can see his father's face growing paler by the second; it is ashen, almost translucent, as though the blood loss will soon cause him to disappear. Suddenly, he realises there is only one way to stop the haemorrhage. He has to take the plastic cap off his own thumb and put it on his father's. Although by now he is aware that this is a dream and that there is no logic to how it will unfold, it seems obvious that the only reason for the presence of this cap is because he has a mission to accomplish. He pulls at it and is surprised to find that it does not come off as easily as expected. He tries twice or three times, then, convinced that there is no time to lose, he brings the thumb to his mouth and sinks his teeth into the cap. It finally comes off and Víctor places it over his father's thumb, although he cannot help but notice a tattered shred of flesh protruding from the hole, nor the wetness that is now soaking down his own arm, and he stands rigid, motionless, bewildered, and sees

27

that he has pulled off half his own thumb, and all he can think to do is scream, scream with a voice that is not even his own, fill his lungs and create a racket loud enough to break through the barrier of sleep, back to life. To wake him up.

The first thing he does when he opens his eyes is look at his hands. Obviously, there is no blood, but a small groove on his thumb makes him think that he may have bitten it while he was asleep. He glances around the dark room. From the smell of tobacco, it seems as though he has barely slept. On the nightstand, a cigarette butt is still smouldering in the overflowing ashtray. Is it possible that he has only just fallen asleep? That this gruelling struggle has lasted only a few minutes?

Fragments of the real world begin to filter through to his brain: he needs to see an optician. And find Galván. He must be expecting an explanation, and probably an apology for his sudden disappearance last night. He needs to focus for a moment, shake off the last wisps of the dream and remember what exactly did happen yesterday, but the very idea panics him. At some point before he fell asleep, for some reason, he warned himself not to remember on pain of some terrible punishment. He knows that if he should take a single step in the direction indicated by memory, there will be no going back, as for someone who leaps towards the first stone in order to cross a river only to find that it is barely big enough to stand on so he must jump to the next and so on, forced to keep jumping from stone to stone towards a far shore he cannot see, which may not even exist. Still lying down, he looks up. If only, at this very moment, the three of invisible diamonds which Galván flicked towards him last night would fall from the ceiling, spiralling like the last dead leaf. If only it would, it might close this unbearable loop in time. Víctor sits up suddenly and turns on the light. Opposite the bed is an enormous black-and-white poster in which Lauren Bacall is holding a match to her face, daring the onlooker to hold her gaze. It has been there for years. The title, *To Have and Have Not*, is written across her chest in red capital letters. If he looks at it with only his left eye, he sees a white halo where the title should be. With his right eye, he can read it, but only thanks to the black outline on the letters. Oh, Víctor.

He gets up and shuffles down the corridor. He opens a door and goes into the studio. Well, studio, museum, junk room. He has never decided what to call the room nor what to do with everything inside it. He has kept it for years, intending to give it all to Galván as a gift, but the maestro has long since given up his plan of opening a museum. Víctor needs to decide what to do with it. Or at least sort it out, organise things, make it useful.

He goes over to the Proteus Cabinet, examines it closely, and is astonished by how accurately he managed to reproduce it in his dream. If only he felt calm enough to revel in the memories evoked by these things. He need only caress the wooden cabinet to conjure the image of his hands and Galván's hands, the plane and chisel, the dirt and the sawdust, all the hours they spent making it, the interminable arguments provoked by trying to settle on the precise model they were going to replicate: the Davenport model, the maestro insisted. No, Kellar's model, Víctor objected. In the end, they followed Kellar's design. But this one has a key. And if he were to open it, the almost inaudible sound of the hinges would take him back to a happier time, more than happy, to one of the high points of his life, since this cabinet came with him on his second world tour, its doors open like a bow, sharing in the applause and the bravos, the thunderous clamour of a success that has continued to this day. But Víctor did not come in here for that. Quite the opposite, he came in to close it. It is a symbolic gesture. There is nothing inside to hide or to protect. It is empty. All it harbours is the dust of time. And this is precisely what he wants to shut inside as he gives the key a full turn and is thankful for the supreme ease with which the bolt slides into place.

Ants Have No Ears

Martín Losa built an ant farm on the terrace in the spring of 1973, convinced that Víctor, who had just turned five, was old enough to learn the basics about the world of ants. It was a glass box, open at the top, half filled with soil. A metre by a metre and a half. From the centre, a small wooden bridge rose up to a transparent box in which the ants' food was placed. It would have been easy to take a colony from any natural anthill with enough worker ants, drones, soldiers and virgin queens, and transplant it, along with the soil, into the glass box. However, Martín wanted to reproduce the natural process that occurs when a recently fertilised queen pulls off her wings, digs a hole in the soil and founds a new colony with only the help of the worker ants that stream from her belly as larvae. He had failed on two previous attempts. For the third, he allowed himself to enrich the soil with nutrients: an egg, two spoonfuls of honey, a few drops of vitamins, some mineral salts, half a litre of water and five grams of Malayan seaweed gelatine. Within a few months the population of the colony numbered thousands.

Martín spent his Saturday mornings on the care required to maintain the colony, and he insisted his son Víctor take part, believing that there was no better entertainment for him: cleaning out the bodies which piled up in a corner; checking the humidity of the soil and regulating when necessary; replenishing the food in the little box and, above all, making sure that there were at least two fingers of water in the little moat that ran around the ant farm. In doing so, satisfying the one condition his wife had imposed before allowing him to put an ant farm on the terrace: that its inhabitants would never invade the house. However, as Martín believed that death was an unnecessarily cruel way to punish the curiosity of the ants, every Saturday he brushed the internal walls of the formicarium with talc. At first, Víctor liked to watch the ants climb over and over only to slip and fall back on to the soil.

Martín tried to turn these chores into a game, and although he was not always able to control himself, he tried not to bombard the boy with too much information. For his part, Víctor never complained, nor did he seem to consider this weekly chore to be some terrible imposition, but he showed only limited curiosity, which invariably related to the three things that could not be seen.

The first was the queen ant. Every week, he asked Martín to show him the queen and his father would have to explain that it was impossible, that the queen spent most of her time underground in the deepest cave of the ant farm and that the survival of the whole colony depended on her being present. He showed him photos and drawings of other specimens and told him he could only see her if, in extreme danger, the worker ants were forced to move her to a new habitat.

The second issue Víctor was curious about was reproduction. Martín had explained to him how a virgin becomes queen ant, explained that it was something almost impossible to witness first hand and frequently promised that one day he would show Víctor a documentary about it. Some day. When he was older.

And then there was the issue of language. It was not easy getting a child to understand that, although they could not hear it, the system of communication used by ants was magnificent in its perfection. Tiny glandular secretions by which an individual could communicate essential information to the whole colony. But only what was strictly necessary: what and where to eat; where and from whom to flee. A chemical code that excluded all subjectivity. A language with which it was impossible to create artworks, but equally impossible to waste time. So perfect that it had taken millions of years to evolve.

Víctor could somehow not believe it. He accepted that it might be foolish to expect articulate speech from an ant, but surely there had to be some sound, if only an almost inaudible chirrup. After all, dogs, cats, birds, frogs, crickets, all the animals he knew made

31

sounds that were more or less appropriate to their size. Even fish made sounds, though you couldn't hear them because of the water. He imagined that ants would make muffled, high-pitched sounds. He asked over and over, marshalling objections against his father's explanations, until one day Martín grew tired of it.

'Come over here,' he called. Víctor stomped over reluctantly. Martín pointed to the magnifying glass in his lap. 'Take that, and wait a minute.' With a pair of tweezers, he plucked one of the ants from the surface of the ant farm and held it up close to the magnifying glass. 'Look carefully. There's no rush. When you see its ear, let me know.'

This was hardly a scientific line of reasoning, but it was difficult to refute: if ants had no way of hearing, there was little point in them speaking. Víctor conceded defeat. He gave his father back the magnifying glass and started tracing figures of eights in the dust with the toe of his left shoe. For the first time, instead of arguing, he said nothing, and resolved to find a way to prove his father was wrong. Since then, every Saturday after he had done his share of the chores, he would bring his face close to the ant farm, close his eyes the better to concentrate and, with his ear pressed to the glass, he would walk slowly around all four sides. When he got back to his starting point, he would set off again. He was convinced that one day, he would hear some sound – a tiny shriek, a pitiful whisper – that would prove he was right. Perhaps, he thought, he needed to goad the ants to make some noise, so he tapped the walls with his knuckles every two or three steps. He was prepared to go on doing this for as long as it took.

Martín mistook his son's stubbornness for boredom and, seeing the boy distracted, he showed him a trick to get his attention. He took a specimen from the formicarium using the myrmecologist's tweezers, made a fist with his left hand, leaving only a tiny hole in the hollow of his thumb, and put the ant inside. Then, he opened his hand very slowly. Nothing ... Víctor stared, open mouthed. Every time, he asked where the ant had gone. Martín told him it was a great mystery, a secret no one would ever know, but so the poor ant would not be lonely, he would send another ant. And then another. Always using the same method. Staggered, Víctor watched the ants disappear. Sometimes he was tempted to put a finger into the hole but he never dared do it or even to suggest it, fearful that this black hole in his father's fist might swallow his whole hand.

They spent the mornings doing chores and tricks. Towards noon, Víctor's mother came to fetch him, put on his coat, gave Martín instructions about how to heat up the meal she had left for him and said her goodbyes, always with the same words:

'We'll be back by half-past seven. And whatever you do, be careful with those little jars. One of these days you're going to kill yourself.'

Every Saturday, as they left, Víctor bowed his head, his body stooped, not because he was sad, but so he could look under his father's chair for some sign of the ants that had disappeared.

Martín, on the other hand, kept his head high so he could watch them until they reached the door; he always smiled, but he associated their leaving with a certain sadness. He felt somehow as though, in spite of all his tricks, he had failed yet again in his attempt to get Víctor interested in ants. It was only a matter of time until the boy started to complain, to beg to be allowed to spend Saturday mornings playing football, riding his bicycle or playing with his friends. And why not. All boys are fascinated with ants at some point, but not all of them translate this passion into the central thread of their lives. This was what Martín had done, he had gone so far as to pursue a career in entomology, specialising in myrmecology. And he made his living killing them. As a young man he had devoted himself to research. He had travelled half the world to study exotic species: to forests, deserts, mangrove swamps, caves. Of that time, he had only good memories. Then, when Víctor was born, he had taken the only stable job he could find: technical director for a laboratory that made insecticides. This was why, on Saturdays, as he watched the door close on his wife and son, Martín went on staring for a moment into the distance and then, with a sigh, he would put the four or five 'disappearing' ants into a test tube, eat the meal his wife had left – almost always cold, in spite of her instructions – then lock himself in the room he had set up as a home laboratory. Perfecting ways of killing. With his little jars.

33

Aces and Kings

alván had been in the profession almost forty years and it had to be acknowledged that he knew a great deal. He had managed to survive the periods in which, for a short time, magic would suddenly become fashionable, only to be consigned once more to the catacombs and strict devotees. People quickly tired of watching a woman in a box being run through with swords as if she were a kebab, only to emerge in one piece and, most importantly, still smiling. To say nothing of money miraculously discovered in a bag wrapped in paper inside a box … what a surprise! He loathed modern magic. For decades now he had not seen anything that had not already been performed by the greats of the late nineteenth century.

In the early 1970s, when everyone assumed that television would revive interest in magic for the nth time, he had predicted a growing infantilisation of the profession: magicians would come to depend on technology, constantly devising ever more spectacular routines, adopting the style of the circus, abandoning their training, their attention to detail and every last vestige of taste along the way. Anyone without the ambition or the talent to make it in the profession had only to flatter the public, tell jokes or persuade his assistant to wear a skirt that came up to her armpits.

Business was another matter. Since the 1940s, Galván had been running The King of Magic, the only professional shop for magicians in Barcelona that had its own workshop, and one of the oldest in Europe. Now, he was faced with a dilemma: the more he despised the superficial flippancy of the magicians who preened for the cameras and pranced like third-rate dancers, the more affluent the customers who trooped into his shop. Some moron had only to perform the latest flashy trick on-screen and suddenly children and their parents came rushing to buy the ingenious mechanical gizmo so they could do it themselves. At the same time, and in equal measure, demand for professional supplies increased: sophisticated trunks for escape artists, floating tables for levitation tricks, cages with delicate mechanisms which could be folded down to a few millimetres wide, making it look as though they had disappeared. Galván made these articles in the workshop at the back of the shop, and those who criticised him for contributing to the success of the sort of magic he professed to despise were not wrong. However, it is only fair to consider the options that were available to him: he had long since realised, in spite of his vast theoretical knowledge and considerable dexterity, that he was not born to be a magician. At least not a magician of the stature he required. He lacked the good looks, the bearing, a lightness of gesture, a gravitas, things that were difficult to explain and impossible to learn. On the other hand, as a craftsman he considered himself the equal of anyone and, above all, he knew that, in Barcelona at least, there was no one to compare to him as a teacher. To use his own expression, he could be the world's best typist, but he would never be a pianist. This was why, in the window of his shop, he still had the little handwritten card, yellow with age, offering to give magic lessons, though by now he did not need the extra money such lessons brought in.

He still had not given up hope of finding a student capable of learning from him the choicest pieces in the history of magic and taking them a step farther, perhaps in some direction that not even he could foresee. A new Houdini, say, though Galván would have despised the comparison and said – as he quickly told Víctor – that Houdini was nothing more than an arrogant bumpkin, feared rather than respected by his contemporaries. Perhaps Peter Grouse was a better example, though history had been unkind to him, and no one now remembered his successes. Let us mention no names, let us just say that he was looking for someone first-class. Could that be Víctor Losa? Had their first lesson been enough for him to sense such greatness in the boy? And if so, what had he meant by his sigh, the sadness, the ambiguity of his prediction?

A number of details counterbalanced these doubts, beginning with Víctor's bearing, the way he moved, his back straight, eyes front, hands open. The glint in his eyes as he picked up the deck of cards. The fact that he lacked the irritating habit of smiling more than necessary. Galván had spent his life telling his students: 'You're performing magic, not telling jokes.' There were other things, too, which only someone of his experience could appreciate, like the fact that Víctor never looked at his hands while performing – a common vice among beginners and one that was almost impossible to correct. The voice was important: the boy had the necessary confidence and roundness of tone, although Galván would have to teach him how to project his voice in large theatres. In spite of the natural diffidence of someone picking up a deck of cards for the first time, Víctor did not need to polish his style, the elegant disdain with which he performed, as though the magic *had* to happen, with or without his intervention.

The sigh, then, was a measure of the weight of his responsibility. To teach Víctor everything that Galván knew and to urge him to surpass his master was comparable to setting him on a rollercoaster with no firm ground waiting for him below, only an abyss, an endless cycle, a constant rushing forward towards something new, something better, always something better, an imaginary goal which, if attained, simply meant starting again from the beginning. The more the maestro fuelled this frantic search, the better a magician his student would become. He was doomed to fall from grace: he might be courageous, enthusiastic, perhaps even brilliant, prize-winning, but he would fall from favour in the end. Did Víctor have the strength and the discipline necessary to ride this rollercoaster without being thrown off?

To judge by the enthusiasm with which he presented himself at his second lesson, he was not lacking in determination. When he saw the boy take out the deck of cards, Galván could not help but smile. The cards looked as though they were about to fall to pieces. Clearly Víctor had been practising Hoffmann's card trick over and over.

'I've been thinking,' the student said as he sat down at the table, 'I could pick up the deck and say . . .'

'Don't tell me what you could do.' The maestro cut him off immediately. 'Show me . . .'

Víctor smoothed the green baize mat several times to gain a few seconds, as though he needed to run through the story before launching into it, then he began:

'Actually, I'm not a magician.'

'Stand up,' Galván commanded.

'Actually, I'm not a magician,' Víctor said as he got to his feet, irritated at the interruptions and clutching the deck tensely in his left hand. 'The thing is, I found this deck of cards and it turns out they have magic powers ...'

Galván's heart skipped a beat. He had heard a thousand different versions of this story. Whenever a magician lacks experience or talent, they play dumb. The most common thing is for the magician to start by saying that, actually, he is not a magician, or he is, but only reluctantly, that objects acquire miraculous powers the moment he picks them up. If it works, it's a double triumph because the magician has overcome his self-proclaimed lack of ability; if he fails, he has set up a logic by which his failure can be viewed as funny, winning him the sympathy of the audience.

Galván repressed the sigh that welled up inside him so as not to influence Víctor, but he could not help but look at the boy pleadingly: don't let me down, make me correct the way you hold your cards as often as you like, pick the wrong card, get nervous, drop the whole pack on the floor, but show me something of yourself, show me some talent.

Víctor carried on with his predictable story, which gave him time to shuffle and cut the cards precisely as the trick required.

'And the best thing is that every single one of these cards has the same powers. To prove it, we're going to pick a card at random. And so you can be sure that I'm not cheating, I'm going to flick them from one hand to the other until you tell me to stop. The card at the top of the deck when you say stop will be our card.'

Galván had the good grace to wait until at least half the cards had been transferred before saying 'Stop.'

Víctor handed him the card and the maestro screwed up his face.

'No,' he said seriously.

'No what?'

'It has to be a different card.'

Víctor did not understand.

'Is it the ace of hearts?'

'Of course.'

'Then it worked, that's what it's supposed to be.'

'That's why it should be a different card.'

'I don't understand.'

'All are children of God. Never forget that. A deck has fifty-two cards and all of them are children of God. The magician's first weapon is chance. And it's not plausible that chance would always pick aces and kings. It makes you a banal magician. Like writers who only tell tales of great feats, or musicians who play only catchy tunes.'

'OK, I get it.'

'What's the next card?'

Víctor turned it over and said:

'The six of clubs.'

'Perfect. Let's suppose chance has picked that one. All are children of God,' he said again. 'Carry on.'

Víctor continued, his voice feeble. Galván had just ignored a feat which it had taken him endless hours to perfect and which he had good reason to be proud of. However valid the maestro's criticism, the fact remained that as an inexperienced student, with no guide but Hoffmann's obscure instructions and an English dictionary, he had managed to execute the fundamental skill required for any trick: forcing a card. What difference did it make whether it was an ace or a six? Didn't he at least deserve some praise? It would be weeks before Víctor realised that this was a deliberate strategy on Galván's part to encourage him to do better: negating every major success with some minor objection. But at that moment, nervous and resentful, he could only carry on because the muscles in his hands knew the routine by heart. When he came to the end, he had to drop the pack on to the table suddenly, from a height of about six inches. If he did it correctly, all of the cards would land face down with the exception of Galván's card, which would land face up on top of the deck. But, instead of a subtle, final movement, he dropped the cards from three feet higher than necessary. Hearing the racket as they landed on the table, he started, and closed his eyes for an instant. When he opened them again, he did not see, as he expected, the pack strewn chaotically across the table, but a perfect pile. It looked as though, while he had his eyes closed, Galván had gathered them together out of sheer compassion. However, the first card, which had flipped over and was lying face up on the others, was not the six of clubs. Víctor stared at the pack. His hands were shaking. He touched them as though looking for some explanation.

'It's OK,' Galván quickly reassured him.

Staring at the face and hands of his student, Galván did not even need to look at the table to know that something had gone wrong. Víctor's eyebrows had just jackknifed twice, signalling the mistake.

'Take off your glasses and try again,' Galván commanded.

Upset, Víctor took off his glasses, set them on the table and tugged at his shirt cuffs. Galván immediately leaned forward, as though trying to discover the source of some hushed sound, and just as Víctor was about to pick up the pack, he slapped his hand down on the pile, like a cat catching a mouse.

'Sing that song for me,' he demanded.

'Song? Which song?'

Something Very Strange

He has been short-sighted since he was nine. Over the years he has had his sight tested dozens of times and, on occasion, his correction had gone up by half a dioptre. Look at the chart. Read as far as you can. OK, that's it. You can go now. Sometimes, he would quickly try to make a word out of the letters before they moved on to the next chart. Once, he needed only an 'I' to spell INSECT and he cried as he left because he could not tell his father.

Now, he does not know where to begin. 'Something very strange.' This is the only phrase that occurs to him when he is asked the reason for his visit. 'Something very strange happened to me.' He prefers not to say that, just before the white halo appeared, he was blindfolded. It would be difficult to do so without explaining that he is a professional magician. If anyone asked him to do a trick now, he would not be accountable for his actions.

They sit him with his forehead pressed against a machine such that his eyes are only millimetres from a visor. If he were in the mood, he would say 'Cuckoo!' as the optician peers at him from the other side of the device. But he is not in the mood. He says nothing. He feels a point of warmth sweep slowly outwards from the inside of his left eye. Then the process is repeated with his other eye. Víctor imagines that this will cure him, that the heat will somehow dissolve the impurities. Easy. A magic laser that can make full moons disappear.

When it's over, a nurse tells him to make himself comfortable, that he will have to wait for a few minutes. His eyes are watering. He would love to be able to burst into tears, into great gasping sobs, but it is simply a physiological reaction to the fact that he has not blinked for too long. He keeps his head down, staring fixedly at a join in the parquet floor to see whether the halo is getting bigger as he waits. The halo in his left eye is still where it was when it first appeared. The one in his right eye comes and goes, a white pulse, a shooting star. He is suddenly struck by a memory of his mother. Her voice: don't stare so hard at the paper, you'll go blind. The ophthalmologist places a hand on his shoulder.

'From what I can see, your eyes are fine. I think perhaps you should see a neurologist.'

'But the white spot ...'

'Human eyesight is a complicated thing ...'

'A neurologist ...' he echoes now incongruously, as though it has taken him some time to process the information.

'That's not to rule out ...'

Is nobody capable of completing a sentence?

'That I'm going blind.'

Blind. There, he's said it. The terrible word hovers over the high plateau of his brain like a hungry eagle, chooses a place to alight, folds its wings against its body and thrusts out its powerful talons. All other thoughts are now just frightened rabbits.

'It's possible that it's psychosomatic in origin. Have you been particularly stressed recently?'

'A little.'

'Well, that might explain it. Trust me, make an appointment to see the neurologist. In the meantime, try to take your mind off it, think about something else. You need to relax.'

The time it takes to process his credit card seems endless. When the moment comes for him to sign, he closes his left eye unthinkingly as though to see what it would be like to be one-eyed.

Stepping out into the street, he bumps into the first passer-by. They don't actually collide; it is barely a brush, a clash between the air each person trails in his wake, but Víctor freezes, stands petrified on the pavement. He is still standing there when the other person crosses the street. Night is falling. Víctor begins to walk, head down, staring at the patch of ground a few inches in front of his feet. People turn to stare. It is impossible to say whether he is trying to walk carefully or steeling himself to bump into someone else. Or whether it is just that his mind is on other things.

41

When he gets home, he goes straight into the kitchen, fills a pan with water, goes out on to the terrace, sits in a chair with the saucepan on his knees and stares out into the distance, across the rooftops. After a while, he places his right hand on the formicarium. For ten minutes he does not move. He does not even blink. He is thinking about the ants. Although, after his father died, he got out of the habit of doing his Saturday morning chores, he has carried on filling the moat with water from time to time. It has been years since he saw a single specimen crawling over the surface, but he has always suspected that there is still something living deep beneath the earth. He pictures the day when the ants realised no one was going to leave food for them in the little box. Perhaps the first envoys dispatched on an urgent mission came back with news that there was no talc on the formicarium walls. Hundreds of worker ants were sent out to find food but only one, half dead, came back to report that there was still water in the moat. Clearly they didn't say: 'We're alone. We're under siege. Somebody do something.' Ants don't talk. They learned to go out only at night. They crossed bridges. Fragile, precarious, made up of tiny twigs found on the surface, pieces of dead leaf and even the corpses of their fellow ants. Every night, dozens drowned on the way out and dozens more on the way back. Only a few made it to the safety of the terrarium with a few crumbs to share, hurrying down into the depths of the earth before they were spotted by that boy – no longer really a boy – who still circled the formicarium from time to time, his ear pressed to the glass, rapping with his knuckles.

What are you doing here, Víctor? Are you waiting for instructions? There are no instructions now, and no maestro to give them to you. The manual of darkness that lies in wait for you has not been written. No one has yet predicted whether you are going to be one hell of a blind man. And you've already got the little wretch thing nailed. Fate, however cruel it may seem, does not wish you harm. It is simply warning you what is about to happen to you. Get moving, get moving now. Stop hanging around. Yes, something very strange is happening to you. And not just to your eyesight. A man is accountable for his time, Víctor. He has a duty to take it with him, close to heel like a ferocious dog that must be muzzled.

You stopped on that stair and set the dog loose. You wanted to stop and survey your life from its happiest moment. Well, this is the result. Time has turned on you, bared its fangs and attacked you with its chaos. One hell of a magician. A little wretch. One of these days you'll kill yourself.

Caught up in memories and predictions, Víctor is oblivious to the present. The present is that the doorbell is ringing. Urgently. Relentless. Five rings and Víctor still has not noticed. He does not even know how long he has been sitting here. His right hand is still pressed against the glass of the formicarium. He thinks he has been tracking the course of the moon but he wouldn't dare swear that the white dot is not in his left eye. Perhaps he has nodded off, sitting with his back rigid, his ankles tense, the toes of his shoes pressed to the ground.

When he finally hears the doorbell, he jumps to his feet, spilling the saucepan of water. He goes to the door and flings it open. Outside is Galván, his finger poised to ring the bell again.

'If you're here for your fifteen per cent,' says Víctor, 'it's not a good time.'

Galván stands, open mouthed, looks Víctor up and down: the scruffy hair, the dark circles under his eyes, his trousers wet. The difference between this slob and the stylish man he has known for years is much more than aesthetic. The worst thing is the tone of his voice. And his words. What he just said. In twenty-two years, Víctor has never once been disrespectful to him. Especially not when it comes to money matters. Why is he being like this now? Who cares about the fucking fifteen per cent? Galván came out of concern for him, to find out why he disappeared from the party without saying goodbye. He is hurt. No one has the right to talk to him like that at his age, least of all Víctor. He turns on his heel and heads towards the stairs.

'Mario!' Víctor's voice stops him. 'Mario, I'm sorry ... Don't go, please ... Come back.'

Galván hesitates for a moment until Víctor's tone, the sadness in his voice, the feeling he might suddenly burst into tears like a child, forces him upstairs again. Hardly has he crossed the threshold when Víctor falls into his arms. It is the second time he has done this in less than forty-eight hours. But the

43

circumstances on the night of the party were different: the excitement, the culmination of the years they had both devoted to reaching that moment, could account for his distress. He had hugged Galván so hard it hurt. But this is not a hug. It is a breakdown. Galván knows that were he to take one step back, were he to let go, Víctor would collapse like a marionette with its strings cut. His arms still around Víctor, he manoeuvres him back into the apartment as though they were staggering back together from a night on the tiles.

It is difficult to get any coherent explanation from Víctor beyond the words 'I'm going blind.' Galván talks to him as one might a wayward child, forcing him to look into his eyes, repeating the same questions over and over until he has managed to elicit some information and make sense of it: the green door, the red card, the full moon in his eye, the visit to the ophthalmologist.

At first Galván tries to play it down. The doctor is probably right, Víctor's just suffering from stress. It's probably because he's exhausted. Then he tries nagging him, trying to get Víctor to react. Since when did whining ever solve anything? Galván tells him that if he's so worried, instead of sitting here snivelling, he should do something. Reminds him that he's not short of money, he could see any number of specialists he wants. He should see the neurologist. Or go to casualty. Galván offers to go with him right now, but he cannot even get Víctor off the sofa.

Then, just as in the old days, comes the lecture. Galván tells Víctor he has no right to go to pieces like this without a fight, reminds him he is the finest magician in the world, not because of some jury's decision at a festival, but because they have both been working towards that goal for years, ever since Víctor was a wide-eyed brat. He has a moral obligation to himself, Galván warns, and to Galván who has led him by the hand all the way and has no intention of letting go now. He lingers over the memories of the tough times, the faith and the tenacity that brought them through. He tries to imply that even if his worst fears are realised, even if he loses the sight in both eyes, Víctor will still be the best magician in the world because the true miracles take place in the mind; performing them is simply mechanics, muscular memory. He does not need to be able to see to be who he is. Until Víctor cuts him off. For the first time, he looks Galván in the eye and says calmly:

'Do you understand, Mario?'

'I understand. You've been thrown a curveball.'

'I'm not talking about that. This is the first time you've been wrong. In all these years, you've always known what was best for me better than I knew myself. You only had to say the word and I knew which way to go. Not only in magic.'

'OK, OK,' Galván modestly tries to interrupt.

'Let me finish.' Víctor cuts him short. He is serious, curt, determined, as though he has spent years honing the words he is about to say. 'I hope you know how grateful I am to you, though I never found a way of telling you that when we first met, I was just a kid who wanted to learn how to do magic. I didn't even know why. A lot of good things have happened to me since and I know better than anyone what it took to make them happen. But I also know that none of it would have been possible if you hadn't always been there, showing me the way. You've been good to me. That stuff about your fifteen per cent was below the belt. I'm sorry.'

'It's forgotten.'

'But this time, you're wrong. You want things to carry on as they were before, but that's not possible. I have to stop, Mario. I don't know how this thing is going to pan out, I don't even know what's going to happen tomorrow, but right now I don't give a fuck about magic.'

Galván flinched.

'Don't say that, Víctor. You owe a lot to magic. You're a magician. I don't just mean that it's your vocation, how you earn your living, that, like me, you probably couldn't do anything else. It's something more. This might sound simplistic, but a man is what he does. And you do magic.'

'But right now I can't perform the one trick I want. To get my eyesight back. There's nothing in my hands, nothing up my sleeve. What do you think? Anyway, you should be happy seeing me like this.'

'I don't know why.'

'Many years ago you predicted I'd be a little wretch. Maybe you don't remember. We never talked about it. You didn't even know

45

I'd overheard you. A little wretch and one hell of a magician. Bingo, Mario. It's all come true, but in the wrong order.'

'Of course I remember. And I'm sorry you overheard. Besides, I was talking about something else.'

'It doesn't matter now. You know why it didn't bother me? Because I was holding a copy of Hoffmann's book. You'd just given it to me so I could practise forcing a card. I didn't know how important it was, but I had the feeling you had just given me the road map to my whole life. At the time, that was all I needed.'

'And you pulled it off, congratulations.'

'But it's not enough. Now, I need a different map. I have to think about the future. About the immediate future, because this thing is moving fast. I have to start planning for the future that will be here before I know it. Instead, I seem to be spending my days thinking about the past. I've been dreaming about my father. I've been thinking about Peter Grouse, about Kellar. Not a day goes by that I don't think about the first time you and I met. I feel as if I'm locked inside the Proteus Cabinet, surrounded by mirrors, about to change into a spirit.'

'A spirit? Well, I always did predict great things for you,' Galván tried to inject a note of humour. 'If you like, we can convene the Seybert Commission.'

'Don't fuck around, Mario, this is serious.'

A Line of Fire

offmann? The most important thing is that you master his work, that you practise it until your hands hurt, but I'll tell you who he was. A little history never goes amiss. Professor Hoffmann's name was not Hoffmann and he was never a professor of anything. He was Angelo John Lewis, attorney. As a magician, he's not worth even a passing mention in a footnote in the appendix of any specialist reference book. But it would be impossible to write a history of magic without citing 1876, the date *Modern Magic* was first published in Philadelphia, as a fundamental watershed.

We know very little about him. He learned magic as a child, but there's no record that he ever performed in public and there's no way to know whether it was crippling shyness that stopped him, or lack of talent. He also liked to write so he decided to combine these two passions and set down everything he knew about the magician's art of his time. What is most surprising is how much he knew, because besides documenting tricks and techniques that had not changed for centuries, beyond the aesthetic changes imposed by fashion, *Modern Magic* also gave an incredibly detailed account of the latest advances in the profession. And we are not talking about sleight of hand, where techniques could be worked out by logic and intuition. We are talking about sheer engineering, illusions so impressive their inventors could sell out the biggest theatres in the world for months on end.

The public of the day adored two illusions in particular: disappearances and levitation. Every magician racked his brains – or paid someone to do it for him – to find some way of making increasingly bigger objects or creatures disappear as the audience watched. As for levitation, a skilled engineer could become a millionaire if he could find a way of fitting everyday objects – chairs, tables, beds, carpets – with an undetectable mechanism that could 'levitate' a magician's assistant for a while. Turn on the television today and it's clear that the passion for these illusions has not died and that a number of magicians have the nerve to perform levitation tricks using the same contraptions described by Hoffmann in the chapter 'Suspension in the Air'.

After publishing *Modern Magic* the bogus professor had to vanish for a while. Had he not done so he might have been killed. It may seem surprising, but the magicians of the day didn't pull their punches when it came to protecting their secrets. Cases of extortion, bribery, industrial espionage and the outright theft of tricks were not uncommon. Intellectual property over devices and contraptions was so jealously guarded that simply changing a nail or a screw would send someone rushing to the patents office.

The atmosphere of intense competition was even worse since magicians were not only competing with one another for audiences. Spiritualism, which had taken off a few years earlier, led by the Davenport Brothers, was threatening to eclipse magic. Magicians and spiritualists performed exactly the same illusions onstage, among them a star turn that might be called 'the magic cabinet' – an ordinary-looking wardrobe in which apparently inexplicable events occurred.

Spiritualists attributed these phenomena to the presence of supernatural forces summoned by them. The public accepted this message with something more dangerous than mere credulity: their need to believe in supernatural elements was so intense that the trick always worked, in spite of the crudeness of some of those who performed it.

Until that point, only the gods – or, at best, their emissaries, the prophets and the saints – had challenged the power of magicians. From the moment the Davenport Brothers and their imitators appeared, magicians discovered that the battle had been brought to earth and must be fought theatre by theatre, seat by seat. Facing down the spiritualists by claiming to have greater powers over invisible forces than they did would not have been clever. And so, they wielded the only weapon that seemed effective against such an onslaught: the truth. If the Davenport Brothers made London audiences tremble with their 'spirit cabinet', the following night John Nevil Maskelyne, generally considered to be the finest magician of his generation, opened his performance at the Egyptian Hall with a direct and brutal reference to them: 'Last night, someone dared to affirm in this same city,' he told the audience, 'that the events we are about to witness are the result of higher incorporeal powers. I propose to prove that they are charlatans. I can equal their feats with the aid of nothing more than science and my own ingenuity.'

It was a sea-change, an act of enormous daring. Having pretended for centuries to possess the ability to perform impossible feats, magicians now saw themselves forced to admit that they performed tricks. In short, that there was no such thing as magic. Rather than fighting for possession of the treasure, they denied the booty existed.

Only in this context is it possible to explain the publication of *Modern Magic*. In fact it is likely that Hoffmann wrote it with the best possible intentions: since everything was based on mechanical science, it made sense to collect it into a manual, a sort of encyclopaedia which might open the eyes of the public, force them to understand, to accept once and for all that the marvels they witnessed did not depend on some occult power.

The truth, however, aside from being a feeble weapon in any argument, frequently has unexpected consequences. A few weeks after Hoffmann's manual was published, in major cities across the Western world, shops selling magical tricks and paraphernalia found themselves obliged to slash their prices. Overnight, they had gone from being the purveyors of secrets to simple manufacturers. As for the theatres, if they did not empty overnight it was only because impresarios had always padded out magic shows with animal circuses, dancers, clowns and charlatans who now took top billing while the magicians relied for their – much-diminished – success on their ability to perform Hoffmann's tricks with finesse.

Of course, regardless of what the bogus professor's intentions were, his contemporaries cursed him as a traitor. There had previously been cases where magicians – in professional publications with limited circulation – had revealed the secrets of tricks they had not invented under the pretext of having perfected them. But it was an unprecedented betrayal that someone should reveal everything in a single book, all the more so when that person, aside from revealing other people's secrets, had never even bothered to put them into practice before an audience. Nor could he be accused of plagiarism, since he was careful to mention – when such information was available – when, where and by whom each trick had been patented, and the costumes and set design usually used in the performance. He frequently included details of the vaudeville plots used as a vehicle for magic tricks. As if this were not enough, he published a second edition in 1879, updated with an appendix which revealed the secrets of the handful of tricks that were not in the first edition.

In all probability, even he could not foresee the chaos his book, *Modern Magic*, would unleash; akin to those moments in nature when an aberrant mutation leads to the creation of a whole new species. The date of publication traced a line of fire that forced magicians to choose on which side they stood. If they chose not to cross it, their fate was sealed: their only glory could be that of skilled practitioners of an art which, though obsolete, was quickly relegated to the category of a craft. In this sense, Hoffmann triggered a purely quantitative increase: since access to the secrets was now available for very little outlay, the number of magicians grew exponentially in the decades that followed.

Those who decided to cross the line were faced with a heroic challenge. To surpass the methods described by Hoffmann was comparable to painting better than Velázquez, being more romantic than Beethoven or giving a more detailed literary reflection of reality than Balzac: it was beyond impossible; it was absurd. They had to invent something different. A few among them tried. Maskelyne came close to succeeding. Houdini managed to do something no less important: he persuaded audiences that he had succeeded. The only person ever to set foot across the line was Peter Grouse, but in doing so, he got burned.

If They Made Me a King

t is impossible for Víctor Losa to think of his father without imagining Louis Armstrong's face. His father was not black, didn't play the trumpet, or flash his teeth when he smiled. And yet, if he closes his eyes and allows memory to carry him along, it is Armstrong's face that he sees. As he does so, Víctor's hips begin to sway in 4/4 time, though it never quite becomes a dance since his feet never leave the ground.

The song is called 'If'. A single note is enough for the lyrics to surge up in his memory. *'If they made me a king/I'd be but a slave to you.'* By the time he was six years old, he knew the lyrics by heart, though he did not understand a single word and – though he often heard the record at home – when he sang it, he made the same pronunciation mistakes as his father. When he was eleven, with the basic English he had learned, his mother's help and long hours spent with a dictionary, he managed to write out a first, clumsy translation: 'If I had everything, I'd still be a slave to you. If I ruled the night, stars and moon so bright, still I'd turn for light to you.'

One might even say that he was able to recognise the melody before he was born. His father had heard or read somewhere that, if you sang the same song regularly, mouth pressed to your wife's belly, after the fifth month of pregnancy, then after the birth the song would help calm the baby when it cried or needed help in getting to sleep. Every night, for four months, he sang 'If', trying to emulate Armstrong's gravelly voice; he even included the rhythmic, meaningless scat Armstrong crooned between each verse: 'If the world to me bowed, yet humbly I cling to you. Baa Daa Doo Dee. If my friends were a crowd, I'd turn on my knees to you. Doo Baa Doo Dee.' When Víctor was born, singing it softly into the child's ear became a routine, regardless of its supposed benefits: it did not always stop the baby crying.

The lyrics hardly seemed appropriate for a lullaby. Perhaps Martín Losa chose the song for practical reasons: if he were looking for a way to calm the child he could not find a better ballad than this, slow almost to the point of solemn but with a swing beat that made it miraculously happy and delightful. It was difficult to listen to it just once. When Víctor inherited the record, the needle of the record player had ploughed the grooves so often that Armstrong's voice sounded as though it were competing with a chorus of crickets. But still he played it. Over the years, he collected every available version of the song, though none seemed to be as good as the original.

The magical effect, if it had ever had one, vanished when he needed it the most. For Víctor, there came a time when his tears were all too real and his father was not there to sing 'If' to him. In fact, it was his absence Víctor mourned, so the very mention of the song made him cry all the more. And yet still he went on playing it, singing it so often that it became a sort of automatic reflex, not only in the face of sorrow, but also when something threatened his peace of mind. Whenever he felt scared or nervous, or when he simply needed to concentrate, the notes to 'If' came from his throat unbidden, so changed that they no longer seemed to form a melody. It was a habit Galván supposedly rid him of once and for all, but one would have to come very close to Víctor to know whether the tremulous sound he makes constantly these days is a whimper of grief or the first six notes of 'If': B♭, C, B♭, A, G, A. Is that it, Víctor? Again? If they made me a king? But they have made you a king. You are king of the world. The finest magician. Dethroned by a song. Song? Which song? This one, Víctor, the same song as always.

Galván made you strip. First the glasses, then the shirt. Then, when your terrified hands sought refuge in your pockets, he made you take off your trousers. He took away the table and the chairs, stepped back into the darkness and commanded you to sing. You wanted to disappear. Why didn't you just pick up your clothes and leave? You stayed in order to side with him. Standing there, bashful. Stripped of everything, even your short-sighted eyes naked, you bowed your head and the blurred pile of clothes at your feet made you think there was a dead body lying there, that it was bitterly cold, that the dead body could be you. You made the sound again, a sound like clearing your throat, but now it is recognisably B♭, C, B♭, and Galván's voice kept hammering in your ears, Sing, sing louder, I can't hear you, Víctor, sing. Perhaps it would have been enough to give form to the melody – after all, he only wanted to make you sing, to make you realise. But then you sang the first line: *'If they made me a king'*. You shivered a little, brought your knees together like the helpless little boy you claimed not to be any more, but you did sing. Softly, out of tune, you sang the first verse almost without moving your lips, and when you reached the second verse, it was not Galván who was urging you on, but Armstrong himself, until you thought you could see his pearly teeth shining in the dark. Or perhaps it was your father. Your father, Víctor. His face, not Armstrong's. His face bending down as though he could press his lips to the belly of time and ask you to sing to put an end to all the tears, so that your voice rose to sing the third verse at the top of your lungs: 'If I ruled the earth, what would life be worth, If I hadn't the right to you Baa-Daa-Baa-Doo Baa-Dah-Boo-Dee'. You thought you could see him smiling, and when you finished you were sure it was him clapping until Galván took a step forward, became visible, his arms wide, and said, 'Come here, come here, you silly boy,' and though three minutes earlier you would have sworn undying hatred, you rushed into his arms, which were Armstrong's arms and your father's arms and your own arms, hugging them all at once. Put your clothes on, Víctor.

It worked. When Víctor bent down to pick up his clothes, what lay there no longer looked like a dead body but a moulted skin he had shed. As he put on his clothes he realised he was tired, but he was thankful for the feeling of relief that came with that exhaustion. Galván placed the chairs back under the spotlight, told him to take a seat and asked him about the song. Before he got to the important part, Víctor described Armstrong, the white teeth, the gravelly voice, the scat. He mentioned Evans, Hargreaves and Damerell, who had written the music and lyrics, remembering their names from the record sleeve read so often during his childhood. He talked about the versions by John Gary, Perry Como, Billy Eckstine and Dean Martin, pointed out that Art Tatum was the only person to record an instrumental version and ridiculed Mario Lanza's attempt to turn it into an aria.

Until that moment, Galván had never heard his student utter more than a dozen words at a time. And so, though this was not the particular information that interested him, he decided not to interrupt, until Víctor mentioned his father for the first time.

'Name?' he interjected.

'What name?'

'Your father. What was his name?'

'Martín.'

'Martín Losa.'

'Yes.'

'Carry on.'

'My father started singing me this song . . .'

'Martín Losa,' the maestro interrupted him again, 'Martín Losa used to sing this song to his son Víctor . . .' then he waved his hand for him to continue.

Víctor understood what the maestro wanted and tried to please him, though he remained unconvinced. He began uneasily, his words disjointed and vague, feigning detachment, as though the story of this Martín Losa and his son Víctor was really about someone else. Gradually, forced through words into some sort of order, the unfortunate events of his childhood began to conform to a certain logic: feeble and governed principally by luck and recklessness, but a logic nonetheless. He had recalled a thousand times his father's death almost ten years earlier. His imagination was so attuned to the uncertainties and the miseries he associated with that period of his life that, when he came to recount it, and though the words poured from his mouth in a torrent, every detail naturally began to find its place and the tale took on a surprising consistency. From time to time, he was astonished to find himself relating something he thought he had forgotten, but he had no time to savour the feeling because, like water too long dammed up bursting its banks, the story hurtled on, carrying him with it. The feeling of relief was so great that Víctor was sorry when he came to the end of the story. He said nothing for a moment, searching his memory, and glanced at Galván as though a question from him might help him rescue some important detail from oblivion. The maestro simply nodded, as though Víctor had just performed some new exercise perfectly, and told him to pick up the deck of cards. The lesson was over. Before he said goodbye, Galván gave him a list of the exercises to practise for the following class and the corresponding page numbers in *Modern Magic*.

An Exciting Case

'**D**o you know what day it is?'
    He has to think. He has to think back to the night of the party in his honour, which, he guesses, was Monday, and count from there, but he picks his way through as though this were a minefield. Thursday? He can't bring himself to say it.

'What day of the week?'

The neurologist frowns and looks at him dubiously.

'Or the date. Whichever you prefer.'

'The date? But I never know what date it is!'

The neurologist glowers.

'Thursday. I think it's Thursday.'

'Good. Do you know where you are?'

'In a doctor's consulting room. At least that's what I thought; right now it feels like a nursery.'

'Don't be impatient. The questions may sound ridiculous, but I have to ask them.'

'It's just that what's wrong with me is . . .'

'I know. Your eye. But I need to give you a general examination.'

For twenty minutes he feels as though he is going crazy. First, the doctor asks him to name three things in the room. Víctor scans it with deliberate care and answers: 'A clock, a bed, a photo of your wife and son. I assume.' Then the neurologist asks him to clap his hands; then clap them again, then look at the ceiling. He keeps Víctor talking constantly as though trying to coax some secret from him. He picks up a stick and holds it by one end. Close one eye and look at the stick. What were the three objects: clock, bed, photo. Now the other eye. Can you see the red dot?

'Really? It's red? It's just that with the left eye . . .'

The doctor sighs. That's it. He's found something. Something

56

serious. Maybe it's not just that he's going blind. Maybe it's something terminal. A brain tumour.

'You see, I have this little spot …'

A little spot, a small smudge, a tiny moon. The diminutives don't make it sound any less serious. From that moment, Víctor interprets every word, every action of the neurologist, as proof that his brain is harbouring some foreign body, something living, deadly, an enemy lying in wait. The doctor systematically checks his motor reflexes, his manual dexterity, strength and sensitivity, his co-ordination and his reflexes. He checks his torso, then begins to examine his legs. When Víctor sees him pick up the hammer to check his knee reflexes, he can stand it no longer. He pushes the doctor's hands away, sits up on the bed and protests:

'Listen, if I'm going to end up paralysed, I'd rather you just told me straight out.'

'Have you been suffering from stress lately?' the doctor asks after a pause, the hammer still hovering in the air. Víctor cannot quite decide whether what he can see in the man's eyes is a glimmer of compassion. 'This kind of condition can sometimes be stress-related.'

'That's what the ophthalmologist asked me. And yes, I've been out of my mind with worry. It's hardly surprising. Look, there's nothing wrong with my knees. Take my word for it. They're fine. It's my eyes that are the problem.'

'Not exactly. It's your eyesight. The reason you're here is because the ophthalmologist ruled out there being something wrong with your eyes.'

'Eyes? Plural?'

'Either or neither. We don't know yet.'

'So what now?'

'Well, now we have to rule out any neurological problem. Eyes are merely the lens of the camera. In reality, we see with this …'

The man brings his hand up to the nape of his neck and massages it with a slight rotary movement. Unconsciously, Víctor imitates the gesture.

'Here?'

'Exactly. Between the eyes and the visual cortex, there are any number of nerve connections that might present a problem.'

'A ... serious problem?'

'We can't know that until we've carried out a series of tests. We'll start with a perimetry test.'

He sits Víctor at a machine and tells him to press a button whenever he sees a light go on. Víctor cannot shake off the feeling that he is taking an exam, and as he presses the button, he desperately wants someone to tell him whether he's getting it right. After repeating the test with the right eye, and having made no comment, the doctor goes back to his desk and starts to write. Víctor waits, trying to remain calm, but he feels his vocal cords quiver and recognises the first six notes of 'If'. He is convinced the man is taking too long over what he is writing. He is convinced he is going to die.

'Do I have a brain tumour?' he asks, finally, his voice almost inaudible.

His throat feels so tight he is not even sure that the words came out. In fact, the doctor keeps writing as though he has heard nothing, and it is a moment before he looks up.

'If I told you I think it's unlikely, would you feel any better? Right now, the important thing is to do more tests: a blood test, a chest X-ray, an ECG and a cranial MRI scan.'

As he lists them, he hands Víctor the forms he has been filling out one by one, as though dealing cards from a deck. The game seems crucial, the stakes high, because there is a glint in the doctor's eye now, an excitement that Víctor did not notice earlier.

'I'm confident these tests will give us the answer. If not, we might need to do a lumbar puncture to rule out multiple sclerosis. Antibodies too.' He suddenly goes back to writing his notes. He makes no attempt to explain to Víctor what he has just said. He does not even look at him. He is talking to himself. 'Maybe genetic screening.' He looks up again as though he has just thought of something he might have overlooked. 'Is there any family history?'

'Family history of what?'

'Of blindness.'

Víctor cannot believe what he is seeing. The guy is licking his lips at the prospect. He can't even bring himself to hide the fact. All the years of studying, hospital rotations, endless bureaucracy and frustrating routine check-ups suddenly became worthwhile the moment Victor stepped through the door. Finally, he has an exciting case.

'Not that I know of.'

'You'll need to get authorisation from your health insurance for the tests. Come and see me when you've got the results. They should be ready in about three weeks. Oh, and take these pills,' he adds, handing Victor one last piece of paper. 'They'll keep you calm.'

Papá is Asleep

Most of the nicotine in a cigarette is eliminated by combustion. The rest is absorbed by the body and the respiratory system becomes accustomed to ever greater doses. However, even for a chronic smoker, nicotine in liquid form is lethal, immediately, whether it is ingested, inhaled or absorbed through the skin. Nicotine is the most common toxic agent in insecticides. Among those accustomed to handling the toxin professionally, there is an urban myth that a single drop in the eye of a horse will cause the animal to collapse within a few steps. Martín Losa would certainly have been familiar with the story. This is why it is impossible that he would not have seen, or, if he were not looking, would not have sensed purely by touch, that he was about to make a terrible, irreversible mistake.

Fortunately, he was alone. Had there been anyone else breathing the air in that room, or anywhere else in the house, they would have died with him, like him: asphyxiated in five seconds. Eight, if we're being generous. Every single second would have been a living hell.

Although there were no witnesses, what his wife and son saw when they discovered his body, together with the medical examiner's report, makes it possible for us to reconstruct what happened with reasonable accuracy. There were six jars on the table. Five of them contained different liquids Martín was testing for their efficacy as excipients. The sixth, which was slimmer than the others and rough to the touch, precisely to avoid any confusion, contained a concentrated brownish solution of nicotine. Even so, Martín took the top off this jar, held it up for a second or two and then put it into the heating block.

Almost immediately the poison began to evaporate and found its way into his lungs.

Martín would have noticed an intense burning sensation in his throat. He might have thought he had a dry mouth, but just then his body would have begun to produce torrents of frothy saliva. Then came the nausea, a pain in his stomach so severe he would have doubled up suddenly as though trying to bite his knees. It is impossible to know whether he had time to realise what was happening to him, but everything indicates that by then his mind would have been in the grip of paralysing confusion. His vision would have become cloudy, his hearing dulled. Convulsions in his right side made him drop the tweezers he had been holding. They landed about three metres away, next to the door, with an ant squashed between the pincers. One last spasm left Martín sprawled on the floor. Immediately afterwards, as though it were some sort of conspiracy, all the muscles involved in the breathing process went into paralysis. And he died.

According to the medical examiner, death took place around 7 p.m. As they did every Saturday, his wife and his son Víctor arrived home half an hour later. In the hall she struggled for a couple of seconds, getting her son's coat off. The nicotine had completely evaporated by now, so it could not have been the smell that alerted her. Perhaps she noticed that her husband had not popped out to say hello as he usually did when he heard the key turn in the lock. Muffled music came from the closed workshop, but there was nothing unusual about that. Martín always liked to have music playing. Without saying a word, his wife buttoned the boy's coat again and led him back on to the landing.

'Stay here, don't move,' she told the boy. 'Everything's fine. *Mamá* will be right back.' She went into the house then quickly popped her head around the door again. 'Did you hear me, Víctor? Whatever happens, you're not to move from there.'

Then she walked down the corridor.

Víctor closed his eyes and held his breath. It was something he always did when he played hide-and-seek. He was not sure whether his mother was playing a game, but he had only to listen to her voice to be sure. 'Martín ... Martín ...' His mother called the name over and over in a whisper that seemed increasingly tremulous until, after the creak of a hinge, she screamed 'Martín!' at the top of her lungs. Then the music stopped. Shortly afterwards he heard footsteps. It has been thirty years since that day and what Víctor remembers most now about those few minutes in which he did not see, did not know, could not imagine what was happening, is the silence that followed, broken some moments later by the sound of the dial on the telephone turning. Then he heard his mother talking in a low voice; there was a sense of urgency but also a weariness, as though she were complaining about something it was too late to change.

Although he remembered that she had told him not to move, Víctor thought that maybe the game had changed now, that maybe it was his turn to find his parents, Or worse, that the game was over and his parents had forgotten about him. So he got to his feet and tiptoed into the hall. His parents had never been very good at hide-and-seek. But he, at six years old, knew all the best places to hide. And so, as he stepped inside, he wore a crafty smile. He reached his father's workshop, pushed open the door as quietly as he could and saw his father sprawled on the floor. He was almost disappointed that it had been so easy. But, engrossed in the ritual of the game, he let out a whoop of joy, threw himself on Martín's lifeless body and screamed:

'Here I come, ready or not, *Papá*!'

When his father did not react, Víctor pushed his fingers into his father's tummy, trying to tickle him.

'Come on, *Papá* ... It's your turn ...'

Bewildered by his father's utter stillness, Víctor made a puzzled face. Was this a different game? Sometimes they played at being asleep, but that was usually later, after dinner, when he had his pyjamas on. Víctor decided to test the theory. He lay down next to Martín, closed his eyes, squeezing them tight, and pretended to snore.

At that moment his mother came in. She didn't scold him for disobeying her. Instead she did something that is still etched on his memory: she rushed across the room, lifting her feet carefully to step over them and, reaching the window, she threw it wide open. Although it was cold. Although it was late. Then she tried to take her son in her arms, but her legs gave way beneath her. She sat down on the floor, gently pulled Víctor away from his father and sat him on her lap. Víctor did not understand what was happening. He looked from his mother's tears to his father's smile: an inexplicable, larger-than-life grimace but a smile nonetheless. Just as he was about to give up, the boy stared again at the mouth, stretched so wide it seemed distorted, the curious angle of the jaw, and then, slowly, he looked his father's body up and down. He thought he had worked it out. Guess the animal. They played this all the time. It had to be an animal, that was the only thing that could explain the unnatural posture, the arms twisted against the solar plexus, the legs drawn up to the waist but completely stiff as though frozen there.

'A cockroach!'

He said it as if it were an incantation, as though the word would not only put an end to his father's game but might also break the spell that held them all motionless.

Instead of congratulating him for guessing correctly, his mother hugged him harder. Víctor remembers the unusual smell of sweat. He remembers being annoyed by his wool jacket chafing at his face. At this point he began to think that perhaps his father was not playing a game but he could think of no other reason for his strange posture. He thinks he remembers struggling for a moment and then his mother stroked his face and said:

'Shhh. *Papá* is asleep.'

She said it over and over: *Papá* is asleep. *Papá* is asleep, darling, *Papá* is asleep. This is how he knows that it was a long time before the doorbell rang. Some men in uniforms took *Papá* away on a stretcher. Then more people came. There was a long conversation with two policemen on the sofa in the dining room, which Víctor remembers because he fell asleep. *Papá* is asleep, Víctor too.

The next day, he woke to the unexpected hum of soft voices. Visitors on a Sunday morning; this was an event so unusual that he had to investigate. He was putting on his slippers when his mother came into his room carrying a large wooden box. She set it on the ground, then sat down on the bed next to him to explain that his father was dead. To *try* to explain to him. You remember *Papá* fell asleep last night? He's still asleep. When is he going to

63

wake up? He might never wake up, *hijo*. Never? But where is he? They took him away, remember? I remember, but when is he coming back? He's not coming back. You mean we won't ever see him again? Well, maybe we'll see him some day, a long, long time from now. Up in heaven? That's right, darling, we'll see him in heaven.

She did her utmost to smile for him, but could not quite hide the grief, the tension at the corners of her mouth. And though at that age he could not have put it into words, Víctor knew it was a grief she would never truly overcome. Perhaps he would not be a little wretch, perhaps he would find the strength to overcome this event, but always, behind every smile, he would see a ghostly trace of that grief and he could do nothing to console her. He hugged her as hard as he could and she, surprised by this sudden role reversal, trembled as he held her. Then she pointed to the wooden box.

'I've brought you some of his things. *Papá* would have wanted you to have them. You don't have to look at them now. Some of them are for when you're a bit older.'

Víctor lifted the lid and glanced inside. The first thing he saw was a finger. A severed thumb that was inexplicably clean. He quickly closed the box and, more disgusted than frightened, said:

'There's a thumb in there!'

His mother kissed him and tousled his hair.

'It's only plastic, silly.'

'You mean it's a toy?'

'It's for doing magic.'

'Magic?'

'That right. Now, you need to get dressed. Some visitors have come to say goodbye to your *papá* and they'd like to see you.'

'There's something I have to do first.'

He went into the kitchen, climbed up on a stool so he could reach the tap and filled a jug with water. He went out on to the terrace and then carefully, without spilling a single drop, he poured the water into the moat around the terrarium.

'Are you going to give them food?' his mother asked.

'No.'

'Aren't you going to put talcum powder on the walls like Dad did so they won't drown?'

'No,' Victor said brusquely, as though annoyed at being asked to explain himself.

An Island

Every Tuesday, as he pushed open the green door, Víctor felt as though he were stepping into a parallel universe. The maestro was always sitting at the table, waiting for him in the gloom. As his student entered the room, finding his way by the faint glow from the small window, Galván would hold up his cigarette lighter, the flickering flame like a prearranged signal to indicate he was there. Then he would turn on the ceiling spotlight and exhale the first puff of smoke. As Víctor took his seat, he watched the smoke roll across the green mat and prepared himself once again to set foot on this island, floating in time, swathed in mist, with a curious sun that always hung high in the sky; a perpetual midday in winter.

He never talked about the classes to anyone. Never mentioned them at school, and gave only basic answers to the questions asked by his mother, whose help he needed in order to pay Galván for the lessons.

Often, the whole lesson would go by without them so much as touching the cards, talking instead about the great magicians of history. On the pretext of explaining some crucial development, some theoretical shift that fundamentally changed the history of magic, Galván would slip into the nebulous, extravagant rhetoric befitting great deeds and legends. And Víctor would listen as though Galván were telling him his own life story.

He knew that Galván had a daughter much older than he was, but nothing more. They almost never spoke of anything that did not concern magic. Yet he felt as though he knew the man intimately. Every furrow, every wrinkle on those hands. He could have drawn the half-moons of those fingernails with his eyes closed. The irritating nicotine stain on his index finger. At some point, usually very late, the maestro would announce that the lesson was over, give him his homework for the next lesson and say goodbye. Víctor would leave, always dreading that he might miss something important, as though some once-in-a-lifetime phenomenon might occur on this mist-shrouded island during his absence. The weeks seemed never-ending. The maestro always stayed behind to tidy up. Víctor cannot remember the first time he ever saw Galván outside this room, but he knows that it was months, perhaps a year, after they first met. And although they went on to share a lifetime of endeavours and success, although Galván became the father life had denied him, even now, the very sight of Galván takes Víctor back to a time when four elements – mist, hands, mat, cards – were sufficient to fashion a world. A world which would quickly become his world.

The Seybert Commission

Since he started taking the pills the doctor prescribed, he feels as though his dreams have changed. They are more peaceful now and, even when he cannot understand what is happening in them, they seem to have some sort of order, some internal logic. What is more, he feels conscious, experiencing every moment of his dreams as though the medication has put him in a state of waking sleep in which he never completely loses control. Today he is walking quickly across a tightrope, a wire stretched across an abyss, but he does not experience any anxiety. If he feels himself leaning too far one way or the other, rather than spreading his arms out and waving them theatrically like a tightrope walker, he stops, takes a breath, then carries on. Suddenly, he hears behind him the flint of a lighter being struck. He turns around. Floating in the air, lit by an overhead spotlight, is a long table at which are seated ten men, nine of them completely motionless, their shoulders hunched, chins resting on their chests. Víctor wonders for a moment whether they are dead or merely asleep. However, the tenth man, seated in the middle, is sitting upright, his eyes wide open. He has Galván's face, but is short and tubby. And he is wearing a cassock.

'Since you have managed to find your way here,' he says, after clearing his throat, 'we can only suppose that you have a basic knowledge of magic.'

'A little, yes,' Víctor answers with a smile.

Simply hearing the tone of the man's voice, he knows he is facing a tribunal, but he does not feel apprehensive. There is no question he fears he will not know the answer to.

'And its history.'

'Of course.'

'Then you will know who we are.'

'The Seybert Commission,' Víctor answers with complete confidence. 'And, assuming that the hierarchy of the commission has not changed, you must be the Reverend Samuel Fullerton.'

'Very good, my son.'

'Don't call me your son.' Even Víctor is surprised by the self-controlled rage in his voice, but continues, 'You are not my father.'

'Forgive me, my son, you are right.'

Fullerton traces a spiral in the air with both hands as though urging Víctor to go on, but before he can speak, the man falls forward, his forehead strikes the table and he sinks into the same sleep as his companions. If he does not split open his head it is only because a thick green mat has taken the brunt of the blow.

'In 1883, the University of Pennsylvania received a posthumous bequest of seventy thousand dollars from a local millionaire named Henry Seybert, for the establishment of an endowed chair in "Moral and intellectual philosophy",' Víctor explains to a non-existent audience. The confidence with which he speaks, while still moving up and down the tightrope, makes him sound, not like a student at an oral examination, but a professor teaching a class. 'One of the conditions of Seybert's will was that whoever occupied this chair should personally, or under the aegis of the university, appoint a commission to investigate all moral, religious or philosophical systems that presume to represent the Truth, particularly Modern Spiritualism.' Víctor took a deep breath and gave a satisfied smile; he is confident that he has quoted the text verbatim. 'It was like a quest for the philosopher's stone,' he adds, 'a remit so ambitious that it was even beyond the scope of the entire doctoral body of the university, with all its knowledge of history. But you, Reverend Fullerton, were the first person appointed to the professorial chair and secretary of the commission because, together with the nine other members here present, or should I say here absent, you were able to read between the lines and focus on what truly mattered to the sponsor.

'At this point we should linger for a moment on the character of Henry Seybert,' Víctor went on with the self-assurance of someone who has told the same story a hundred times and knows how best to relate the sequence of events, which inflections to use for maximum effect. 'Seybert was the son of a prominent chemist and mineralogist, a Republican member of the House of Representatives for several terms. Henry also studied chemistry but abandoned this at the age of twenty-two when his father died, leaving him an orphan with a considerable inheritance. His mother had died giving birth to him. Henry Seybert's calling card never mentioned a profession; in directories, his occupation was listed as *Gentleman*. Meaning rich, and idle. However, if one can judge from appearances, he was not happy. There is no reliable evidence to explain why this young man of scientific bent became a follower of spiritualism, so we can only speculate. Perhaps he believed he saw the ghosts of his parents at some point. Perhaps he fell into the clutches of one of the many spiritualists practising at the time, who, exploiting the moral and intellectual doubts of their victims, used crude trickery to convince the latter that the dead wished to communicate with them. Perhaps not. All we can say is that he spent his whole life yearning to make contact with the great beyond, and it was precisely because he did not succeed that he bequeathed his money so that the search might carry on. Or maybe, terrified that he might one day find himself a soul in torment, he wanted to leave the door open for his own return.

'Although I think I know a great deal about this episode in the history of magic, it would be stupid to claim I know more than you do, since, after all, you were involved in it.' Víctor turns to look at the table and does not seem to think it remarkable that all of the members of the commission are still asleep. 'Anyway, you worked out that the only thing Seybert was interested in was the truth about spiritualism and that, if he had lumped it together with other religious, philosophical and ethical systems, it was only to place it within a scientific context. As you know, before inviting self-professed spiritualists to demonstrate their powers before the commission, you decided to limit the enquiries to two concrete points.'

Víctor stops walking and looks up. For some reason, he feels the need to prove to the tribunal that, in spite of the exactness of his account, he is not referring to any notes.

'Firstly, you had to determine whether the phenomena in question were real or imaginary. By which I mean, whether they were something that could be seen, touched or heard or whether they existed only in the mind of the witness. Secondly, you assumed responsibility for confirming what produced these phenomena. Natural forces? Supernatural? Human intervention? Spirits?'

As he says the word 'spirits' he hears a strumming behind him and notices a sudden change in the air temperature. He turns and sees an amorphous mass in the sky, like a cloud that is not fully formed, trailing behind it a line of chalk which reads 'Preliminary Report of the Commission appointed by the University of Pennsylvania to investigate Modern Spiritualism in accordance with the request of the late Henry Seybert with a foreword by H. H. Furness, Jr, 1887'. He is not particularly surprised, he knows the document almost by heart.

Víctor waves his hand like someone turning the page of a newspaper and begins to recite the introduction: 'The commission is composed of men whose days are already filled with duties which cannot be laid aside, and who are able, therefore, to devote but a small portion of their time to these investigations. They are conscious that your honorable body looks to them for a due performance of their task, and the only assurance which they can offer of their earnestness and zeal is in thus presenting to you, from time to time, such fragmentary reports as the following, whereby they trust that successive steps in their progress may be marked. It is no small matter to be able to record any progress in a subject of so wide and deep an interest as the present. It is not too much to say that the farther our investigations extend the more imperative appears the demand for these investigations. The belief in so-called spiritualism is certainly not decreasing. It has from the first assumed a religious tone, and now claims to be ranked among the denominational faiths of the day.

'What chutzpah!' Víctor cries. 'But it was a brilliant tactic.' When he turns he discovers that the ten men have vanished, together with the table at which they were sleeping, yet he continues to address them, his tone accusatory: 'In other words, you made no progress but wanted to continue with your investigations for as long as a single dollar remained to be spent.'

He continues turning the pages. His fingers are covered in chalk dust. When he comes to the index, he realises that his suspicions are unfounded. The chapters of the report are in fact the minutes of dozens of meetings held by the members of the commission with so-called spiritualists, during which time they rigorously recorded every statement by those present, every movement perceived or intuited, from notes taken by Fullerton himself in his role as secretary. Faced with the need to systemise the investigation, they decided to divide up the subject according to the most prevalent manifestations of the time. The first of these was referred to as 'independent writing', in which messages from spirits were transcribed on the concealed surface of a slate held by the medium. For these, they used two pieces of slate, hinged so they could be closed like a book. A piece of chalk was placed inside and the slates were sealed with a screw so that it was clear that any writing that appeared would have occurred without the physical intervention of the spiritualist.

The first two chapters give an account of two sessions held with a Mrs Patterson, a local star in the field of 'independent writing'. In both cases the supposed medium held the sealed slates in her trembling hands for an hour and twenty minutes, under the table and out of sight of the investigators, but she proved incapable of anything but an almost illegible scrawl. Attributing this failure to the supposed negative energy generated by some of those present, she asked to be allowed to make the attempt alone, in her own home. After long deliberations, the commission gave her a pair of hinged slates sealed in such a way that any tampering would immediately become apparent. Patterson took the slates away and brought them back six months later, after considerable pressure on Fullerton's part. She even had the nerve to ask for another pair of slates and the commission agreed. When she returned them after two months, with clear evidence that the seals had been tampered with and marks where a knife had been inserted into one corner, Fullerton noted that 'The Spirits had not taken even the precaution to wipe the broad knife clean from rust or dirt.' Víctor looked up and was disappointed that Fullerton was not there so he could congratulate him on his irony.

The second spiritualist summoned before the commission was Dr Henry Slade, the highest authority on independent writing, for whom they had to pay travel expenses and a two-week hotel stay, sufficient time to determine that his mediation with the spirits was more effective but just as fraudulent as that of Mrs Patterson. Suffice it to say that one of the investigators, exasperated by all this trickery, concealed a pocket mirror in his hand so that he could observe what was happening under the table. In the report, he described seeing 'the reflection of fingers, which were clearly not Spiritual, opening the slates and writing the answer'.

As he reads, Víctor wavers between laughter and indignation. In spite of the good intentions of the commission, the report is a catalogue of cheap con-artists performing tricks worthy only of a sideshow puppeteer. Third-rate typists attempting to pass themselves off as pianists. By contrast the commission's tenacity and consummate zeal in pursuing the investigation seem both admirable and irritating. The report is offensive to his passion for doing things properly. Víctor knows what the spiritualists of the time were capable of.

Fullerton himself, in a separate chapter dealing with the difficulties of his task, explains that they could not find a spiritualist who could justify the considerable success achieved by the movement. From time to time, they would put an ad in the Boston magazine *Banner of Light*, the leading spiritualist publication. These ads were answered by curious characters such as a Dr Rothermel, who claimed to be able to produce sounds from a series of musical instruments merely through psychic force. The instruments were housed in a small portable cabinet covered at the back by a black screen. Rothermel sat on one side, his hands tied to a chair, covered from head to foot with a black curtain. After a few seconds, there was the clear sound of scissors. 'The Spirits are cutting me loose,' the charlatan exclaimed, pretending through various twitches and convulsions to be in a trance. Then a hand suddenly appeared in the cabinet and played each of the instruments in turn. 'We had no difficulty in believing,' Fullerton wrote in the report, 'that the hands which were dexterous enough to play the zither with very remarkable skill, under such conditions, behind the curtain, were deft enough to sever the cords.'

The next chapter of the report is devoted to a Mr W. M. Keeler, famous for his mastery of what at the time were called 'Spiritual

Photographs', in which mysterious figures of angelic or diabolical aspect would appear next to the subject of the photograph. Receiving a letter inviting him to appear before the commission, Keeler responded, agreeing to perform three séances for the sum of $300, payable in advance, the fee to be non-returnable whether or not his efforts proved satisfactory. He also clearly stated that there might be no results because of 'the antagonistic element which might be produced by those persons not in perfect sympathy with the cause'. In addition he wanted guarantees that he would be alone when developing the images in the dark room since the spirits were particularly vulnerable at such moments.

Víctor is growing impatient. He doesn't believe in spirits, nor did he expect that he would stumble on some astonishing revelation in the report, but he did expect a modicum of professional dignity. He goes back to the first page and checks the date again: 1887. It seems impossible that the commission could not find anyone capable of doing a decent job. It is as if a literary commission could not find a single decent poem in the whole of the seventeenth century. He begins to skim through the report, lingers only over the beginning of a paragraph or the capital letters indicating someone's name, until he gets to page 77, where he stumbles on Harry Kellar. Knowing that he performed an independent writing illusion in his stage show with sealed slates similar to those used by Slade, the commission asked him to appear. Kellar, it goes without saying, did not pass up the invitation. On the contrary, he was more than happy to impress the commission, and he did not do so with some illegible scrawl, but with seven sealed slates on which appeared sentences in English, Spanish, French, Dutch, German, Chinese, Japanese, classical Arabic and Gujarati. The report even includes good old Fullerton's regret that the last three cannot be reproduced since his machine does not have the requisite characters.

Víctor stops reading and thinks about Galván. The maestro always insisted that Kellar was little more than an imitator and a braggart, but he must be given credit for his ambition: when he set himself to a task, he pulled out all the stops. Víctor goes back to his reading. It seems that one of the investigators dared to voice an objection: clearly the texts were quite long and exquisitely calligraphed, had been written beforehand, and Kellar had made them appear by some simple sleight of hand. Unruffled, the magician took out a double-sided slate, showed both sides to those present to prove that it was indeed blank and handed it to the investigator, asking him to write down a question, which he did, handing it back face down so that Kellar could not see it. The investigator wrote: 'How tall is the Washington Monument?' Kellar took the slate and a piece of chalk, and held it beneath the table for only a few seconds, during which time the investigators noticed no suspicious movements on his part. When he showed it to them again, on the other side of the slate were the words 'We have never visited the Washington Monument, therefore can not give its height.' Brilliant. In spite of his insolence, it has to be said that of all those summoned to appear before the commission, he was the one who did a good job. Although the report never deviates from its neutral, pseudo-scientific tone, it is possible to detect the investigators' pleasure that, after decades of cheap tricks, they have finally witnessed something pure. Not because Kellar did not use trickery. On the contrary, of all those who appeared before the commission, he was the only one to admit to doing so. And his frankness proved such a devastating blow to the spiritualists that the investigators never met again. Only one of them, a man named Horace Howard Furness, continued with the investigation on his own. Although the basis of the commission was such that only those sessions at which all members were present were valid, they granted Furness the right to add a series of appendices to the report, in which he recounted his attempts to obtain one single proof of communication with the spirits in whatever form. Moochers who claimed to be able to read a letter without taking it from the envelope only to return it, with a sizeable invoice, and clear signs of tampering; queens of the underworld who charged recently widowed women exorbitant sums for reciting supposed messages from the beyond, closing their throats to produce voices that sounded both masculine and ghostly.

Víctor is sorry the tribunal has disappeared; he would like to see Furness's face right now. The tone of his appendix is ruthless and cynical and there is a barely controlled fury when he comes to describe the various crude methods used by spiritualists to profit from other people's grief. He wants to go on reading, but the chalk marks disappear. Víctor protests:

'Fullerton! Tell me something – according to the title, this is only a preliminary report!' He waits for a few seconds but there is no reply. 'There has to be something more! A definitive report, a list of conclusions ... You spent all the money, the least you could have done was adjourn the commission. No? Nothing?' When he realises that the commission will not rematerialise, his voice drops to a whisper and he says, almost to himself, 'It's not possible. Long ago, Galván told me that the commission met one last time, about two years later. Peter Grouse summoned them. I'm just a student, but Galván ... He can't be wrong. Bah!' He heaves a sigh. 'Grouse hoodwinked them. That's why they're playing possum.'

As he says the word 'possum', he falls into a deep sleep, one mercifully devoid of images, though he is still walking on a tightrope.

Peace

When they ask whether he is claustrophobic, he immediately says no. It is hardly likely that the MRI scanner will be as dark, as cramped, as airless as the inside of the Proteus Cabinet. As the table moves into the tunnel, Víctor thinks of the countless women, magicians' assistants, who, down the centuries, found themselves confined in boxes and trunks of every shape and size. Beautiful women, though usually petite. Anonymous women. Women with small heads. The human head is the one thing no magic trick can shrink or fold or reduce in size. Víctor could not possibly work as a magician's assistant because from the nape of his neck to the tip of his nose measures more than twenty-two centimetres, the maximum depth of the hidden compartments in every stage contraption.

They have him remove all metal objects, including his glasses, so now he cannot see clearly this machine which is slowly devouring him. Everything is white. Or perhaps it's just the light that seems milky, as though filtered through a white curtain. The final instructions come over the speakers just before the MRI scan begins: he is to keep still, try to relax, keep his eyes closed at all times. He should let them know if it gets too much for him, though if that happens they would need to start over again. He closes his left eye and immediately a lump comes to his throat: he could swear that the halo, the veil, the full moon, the wafer, is now also in his right eye. It's not possible. He is about to scream for them to get him out of there, to lash out with his arms, his feet, kicking nervously, but a reassuring voice once again commands him to close his eyes and relax. We're about to start, it says. He does as he is told. Or tries to. Five metallic taps indicate that the magnetic resonance imaging has started. In the fifteen minutes that follow, all he senses is the table moving back and forward slightly and a series of irritating noises. Like a terrible piece of disco music from which everything but the percussion has been stripped away. Or worse, like a washing machine full of screws. It is strange: his whole body is relaxed, he does not move a muscle, does not even blink. He could be at home, in bed, asleep. If he were to open his eyes now, he thinks, Lauren Bacall would greet him from the opposite wall. He thinks about tombs. About white cradles. He thinks about Galván's island, the white light spilling from the ceiling, can almost hear Galván's voice saying, 'Pick a card.'

Pick a card. Víctor dares not smile, afraid he might interfere with the MRI scan. Every Tuesday, during the first year of their lessons together, Galván crushed him, forced him to practise again and again until he finally mastered the technique of forcing a card. There are many ways to make the victim in a trick believe he is freely picking a card when in fact he is choosing one previously selected by the magician. There are mathematical methods in which the magician pretends the selection depends purely on numerical chance. Others are mechanical: the card is marked, or has a corner cut away, or is in a particular position in the deck. But a good magician, a real magician, one of the scant few who, in Galván's words, are worthy of the name, cannot resort to such crude bungling. Such a magician has to fan out the deck, to pass the cards from one hand to the other, bringing them close to the victim at precisely the right moment, making his voice hypnotic, pick a card, any card, any one at all. He has to put himself in his victim's shoes, to know exactly what he is thinking and act on that knowledge, speeding up or slowing down so that when the victim finally closes his nervous fingers, it is on the predetermined card and no other. Every Tuesday, Galván would demonstrate the trick once. Pick a card, he would say. Time after time, Víctor tried by any means possible to ensure the maestro failed: he would pick the first card, the last, pretend to choose one only to pick the next at the last minute; allow the whole deck to be dealt out so that Galván had to start again from the beginning. Never, not once, did Galván fail to identify his card correctly. He would tell him what it was even before Víctor looked at it: two of clubs, he would say, almost always in a whisper, his mouth half closed, lips

78

clenching one of his endless cigarette butts. King of hearts, five of spades. He was always right. And whenever Víctor asked him to explain the trick once and for all, the maestro would merely bring his hand up to his forehead and say: 'It's all in here. There is no trick.' Then he would ask Víctor to do it.

For a long time, Víctor thought Galván was cheating. It took a whole year, but in time his hands became just as skilled. Galván had been right. It was possible. Nor was it definite that his mind had anything to do with his success. It was sheer manual dexterity. The hands knew. The hands knew which card the victim wanted to pick and simply offered it to him.

Why am I thinking about all this now? Oh yes, the white light. The island. 'Here are your glasses, señor,' a voice says. 'Señor,' the voice comes again and with it a gentle tap on his shoulder, 'your glasses.'

The table, with Víctor lying face up, has emerged from the scanner. He takes the glasses the nurse is holding out and puts them on. In only a wink, he knows that the halo is still there in his right eye but, rather than being panicked, he feels a mysterious sense of peace. Fate has forced a card on him and on it is written his future. His immediate future. He is going blind. It is only a matter of days. It seems futile to resist. He cannot change the card. He picked what he picked; it was always going to be the one that fate dealt him. There is no more frenzied pursuit in his brain, no more useless running away. Blind. There is peace, even if he knows that it is the meek, regretful peace of those who surrender in the face of defeat. Like a conquered village, he must stop dreaming of some unattainable victory and begin to think about survival.

Children of God

After six months of lessons, Galván suggested he make his debut at a children's party. Víctor immediately agreed and the maestro did nothing to curb his excitement, though he knew that children were the toughest possible audience. Contrary to what most people believe, children are not remotely innocent when it comes to magic; they treat magicians with scepticism and laugh at even the smallest failure. Perhaps in order to lessen the chance of stage fright before his debut, or perhaps because he thought the time had come for him to fend for himself, Galván spared Víctor these details, telling him only the date and time of the performance. Víctor would have to entertain the guests for forty-five minutes. The party, to celebrate the eleventh birthday of a boy named Manuel, was to take place on the outskirts of Barcelona.

He had less than two weeks to prepare himself. In the months he had been studying, aside from getting the benefit of the maestro's advice, Víctor had memorised and rehearsed Hoffmann's techniques. Those within his powers. Galván had not yet allowed him to attempt tricks that required complicated equipment, professional staging or those involving animals. Together, they made a list of the tricks he performed best and a second list of the materials he would need to perform them.

He worked harder than ever before. He faked a sudden stomach ache in order to skip school. The following Tuesday, he proudly demonstrated the results, and for three-quarters of an hour he smoothly performed the tricks he had prepared. Galván allowed him to perform without interruption, and when he had finished, praised his fluidity and his technical precision. He made a few comments concerning Víctor's posture and his voice, pointing out that the party would be in the garden, so he would need to speak loudly and project his voice. He also made one or two suggestions about his rhythm.

As Víctor began to gather up his equipment and put it in his backpack, Galván went to the back of the room and returned with a small leather case, like those once used by country doctors. It was old, but well preserved. The leather and the buckles were freshly polished and a braided leather strap hung from the handle.

'I'd like you to have this,' he said, giving it to Víctor. 'This is so you can tie it to your wrist,' he added, nodding at the leather strap.

'If you lose it, I'll cut your hands off. It's not very big, but I think it'll do,' he said, cutting off any attempt by Víctor to thank him for the gift. 'Stick to your routine. Don't be tempted to try something you haven't planned to do. Otherwise, you'll become flustered and end up getting yourself into a fix.'

Víctor stood, staring at the case, while Galván continued with his advice.

'Don't be obsessive. You don't need to practise any more. Sooner or later a routine loses its sparkle, it becomes mechanical.'

His words were futile. They both knew that Víctor would rehearse the routine at least a dozen times in the three days that remained.

'Who's Peter Grouse?' Víctor asked.

There was a tiny inscription stamped into the leather of the case: PETER GROUSE – EGYPTIAN HALL.

'A magician. I'll tell you about him some time.' He handed Víctor a piece of paper. 'That's the address. The party is in Malespina. It takes about an hour to get there by train, but it's best to give yourself plenty of time. You can give me chapter and verse next Tuesday.'

'What? You mean you're not coming?'

'No. They'll give you an envelope with your fee, four thousand pesetas. Don't forget to bring me my fifteen per cent.'

Too many surprises. It hadn't occurred to Víctor that he would be paid for the privilege of performing. In fact, it was not good news, it simply heightened his sense of responsibility. Knowing that Galván would not be there was worse still, though he knew the maestro too well to raise any objection.

As he was about to leave, Galván hugged him goodbye, but, before letting him go, he whispered in his ear:

'What do you do if they ask you to do the same trick twice?'

'I refuse. And they're not called tricks.'

'And if they insist?'

'I refuse again.'

'And what if they won't drop it? They're only kids, Víctor.'

'I'll pretend to give in. I'll start over, then quickly change the end of the trick so they'll be doubly surprised.'

'Good.' Galván still did not relax his embrace. 'How will you spot the little shit who wants to ruin the act?'

'He'll be sitting in the front row.'

'And . . .?'

'He won't take his eyes off my hands.'

'Good. So what will you do about him?'

'Go over and casually ask him something. If I can get him to look into my eyes, I can make the most of the moment . . .'

'And if you can't?'

'I drag out the first couple of tricks and wait for his attention to wander.'

'And if that doesn't work?'

'I snub him. I don't look at him at all.'

'What else?'

'Whenever I need help from the audience, I pick someone sitting behind him. I make some joke so he thinks it's not me he should be watching but the rest of the audience.'

'And if he doesn't stop? He's a little shit, remember?'

'I forget about him and start praying.'

'Perfect.'

Having concluded his interrogation, Galván relaxed his grip, but now it was Víctor who clung to him.

'What if I mess up, Maestro?'

Silence.

'What if I make a mistake? What if it all goes wrong?'

Galván placed a kiss on his forehead and answered:

'Then you come back here and you tell me about it. We'll both cry a little and then we'll start again. But that's not going to happen.'

On the Saturday, he arrived at the house so early that he had to walk around the block several times before he rang the doorbell. A rather ugly girl answered, holding a freckled little boy of about three in her arms. She looked him up and down: he was too old to be invited to the party; too young to be the father of one of the guests.

'Hi, I'm Víctor,' he said, to break the silence. 'Víctor Losa,' adding, with a trace of embarrassment, 'the magician.'

'Oh ... come in. I'm Silvia, Manuel's sister. And this is Pablo, he's the baby of the family.'

She smiled a little condescendingly as though she had decided at first glance that Víctor was an obnoxious twerp who was far too young to be a magician. She was about two or three years older than Víctor, though the disdain in her eyes made her look even older.

The shrieks of the children playing in the garden sounded like the war cries of some tribe of cannibals. He asked Silvia whether she could give them a snack indoors so that he could set up without anyone watching.

Before leaving him, she looked at the case.

'I thought you told me your name was Víctor?'

'It is.'

'So who's Peter Grouse?'

'A magician. I'll tell you about him later,' he said, as though he were in a hurry. 'I have to set up now. I'll let you know when I'm ready.'

There were about thirty folding chairs set out in four rows in front of a teak table. Víctor placed a black cylinder on the table, along with three boxes of different colours, and covered them with a red silk handkerchief. There wasn't a cloud in the sky. A perfect line of ants was marching across the lawn, towards the table, from one of the hedges that bounded the garden. Víctor bowed his head and stared at them for a moment. He did not know whether to take their presence as a good omen.

Getting the children to sit down and be quiet proved difficult, but finally, Víctor lifted the silk handkerchief and the show began.

'You've probably been told I'm a magician, but actually, that's not quite true.'

He stopped abruptly. He was talking loudly and, rather than masking the quavering of his voice, the volume simply amplified it. Silvia had taken a seat in the middle of the front row and was staring at him expectantly. Víctor had to remind himself that the party was not for her but her brother Manuel, who was sitting beside her. Between them, little Pablo sat cross-legged on the grass, holding a multicoloured lollipop, and completely uninterested in the show.

'The thing is, I was once in China, and I was given these antique boxes which have a long and strange history ... As you can see, the cylinder is empty.' He held it up so the audience could inspect it. 'A long, long time ago ...'

Something was happening. Or more precisely, something was not happening. In front of a mirror, Víctor had rehearsed every look, every gesture, every piece of patter designed to win over his audience. He thought he had a comeback for any reaction; but he was not prepared for indifference. The children were looking at him, but their faces were blank, as though they felt it had been a terrible idea to take them away from the party food and force them to watch something that felt like being in school.

In theory, the Chinese Box Trick was the perfect trick to start off with. It was a classic. It worked every time. The silk handkerchief magically disappeared, reappearing in one box after another as the order of the boxes inside the cylinder changed and he recounted a strange and mysterious story. Furthermore, the first magic tricks happened within seconds. The dramatic pause so people could clap felt endless and awkward since no one in the audience said or did anything. Forcing a smile, Víctor accomplished the labyrinthine series of movements so he could manipulate the cylinder and carry on with his story about the powerful mandarin, the little thief and the handkerchief endowed with magical powers.

Although his hands rose above the temptation to tremble and, one after another, managed to perform all the necessary steps to perfection, he could not shake off the horrible feeling that he was making a fool of himself. When he concluded the trick, waving the handkerchief in the air, a single person applauded sadly, as

84

though taking pity on him; three or four slow, booming claps that could only be made by the hands of an adult. He did not need to look up to confirm that one of the children's parents was standing behind the rows of chairs, making sure the children behaved themselves, rather than watching the magician.

'It was at that point,' he carried on, his voice now shaky, 'that the handkerchief came into my hands. I felt a strange power surge through my fingers like an electrical current. From that moment on, everything I touched acquired magical properties. This pack of cards, for example . . .'

At that moment, Pablo started to cry. Annoyed by the interruption and convinced that he would never recover his rhythm, Víctor looked up and saw what had happened. The lollipop was completely covered in ants. Some of them were darting crazily across the toddler's cheeks. Silvia tried to pacify the child, but Víctor got there before her. For the first time, he acted without thinking and did what he needed to do. He scooped the child up into the air, took the lollipop away and dropped it on the ground, kissed the boy on the cheek and wiped away his tears with the handkerchief from the Chinese boxes.

'You'll be OK . . .' he said, more surprised than anyone at the sudden authority in his voice. 'When I was your age, I used to get scared sometimes too. You know what my father used to say to me? My father used to say that the way to deal with nasty things is to make them disappear.' With his free hand, he took three ants which were still looking for traces of sugar on Pablo's cheeks. He had only to wink at Silvia for her to take the child from his arms. 'Ants, for example. People are always trying to think of ways to kill them. But you don't need to.'

He made his right hand into a fist, leaving only a small opening by the ball of his thumb, just as he had seen his father do so many times. He then put one of the ants into the hole and looked at the audience. For the first time, they were all staring at him open mouthed. The problem was, he didn't know what to do next. He noticed that his glasses were jiggling on the bridge of his nose and thought about Galván and about his father as he slipped his finger into the hole and squashed the ant into the gap between his fingers. He did the same thing with the other two ants. Only when he suddenly opened his hands, holding his palms out for the audience to see, did he realise the trick had worked. The squashed bodies of the ants were on the back of his hand, facing him. One of the ants was still wriggling. He did not grieve for it, even for a second.

'You can do exactly the same thing with tears,' he said. 'Pablo's tears are on this handkerchief, but I'm going to make them disappear.'

Very slowly, working close to the toddler's face as though he were trying to hypnotise him, he pushed the silk handkerchief into his left fist. Then he opened both hands and showed them to the audience: they were empty. At last there was a burst of genuine applause and Víctor did not make the mistake of pausing to revel in it. He had barely found his rhythm, but he pressed on.

'He was a big guy, my father. Make your problems disappear, invent your own solutions, that was his motto. He used to tell me that even poor people don't have to worry because you only have to dig into your pocket and . . .'

He made coins appear, and balls and flowers. He made impossible flames leap from his fingertips. One after another he performed the tricks he had planned, combining them with the freedom only afforded to those who know exactly what they are doing. Nothing went wrong. Not a single trick went unapplauded and more than once he heard the magic words 'It's not possible!' He was like an infallible robot. He didn't know whether he had been performing for ten minutes or three hours and he didn't care. He noticed that Silvia kept trying to catch his eye, tapping her wristwatch insistently.

'Your parents are all standing at the back laughing because they think they're brave. But sometimes they get scared too. When there's bad news in the papers, for example. Before I finish, I want to tell you what my father used to do when that happened . . .' He pulled the case towards him, took out a double page from a newspaper that he had prepared that morning and showed it to the audience. 'He'd take the paper and tear it in half. Like this. And then in half again. He liked to make sure he'd really ripped it to shreds.' He tore the paper four times, then placed the eight pieces on top of each other in the palm of his hand. 'But then he'd think maybe there was some good news on the other side of the page, so he'd open it out again like this ...'

As he unfolded the torn fragments, the page reappeared intact. There were shouts and whistles and laughter from the audience and this time Víctor made no attempt to silence them.

From the moment he tossed the paper in the air and took one last bow until the point when Silvia offered to drive him back to Barcelona, his memory was a complete blank. They had probably given him something to drink and he had probably had a piece of birthday cake. He assumed he had talked to some of the children and the parents as they came to collect them. He liked to think that at some point he had stood on his own in the garden, which was dark by now, going over in his mind what had just happened. He couldn't get over the fact that fate had transformed the ancient typewriter on which he had been wearing out his fingers into a magnificent, perfectly tuned piano. A piano he had been able to play with his eyes closed.

On the other hand, he distinctly remembered the moment when Silvia appeared in the garden, the car keys in her hand. When she offered to drive him home, he came down to earth with a bump and realised the hair at the back of his neck was damp and matted with sweat. He also suspected his breath stank from talking so much and felt sorry that there had been no miraculous transformation in his adolescent body during the brief period when his mind had been taken over by the mind of a magician.

'Don't worry about it, thanks,' he said, 'I have a return ticket for the train.'

'Maybe, but the last train left at nine,' Silvia insisted. Víctor was about to check his watch, but she took him by the arm. 'It's quarter-past. Besides, I need to go into Barcelona anyway.'

They spent much of the journey in silence. Víctor was experiencing the after-effects of triumph, not unlike a hangover, but he was also completely bewildered. He couldn't work out why everything had gone wrong at the start, still less why fate had quickly taken his side. Nor had his luck abandoned him, to judge from the way, when she changed gears, Silvia let her right hand graze his thigh. The inside of his thigh. Víctor may have been a virgin, but he was not stupid. When she stopped the car on the hard shoulder a few kilometres outside Barcelona, he knew what was coming next and he thought he was ready. Too ready: for a while now, the pain in his crotch had been unbearable. Silvia straddled him without a word and he concentrated on living up to her expectations. He felt exactly as he had done a couple of hours earlier: once again, for the first time in his life, he was about to do something he had been dreaming about for a long time. Something he knew about only in theory. Something he had often practised in front of a mirror.

Although it was cramped and uncomfortable, Silvia seemed to know what she was doing. As he entered her, Víctor was surprised by two things: the first was the throbbing he could feel, as though he had penetrated all the way to her heart. The second was the transformation that took place on Silvia's face as the corners of her mouth rose a few millimetres in something like a simulated smile. Never had a woman seemed to him more beautiful.

They barely spoke during the rest of the journey to Víctor's house. He attributed the silence to Silvia's disappointment: there was a difference between the idea of making love to a magician and the reality of being awkwardly penetrated by an adolescent virgin that saddened even him. When he got out of the car, she rolled down the window and called him back, nodding to the case he had left on the back seat.

'You never did tell me who Peter Grouse was.'

'Ah.' Víctor looked at his watch. 'Next time, OK?'

'Sure.'

They both knew there wouldn't be a next time. They said goodbye again, but just as he got to the door and was about to go in, she honked the horn. Víctor walked back to the car and Silvia handed him the white envelope containing 4,000 pesetas.

'Here,' she said, 'from my father. You've earned it.'

Víctor watched the car pull away and stood in the doorway, the envelope in one hand and the leather case in the other. He had spent the afternoon on a rollercoaster, hurtling round and round between despair and euphoria. He felt exhausted. He was incapable of explaining what had happened, even to himself. Magic . . . Well, he had acquitted himself with dignity. He could face his teacher with his head held high. For a few moments, he had even felt the thrill that Galván so often talked about; a curious disparity between feeling absolutely in control of every movement and the notion that everything was being controlled by another, higher, power. But he was not about to allow himself to be taken in. It was only a kid's birthday party. He expected much more. Of magic, and of himself. He felt much the same about Silvia. He had made love for the first time and he was happy. But he could not help but sense that there had to be a huge difference between their awkward fumble and real sex. In both cases, he felt as though he had managed to force the door to a palace only to find himself standing in the hall. He was eager to take possession of every room.

The party had been banal. The girl, ugly. Before he put his key into the lock, he thought about Galván with a smile and said in a soft voice: 'All are children of God.'

A Map of the World

Something wakes him in the middle of the night. Some worry, some urgent need for order. Everything is a mess. Not just the apartment, which he has not tidied for days now, but his life too. Light, time, everything proceeds from a different place to what we expect. And, as Víctor will soon realise, position is everything. The point of departure. I am here and I want to get there. This is in front of me and that is behind me. This comes before, that comes after.

Order. He has a lot of things to do and he doesn't know how much time he will have before blindness darkens his days completely. 'Make a list of everything you need to do. Then tick things off as you go along. You'll see, it's a relief.' His mother's voice. What a blessing it would be to have his mother with him now. Her voice, her simple presence, her heart, which was always so big. But he cannot think about the past now. The present is taking up all his time with its arrogance, its niggling constraints. Make a list.

He takes a sheet of paper and draws a horizontal line, dividing it in two. In the top section, he writes the title: 'Done', and below it: '1. Diagnosis 2. EEG 3. MRI Scan'. Below the line he writes: 'Pending'. He stops for a moment and thinks; he puts the pen down on the piece of paper, right in the middle, then gets up and walks to the door, counting the steps as he goes. He turns out the light and, in total darkness, walks back to his chair. Sitting down, he feels his way across the table. With his left hand he brushes the piece of paper. It seems as though he is trying to smooth it out when, in fact, he is measuring it, trying to fix its boundaries in the memory of his hands. With his right hand, he picks up the pen and presses the tip at a point he estimates to be below the horizontal line. It feels very much like writing a poem, though all he wants to do is write the words: 'Take test results to neurologist.' A change in texture and a subtle shift in the sound made by the pen let him know that he has written the last two syllables on the table.

Grouse, according to Galván

I n London in 1880, Peter Grouse was recognised by the many colleagues in his profession as the finest pickpocket of his generation, perhaps because, unlike them, he brought to his profession extraordinary effort and dedication and he never gave up. While his colleagues spent their pickings on whores and drink, he spent his nights practising. He devised new techniques which, naturally, he did not put into practice until he had completely mastered them and rehearsed the methods he already knew in order to perfect them. Then, he ensured he got a good night's sleep so that his mind and his fingers would be fresh the following morning.

Late one afternoon he encountered John Nevil Maskelyne near the Egyptian Hall. Maskelyne was the most famous magician in Victorian England and his appearance was far from ordinary: he was short and very plump, almost stumpy, and he had a thick moustache that you could see even from a distance. The Egyptian Hall, which he managed, had been a museum of exotic curios but was now converted into a hall for exhibitions and performances. Given that he was more interested in material things than in magic, there was no reason why Grouse should recognise Maskelyne, but he stared at the little man, eyeing the leather case he was carrying. As if it were not enough that Maskelyne was clutching the case so tightly that his knuckles were white, Grouse, who was well trained in such matters, noticed a braided leather strap which was securely knotted around the man's wrist.

He was sorry he could not treat this challenge with the respect it deserved: he could cut the strap and substitute the leather case for something similar, something heavy so that the switch would be almost imperceptible. He had accomplished more difficult feats, but this would take time to prepare – time he did not have. He reluctantly decided instead to lift the wallet that bulged in Maskelyne's breast pocket. Before proceeding, as was his habit, he smoothed down his coat to get rid of any unsightly creases. Physical appearance was important. Grouse always invested a portion of his earnings in elegant, but not ostentatious, black clothes, and though he never knew what the day would bring, he always left the house looking neat and tidy.

Seeing his victim turn into Duke Street towards Piccadilly, he quickened his pace. He deliberately bumped into Maskelyne and, as he apologised for his clumsiness, he patted the man's chest as though to make sure he was unhurt, or to brush away some imaginary piece of lint. It was a classic manoeuvre and one he knew so well he could do it without thinking. The guilty parties in the theft were the fingertips of his left hand, but his right hand was the true protagonist, responsible for providing distraction, straightening the lapels, patting the sides and the shoulders and, if necessary, going so far as to stroke the victim's cheek.

Only this time his left hand, rather than encountering the expected wallet, found a folded piece of paper. Maskelyne, unruffled, took a step back and, judging from his smile, suspected nothing. He placed his hand on Grouse's side as though to move him aside and said:

'Don't worry, I'm fine. I'm terribly sorry, but I'm in rather a hurry.'

And he walked off.

Grouse watched him go, with a mixture of frustration about the leather case, regret about the wallet he had not managed to lift and a little curiosity as to the piece of paper that had changed pockets. When Maskelyne finally disappeared from view, he glanced at it and, in the twilit street, he could just make out a diagram depicting some sort of bust placed on a large trunk. Disheartened, he stopped for dinner in his usual pub and did not realise what had happened until, when he came to pay, he slipped his hand into his pocket and discovered he had no money. At that moment, in a painful flash, he remembered Maskelyne's step backwards, the ironic smile as he took his leave, the hand on his side. Grouse almost felt ashamed. Not only had he been unable to fleece his victim, he had allowed the little bastard – there was no other word for him – to pick his pocket. Anger gave way to a curiosity he found mortifying.

Who was this guy? Grouse prided himself on being able to recognise his cohorts in the trade at a single glance. He never forgot a face. The very possibility that he had been robbed by a beginner, or someone who had just arrived in the city, was deeply humiliating. He took the piece of paper from his pocket, the meagre spoils of his encounter, and unfolded it on the table. With more light he could examine it now in detail. From the ragged edge of the paper he worked out that it was a page torn from a book. In the top right-hand corner was the number 537. The illustration showed a man sitting on a trunk, his legs crossed and his right arm extended. Only his head, turned to the right and wearing a curious turban, seemed solid. The rest of his body, and the trunk on which he was seated, was outlined with a dotted grey line to create the illusion of transparency. Inside the outline was what looked like an anatomical drawing in which every organ had been replaced by mechanical parts: gears, pistons, levers and pulleys. Every piece, every joint, every socket was labelled with a capital letter from A to X.

Above the diagram were four short paragraphs. Reading was not exactly Peter Grouse's strong suit. He could recognise the alphabet and decipher short messages without too much difficulty, but these long sentences made him hesitate. To be able to recognise a tree was one thing; to find one's way through a dense forest was altogether different. He tried to focus on the last paragraph, which seemed to shed some light on the illustration:

'One very ingenious solution of the construction of Psycho was offered in November 1877. I partly reproduce it not because it is a solution, but because it will enable the practical and ingenious reader to construct a figure something similar, although not at all equal, to the Whist Player of Messrs Maskelyne and Cooke.'

Beneath the drawing was a rambling explanation of the workings of the contraption, explaining the nature and the mechanics of each part and giving the necessary instructions for assembling it. Grouse turned over the page and saw that the text continued on the reverse with a list of incomprehensible instructions like

'The lever being pivoted at *c*, it is obvious that by depressing the end, N, B will be set at liberty, and the hand will move along the cards ...' All this simply to make the little oriental-looking mannequin move its right arm and open and close its hand.

Peter Grouse screwed the page into a ball and angrily tossed it on to the floor. He considered himself to be a man of great imagination and he had undeniably brought considerable creativity to his chosen profession, but such fanciful displays as this, which had no practical application, made him nervous. Having been the victim of a madman or a fool did not alleviate his indignation. To make matters worse, he now had to ask that dinner be put on his slate. He did not expect this to be a problem since he was a regular at the pub, but as a matter of principle, it irritated him. As he got to his feet and was about to kick the ball of paper across the room, he spotted a scribble he had not noticed before. He picked up the piece of paper, and smoothed it out on the table once more. At the bottom of the page was a handwritten note: 'Hoffmann has no idea. Raise the Egyptian Hall bet to 3,000.'

He examined the drawing again but this cryptic note offered no new insight. And yet, for the first time since his unfortunate encounter with Maskelyne, Peter Grouse took a deep breath and his lips widened in a tense smile. A bet? Three thousand what? Three thousand pounds? That was a fortune. If he could find out where this Egyptian Hall was, he would know where to start.

A Trick at Every Table

Galván offered him his first real job, but warned him not to have great expectations. It wasn't in a theatre, nor even one of the nightclubs which, in the mid-eighties, organised cabaret-style performances of magic. No one would be paying to see him and his name would not appear on the bill. He would earn only what he received in tips. La Llave was a modest little bar in the centre of Barcelona and it made a respectable profit, basing its opening hours around the schedules of the local office workers: two sittings at breakfast, a lunch special, beer and slices of tortilla in the afternoon.

Víctor went there for the first time on a Friday just after 9.30 and, since there were no customers, he could size up at a glance the place where, according to Galván, he was to work six nights a week for the next two months: a bright polished stone floor, a small bar with a grill and a coffee machine, three whole hams hanging from the ceiling, recessed halogen lights. There didn't seem to be much sense in opening the place in the evenings.

The owner pressed him to get changed quickly in a small basement which was part stockroom and part wine cellar. Surprised at being asked to hurry, Víctor studied the excellent selection of wines as he buttoned his black jacket and slipped into his pockets the various things he had brought in Peter Grouse's case. Suddenly, the basement ceiling started to shudder as though there were a stampede. He climbed the narrow wooden staircase and, when he reached the door, he had to lean all his weight against it to open it a crack. The place was heaving. Though he had been downstairs less than five minutes not only were all the seats at the tables and the bar occupied, but every inch of standing room too. The noise was unbearable. Two waiters had to shout to get past, moving through the crowd as gracefully as tango dancers, each holding aloft a tray. Behind the bar a small woman was preparing tapas at such speed that, seen from behind, she looked like some Hindu goddess with six arms in perpetual motion.

Víctor stood, confused, wondering how he was going to clear a path through the crowd until suddenly the owner appeared next to him and shouted in his ear.

'Follow me. And get a move on, you've only got an hour.'

As he followed the owner, Víctor went over the list of unforeseen problems he now had to deal with. He didn't like being rushed. Working with barely enough space to move his arms would be a challenge, but the most difficult thing was there would always be someone behind him. However good, however subtle a magician, he is always vulnerable if someone watches him from behind. He cursed Galván, who he assumed was aware of the situation but had not told him so he would be forced to come up with solutions. In fact, the teacher had given him little advice. He hadn't even wanted to help choose the routine. 'You get to a table, you sit down, you do what you have to do, then you move on to the next table. You have to work quickly or they'll leave before you've even finished. If all goes well, they'll ask you to stay and do another trick. They'll offer you a drink. But you'll get up and leave. A different trick at every table for as long as there are customers. Prove to me you're up to it and we'll think about doing real magic.' These had been his only instructions; this was the challenge.

The first problem was finding a seat. There wasn't a single empty chair. Víctor fumbled his way to the first table, where he did not even have time to introduce himself before one of the diners, assuming he was selling something, waved him away without looking and said, 'No thanks, we're fine.'

Víctor snorted, raised the hand holding the deck of cards to shoulder height and dropped it in the centre of the table.

'Anyone know how many cards there are in a pack?'

After a good start, everything became easier. He finished his first round feeling as though he had achieved his aim. The tricks worked and the cries and applause at one table guaranteed him a warm reception at the next. Every time he moved, he created a small

97

procession since some of the customers followed him around so as not to miss anything.

When he got back to the first table, there was an empty chair for him and the diners were waiting expectantly. Someone called for silence and although the clamour elsewhere in the bar continued, for the first time he found he could perform without shouting. The second round went better than the first because Víctor had used the first as an opportunity to select objects at each table that he could adapt for his second trick. One of the diners tore a card into four only to find it, apparently whole again, under their soup plates; a handbag with its buckle fastened turned out to contain the card on which its owner had signed her name. Víctor heard the words 'It's not possible' and he knew he was on the right track. In fact he was euphoric. At one point he felt as though, floating above the noise and the crowd, he could see himself, see the pleasure, the joy, if it could be called that, on the faces of those around him. He had just turned eighteen. In a month, it would be one year since he had started taking lessons and here he was achieving what, by any standards, was a resounding success.

And the best was yet to come. As he finished his second tour of the bar, he made a mental inventory of the items in his pockets and decided that this was the perfect moment to move on to more spectacular tricks. He had powdered phosphorus which, with a subtle flick of his index finger, could cause spectacular flames to leap; harmless dyes a single drop of which could change the colour of a drink in an instant; a tiny saucepan into which he could put a raw egg and, with a wave of his left hand, transform it into a steaming omelette.

When he came to the last table, surreptitiously patting his pockets to check that everything was where it should be, he felt a blast of cold air and noticed a sudden silence. The door was open and people were streaming out into the street as though someone had shouted 'Fire!' The waiters quickly collected the plates and the tips. The woman who had been preparing tapas had come out from behind the bar and was sitting at a table, massaging her aching feet. At the far end of the room, a swing door Víctor had not noticed opened suddenly and a chef arrived carrying trays loaded with croquettes, Russian salad, ham and tuna *empanadillas*.

'Did it go well?' she asked him.

'I think so,' Víctor said, still in shock.

'Come on, sit down with us and have something to eat. But you'll have to do a little trick for us too.'

Before he did so, Víctor asked for an explanation. The secret to La Llave's popularity at night was its proximity to Scala Barcelona, a ballroom which dominated the nightlife in the city at the time, with its spectacular shows featuring contortionists, acrobats, ventriloquists, magicians and, above all, two dance troupes capable of performing the most complex routines as long as they required the wearing of almost nothing or, failing that, the removal of a costume piece by piece. The early show offered dinner at nine o'clock, but was so expensive that many people, especially the younger audience, preferred to have a snack at La Llave and then go to the second show at 11 p.m.

'So that's it, they bolt down some food and then head off?' asked Víctor.

'Not quite. Now we get our second sitting – the people who went to the first show and spent so much on dinner that, instead of having a drink in the Scala bar afterwards, they come straight here. It's one of the advantages of being cheaper. They'll be streaming through that door in half an hour.'

This explained why the waiters were wolfing down the food the cook had brought out. Víctor complimented her on the croquettes and did as they did, gobbling his food with one hand and performing simple magic tricks with the other. When the first customer came through the door, the staff all got to their feet.

Víctor discovered that things went much more smoothly when customers were not eating. All he needed to do was take an empty chair and start performing and the customers would come to him. He felt completely at ease. Most of the customers just came to have a quick drink and then head home, or go on to some other bar, but one or two hung around to see another trick, and then another, until suddenly it was two o'clock in the morning and Víctor realised he had been sitting in the same chair for over an hour, performing for a group of about forty people who seemed in no hurry to leave. The shutters came down at half-past and even the owner sat and watched him perform while the waiters cleared up. Víctor brought the show to a close, only to hear the inevitable request for just one more trick.

'What's your name?' he asked the woman sitting next to him.
'Inés.'
'Inés, can I borrow your hand?'
'With pleasure.'
'Don't worry. I won't make it disappear,' he announced, taking her hand gently. 'I just want to write your name so it's imprinted on your skin and will remain with you for ever.'

He told her to make a fist, then he dipped his finger into an ashtray and, on the back of her hand, traced the letters 's-é-n-i' in ash.

'As you can see, I've written it backwards. It's like a nickname. The only people to know your real name will be those who know you like the palm of their hands,' he said, as he turned her wrist and, stroking her fingers, asked her to open her fist.

On the palm was the name 'Inés', written the right way round, as though the letters had travelled through skin and bone. Víctor got to his feet as the audience applauded and gave a little bow, which seemed to bring the performance to an end. Suddenly Inés looked at her hand and screamed:

'Oh my God! My ring!'
'Don't look at me,' said Víctor. 'I think your husband is the jealous type. Maybe he decided to look after your wedding ring while you did me the honour of lending me your hand. If he denies it, tell him to look in his left-hand jacket pocket.'

The man sitting on Inés's right looked startled. He slipped his hand into his pocket and piled the contents on the table, a handful of coins and his car keys: Inés's ring was threaded on to the keyring. Before taking it back, she looked at Víctor and said:

'Not bad! There's just one problem. He's not my husband. I've never even met him before. Besides, it's not a wedding ring. I'm not married.'

Víctor held her gaze. She was short, a little plump. She had narrow lips and her face was tense. It was almost 3 a.m. and he was exhausted. 'What the hell,' he thought, 'tomorrow's Saturday.'

For his last trick, he decided to put a smile on that face.

Before they left together, he slipped the envelope of money the owner had given him into his leather case. He hadn't counted it, but the jingle of coins told him it wasn't much.

One Bloody Nerve, Victor

'The cause is in your DNA, it's a mitochondrial mutation. Until recently the only way to diagnose it was by a process of elimination but nowadays we can confirm it by molecular analysis,' the neurologist says, as though this were good news.

Twenty minutes of incomprehensible technical jargon. Now more than ever Victor envies the efficient language of ants. He makes a list of useless words: the haloes are cecocentral scotomas; there are signs of retinal vascular tortuosity in the blood vessels supplying the eyes; the fundus of the optic nerve is swollen and, most seriously, the nerve itself is suffering from irreversible atrophy.

He assumes it will not be long before the neurologist finally utters the word 'blind' and he knows that, at that moment, the eagle in his brain will have a field day.

Even more than the technical jargon, the numbers bother him. The percentages the doctor intones like a litany. Fifty per cent of men with this genetic mutation go on to develop the disease. Only 10 per cent of women, however, contract it. In 25 per cent of cases, sight is lost in both eyes simultaneously; in 75 per cent of cases it is sequential.

'In twenty per cent of cases,' the doctor goes on, 'the optic nerve head ...'

'What is it called?' Victor asks, shifting in his seat as though he has suddenly decided to take part in the conversation.

'Sorry?'

'The disease. If I have to deal with some monster that is going to leave me blind, the first thing I need is a name, don't you think?'

'The full name is Leber's hereditary optic neuropathy, but it's generally referred to as Leber's for short.'

'Leber.'

'Yes.'

'Who was Leber?'

'Theodor von Leber was the ophthalmologist who first described the disease.'

'When was that?'

'1876.'

'Jesus! What a coincidence.'

'How so?'

'Nothing, it's just something personal ...'

'Tell me about it ...'

'How long before I go completely blind?'

'Look, let's not get ahead of ourselves.'

'I'm sorry ...' Victor gets to his feet and begins to pace around the room. He is trying to keep calm but he looks like a caged animal. '... but I've heard those words a little too often lately and I can't say I agree with them. There's a runaway train bearing down on me, and if I don't get ahead of myself, it's going to run me down. If you don't mind, I have a couple of questions I'd like to ask and I want straight answers.'

'Fire away.'

'And no jargon.'

'Ask away, I'll do my best.'

'Is there any treatment?'

'There are clinical trials to see whether Vitamin B12 and Vitamin C supplements together with quinine analogues ...'

'Doctor ...'

'No, there are no tried and tested treatments.'

'Am I going to go blind?'

'Yes, but to what extent is difficult to predict. Twenty per cent of cases retain up to fifteen per cent ...'

'Enough with the percentages, please!' Victor protests. 'How long do I have?'

The neurologist checks the file in front of him to see when the symptoms had first appeared.

'It's difficult to say exactly. It starts out with problems

distinguishing red and green. Then the halo gets bigger ... With the spot in your left eye, I think it's only a matter of days, a week at most. After that ...' He takes a deep breath and, for the first time, sets his face in something akin to an expression of compassion. 'Between losing sight in the first and second eye there is usually a gap of about eight weeks.'

'From now?'

'From the moment the symptoms first appeared.'

'In other words, I've got about a month.'

Víctor cannot help glancing at the calendar on the doctor's desk. Then he turns and pretends to study the diplomas that hang on the wall.

'Can you explain in simple terms exactly what it is I've got?'

'The optic nerve has atrophied and can't function properly any more. Your eye is perfectly fine, as indeed is the part of your brain that processes visual information. Imagine there's a petrol station on one side of a river, and all the cars are on the other side. Now imagine the bridge is out ... Or an engine, when the transmission cuts out ...'

'All right, I get it. What I don't get is why. I mean why now? I know, I've always been a little short-sighted, but ...'

'It has nothing to do with that. As I said, it's a mitochondrial mutation. It's passed down through the maternal line and can develop any time between the ages of ten and seventy.'

'But my mother wasn't blind.'

'Look, I know you hate the whole percentages thing, but this is like the lottery. Your mother must have ...'

'Had.'

'OK, had the same mutation but, like ninety per cent of women, she never developed the disease. It's likely that a couple of generations back there was someone blind in your family, but it's so far back that no one remembers. And because you're a man, when you drew the same lottery ticket, the situation was different because half the balls in the drum had your number on them.'

'Fifty per cent,' Víctor says. 'That's a lot.'

Slowly, as he digests the information, he comes back towards the desk. He is going blind. That little wretch ... It's not a prediction, it's a statement of fact. The future has just come crashing down on him with such violence that it is already almost a memory.

'Is there anything else? What I mean is, is there anything else I should prepare myself for, apart from the blindness?'

'In principle, no.'

'I see ... in principle.'

'Leber's is a mitochondrial point mutation related to respiratory chain complexes. In some cases, patients have been known to develop other symptoms including movement disorders, tremors, peripheral neuropathy and even cardiac arrhythmia, but there is no proof they are directly related to Leber's. In my opinion they are often stress-related.'

'That's understandable.'

'There is one other percentile group that might interest you, though the last thing I want to do is give you false hope. In about 0.2 per cent of cases, for reasons we do not understand, some degree of vision has been recovered.'

'At least there's some hope,' says Victor. And he says it again, 'Some hope.'

There's nothing more to talk about, Victor. Leave now. Get out of here. Take that crumb of hope, go home and lick your wounds. Or better still, make the most of what little time you have left to prepare yourself. You are about to enter a world peopled by ghosts, by illusions, and the frontier has already been marked: you have one month. There is no line of fire now, it is a line of shadows. The day you cross it, your eyes will see no more. Worse still: we know that they will go on discerning light, movement and the whole panoply of physical manifestations implicit in the verb 'to see', but your brain will be like a wheel spinning in the void. The doctor explained it perfectly: there is no bridge. All that will remain is that mocking 0.2 per cent chance of hope and a faint curiosity as to what happens to all those images you see without seeing. Are they lost in some forgotten corner of your brain? Who cares? Maybe the eagle that is your blindness devours them. See how hungry it is? You can ask yourself a thousand times: 'Why me?' Because of a nerve, Victor. One bloody nerve. The one you leave on the side of your plate when you eat your steak.

Dust Thou Art

Although he had no reason to hide, Peter Grouse took cover in a doorway in order to observe number 22 Piccadilly on the opposite side of the street. He had passed the outlandish building many times but, assuming it to be a museum, had never stopped to give it a second glance. Somewhat narrower than the surrounding buildings, it was notable for the opulent pilasters that flanked the doorway and for the two enormous statues above the entrance. He had no possible way of knowing that they depicted Isis and Osiris, but anyone with even a minimal education would have been able to identify them as Egyptian. This was how he knew he had found the right place, since nowhere on the building were the words Egyptian Hall. The only word carved into the stone was EXHIBITION.

The figure of John Nevil Maskelyne came around the corner of St James's Street, threading his way through the traffic towards the entrance. Let us give Grouse due credit for what might otherwise be taken as chance: since his encounter with Maskelyne had occurred the previous day at about 6 p.m., he had stationed himself there since five o'clock. As soon as he saw the magician, he threw himself back and dissolved into the shadows. One could never be too careful. All his attention was focused on the case, once again attached to the man's left wrist by the braided leather strap.

Maskelyne opened the front door with his own key and then locked it again once inside. Grouse thought it prudent to wait before approaching any closer, and even then, he went to the next corner before crossing the street so that nobody might see him arriving directly and conclude that he had been waiting. Ever the professional.

He stopped and read the poster next to the entrance:

MASKELYNE & COOKE

ENGLAND'S HOME OF MYSTERY

EGYPTIAN HALL

EVERY EVENING AT 8.

TUESDAY, THURSDAY AND SATURDAY AT 3.

SEVEN YEARS IN LONDON OF

UNPARALLELED SUCCESS.

A MAN'S HEAD CUT OFF WITHOUT LOSS OF LIFE

A STRANGE STATEMENT, BUT NO MORE STRANGE

THAN TRUE.

This was followed by a promotional text which guaranteed unrestrained laughter and the verisimilitude of the decapitation. Grouse scanned the text to the next paragraph in bold type:

THE FOUR AUTOMATONS

PSYCHO, THE WHIST PLAYER; ZOE, THE ARTIST;

MUSIC BY MECHANISM, ILLUSTRATED BY FANFARE ON THE

CORNET; AND LABIAL, THE EUPHONIUM, ARE ATTRACTING

VISITORS FROM ALL PARTS OF THE GLOBE.

He was confused by what he read, but the name Psycho told him that this was indeed the right place to try to shed light on what had happened the previous evening. Although 'magic' did not appear on the poster, the word certainly summed up what was written and moreover explained the skill with which Grouse's intended victim had picked *his* pocket. He felt one step closer to avenging this slight, though he had not yet decided what exactly he was going to do to the man when they came face to face once more. He immediately dismissed the idea of resorting to violence. Not only because he was peaceable by nature, but because he took pride in the fact that he had made a living from his profession without ever having to shed a drop of blood. However, he needed to think of some means of recovering the money he had lost. More than that: he licked his lips at the prospect of multiplying his loot by robbing the man of everything he possessed, though he could not begin to plan his revenge until he discovered what exactly went on in the Egyptian Hall.

He wandered around the area until the box office opened then willingly paid five shillings for a front-row seat. It was a good investment. When the theatre doors opened, he waited for a large crowd to come inside so he could mingle with them and make his way to his seat. The walls were decorated with vast murals depicting dogs, huge birds, snakes and Egyptian gods. He recognised one of the signs of the zodiac. The show took place in a large room on the ground floor. Grouse counted the rows and estimated that the place seated at least two hundred people, although tonight the audience barely numbered one hundred. Judging by their appearance, most were visitors to the city. In Grouse's profession, the ability to recognise a tourist was crucial.

Music began to play and the curtain rose. As their eyes adjusted to the darkness the audience noticed that, aside from the pianist, all the other musicians were automata. A harp flew above their heads and for a moment Grouse thought he saw the light glinting on a piece of wire or rope that was holding it aloft. The orchestra were playing a merry tune which seemed to go on too long; only when the last notes died away did the man with the leather case finally appear and begin to speak. First he introduced himself as John Nevil Maskelyne, thereby confirming what Grouse had suspected when he read the poster at the entrance. Then a second man appeared, whom Maskelyne introduced as Mr Cooke, his assistant.

Onstage, Maskelyne looked even shorter and his walrus moustache seemed all the more ridiculous. His voice had a grating quality and his attempt to sound authoritative served only to make him sound unpleasant. What most surprised Grouse was his refusal to use the word 'magic' or anything similar. On the contrary, he insisted on warning the public that everything they were about to witness had a scientific explanation: 'Pure science, ladies and gentlemen,' he said between bows, 'the only marvels you will see here are those the human mind is capable of creating when it understands the laws of physics, mechanics and optics.' Since he knew nothing of the controversy surrounding the spiritualists at the time, Grouse did not understood why Maskelyne was saying this. Where was the mystery? What was the point of paying to see something which, in the words of the inventor himself, could be performed by anyone with the necessary knowledge? Why was the audience applauding? Clearly the spectacle had not been conceived for minds as pragmatic as his. And since he did not care much for the music, the first half-hour of the show, during which each of the automata performed long solos, seemed interminable.

When Maskelyne announced that the moment had come to introduce Psycho, Grouse started in his seat. As the assistant pushed a large bundle swathed in black cloth to the centre of the stage, the audience gave their loudest ovation yet. Apparently this was the part of the show they had come to see. Maskelyne removed the cloth and finally Grouse could see in three dimensions the figure that had so perturbed him the night before. He took the illustration from his pocket and surreptitiously glanced at it to compare the two. Introducing the piece, Maskelyne asked the audience to note that the trunk was standing on a glass cylinder which was completely transparent and consequently was not connected to any ropes or cables. Although the cogs and pistons visible in the illustration were not apparent onstage, Maskelyne was not trying to pass this off as a man of flesh and blood. On the contrary, he was emphasising the fact that it was mechanical. Its great achievement was the ability to play cards unaided. With slightly stiff movements, accompanied by the suspicious hiss of valves, one of its hands would systematically run along a metal shelf on which a dozen cards were laid out and, at the magician's request, would hand him a card in order to play a game of whist. Maskelyne deliberately exaggerated the movement as he stretched out his arm to take the card so the audience would discount the possibility that he was influencing the automaton's movements in any way. Every move was greeted by a round of applause Grouse thought excessive. When the hand was over, the magician turned to the audience and issued a challenge: for years, he had offered a reward of £1,000 to anyone who could show him a similar apparatus capable of playing cards that was genuinely automatic. But that evening, he was feeling particularly generous and felt disposed to increase the reward to £3,000. Having said this, he covered Psycho with the black cloth and announced there would be a short interval.

It was a tempting figure. For the first time Grouse began to believe he might recoup his money with interest, and in doing so heal his wounded pride. His mind immediately began trying to work out the mechanics of how Psycho moved and how to get the automaton to choose and present the appropriate card when requested. Magnets, maybe? Some hydraulic mechanism. Perhaps Maskelyne had managed to hide a cable connected to it in spite of the transparent glass cylinder. Grouse did not move from his seat and spent the twenty-minute interval racking his brains.

When the curtain rose once more, there was a round, three-legged table in the middle of the stage bordered at the back and on both sides by a thick black canvas screen. After a moment, Maskelyne appeared at the back of the stage. In his left hand he held a box by a bronze handle. In a tone intended to be comical he told the audience that, given Mr Cooke's frequent blunders when repairing the automata, there was nothing for it but to cut off his head. As he spoke, he moved towards the table and placed the box on it.

'I am reluctant to pass up this magnificent opportunity to demonstrate for you one of the latest advances in science,' the magician went on. 'Because today, ladies and gentlemen, the simple presence of a part of the body of someone who has passed away makes it possible to summon, for a brief moment at least, that person's spirit.' As he said this, he removed the front section of the box and stepped to one side.

Inside the box was Cooke's head, completely dishevelled as though the man had indeed been decapitated after a brutal fight. There was even a trickle of blood on the neck. At first, Cooke's eyes remained closed. Then slowly he opened them and glanced to either side as though he had just woken up and did not know where he was. Maskelyne immediately engaged him in conversation.

Though his mind was still preoccupied with Psycho, Grouse began to feel a genuine curiosity about what was happening onstage. This truly was magic. Cooke's body could not possibly be hidden beneath the table as he had first suspected because you could still see the black screen between the three legs of the table.

He had to force himself to turn away from the stage. He had come to the Egyptian Hall to recoup his money and avenge a slight, and the information he needed to do so was not to be found up there but might well be waiting in the wings or in the flies. He apologised to those sitting next to him and crept out into the aisle. When he reached the hall, he quickly found the door he was looking for: it was the only door that was locked. As the levers of the lock fell to his picklock he thought of Maskelyne and smiled sardonically: pure science, ladies and gentlemen, the only marvels you will see here . . .

He found he had to grope his way along a dark corridor but he knew he was headed in the right direction because as he advanced Maskelyne's voice grew louder. At that moment, he was encouraging the audience to ask Cooke – or rather his head – any question they liked. Grouse finally came to the end of the passageway and found a small room next to the stage. He glanced around and recognised the shapes of the musical automata covered by tarpaulins. The only unexpected object was a strange cylinder more than three feet tall topped by a headboard covered in tubes which ran down to the ground then disappeared through a trapdoor. Farther away was a table strewn with papers, tools and small contraptions he could not make out in the half-light. And at the foot of the table was the leather case. Open. Fearing that the magician might hear his movements, Grouse peeked through the curtains to see what was happening onstage. The magician approached the table, closed the box and picked it up to carry it away. In the thunderous applause that followed there were shouts for Maskelyne to perform the trick again. He set the box on the table once more and went to the front of the stage to deliver his last words to the audience. Seeing that the show was almost over, Grouse crept over to the leather case and fumbled blindly inside it, all the time listening carefully to what Maskelyne was saying: 'Ladies and gentlemen, unfortunately the march of science, though sure, is slow. Though the day has not yet come, it cannot be long before we triumph over death completely.'

All that was inside the case was a book. Grouse cursed silently, then took it out and slipped it into the waistband of his trousers. Disappointed, he crept back to the curtains in the hope that, from this privileged position, he might discover where and how Cooke's body had been concealed.

'For the moment,' Maskelyne went on, 'the charm by which I am enabled, as you have seen, to revivify the dead lasts but fifteen minutes. That time once expired, not only does the mind vanish, so too does the head wherein it was contained, in accordance with the words of the Bible: *dust thou art, and unto dust shalt thou return.*'

As Maskelyne said this, he opened the box once more, lifted it up so that the audience could see it was empty and, as he blew into it, a small cloud of dust appeared.

The ovation was so deafening that Grouse was able to run away without worrying that the magician might hear his footsteps.

The Queen Mother

Careful with that or you'll burn yourself. Don't look at the sun. Come over here right now. Close your mouth when you're eating. Don't talk with your mouth full. Don't tell lies. That's not how you ask for something. Don't drag your feet. If you don't know, ask. Don't make fun of people. Don't sit so close to the TV. Make your mind up. Aim at the bowl when you do a wee and don't forget to flush. Your eyes are bigger than your stomach. Look at me when I'm talking to you. Don't shovel your food. Don't talk back to your elders. Knives are not for playing with. Don't waste water. Sit up straight. Don't leave everything to the last minute. Don't play with your food. Stop biting your nails. Wrap up warm, it's cold out there. Don't slurp your soup. Tidy your room. Don't use dirty words. Didn't I tell you to tidy your room? Is it too much to expect a civil answer? Be on time. Blow your nose. Answer me when I talk to you. Don't pick your nose. Do your homework. Look me in the eye. Don't leave your stuff lying around. Polish your shoes. Don't interrupt when the adults are talking. If I've told you once, I've told you a thousand times, tidy your room. Turn that music down. Do as I say. Don't be home late, darling.

In spite of the frustrations, in spite of the tedium, the constant need for patience, in spite of the fact that no one did a hand's turn and she was constantly wearing herself out, trying to do everything in what little time she had before she had to go back to work so she could support her son, Víctor's mother managed to write for him, in clear, neat writing, the one true book about life. A text that made no mention of the loneliness she must have felt, of her helplessness, of the silent grief that scarred her. An instruction manual filled with slip-ups and crossings-out, with uncertainties and second thoughts, with rejections and capitulations, but all dispensed with enough love to look after her son until he felt the need to set off and find new instructions elsewhere. Anywhere: at university, at work, on the curious island he returned from every Tuesday afternoon with that gleam in his eyes. Afterwards he'd shut himself away in his room to practise without so much as a word. Don't call them tricks. Don't ask how it's done. Don't raise your eyebrows. You hold the pack like this. Sing that song for me.

Later, when Víctor was old enough and wise enough to begin to write the story of his own life, his mother learned to be a passionate, even critical reader, but one prepared to accept that the only instructions she could now offer had to be couched in parentheses, or followed by a question mark. Just because you're earning a lot of money, don't think that means you've got life all figured out. Magic isn't everything, son, you have to do other things. Isn't it about time you got yourself a girlfriend and settled down?

Víctor still has an image of his mother sitting in the front row, on the day of his first performance in Barcelona. He remembers the mental short circuit, the four interminable seconds of silence, before he addressed the audience with the words that would one day be famous: 'My father died when I was seven years old'. Truth be told, at that moment, he would have liked to say: 'My mother is here. Look at her. She brought me this far. Everything I know, I owe to her.' But he carried on with his monologue as it was written, focused on his work, did not look at her or even think about her again until afterwards, in the dressing room, when they hugged each other and did not say a word. And after that, everything that happened, happened, and Víctor began to go off on world tours and whenever he came home, never for more than a few days, his mother would hone her instructions: You need to eat more, you're looking very thin; relax for a while, I don't understand why you have to work all the time; I hope you wrap up warm when you're over there; words that were now no more than footnotes in someone else's story, or an epilogue, since they were her last words, almost her last. Though no one suspected it at the time, her heart would not go on beating for much longer.

*

'My mother died when I was twenty-six years old,' Víctor says aloud. 'Her heart was always too big. She left me the house where I still live, an instruction manual for life which over time has proved to be quite useful and, according to my neurologist, a lottery ticket in the game of darkness.' It would make a good opener for future shows, he thinks. He imagines the curtain rising to reveal him, as always, standing alone in the middle of the stage, his hands balled into fists. He opens them and in his right hand he holds a heart. A living, beating heart that is too big. Because that was what did it. Those were the words Galván used on the phone, too big, you have to cancel the show and catch the first flight back, fuck the tour, you're coming home now, she's in a coma, she can't hold out much longer. It's not uncommon, the cardiologist told him later, the heart grows too big and each beat requires twice as much energy.

Víctor sat with her in the hospital for thirteen hours straight, as though by doing so he could somehow make up for the long absences of recent years. He did not even leave her bedside to get a solitary bite to eat. And at some point, he realised that she was dead. There was no death rattle, no choking, no spasm, nor were there any last words. Having checked that the weak, erratic pulse of her last days was gone, Víctor pulled the sheet up over her shoulders and went to find a nurse, utterly unaware of the sym- bolism of the gesture, the belated homecoming of a mantra he had heard a thousand times: wrap up warm, son, it's cold out.

He picks up the remote control, but before the parade of images begins, he decides to move his chair six feet away from the TV screen. He turns down the sound so he cannot hear the voice. Nobody is going to say anything he doesn't already know. He places a hand over one side of his glasses, covering his left eye to avoid any interference. He doesn't want to miss anything. After the opening credits, the screen is filled by a vast expanse of untilled land with only a handful of weeds blown by the occasional gust of wind. This is a scientific documentary, there's no big budget, no special effects. In fact, there is only a single camera fixed on this general shot and another which will give a close-up of what comes next. Suddenly, from several different points, a black torrent streams out of the ground. At first there are two or three puddles of darkness, but soon almost the entire surface, the whole screen, is black. You need a sharp eye, or, like Víctor, to know the film by heart to realise that what you are seeing is ants. Dozens, hundreds, thousands. This has been shot on the day they reproduce. Or rather not a day, since reproduction takes barely fifteen minutes.

As a result of a genetic command whose trigger and means of transmission have not been wholly determined, a host of sterile females have decided, at this precise moment, not to be so any more. They swarm from the anthill in an explosion of wings so violent that it leaves them stunned, and they fall back to earth, the males throwing themselves on top of them, four, five, as many as eight for every female. Even in the close-ups, it is impossible to see clearly what is happening. The place looks like a war zone. The males become furious, they fight, they bite, and even after they finally manage to conquer a female in the briefest of thrusts, they still stagger about wildly, drunk on hormones.

Although there has been no change in their appearance which might alert the males to the fact that they have been fertilised, once the females have been impregnated, they are left alone. They have a short time to distance themselves by a few metres, dig a hole in the ground and establish a new colony, a task in which only a few will triumph. But before they do so, before they say farewell for ever to the light, they rip off their wings. If all goes well, the fertilised female ant, now a queen, will spend the rest of her life buried several metres underground and wings would simply be a hindrance. The first time he saw this part, Víctor found it so violent that he couldn't stop trembling and had to hug himself as though someone were trying to rip off his shoulder blades.

The screen begins to clear. Patches of ochre earth reappear amid the black, which, in a matter of seconds, vanishes completely. Soon all that will remain on the surface will be the dark smudges of dead ants that have failed and the dusty gossamer of torn wings.

His mother showed him this tape for the first time when he was twelve. 'I want to show you something your father filmed before you were born, when he was still involved in research,' she told him. 'He never showed you himself because you were too young and I suppose I didn't put it in the box with the rest of the things I gave you for the same reason. But you're old enough now to understand it.' The tape should have reminded him of Martín Losa, and not simply because his father had filmed it, but because it was a meticulous, tangible, scientific response to one of the three questions that had obsessed Víctor during the Saturday mornings they spent together tending to the ant farm: the queen mother, the silence of the ants, their reproduction. And yet every time he watches the tape now, it is his mother who comes to mind. He is thinking about her as he imagines the one thing not shown in this documentary, what it should show: the lives of the mothers holed up in their dark corners, slaves, though they are called queens, subject to the dictates of evolution, oblivious to the fact that if the drones clean and feed them, it is not out of gratitude but to make sure that they go on teeming with life, go on spilling from their bellies larvae in their thousands. Some will be male, others will have wings, though they will not know why until the moment comes, and some will inherit a defect, a genetic mutation, a cruel percentage that dooms them to be crippled or useless. Or blind. Because that, too, is our subject.

Double Feature

La Llave was closed on Mondays so Víctor made the most of the opportunity and went to the cinema. He loved the fact that, at least once a week, he could be part of the audience, exchange the spotlight for the shadows. The Casablanca Cinema, which had opened not long before, lived up to its name that summer by showing a Humphrey Bogart retrospective. The elegance of black and white harked back to times more in keeping with his parents' generation than his own. Víctor was very taken by Bogart's easy charm and, without realising it, struck much the same pose when he was smoking, but he could not help but see him as a hackneyed and slightly improbable hero. Although he enjoyed these films, Víctor watched them with the detachment of someone watching an old documentary. Until he saw *To Have and Have Not*. Lauren Bacall's first appearance on the screen, late in the film, left him speechless. He saw the film fourteen times. More than once, he showed up at the cinema for the afternoon showing and then, after wolfing down a snack, would return for the evening performance as well. He learned the lines by heart. He bought and devoured the Hemingway novel on which the film was based only to forget it immediately, since Bacall's character did not appear in the book. He bought the poster and put it up in his bedroom. He collected all the stories, all the gossip about the shooting and the writing of the screenplay. For the first time he envied Bogart, and not because of his screen presence or because in every film he managed to get the booty and, usually, the girl, but because, as Víctor discovered, shortly after filming *To Have and Have Not*, he married Lauren Bacall. She was only eighteen and he was on the rebound from his second marriage to a woman given to alcoholism and bouts of violence. They were together until cancer carried him off. Another person who died because of nicotine. He read Bacall's memoirs and cherished the anecdotes she recounted with nostalgia: when Bogart pinched her bottom on set, knowing the camera was filming them only from the waist up; the crippling shyness she felt when she had to look directly at the camera and which, according to critics, explained the ambiguity of her gaze. He wanted to know everything about her. This was not the classic crush teenagers have for actresses. To see her in close-up, hear her husky voice, as assured when talking about love as when humming a blues melody, did not trigger a hard-on or some shameful desire. It never occurred to him to compare Bacall to the women he dated at La Llave. He knew perfectly well that what fascinated him was not a woman, nor even the image of her body on film, but a fantasy. Bacall did not exist. What truly did fascinate him, what prompted him to see over and over a story he already knew by heart, was the light. The way the light glanced off her cheekbones, sank into her eyes, traced the outline of her hips, the way it seemed to pick her out in every shot regardless of how many people were in the frame and accentuate her presence. Whenever she appeared, all the technical phenomena that made her presence on screen possible simply fell away: the spotlights, the camera, the characters on the page, the direction, the brilliant lines Faulkner wrote into the screenplay for her and which she spoke with the same playfully insolent smile; everything. The typewriters were silent and music began to play. Suddenly, he was not watching a film but a living being cradled by light. Every time he saw the film, he emerged from the cinema feeling exhilarated and astounded in equal measure. This was the feeling he wanted to create when he performed, something that went beyond the simple pleasure of seeing some baffling trick flawlessly executed. This was why he was not content simply to witness the expression of amazement on the faces of his audience for the other six nights of the week. He wanted more.

0.2 Per Cent

Such a small degree of hope is like a minuscule balcony in a poor man's home. Perhaps it looks out towards the bleak north, perhaps it is not large enough even for one miserable chair and perhaps, over time, it serves only to house three empty flowerpots that once upon a time contained something living. It extends the space of the apartment only in the mind of those who live there. This is its meagre function, and even if it succeeds in this, it is a miracle. Víctor spends little time nurturing this vain 0.2 per cent of hope, and whole days, many of them, regretting that it will not come to pass.

Mr Lápidus

After his first month working at La Llave, Víctor had every reason to be happy. His success on the first night was merely a taste of things to come; so many people came to the second sitting that barely had they opened, than the owner had to start turning people away. Every night the envelope of money was thicker and over the weeks, as he slipped it into his pocket, Víctor no longer heard the jingle of loose change. He always set aside 15 per cent to give to Galván the following Tuesday as soon as he arrived at his lesson. The maestro congratulated him, but he did not ask for details. All he wanted to know was whether the owner of La Llave was happy, a question that was more than answered by the steady increase in the contents of the envelope Víctor gave him each week.

Víctor had had so much practice now that he could perform any piece of close-up magic with his eyes closed. More importantly, he had learned how to handle an audience. He knew exactly which tables he should linger at to perform his best tricks, and those at which he should pause long enough only to go through the motions. With a single glance he could tell who was gullible and who was sceptical, and with a single phrase he was more than capable of dismissing the killjoys, the jokers and those whose sole intention was to sabotage his routine.

He had also learned to work out whether one of the women present would end up sitting next to him, letting him know she was available. When this happened, and it happened often, he would pretend to ignore her until the end of the evening. Only then would he go over and perform a trick just for her. It never failed.

He was enjoying himself. He was young and ambitious and he

was in a hurry. He slept little, even revelled in the exhaustion as proof of his passion. He was not in the least worried that things were moving so quickly. He switched partners the way he switched cards. Performed and disappeared without even taking the time to acknowledge the applause. He was constantly surprised by how similar these things were. In sex, as in magic, everything depended on the effort he put in, the groundwork, and as his knowledge increased, he was able to establish general rules which only had meaning when they were successfully applied to a particular case, when they crystallised for a brief but unforgettable moment: an ovation, an orgasm, an embrace.

But such moments were not enough for Víctor. The more confident he grew with the deck of cards in his hands, the more conscious he became of the vast gulf between this work and the great feats he had laboured so hard to prepare himself for. More than once, when he arrived at La Llave, he stood watching the woman preparing the tapas and was forced to accept that there was little difference between the jobs they did. In both cases, the hands displayed a fluid dexterity that seemed almost entirely dissociated from any intervention by the brain.

Galván's speech about the difference between a typist and a pianist – repeated so often at their lessons that it had become a cliché – now intrigued him. What difference was there exactly? After all, even if a pianist is playing his own work and therefore feels entitled to call himself an artist, when it comes down to it, he is displaying no skills that could not just as easily be attributed to a typist: technical dexterity, speed, accuracy, a sense of rhythm, memory. Obviously we all prefer music to typing. In other words, to put it in terms more relevant to him, you'd have to be starving to prefer tapas over a good magic show. But this simply underscored the problem rather than answering it. Did it all depend on how the performance was received? Was applause the only measure of worth? Even the audience's amazement, even the astonished gasps of 'It's not possible', no longer had the miraculous effect they had had at first. Because he knew that it *was* possible. That it was real. That all it required was a little manual dexterity. The euphoria of the first night at La Llave had become simple satisfaction at a job well done.

To Víctor, these doubts were not merely rhetorical. He knew that he was coming to the end of his residency at La Llave and he realised he would have to decide on a new direction for his career. He took it for granted that he wanted to be a professional magician and was surprised to discover that he could make a decent living doing so. But he did not want to spend his life making metaphorical tapas, however much he was applauded.

A second, more concrete and more pressing problem overshadowed the first. It concerned an irritating sound, a name he had heard whispered constantly ever since his first performance at La Llave; the ludicrous name of Mr Lápidus. Often people would come up to congratulate him. 'Just like Mr Lápidus,' they would say, 'You should meet Mr Lápidus.' 'If Mr Lápidus could see you . . .'

He knew who they were talking about. It was impossible not to know: the whole neighbourhood was plastered with photos of the man on posters for the Scala Barcelona: he was bald with a goatee beard, wore a black tuxedo and wire-framed glasses. A flashy shower of gold stars streamed from the magic wand he held, one of which seemed to have landed on his left eyelid, giving him a magical wink. His name was printed in large bold capitals – also gold – across his chest, with the motto: 'He could steal your soul.'

Rather than being flattered by the comparison, Víctor felt a twinge of scorn when he heard the name. There came a point when the mere mention of it brought a contemptuous smile to his lips. He decided that he had to do something. The following Monday, instead of spending his day off at the cinema, he went to see this Mr Lápidus perform. He was good. Banal, a bit tacky, a little too slick and self-satisfied, but good. He started off with a series of card tricks which, in spite of his appalling habit of strutting around the stage fanning himself, and his tendency to make the cards fly through the air like an acrobat, demonstrated a profound understanding of his craft and an astonishing dexterity. After this, he invited various members of the audience to come onstage to assist in a number of classic, and to Víctor, superfluous tricks: the chest speared by daggers; a number picked at random by a member of the audience which miraculously turns out to be on the magician's slate. As Lápidus performed he kept up a patter which to Víctor's ears sounded corny and completely contrived, but which drew gales of laughter from the audience. He constantly brandished a magic wand which he used to embarrass his victims: poking them in the belly if they were fat, tapping them on the nose if they looked confused. After what seemed like nothing more than a piece of clowning he would send the member of the audience back to their seat, only to call them back as they were about to leave the stage:

'Excuse me, sir, I believe you've forgotten something ...'

Then, one by one, with astonishing self-assurance, he would hand back various items he had managed to pinch during the conversation. The first items, usually a watch and a wallet, provoked only lukewarm applause, but as the objects became more peculiar, more outlandish, the audience went wild. Even Víctor, carried away by their enthusiasm, almost shouted out 'It's not possible' when the man handed back a tie he had managed to take from his victim. The following day, he told Galván, who gave a mocking smile and said simply: 'Oh, yes, he has nimble hands, Mr Lápidus.' After that he refused to be drawn.

Víctor became obsessed with Lápidus. He went back three Mondays in a row to watch him work. He stayed for both performances and each time he chose a different seat so he could watch from every possible angle. Above all, he spied on Lápidus during the interval when the magician sat at the long bar to have a drink and chat with the waiters, who were constantly on their guard. Even so, as he left to do the second show he would hand back their watch, or the pad and pen they used to jot down orders. Then, as the audience arrived for the second performance, Lápidus would stroll through the theatre. Anyone observing him would think he was simply relaxing between shows, but it was a decisive moment in his performance. This was the point when he chose his victims. Having seen him do this several times, Víctor drew a number of conclusions and began to hatch a daring plan: he would get Lápidus to choose him.

Statistically, a high percentage of those the magician chose wore glasses; this for the simple reason that the audience loved it when he said: 'Here, you'll need your glasses, we don't want you tripping on the stairs on your way down from the stage.' He probably chose people whose lenses were not too thick; it's impossible to steal glasses from someone as blind as a bat without their noticing. Being slightly short-sighted gave Víctor a distinct advantage. He would need a watch with a metal clasp – much easier to open than the buckle on a leather watchstrap and consequently more tempting to a magician. There were other useful ruses: he could show up with a girl and seem completely absorbed in her, he could say he was celebrating something. Often, the magician would ask for a round of applause as he called someone up on stage, telling the audience it was their birthday, or that the person was getting married the following day. And when he teased his victims, there would invariably be a few salacious comments about the girlfriend still sitting in the audience. Although Víctor never knew for certain, he suspected that in picking this type of person, Lápidus was making sure the victim was aware that his partner was watching and he would consequently be more distracted. One last, minor detail: it was best for the victim to be seated at a table near the centre aisle so that he did not disturb too many other people when he got up.

On the fourth Monday, Víctor prepared carefully. He invited the girl he had picked up at La Llave the night before to come with him and made sure that the magician saw them gazing into each other's eyes. He spent the break passionately kissing his date, and pretending not to notice Lápidus, who, as always, was watching the audience. In addition he had managed to get a good table, and as he ordered a bottle of champagne, he let it slip that it was his birthday.

During the first performance, six members of the audience were invited on to the stage and Víctor watched them enviously, but he remained calm. He was prepared to do this every Monday for as long as it took. In fact, the longer it took Lápidus to call him up onstage, the better prepared he would be. During the second half, the magician came to the front and said:

'Now, I'll need someone from the audience to assist me.' A number of people immediately got to their feet. Víctor gave a start but decided to hold back for a few seconds so as not to draw attention to himself. Lápidus brought his hand up to shield his eyes and pretended to survey the room: 'No offence, madame, but it has to be someone young and strong ... How about you, sir?' Víctor shrugged slightly but did not get up. 'Yes, you there. Don't go all shy on me ...'

As Víctor stepped on to the stage, the magician spoke to him in the disparaging way the audience found so funny.

'Wow ... I was hoping for someone young, not a baby. Are you sure you're eighteen, sonny? I don't want your *mamá* giving me grief!'

'Absolutely. In fact, I just turned eighteen today.'

'What a coincidence. I think that deserves a round of applause.'

The audience obeyed and Víctor stood, motionless, on the stage. Lápidus came over to him, pressed a hand gently to his side and suggested he take a bow.

'Say thank you to the audience! Young people these days ... they have no manners.'

As he bowed slightly, the punchline to Lápidus's joke, Víctor took it for granted that his wallet had now been purloined. Not because he felt the flutter of Lápidus's fingers, but because he had put it in his right-hand jacket pocket so it could be taken and he now understood how the magician worked. Lápidus continued to use Víctor as the butt of his jokes, and told the audience that the young man was about to witness the classic Chinese Linking Rings. He used every cliché in the book: 'This is the real deal,' he said, sliding one ring over the other and announcing that they would be joined together 'like two hearts in love'; he even found a way to use the execrable phrase 'Now you see it, now you don't ...' From time to time, he handed Víctor a ring so he could check it and tell the audience that it was completely solid. The more Víctor listened, the more he loathed the man. But he had to acknowledge the skill and ease with which Lápidus performed a dazzlingly fast, complex series of manoeuvres, shaping the rings into the symbol of the Olympic games, then uncoupling them again. Víctor, too, knew how to perform the Chinese Rings illusion, though he was much slower. Galván had shown it to him as an old-fashioned curiosity, unworthy of being performed onstage nowadays. Víctor tried to keep a surprised look on his face while focusing all his attention on every movement Lápidus made as he lifted another object from him. After all, that was why he was wearing them.

Though he noted how Lápidus took his watch, he had to admit that an innocent observer would never have noticed. He could not help but smile when he saw Lápidus's fingers take his tie-pin. When he had put it on, he knew that it was distinctly lacking in taste, but he had also been aware that the magician would be unable to resist the temptation.

When the time came for him to leave the stage, he walked quickly towards the steps and only began to gloat when the magician called out:

'Hey! Our little man seems to be in a hurry. Hardly surprising, since he's not wearing a watch . . .'

With the same theatricality, Víctor stopped, looked at his bare wrist, slapped himself on the forehead and walked back to Lápidus, who gave him the watch. As he did, he added:

'Don't forget to bow before you go. And enjoy your birthday, the champagne is on me . . .'

Once again, Víctor did what was expected of him. He even applauded before he turned to leave the stage a second time and did his best to look surprised when he heard the magician's voice.

'. . . because if you had to pay for it yourself, you'd be hard pressed.'

He didn't need to turn round to know that Lápidus was holding up his wallet. The audience were splitting their sides as though they'd never seen this trick done before. Unless the magician's nimble fingers had been skilful enough to escape Víctor's keen attention, only the tie-pin and his glasses remained.

'Thanks, kid,' Lápidus said. 'You've been a great assistant. I hope you didn't mind me pulling your leg. As a token of goodwill, I'd like to give you this beautiful tie-pin. Yes, I know it's yours, but I could have kept it for myself.'

The moment had come to act. Víctor found he had to raise his voice to drown out the audience's laughter.

'Thank you very much, Mr Lápidus. In any case,' he turned brazenly to the audience, suddenly taking over the role of ring-master, 'it wouldn't be much use to you, since you always wear a bow tie.' He held up the tie-pin for the audience to see, glanced at the magician, then added, 'Because you do always wear a bow tie, don't you?'

Taken by surprise, Lápidus brought his hand to his collar. For several seconds, the audience fell silent, only to burst out laughing again as Víctor put his hand in his trouser pocket and drew out Lápidus's bow tie. He dangled it in the air as though he were holding a snake. The magician quickly attempted to improvise.

'Are you sure it's mine? Take a good look, you might be mistaken. Though you might need these,' he said, proffering Víctor's glasses.

'No need, I'll use yours,' Víctor countered, putting his hand in his breast pocket and taking out the magician's wire-framed glasses. 'I think they're about the same strength.'

The audience was in stitches now. Lápidus glared at him and Víctor knew he would have strangled him with his bare hands had he been able. But the man was a good sport. Lápidus raised his arms and took a step towards Víctor as though to hug him. Víctor went with the flow and as they hugged the magician whispered:

'What's your name, you little son of a bitch?'

Víctor hesitated for a moment before answering.

'Don't fuck with me or I'll kill you,' Lápidus growled, still clapping Víctor on the back. 'What's your name?'

'Víctor,' he said finally.

'Víctor what?'

'Víctor Losa.'

Lápidus took a step back and, gesturing to Víctor, asked for a round of applause.

'Víctor Losa!' he announced. 'Víctor Losa, ladies and gentlemen!' he said again, as though announcing the name of the winning horse at a racetrack. 'A new star in the Lápidus constellation. A brilliant pupil. We'll be hearing a lot more from him in future. Don't forget, you saw him here first. Víctor Losa!'

It was a brilliant ad lib, and the audience seemed completely convinced that Víctor had been following Lápidus's orders from the outset. Víctor still had a surprise up his sleeve, but he decided to play along.

'Thank you, thank you,' he said, bowing. 'But, to be honest, the pupil can't take all the credit. Most of it goes to the master's magic wand!' He rummaged in the sleeve of his jacket, pulled out Lápidus's wand and handed it back to him. As he came over to take it, the magician blocked Víctor's path to the short flight of steps leading down to the stalls. He announced Víctor's name again, one hand firmly clutching the boy's shoulder, forcing him to leave the stage via the wings. Víctor had no choice. As he stumbled through the side curtain, two hefty thugs appeared and invited him to stay exactly where he was. His legs suddenly turned to jelly and his pounding heart leapt into his mouth like a hunted frog. He had to sit down on the ground. Not that he was afraid of what might happen next. After all, even if they did give him a good kicking, it was no more than he deserved. The wooziness he was experiencing was the tension draining away, a floating sensation similar to what he had felt on his first night at La Llave, exacerbated by the torrent of adrenalin surging through him. From his position on the floor, he listened as the magician brought his act to a close.

The audience was still applauding when Lápidus planted himself in front of Víctor. He lit a cigarette and, without saying a word, gestured for him to get to his feet. Then, he had only to nod and the two thugs came over and grabbed Víctor, twisting one arm behind his back and pushing him down the corridor. When they reached the emergency exit, they stopped and waited for Lápidus, who was following slowly behind.

'So, you are Víctor Losa, are you?' he said.

'Yes.'

'Give my best to Galván when you see him.'

'How do you know that ...?'

The sentence was never finished. Víctor could not protect his stomach since the thugs were holding him by both elbows and, though he tensed his abdominals, Lápidus's punch still left him gasping for breath.

'That's how Houdini was killed,' the magician said as he lashed out again. 'Tell the maestro, so he knows I haven't forgotten his history lessons.' Then he grabbed Víctor's right thumb. 'And this is more or less how Peter Grouse invented the false thumb.' He twisted the digit, bending it back until he heard a crack. Then the door was opened and the thugs tossed Víctor out into the street. Sprawled on the ground and doubled up in pain, Víctor thought the beating might not be over when he saw a shadow suddenly loom over him. As someone once again grabbed his throbbing thumb, he noticed the unmistakable smell of Galván's tobacco.

Without saying a word, the maestro jerked the thumb back into its normal position with another loud crack. Víctor covered it with his other hand and squeezed, but he noticed that the pain had subsided. Still gasping for breath, he hauled himself on to his knees. Just then Galván slapped him across the back of the head.

'Hey!' Víctor turned to stare at Galván, 'Why di—?'

'Because you deserve it. Because I've told you a thousand times not to improvise. Because you can't pull that sort of stunt unless you've planned your escape.' Galván's voice sounded more serious, more professorial, than ever, but he took a step forward, bent down and hugged his pupil hard. 'And because you're a genius, you little bastard.'

Víctor said nothing. Suddenly all the pent-up tension, all the aggression of his encounter with Lápidus, drained away, leaving him trembling. He did not answer. Or could not.

Galván broke the hug, pressed a finger under Víctor's chin and helped him to his feet.

'Did they do much damage?'

'Nothing that won't heal.'

Víctor suspected it would be some time before the pain and the swelling disappeared, but he did not care. He could do magic with one hand. With no hands. It was all in his mind. At that precise moment, he felt he could perform miracles.

Galván silently held his gaze.

'I didn't know you were here.'

'I'm always here, Víctor, you should know that by now.'

'Lápidus said to give you his regards. Something about Houdini and Peter Grouse.'

'I don't care about Lápidus. It's time to go. I think your girlfriend is waiting for you in the entrance.'

Víctor had not given the girl a single thought since Lápidus had called him up onstage.

'Wait. There's a lot of things I need to ask you.'

'This is not the time, Víctor, we'll talk about it in class.'

'At least tell me about Lápidus.'

'What about him?'

'You taught him?'

'Fifteen years ago.'

'What happened?'

'It didn't work out.'

'I've seen him do astonishing things.'

'He has talent, I'll grant you. He's a great typist. But he wouldn't recognise a piano if he saw one.'

'You sent him away.'

'Not exactly, I told him to come back when he was prepared to cross the line of fire.'

'Hoffmann,' Víctor muttered, 'fucking Hoffmann.' He bit his lip; now was perhaps not the time to ask this next question. But eventually, he looked Galván in the eye and said: 'Mario ... I've been working at La Llave for more than a month now.'

'Very successfully, from what I hear.'

'Yes. But you said that if I proved I was up to it, we could start doing real magic.'

'We will start. Very seriously. But it will have to wait until tomorrow.'

Together they walked back to the front of La Scala. As soon as she saw him, the girl threw herself into Víctor's arms, half overjoyed, half bewildered. As she hugged him, Víctor realised he hadn't even said thank you to Galván. He glanced around, but the maestro had disappeared.

Counting Steps

The first step is to accept the strict limitations of this ruined new world, the closed borders, the permanent curfew. To act accordingly. Make no grand plans. Or at least start with small steps. After all, when the future is as imminent as this, it requires little imagination to adapt to it. Can he do so? Is he capable of seeing himself – apologies for the tasteless use of that verb – as a blind man? Can he imagine living out this little life with dignity? Yes. In spite of everything, he can. And he must. He knows every square inch of his apartment like the back of his hand. He can now move around it with his eyes closed and without stumbling. He has lived here since he was born. He needs to hole himself up here, make the most of the few days he has left to buy everything he needs, make sure he has everything necessary to survive. Eat, sleep, shower, a fresh change of clothes every day.

What else. The world. Small, Víctor, think small. His local area, at least. Or smaller still: his block. Would he be able to make it around the block with his eyes closed? Probably not, but he can prepare himself. Prepare himself to be one hell of a blind man. And now would be as good a time to start as any. He jumps out of bed. He puts on the clothes he wore yesterday. He goes out, determined to circle the block, every sense on the alert, making a mental note of the details which, when he loses what little sight he has left in his right eye, will have to be enough for him to find his way around. Don't think about it, Víctor. Do what Galván always taught you; don't tell us what you are about to do: just do it.

He walks, trailing his left hand along the wall, but surreptitiously. He quickly passes the first shops and two houses. The last door before he comes to the corner is that of a bakery. He stops as though simply curious, alert to every sense. It is a glass door, like any other. He closes his eyes and takes deep breaths through his nose, twice, three times. He should be able to smell bread. The place probably doesn't even have its own oven any more; the bread is probably delivered from some factory first thing in the morning then the bakery simply sells it. It's a sad day for a blind man, thinks Víctor, when the overriding smell in a baker's doorway is that of dog piss rather than bread. Maybe he should have counted the number of steps from his own door. Some other day. He's not going back now.

El Paqui. The good old corner shop. There's an unmistakable fragrance. Open every day until 11 p.m., including Sundays and holidays. Everything you could ever need, just round the corner. Without realising it, Víctor quickens his pace. It would be ludicrous to say he feels euphoric, yet he blesses the benefits of this little world. Everything within easy reach. Everything easily memorisable. Who could ask for more? He moves away from the wall to step around a pile of dog shit and for an instant his imagination conjures a scatological vision of hell. There are lots of dogs in the area, Víctor. And lots of not very civic-minded dog-owners. Well, if necessary, he can always leave his shoes on the landing every time he returns home.

He speeds up, turns the second corner, makes a mental note of the smell of sawdust coming from the upholsterer's, and a few steps on, the smell of wine from the barrels in the winery, and he begins to think: yes, he can do this, everything he needs is just round the corner; a corner he can turn without seeing, he could walk round the block with his eyes closed even now, and if he can navigate the block, he can navigate the area, the world, the universe, because it's all fairly much alike, you can recognise anything if you're prepared. He has just turned the third corner; for some time now he has not been looking or smelling or listening, for several metres he has been making no notes for his mental map of the future. Keep walking, Víctor. Keep going. And count the steps you take. Don't stop to think how deceptive, how fragile, how short lived is the peace of those who have been vanquished.

Nothing More Invisible than Air

When he first saw a tank of compressed air in the cold light of day, it was proof that Peter Grouse had already stopped thinking like a thief and begun thinking like a magician. The metal cylinder was just like the one he had seen at the Egyptian Hall, though it looked thinner and appeared to be less heavy, although in fact two men were needed to carry it. Throwing caution to the wind, he went straight over and asked them what they were carrying. Compressed air was a recent innovation and although it had been used in factories for some years now, the idea of storing it in relatively small quantities for use in workshops and on building sites was only just taking off. When he found out what it was, he did not, for a moment, think about how much it might be worth if he could steal it. On the contrary, his first thought was about its practical applications in magic. More precisely, how it might be used to operate Psycho the automaton. Nor was it a particularly detailed deduction. He was simply struck by the words 'Nothing more invisible than air'. He started to run.

He got back to his room, excited and out of breath, but before opening his copy of *Modern Magic* for the umpteenth time, he tried to calm himself a little. Eleven months had passed since his first visit to the Egyptian Hall but he still remembered the absurd joy he had felt that night when he got home and realised that the torn edge of the piece of paper he had stolen from Maskelyne matched the thin ragged strip where pages 537/538 had been ripped out of the book. He immediately sat down and began to read, convinced that in his hands he held the key to claiming Maskelyne's £3,000. He was quickly, and brutally, disappointed. Having read the whole chapter, all he could do was agree with

Maskelyne's scrawled note: Hoffmann has no idea. Worse still: Hoffmann masked his ignorance by larding his text with technical terms. Though he now knew the entire chapter by heart, Grouse still resented the convoluted prose, full of deceptions, insinuations and deliberate evasions.

That first night he had not been able to get a wink of sleep so he profited from his insomnia by making one of the most important resolutions of his life: whatever it took, he would reconstruct Hoffmann's diagram in three dimensions. He knew from the text that he could not possibly replicate the way the automaton functioned and consequently he was a long way from being able to claim the magician's £3,000, but he needed to see it. To see, to touch, to have something concrete, something tangible, which might act as a springboard for his imagination. Provided he succeeded, it did not matter to him how much he spent. Or, rather, what crimes he might have to commit, since as a matter of professional pride he did not pay for anything he could get free. His most spectacular crime had been breaking into a tailor's shop at night and stealing a wooden dummy, a head and torso which were conveniently hollow. In just two days he had managed to lay his hands on dozens of tools, many of which he would not even need. With these, he had handmade most of the pieces. Others he had seized from poorly guarded bicycles which he had abandoned after he had done with them. For the more complex parts, he had had no option but to entrust his request to a blacksmith and pay for them. As the expenses began to eat into his earnings, he was obliged to extend his working hours. The few free hours he had left, he spent at the table in his room, assembling pieces which he then fitted into the dummy by the light of two candles.

It had taken him five months to build something that vaguely resembled Psycho. It was a poor copy and the movement lacked the precision of the original, but at least he had managed to get the arm to move. To do this, he had only to turn a crank set into the hollow body of the mannequin. Grouse was particularly proud of the way the gears meshed silently and he would frequently take them out and oil them again.

But he still did not have the most crucial piece of information;

the detail over which Hoffmann shamelessly equivocated: how to move the crank remotely. In the Egyptian Hall, no one had come within two metres of the automaton while it was working, a fact that Maskelyne had not only mentioned, but had rather pretentiously and theatrically demonstrated. Grouse spent night after night with the crank in one hand, spinning it in the air as the imaginary gears in his brain turned round and round.

He had his first success using a bicycle from which he had removed the wheels. He screwed the frame to the floor and attached the crank handle to the chain. This gave a distance of barely two feet. The arm of the automaton still moved, though the movements were more spasmodic and less precise than before. Next, he tried making the chain longer so as to increase the distance but, although he extended it by only a few inches, it didn't work. Now that it was longer, the chain lost tension after the first turn of the pedals. It was logical, he thought; after all, bicycles otherwise would be fifteen feet long.

As the weeks passed, his room began to seem smaller and smaller. Every inch of space was covered with tools and spare parts which he went on collecting even if he had no specific use for them. By now, not even his bed, which was pushed back against the wall, was immune to the invasion. One night, stumbling into his room in the dark, he tripped over the bicycle chain and, in a rage, he lashed out, kicking and stamping. He didn't quite manage to destroy the mannequin, but it was a close thing. When he finally calmed down, he was frightened. He was not accustomed to losing his head. Lying back on the bed, it took him only a few moments to work out what had caused this reaction: the closer he came to the solution, the more impossible it seemed. Even if he could find a way to extend the chain by several metres and keep it taut, he still had to deal with the most intractable problem of all: making it invisible. In the end, even allowing for a trapdoor and a space beneath the stage, which probably existed at the Egyptian Hall, the chain still had to connect with the body of the mannequin. Through a transparent cylinder. This phrase was carved in capital letters on his brain: A TRANSPARENT CYLINDER. He was as far from his goal as he had been the day he started.

There was no way to make a chain invisible. He had to start over again.

Something invisible, something invisible. These two words had been plaguing him for weeks. Determined not to squander any more time or money, he forbade himself to pick up another tool until he had worked out the theory. He would draw. That's what he would do. Draw as many diagrams as he needed, make lists of every substance he was aware of until he came up with one that was invisible but still capable of moving the mechanism of the automaton. He was not stupid, he knew that, in this case, 'invisible' meant 'transparent'. He continued to throw himself into the task, but the thrill of the first days was gone because he was faced with an insurmountable obstacle. He never forgot that his initial desire had been to see. To see something similar to the original so that he might use this as a springboard to imagine a solution. Now that he could see it, he had to imagine something invisible. He had to see something that was invisible.

Two months later, he was still turning the problem over in his mind, but now he no longer drew diagrams and, though it pained him to admit it, he was thinking about giving up. The *coup de grâce*, when it came, was not the result of long nights of mental gymnastics, but a complete accident, a piece of information he stumbled on while going about his ordinary business.

Grouse always kept in touch with various officers in the London courts. It was useful to know who had been locked up, what sort of sentences were being handed down for which crimes, which judges were harsh and which were lenient with those who worked the streets. All in all, information that was of secondary importance, but useful in making decisions with regard to his profession and which only entailed buying a pint of beer from time to time for clerks and junior officers of the court. It was during one such meeting that he discovered Maskelyne had been to court a few weeks earlier. And not as a plaintiff – something he frequently did if he felt someone was making use of one of his patents – but as the defendant. It seemed that someone had come up with, or thought they had come up with, the solution to how Psycho worked and had claimed the £3,000 reward. Maskelyne had refused to pay. The case had caused something of a stir among the court officers because the plaintiff had brought his automaton into court. Maskelyne had not. He had nothing to prove and the judge accepted that forcing him to demonstrate how Psycho worked was tantamount to making his invention obsolete.

Since the hearing had been held *in camera*, Grouse's informant did not know how the plaintiff's automaton worked. What he did know was that the verdict had been decided on a linguistic nuance. During opening remarks, witnesses for both sides had agreed on Maskelyne's exact words when he made the challenge: 'A similar apparatus capable of playing cards that is genuinely automatic'. In other words, what was important was not that the competing automaton should look exactly like Psycho, nor even that it should function in the same way, but that it do so without any human intervention whatsoever. This, according to Maskelyne, and apparently to the judge, was the meaning of the word 'genuinely'. It was not enough that someone should be able to operate the automaton secretly or remotely. In simple terms, the machine had to function by itself. The plaintiff therefore demanded that Maskelyne reveal how Psycho worked in order to prove that the challenge was possible. Or, if not, that he should publicly admit that he had been fooling his audience. The judge, however, poured scorn on this request, in words that quickly spread throughout the courts: 'If I claimed that I had visited the moon and offered a reward for anyone capable of doing likewise, I would be insane. But nobody could insist that I prove it, still less that I pay up. And being insane, as far as I know, is not a crime.'

Even Grouse had to accept that the decision was legitimate, and, with a heavy heart, he felt he had to abandon his attempt. A substance that, besides being invisible, was capable of moving by itself? It seemed easier to accept the judge's challenge and try to come up with some means of propelling himself to the moon. Until his conversation with the two workmen in the street. At that moment it was as though a light had switched itself on in his mind and, for the first time, he saw the solution he had been seeking for so long. The rubber tubes from the tank could run under the stage to a simple trapdoor, which would allow air up through the cylinder when required. Nothing was more invisible than air.

The Future

'Let's leave it at that,' Galván announced.

He had been telling the story of Psycho and had just come to the point where Grouse discovered the existence of compressed air and its possible uses for automata. Halfway through the story he had got to his feet and his voice continued its narration from the darkness. These sudden, increasingly lengthy disappearances had ceased to worry Víctor, but it did bother him if Galván moved around as he was talking because it forced Víctor to swivel round in his chair in order to be able to hear. Most of all, he was irritated by Galván's tendency to break off in the middle of his stories.

'Why?' he protested. 'Go on, just a little more ... It's not late. I still don't understand what this has to do with Grouse's thumb ...'

'There's too much left to tell,' the maestro said. 'Right now, we need to talk about the future.'

At that moment, there was a noise and the lights came on.

Víctor rubbed his eyes and blinked before looking around the room. The island, these two square metres within whose borders he had been confined every Tuesday afternoon for almost two years suddenly became a vast, diaphanous space. Galván, dressed in black, as always, was standing with his back to Víctor near the door in front of a large bank of switches. Every time he pressed one, another section of the hall lit up, finally revealing a small stage right at the back of the room. In this new context the table and the two folding chairs looked like toys. The walls were plastered with old magic posters. Without moving from his seat, Víctor recognised several names: Maskelyne, Kellar, Stodare. Near the stage, the walls and the floor were completely black. At the other end of the room, on the wall with the small window, were half a dozen objects which Víctor at first assumed were pieces of furniture until, taking a second look, he recognised the famous Sword Cabinet and an escape-artist's trunk circled with stout chains and heavy padlocks.

'Shit ... this place is a museum.'

'Not yet,' Galván said. 'But that's what I want to talk about.'

He came over to the table, moved his chair next to Víctor's and sat down. He smoothed the green baize tablecloth before carrying on.

'I have emphysema,' he announced matter-of-factly, as though he were telling someone it was raining outside. As Víctor opened his mouth, the maestro raised a hand to stop him. 'It's not going to kill me just yet, but I need to make a few changes. At my age ...'

'I don't even know how old you are,' Víctor objected.

'Too young to die,' replied Galván. 'And too old not to face the fact that I'm dying.' He put his hand in his pocket and took out his pack of cigarettes. Víctor could see the determination in his eyes and did not even try to comment. 'I'm not going to bother you with all the gory details. Let's just say it's like having a hole in my lungs. Or rather, a tunnel. I can't breathe properly. I tire easily.'

'But, Mario ...'

'Let me finish. I've wanted to change some things in my life for some time, and this is exactly the opportunity I've been waiting for. I'm tired of giving lessons.' Seeing the fear in Víctor's face, he quickly clarified his meaning. 'Not to you. It's the others I want to give up. In fact, I've told them I'm not teaching any more.'

Víctor, who had not even realised that Galván had other students, breathed a sigh of relief.

'I don't really care about the shop either. I don't want to get rid of it, because I've spent my whole life there, but from now on, my daughter will manage it. Right now, there are only two projects that interest me. One is the museum. I have a lot more old things in the workshop. I'd like to restore them and exhibit them. If I put in seats from here up to the stage, I think the place could hold just short of a hundred people.' It was clear he had everything planned. 'It could be used as a lecture hall for conferences, exhibitions, masterclasses. All of this will take time that I haven't had until now.'

'And the other project?'

'The other project is you.'

Víctor could not suppress a smile.

'When do we start?'

'We started two years ago. You've learned a lot. So much, in fact, that if you never set foot in this place again, I guarantee you could make a good living.'

'Like Lápidus.'

'More or less. All I need to know is whether you have the talent and the determination that he lacked. Whether you're prepared to take the next step, prepared to think big, whether you're interested in doing something that will make a difference.'

'What do you think?'

'I think you are. But that's not enough. What I need from you is a commitment. If we're to carry on, I'm going to put a lot of pressure on you. We'll have to work, Víctor, *really* work. And if you fail me, I'll never forgive you.'

'Shit, Mario, you make it sound like we're getting married.'

'I'd never do that. You never stay with anyone for more than a couple of days.'

'Anyway, the answer's yes. Yes, I want to.'

For the rest of the conversation, Víctor had a smile on his face. He had spent two years waiting for this moment. He got up and hugged Galván, hopping from one foot to another like a little boy.

'If everything goes well, you'll make a lot of money. A lot. Even after I take my fifteen per cent. If not, it's still worth having tried.'

'Real magic.' Víctor sat down again. Though he had returned the hug, Galván's face was solemn, as though he was determined to ignore the magnitude of the moment. 'At last.'

'Yes,' the maestro said. 'Imagine. You wanted to talk about real magic. I wanted to talk about the future. As it turns out, they're the same thing. But we can only make it happen if we go back to the past.'

'Don't start with the word games, Mario. Please.'

'You're right.' Galván paused for a second and thought. 'It's time to act. Stay there, don't move and keep your eyes closed until I tell you.'

Víctor did as he was told, but he listened as Galván's footsteps moved away towards the stage at the back of the hall. After a few moments, he gave Víctor permission to look. When Víctor opened his eyes, he could not see hide nor hair of the maestro.

'We are in the Berlin Panoptikon. The year is 1886, ten years post-Hoffmann.'

Víctor searched the room but still could not see Galván anywhere, although he could not possibly be hiding unless there was an invisible trapdoor in the back wall. After a few seconds, a small table suddenly materialised in the middle of the stage. Víctor started as though someone had pricked him. It was not possible. Ignoring Galván's orders, he got up and moved closer, only to stop, frozen in mid-stride, when he saw a red cup appear on the table. It did not simply appear, it seemed to have sprouted there. In a fraction of a second. As if this were not enough, at that moment a trickle of white liquid was spirited out of the air, filling the cup. Víctor crept closer, almost on tiptoe, as though the least sound would cause the illusion to vanish. He arrived at the stage, reached out and touched the table, the cup. Despite their solidity, he still believed they might be holograms. At that moment a strong hand grabbed his calf and Galván's voice thundered:

'I thought I told you not to move!'

Víctor let out a scream and stumbled, knocking over the cup and spilling the milk. Galván's booming laugh echoed round the room. Still Víctor did not understand until he saw Galván's hands in black gloves holding up what looked like a hood. As his student's eyes lit up with the sheer simplicity of the illusion, the maestro said:

'Welcome, Víctor Losa, to the Black Art.'

It was so simple it was insulting. Galván removed the gloves and explained the few details he had not grasped.

'Apparently the illusion was discovered by a German actor, Max Auzinger, in 1885. According to him, the idea came to him by chance while he was watching a play his rep company were performing. At the climax of the play, a black man was supposed to appear suddenly at the back of the stage to rescue the kidnapped heroine. On opening night, when the black man appeared – though of course it was actually a white actor blacked up – the audience didn't react. Auzinger, who was sitting in one of the boxes since he wasn't in the scene, immediately realised the problem. Since the backcloth was black, all the audience could see were the whites of the actor's eyes.'

'But . . .'

'Hold on . . . I've told you this because it's a charming story and it's tempting to believe it, but all the research indicates it may not be true. The Black Art was well known long before that. In fact, this is the way puppet shows were done in Japan centuries ago. The background was always black and the puppeteer was dressed in black – he didn't even try to pretend to be invisible, he simply dressed in black so that his presence didn't interfere with the story. Some magicians had used it before too, but only as a minor illusion in the middle of a show. Maybe this is why Hoffmann only mentions it in passing. This was how Maskelyne's floating harp worked. It was held up by a black cable.'

'So Auzinger had read *Modern Magic*?'

'Maybe. If so, there's no record of it. It doesn't matter. What matters is that Auzinger, perhaps without realising it, had discovered one of the ways of crossing the line of fire. Taking a minor technique, something Hoffmann barely mentions, and elevating it to an art form. He spent months perfecting the illusion, tested it with magicians who allowed him to take the stage briefly, but still it excited little enthusiasm until he came up with the final touch, the detail that made the illusion perfect: a series of spotlights at the back of the stage pointing towards the audience. Not enough to blind them, but enough to force them to squint a little.'

'Didn't it bother them?'

'Absolutely. But you've just had the same spotlights pointing at you and you didn't even notice.' Galván nodded towards them. 'Auzinger had crossed the line of fire and so collected the prize. For years, he toured the world with his Black Art illusion. And since orientalism was in fashion, he dressed in Arab costume, wore a turban and called himself Ben Ali Bey.'

'I don't understand. I thought he had to be dressed in black?'

'That was another of his improvements. He wore bright, garish colours and all he did during the illusion was speak. Onstage with him was an assistant, dressed completely in black, and consequently invisible as far as the audience was concerned. Auzinger would move about the stage, talking as he went, and from time to time he would raise his hand. He kept this hidden in his fist.'

Galván showed him a shiny, red metallic cylinder. Víctor took it, gauging the weight of the thing in surprise.

'It's very heavy for such a small object, isn't it? Squeeze it in the middle and you'll see why.'

Víctor closed his fist. There was a cracking noise and the cylinder shot out, becoming a long telescopic cane. Galván took it back, squeezed again and, with the same crack the cane telescoped back and disappeared into his fist.

'I still sell a lot of these in the shop, though these days they're made of plastic. They've become little more than toys. People only use them for cheap tricks, they attach something to the tip: a spray of flowers, a silk handkerchief, something like that. But Auzinger used the case as it should be used – as a signal. He would raise his hand and squeeze the cylinder and at that moment, his assistant would whip aside a black cloth and some object would magically materialise exactly where the rod was pointing. From the audience's point of view, this enhanced the whole performance. Not only did things magically appear, but the magician seemed to have complete control over where and when they did so.'

'I'm surprised I've never heard of him.'

'You're right. He could have been as famous as Maskelyne, or as that moron Houdini, but only real aficionados are aware of his existence. And do you know why?'

'No, obviously, but I feel a lesson coming on.'

'It's an important lesson. It's not enough simply to cross the line of fire. From time to time, you have to go back, get new material and cross the line again. If not . . .'

'Kaput.'

'Exactly. Kaput. Auzinger was happy to rest on his laurels. After a couple of years, he had imitators the world over. But there are other lessons to be learned from him. Maybe the most important is that Auzinger wasn't a magician. He was an actor who for a couple of years made a good living performing an illusion. When

144

it didn't work, he gave up. Cinema was the new thing for actors at the time. Auzinger, who was certainly no oil painting, managed to get a part in a silent horror film; later on he even appeared in Dreyer's *Mikaël, Chained*. What I need to know is whether you are a real magician.'

'Put me to the test, Mario. Put me to the test.'

A Madman Walking

He still has some vision in his right eye, but he is ready to walk as a blind man and trust himself to his sensory memory. Or he thinks he is. After all, he has spent his whole life trusting in his fingers. He opens the wardrobe, finds the black jacket he last wore at the party, and from the pocket he takes the black scarf he used to blindfold himself. It is three o'clock in the morning. Nobody is going to notice a lunatic walking around wearing a mask. As he knots the scarf behind his head he thinks of Galván, who did this for him the last time . . . Can it only be two months ago? Can the time have passed so slowly?

He starts to walk, hugging the wall. This is something anyone can do at home. We all manage to go to the toilet in the middle of the night without turning on the lights. Besides, Víctor has moved confidently across a hundred different stages blindfold. He can trust his sense of direction. Without realising it, he adopts a rather faltering gait. He hunches his shoulders slightly and, from time to time, he puts his arms out in front of him. He looks as if he is chasing invisible insects. He also stoops as he walks, as though expecting the roof to fall in at any moment. He gets to the door without incident and stops for a moment, his hand on the latch. This should be enough to prove his point. But something, perhaps something that might be called hope, urges him on.

He opens the door, crosses the landing, hesitates for the first time as he comes to the first flight of stairs, then starts his descent. Walking down six flights, he stumbles only once. In fact, he does not even stumble, he missteps, forgets to bend his knees. There are three steps in the middle of the lobby. He hugs the wall for support that he does not actually need and slows down a little. He negotiates them easily, then reaches the front door and throws it open.

He closes it immediately.

There is no traffic at this hour, there are no pedestrians. It is nothing but a gust of wind, the night's cold breath, but it is enough to confound his senses. The closed door is not enough to protect him from the onslaught. He needs to get back to the safety of the walls. His heart in his mouth, he starts to run as though some hideous beast has crossed the threshold after him. He trips on the first step. He quickly gets to his feet and lashes out, then climbs the stairs as best he can, clinging to the banister. If Galván could see him now. What has become of his elegance now, his celebrated poise?

He gets to the top floor and hurls himself against the door. It is closed. He does not need to put his hand in his pocket to know he has come out without his keys. He pounds on the door as though there were someone inside. He turns round, leaning against it, bends his legs and allows himself to slide down until he is sitting on the landing. Then he puts his elbows on his knees, his face in his hands. Only when he is about to burst into tears does he remember he is wearing a blindfold. See how easy it is, Víctor? You wanted to put yourself in a blind man's shoes. The same shoes that will all too soon be your own. This was a test. You just wanted to dip your toe in the water and you've ended up drenched to the bone. You have just discovered that the frontier that separates you from the world works both ways. You wanted to go out into the world, but the world has come in to you. You wanted to understand the blind man, and you have found him inside you. Take the mobile phone from your pocket and call Galván, he has a set of keys. All you need to do is press number two. Find it with the gift of sight your right eye still affords you, press and hold for a few seconds. And get a grip on yourself. The only beast here is the one inside you. A blind animal.

A Sausage Inside a Sausage

When he realised there was not one but three locks on the door which led backstage, Peter Grouse stopped to think. He was not particularly bothered by this hitch, which at worst meant it would take him three times as long to get through, but he was worried by what it meant. Obviously Maskelyne, suspecting that someone had stolen his copy of *Modern Magic*, had decided to double his efforts to protect his secrets. Maybe someone would be waiting for Grouse on the other side of the door. Or worse, they might be watching him right now, in which case he would be caught the moment he set foot in the corridor. It was not a particularly pleasant thought. He turned and quickly surveyed the entrance.

He had spent several weeks perfecting his automaton and although he still had some doubts as to how rigorously the words 'genuinely automatic' might be interpreted, he was satisfied. He had not managed to steal a tank of compressed air for the simple reason that he did not know where to find one. At some point he had even thought of breaking into the Egyptian Hall in the dead of night and stealing Maskelyne's, but he quickly dismissed the idea: it would set off alarm bells and jeopardise his objective. However, he believed he had found a simple solution to the problem: reefing all the pieces to make them lighter so they would move at the slightest burst of air which he would provide by blowing into a tube. Though the automaton's hand moved very slowly, despite Grouse filling his lungs to bursting point, he considered the concept proven. Explosive bursts of compressed air, he was certain, would resolve this issue.

However, he knew that Maskelyne could make a host of technical objections to his invention and Grouse did not want to find himself in the position of being forced to deal with these in a courtroom. In spite of his consummate skill as a pickpocket, he had a number of prior convictions and knew all too well how judges would react to someone like him. Consequently, he had devoted the past few evenings to the thought experiment he enjoyed the most: putting himself in his victim's shoes. Anticipating Maskelyne's every possible reaction. He was certain the magician would refuse to pay. Even if Grouse created a precise replica of Psycho piece by piece, Maskelyne would find some excuse to avoid having to pay out. Unless Grouse could forestall his every move and back him into a corner. He needed a little more time to think and, above all, he needed to gather information. This was what had brought him back to the Egyptian Hall.

Maskelyne and Cooke's performance had been exactly the same as the first time except for the fact that, now the element of surprise was gone, Grouse found the show rather boring, Maskelyne's pompous tone faintly ridiculous, and his scientific pretensions barely credible. The only thing that was new was that when he introduced Psycho, Maskelyne spelled out the conditions for claiming the reward and implored the audience not to waste his time with 'spurious automata which, at the moment of truth, cannot function without human intervention'. Grouse made a note of his exact words. It was clear that Maskelyne felt he could not depend on always having a sympathetic judge. However, the magician's speech did not prevent Grouse from noticing something he had failed to spot on his first visit: Cooke was entirely absent from the stage during Psycho's performance. If Grouse now found himself, picklock in hand, in the entrance of La Scala, it was not simply to gather more information but in defiance of what was, the more he thought about it, nothing more than a crude and ugly scam. Psycho was not a genuine automaton! It required human intervention in order to function. The arm was made to move using compressed air, but someone had to operate it. Somebody had to open the stopcock on the tank every time Maskelyne asked Psycho to choose a card and close it again so the arm would stop moving. And that somebody was George Alfred Cooke.

This was why he did not force the door. To dash down the corridor and find Cooke standing next to the tank would only confirm what he already knew. It was too big a risk for too little reward. Besides, as often happens when we think we know all the answers, a new question had formed in his mind: could he improve on Maskelyne? Could he find a means by which the compressed air regulated itself? He thought perhaps he could, although he needed to collect more materials to do the relevant tests. He turned and left the Egyptian Hall. He felt euphoric. If he had finally found the answer, only one marvellous question remained: how would he spend the £3,000?

It took him a few days to organise everything. The following Monday, he planted himself outside the Egyptian Hall armed with courage and, more especially, with patience. He knew this would not be his last visit. At 6.30 p.m., Maskelyne came round the corner, heading for the theatre wearing his black coat, carrying his leather case. Grouse smiled: he liked men who stuck to their routine. When the magician arrived at the door, Grouse did not say a word. He simply stood next to him, leaning nonchalantly against one of the enormous pilasters of the façade. Maskelyne, alarmed by his silent presence, returned his gaze and, with none of the artifice or pretension of his stage performance, he asked:

'May I be of some assistance?'

'I hope so,' replied Grouse.

'Go on ...'

Maskelyne's frown indicated that his patience was already wearing thin. From the way the man was scrutinising him, Grouse thought that perhaps Maskelyne remembered his face from their first encounter, but as the conversation developed he quickly realised this was not the case.

'I am here as a representative of Mr Grouse.'

'I have not had the pleasure.'

'You shortly will.'

'Ah ...' Maskelyne gripped the key, clutched the handle of his leather case and took a step back. 'And how precisely might I be of assistance to this gentleman, this Mr ...?'

'Grouse. Peter Grouse. You might give him the three thousand pounds that he considers to be rightfully his.'

'I see. Another nincompoop who believes he has solved the riddle.' Maskelyne could not help smiling. 'Tell him my answer is no. And tell him not to waste my time. If, of course, he wishes to take the matter to court, I shan't stop him. Now, if you don't mind ...'

'You have things to do. I can well imagine. Mr Grouse asked me to give you this.'

He handed Maskelyne a folded piece of paper and, without waiting for him to open it, took his leave and set off east along Piccadilly. Hardly had he taken a few steps before the magician called out to him:

'Hey! Wait a minute. Tell Mr Grouse that I am prepared to meet with him here, tomorrow, at the same hour.'

'I shall do that, sir.'

Mission accomplished. Grouse suppressed a smile. This was precisely the response he had been expecting. On the sheet of paper there were only two words: 'compressed air'. He had made two attempts at writing them, his tongue sticking out as he concentrated, persuaded that writing was clearly a more difficult task than reading.

The following day he arrived fifteen minutes before the appointed time and once more took up his position against the column.

'What of Mr Grouse?' Maskelyne asked when he saw him.

'He is about his business. But I shall take your reply to him promptly.'

'My reply is the same as it was yesterday. Now ...'

'I know. You have much to do. And no, I don't mind. On condition that you be so good as to take this.'

Once again, Grouse handed him a folded sheet of paper, but this time he made no move to leave. He wanted to see Maskelyne's face as he read it. Though it was not exactly a long text, it had taken much more effort to write than the previous one. The magician unfolded the paper and read: 'Genuinely automatic. I don't need Cooke to make it function.' Maskelyne's face showed annoyance and curiosity in equal measure. The man frowned, pondered for a moment, then said:

'Tell him ... tell Mr Grouse that he will have to demonstrate his claim. Tell him I wish to see him here, at the same time tomorrow. In person. Without fail.'

Grouse resisted the temptation to feel sorry for Maskelyne. If he persisted in giving the expected response at every step, Grouse would soon have him cornered like a rat. But he could not afford to drop his guard: cornered rats were known to bite.

'Very well. However, I have another message. Like you, Mr Grouse is a busy man and as a result he, too, cannot afford to waste his time. He has asked me to insist that you come with the money.'

'He has my word on it. But he has much to prove to me before I hand it over.'

On the Wednesday, Grouse arrived several hours before the appointed time. In fact he arrived even before the sun had risen. He forced his way into the Egyptian Hall without substantial difficulty and when he came to the tank of compressed air, he set down the heavy sack which contained his tools and materials and gave a sigh. This, he thought, was the happiest moment of his life, but he could not stop to enjoy it. He had work to do.

Much later Maskelyne arrived and, not finding Grouse by the entrance, took this to be an auspicious sign. But when he slipped his key into the lock and found the door already open, a shudder ran through him. He turned quickly and gestured for the two boorish men who had been following him to come closer. Grouse, who had been watching from a safe distance at the rear of the entrance hall, walked calmly towards the stage, stopped for a second in the wings to open the tank of air and, before he concealed himself beneath the table Maskelyne used for the 'Decapitated Head' illusion, he silently gave thanks to Hoffmann – he had found the solution to this trick in *Modern Magic* and, unlike the entry for Psycho, the diagram was so clear and comprehensible that he had not even had to decipher the text. Between the legs of the table, two pieces of looking-glass are set at such an angle that the spectator sees what appear to be the curtains at the back of the recess, but are in fact a reflection of the curtains at the sides. Simple as that. During the interval, Cooke took up his position under the table, concealed by the mirrors, and waited for the second act to begin. Maskelyne appeared on stage holding an empty box which he held up for the audience to see, but was careful that they did not see it was hollow at the bottom. When he placed it on the table, Cooke had only to release a trapdoor and poke his head up into the box. Just before Maskelyne opened the box to reveal him to the audience, he would close his eyes and adopt an otherworldly expression.

As soon as he stepped into the theatre, Maskelyne saw that the lights were on and that Psycho was in position onstage. He dispatched his thugs to either side of the automaton, while he went back into the wings, where everything seemed to be in order.

'Grouse!' he roared, standing at the front of the stage once more. 'Enough of these games! I'm warning you . . .'

He trailed off in mid-sentence, alerted by the familiar puff of air and the grinding of gears that heralded Psycho's movements. He quickly turned and saw the arm of the automaton moving towards the rack that held the whist cards. Maskelyne was dumbfounded: he had just checked to make sure there was no one near the tank of compressed air. Only when Psycho's hand stopped in mid-air did he notice that it was not holding a card, but a piece of folded paper suspiciously similar to those Grouse's emissary had delivered. Still glancing around the theatre furiously, he came closer, took the piece of paper and read: 'As I said: genuinely automatic.' Maskelyne screwed the paper into a ball, threw it on the floor, and attempted to invest his voice with a calm he did not feel.

'Grouse!' he called. 'We need to talk. There's no need for you to hide. We can settle this matter like gentlemen.'

Maskelyne jumped, startled by another burst of air. By the time he turned round, Psycho's arm was already proffering a second slip of paper. 'I have made three copies of the plans which I have entrusted to my associates. Should any mischief befall me, they are instructed to register the patent this very day.'

From his hiding place, Grouse could not see Maskelyne, but the hail of insults and blasphemies was enough for him to know that the man was still following the script he had penned for him. Slowly, Grouse smoothed the creases of his black jacket. He would soon be making his entrance.

'You win, Grouse. I am a man of my word.' As he spoke, the magician's head jerked about like a fretful bird, trying to find his rival. 'I have the money here.' He slipped a hand into his pocket and took out an envelope. 'But you must understand that I cannot pay you unless . . .'

Another burst of air. Infuriated, Maskelyne did not even wait until Psycho had completed its move. He marched over to the rack, took the next piece of paper and read it: 'Place the envelope on the card rack and withdraw to the back of the stage.'

Maskelyne did as he was ordered but, unable to contain his fury, he lashed out at Psycho's metal arm as he passed. It now hung limply at the elbow as though a tendon had been broken and there was a sudden whistle of compressed air as it escaped the entrails of the automaton. The moment had come for Grouse to play his starring role. It would have amused him to pop his head out of the trapdoor in the table and speak, but he was afraid that in such a vulnerable position he would be at the mercy of the magician. Instead, he emerged from behind the table and rose to his feet.

'Tell your thugs to stand next to you, Maskelyne. I have as much concern for my health as you do for your patents.'

The magician gestured to his henchmen to move to the back of the stage. When Grouse was still some paces from Psycho, Maskelyne came forward and stood ten feet away from him.

'Don't touch the money yet,' the magician warned, attempting to invest his tone with what meagre authority remained. 'In the first instance, there are a number of matters to be settled.'

'Of course,' Grouse replied, but his every muscle was tensed and primed. '. . . like gentlemen.'

'Like gentlemen. I cannot pay Mr Grouse unless he comes here in person and surrenders all copies of the plans.'

'I regret that will not be possible, sir. Moreover, it would serve little purpose. I have seen Mr Grouse working on this project and, believe me, he could walk out of here and draw the diagram again from memory. Right down to the last nut.'

'How can I be sure that he will not attempt to steal my patent?'

'Mr Maskelyne, I truly believe you have not quite understood the situation. There is no theft here. On the contrary, it is a gift. Mr Grouse is giving you the gift of integrity. Because from now on, every time you utter the words "genuinely automatic", every time you boast about how your automaton works without the need for human intervention, you will be able to do so with a clear conscience. And that, I think you will agree, is priceless.'

Maskelyne reflected for a moment in silence. He had just witnessed his invention functioning completely independently. Three thousand pounds was a considerable sum, but it would put him several steps ahead of his rivals and extend Psycho's lifespan, and consequently his earnings, by several years.

'You yourself put a price on the invention; so it is only fair that you should pay it,' the thief went on. 'In addition, Mr Grouse is offering you a significant improvement, and his silence on the matter for the remainder of his life, for which he asks only the modest additional sum of four and thruppence.'

'Four shillings and ...' Maskelyne looked him up and down, a look of contempt that suddenly changed to a flash of recognition. 'Ah! I see ... It seems I have been dealing with Mr Grouse in person all along. I confess, it was somewhat irksome, parleying with a ghost.'

'They say he who robs a thief is pardoned for a hundred years, Maskelyne. But you should not believe everything you hear.'

'That much seems incontrovertible,' the magician replied, 'but one important detail remains.'

'There is nothing, I'm sure, that we cannot settle here,' said Grouse, 'as gentlemen.'

'This gift that you speak of ... I cannot take full advantage of it unless you explain to me how it works.'

'You are right. However, I'm sure you will agree that the problem cuts both ways. The moment I show you how it functions, I lose all legitimate claim to the money. This, I suspect, accounts for the presence of your friends.' He nodded towards the back of the stage. 'But this can be resolved by the order of events. Shall we begin with the matter of the money?'

With an irritated expression, the magician rummaged in his pocket and began counting.

'Leave it, Maskelyne. We are not going to haggle over loose change. After all, on the night in question, you were merely acting in self-defence. But I shall take the envelope. And I would like the leather case, too. I took a liking to it the first time I saw it.'

'You're mad. The case contains nothing of any val—'

'I don't care what it contains,' Grouse interrupted him. 'It could be empty for all I care. It is symbolic.'

It took a little longer than expected for Maskelyne to untie the leather strap attached to his wrist. Perhaps because he was stalling for time, perhaps simply because his hands were trembling with rage. But finally he untied it, and when he turned it upside down some papers tumbled out, together with two or three small metal parts which rolled across the stage. Grouse moved closer, took the envelope from the card rack, placed it inside the leather case and tied the strap about his wrist.

'And now, if you don't mind ...' he said. 'I have things to do.'

'You're playing with fire, Grouse,' the magician said, grabbing him by the sleeve of his jacket. 'Tell me the secret ...'

'Had you not interrupted Psycho in his duties, you would have discovered it some time ago,' Grouse said, gesturing to the card rack in front of the automaton on which there were two more pieces of paper.

Maskelyne turned and reached towards the metal rack. As he did so, Grouse jerked his arm away, freeing himself. He leapt from the stage and ran off between the tables.

'Don't worry, Maskelyne!' Grouse called out before vanishing into the hallway. 'At least I am a gentleman.'

The magician watched his henchmen disappear after Grouse, and though they had no hope of catching him, Maskelyne made no attempt to stop them. He held both pieces of paper in his hands. One read: 'Open the tubes'. The other: 'Pig's intestines. A sausage inside a sausage.' These words were enough to give him a general idea of how Grouse's improvement worked. He ran into the wings, closed the stopcock on the tank and reeled in the tubes that ran under the stage. He found a sharp knife among his tools and made a cut lengthwise into one of the tubes. As he pulled the rubber apart, Maskelyne silently cursed Grouse: he could see nothing inside. But when he got to the other end, he cursed again, aloud this time, because the trick was so simple, so brilliantly simple, that he was both astonished and insulted. With a pair of tweezers, he removed the transparent tangle that stopped the tube and held it up to the light. Pig's intestines. Exactly what was used to make sausages. He sniffed the material, touched the tacky surface with his fingertip. The little pop he had heard before each of Psycho's movements helped him deduce how it worked. Grouse had used the pig's intestine to create a valve in each of the tubes. When the stopcock was opened, the flow of air was blocked by the valve. In a matter of seconds, the compressed air popped the valve, but the force of the air pulled it along such that, reaching the narrow end, it clogged the tube completely. During this brief period, a blast of air hit the workings of the automaton and set Psycho's arm in motion to select the first card. Now that the first tube was clogged, air could move only through the second, where the process was repeated: another pop, another blast of air, the tube became clogged and the arm stopped over the second card.

Bravo. Maskelyne used the knife to cut along the second tube, in no hurry now, knowing what he would find. The only complication was calibrating the position of each tube and the various valves to precisely regulate Psycho's movements. If a common pickpocket had been able to do so, Maskelyne, who considered himself a scientist, could surely replicate the process easily.

Meanwhile, Grouse, safe from his pursuers, had taken refuge in a darkened doorway where he stood contemplating the coveted leather case. With a finger, he traced the gilt inscription that glittered next to the lock: JOHN NEVIL MASKELYNE – EGYPTIAN HALL. Any leatherworker, he thought, could replace this name with his. He was prepared to pay to have it done. Although, thinking about it, he could just as easily buy the tools and do the work himself. He enjoyed manual labour, he realised, and for the first time in his life, thanks to the contents of the envelope, he would have time on his hands.

Sparks in his Hand

In his right hand are the sleeping pills. It feels strange holding them in his palm, feeling their heft yet not seeing them. Not for a moment has he considered taking them all at once. He simply wanted to see them, to toy with the idea. But they are green and he cannot see them. There are shadows in his hands, and a scattering of sparks. It is difficult to take an overdose of shadows. He does not know whether to laugh or cry. One by one, he flicks them into the air, hoping they will fall into his mouth, the way he always ate popcorn as a boy. Only three find their mark. He sleeps through the night and does not dream. Or if he does, he cannot remember.

Burn, O Earth!

When he sees him, Galván is terrified because his face, the grin that all but dislocates his jaw, the hearty greeting, the sing-song tone and, most of all, the way he launches into a conversation on the landing without so much as inviting him in, offering him a seat, letting him take off his jacket, does not lead Galván to think that Víctor is his old self again, but rather that he has gone completely mad.

Víctor has had an idea. A brilliant idea. Come on, he says, come in. He takes Galván by the elbow and drags him to the bedroom. Though he needs to put his arm out and feel his way along the wall, he walks quickly, almost fitfully. Come on, look, I've packed my suitcase. We can leave today. I'll take care of everything, the flights, the hotels, everything. For a moment, Galván stops listening to him. He takes a step back, looks Víctor up and down, notices how his eyebrows are bobbing around, how he is tugging at the cuffs of his shirt. He tries to focus his attention, to fill in the holes in what Víctor is saying with something akin to logic, but he barely makes out a few random words: Java, Tasmania, Calcutta and the South Seas. Inventory. Journey. And Kellar. Most of all, Kellar.

It takes some moments before the pieces of the puzzle fall into place. Víctor is suggesting that they recreate Harry Kellar's grand tour, which took him halfway round the world. A month, he says. Kellar went by boat and it took him two years, but we can fly. A month will be more than enough. We can take his book along as a guide. We'll see everything he saw, see it through his eyes. Can you imagine? We'll discover the world. You can't tell me it wouldn't be fantastic. Víctor's voice is insistent, imploring. He promises every possible creature comfort, assures Galván they will stop and rest for a few days in every city so they can get over the jet lag. He promises him jungles, undiscovered lands, lakes, tribes. He is babbling faster than ever now. He says he needs to make an inventory of the wonders of the world. Ever since this shit started, he says, you've been telling me to be brave, to accept my situation, to do something, to look to the future, not to give up on magic. OK, well, now I'm doing it. The key to the whole thing is Kellar. Kellar's great lesson is that it's never too late to start again. I have only a little sight left in one eye, but at least it's something. And if I can't do it, if I can't see something that really deserves to be seen, you'll be there to explain it to me. This is what you wanted, isn't it? For me to face up to things, to stop deluding myself: I'm about to go completely blind. This is the line of fire, and like all the magicians of 1876, I can choose whether or not to cross it, to pretend it doesn't exist and carry on as before. I can become a pale imitation of the man I was, I can perform from memory, go on performing what has already been written, again and again for the rest of my life. Or I can take a step forward, and cross the line. To do that I have to see something new. I have to build up a store of new, beautiful sights in a dusty corner of my memory because soon, when darkness engulfs me, the past will be the one window I can stick my head out of in search of consolation. Memory will be the only store with which I can feed my imagination. I need to fill it to the brim, and I can't do that without your help. We have to set off today. I'll come with you back to your house, we'll pack a suitcase for you and . . .

Galván opens his mouth but he cannot bring himself to say a word. He crosses over to the bed, sits down and says nothing. For the first time Víctor, too, is silent. It is impossible to know whether he is still expecting the maestro to answer or whether he has registered the refusal implicit in his silence. Víctor sits down next to him. Or rather, he slumps, he falls back as though someone has suddenly yanked away the cable that has been supplying him with this frantic energy. Galván puts an arm around his shoulder. Before he speaks, the maestro takes several deep breaths. 'Listen,' he says, 'I've been here for a while now and I still haven't recovered from climbing the stairs. All the air disappears out of the holes in my lungs and I can't seem to get my breath. You're talking about going halfway round the world and I can barely manage a few steps.'

Galván could leave it at that. He could pretend this is the only reason to reject the suggestion, assume that his terrible health might at least invoke Víctor's sympathy. But he knows he is going to say more. He cannot help it. After all, he is Víctor's teacher. Much more than that: he is his friend, his mentor, and – why not admit it? – his father. 'Besides,' he says, and perhaps he squeezes Víctor's shoulder before continuing, 'maybe you'll never forgive me for this, but I have to tell you it's a stupid idea. It's a mistake. You're in no fit state to travel, Víctor. Look at you – you're wearing one black sock and one brown one. You haven't shaved in over a month. You're looking to the past to create a future. But the only thing that matters now is the present. And the present is already set in stone. For both of us. Mine is simple: I'm going to die. Today, tomorrow, next month, before the year is out. And I'm going to die properly. In my own home. Your present is to call ONCE, the National Organization for the Blind, they're the only ones who can help you now. They know about these things. They have specialists, people who can teach you. You want a magic wand, you want to take it with you to the ends of the earth, drive it into the ground and roar "Burn, O Earth!" just like Kellar. But you don't need a wand, Víctor, you need a cane. A white cane. And someone who can teach you how to use it.'

They do not argue. Mercifully. Víctor gets to his feet, goes out into the corridor and walks to the door, dragging his feet as though Galván's words have brought him down to earth. He throws the door open. Galván understands the gesture. He follows Víctor and stands in the doorway, trying to think of some parting words, something that might take away some of the bitterness of this fruitless encounter. There is nothing to say. He brings his hand up and strokes Víctor's face, his coarse beard. Víctor takes his hand, perhaps to push it away, but maintains contact for a moment. They are antennae. They are almost like ants.

The maestro slowly heads down the stairs. He has already gone three flights when he hears Víctor close the door. Then he takes his mobile phone from his pocket, calls directory enquiries and asks for the number of ONCE. It is the only thing he can do for him.

Víctor goes back to his room and sits on the bed. He knows Galván is right. He tries to think about the future, but his imagination is tired, filled with nostalgia, it is suspended on the step where he stood two months ago, twenty-two years ago, more than a century ago, lost in the secret compartment of a cabinet, hounded by shadows and spectres. He stares at Lauren Bacall. He cannot see her, but he knows that she is there. There are those who believe in ghosts. He points to the floor. His lips curve into an ignoble, disbelieving smile and in a barely audible voice, he says: 'Burn, O Earth!'

Starting Over

iven his difficulty with long sentences, it is hard to believe that Peter Grouse developed a taste for reading. On the other hand, it is possible that the simple fact of getting through Hoffmann's indigestible prose convinced him that he was capable of swallowing anything. Or perhaps books were simply the answer to the question of how he intended to spend Maskelyne's money. Whatever the case, the only traces of him in the decade following his triumph at the Egyptian Hall derive from the four fundamental books on the history of magic published in England at the time. Two of these were memoirs by famous magicians: those of Jean Robert-Houdin, a Frenchman who is universally considered to be the father of modern magic, and those of Colonel Stodare, inventor of many of the popular illusions of the period, among them the Decapitated Head trick that made Maskelyne such a handsome profit. The other two were academic studies of the theatre and prestidigitation, both published in 1881. In all four cases, the authors agreed to reveal the workings of a number of important illusions that had become obsolete – either because they had been overperformed, or because they had been superseded by some new method. There is, of course, no proof that Grouse read any of these writers, but one would have to be a firm believer in coincidence to come up with another way to explain the fact that, between 1880 and 1890, he made his living from the phenomena they described. For the only trace of him during the decade is the series of improvements he devised for classic illusions, registered by him at the Patent Office in London. Though, in general, these consisted of seemingly minor technical enhancements, they breathed new life into the illusions: a velvet sheath on a wire muffled the sound which might attract the audience's attention, pulleys attached to a trapdoor made it easier for ghosts, as they appeared from vaults, not to be so pitifully motionless. It would not be accurate to say that Grouse changed the profession, since, in the end, he was still a thief. The difference was that now, he stole ideas rather than objects and gave them back much improved. He paid in advance, naturally. It appears that learning to read, however difficult it may have been, proved to be a good investment. Now he did not have to go out to steal. It is easy to imagine him spending his nights shut up in his room reading by candlelight, and his days perfecting technical improvements and patenting them.

Galván had bought first editions of all four books for exorbitant sums at antiquarian book fairs. He kept them under lock and key in a display case in the workshop, together with a first edition of *Modern Magic*, and unlike with the rest of his vast collection, he never loaned these books to Víctor. At best, he allowed him to look through the glass, as though contemplating a sacred relic. 'Even I don't touch them,' he would say. He did, however, persuade Víctor to read Harry Kellar's *A Magician's Tour*, which, according to the available evidence, was responsible for Grouse's next appearance in public.

'It's a recent edition,' Galván said. 'It's not likely to fall apart in your hands like the others. Besides, this one is much more important; this is the book that brought Grouse out of his decade of darkness.'

Víctor read the title page, where, next to the information that it had first been published in Chicago in 1890, it gave the author as 'HARRY KELLAR, EDITED BY HIS FAITHFUL "FAMIL-IAR," "SATAN, JUNIOR"', a device that allowed him to refer to himself in the third person, so that he would not have to deny himself praise.

Kellar had been a real character. Born to a poor family in Erie, Pennsylvania, he had been a seminarian and as a boy had earned his living as assistant to the Fakir of Ava. He toured with the Davenport Brothers when they began their career as spiritualists and must have learned something from them to judge by the facility with which he appropriated other people's illusions later in his career. Although his fictitious, satanic familiar is careful not to mention the fact, accounts by his contemporaries confirm that he was a terrible magician; or rather, he was all thumbs, incapable of performing the most basic sleight of hand using coins or cards or cubes, which any aficionado is required to master. Even with something as simple as palming a card, he was obliged to resort to clumsy mechanical solutions. And yet, perhaps through the audacity of ignorance, he managed to hold his audience spellbound.

Though he knew many triumphs and was, for decades, considered the finest magician in the world, he bankrupted himself several times over but always found the strength to start again. In 1867 he claimed to have left Chicago by train, but he had barely made it as far as Rose Hill cemetery when the conductor forced him to get off since he did not have the money for the ticket. He walked for hours along snowy roads, keeping his spirits up by noting the fact that there were twenty-seven lamp-posts for every mile. He finally arrived in Waukegan, where he persuaded various people to extend him credit for the rental of the Phoenix theatre, the printing of the posters, the four dollars he needed for a performer's licence, even the two packs of cards he required for the show. Three weeks after he opened, the theatre was still sold out every night.

In August 1875 he survived the shipwreck of the boat that was taking him from Rio to London via Cape Verde. Kellar had embarked after a long tour of Latin America, and when the ship went down, he lost not only all the props for his stage show, but two huge trunks containing a myriad objects collected during his tour: stuffed birds, a Mexican suit valued at $500 together with gold and silver coins from the countries he had visited. The last straw, however, was that, having been rescued by a French ship, he arrived back in London to discover he was utterly penniless: his bankers, Duncan, Sherman and Co., to whom he had sent the substantial receipts from his American tour, had been declared bankrupt. And yet a few short months later, he was once again performing in Lima to great acclaim. He survived an epidemic of Java fever, which forced him to take to his bed, where he spent two months in delirium, and, no sooner was he well, than he immediately set off on a tour of Australia. Starting again was his speciality.

If there is one thing Kellar cannot be accused of it is a lack of ambition. In 1871, he toured Mexico with a show so spectacular he was forced to reserve an entire train to carry his equipment. Aside from Mexico City, he visited Pueblo and Veracruz. The press accused him of being 'the devil himself' and his fame spread so quickly that even the *bandidos* did not dare attack his train. In Cape Town, people wrote letters to the newspapers complaining that this man, who was manifestly capable of bending supernatural forces to his will, should dare to present himself as a mere performer of mechanical tricks.

He was a much better self-publicist than he was a magician. Shortly after arriving in Calcutta, at the invitation of a British colonel's wife, he met with Englinton, a well-known spiritualist at the time. The object of this meeting was to convince Kellar that spiritualists were indeed capable of controlling the forces of nature and to discourage his mission to expose them as charlatans. On 25 January 1882, the magician wrote two letters to the editor of the *Indian Daily News*. In one of these he wrote that Englinton had apparently caused a series of slate writings to appear from former acquaintances of Kellar who were now dead. In the other, he recounted a seance in which the spiritualist caused the entire group to levitate. In neither case did he directly attribute the phenomena to spiritual intervention; he admitted that he had thoroughly examined the room in which the seances were conducted and confessed himself unable to find a logical explanation for the events. A week later, however, in another letter, he announced that he himself would perform these illusions, which he had since decided were mere trickery, in a theatre in the city. Which theatre was, of course, immediately sold out without the need to pay for a single advertisement.

Some of the feats that were to make him a legend were the result of a basic understanding of chemistry. In 1874, for example, in deepest Patagonia, the commandant of the penal colony in Punta Arenas asked him to perform something that might impress the natives, whom he refers to in his account as 'half-naked savages'. Kellar *'began to harangue them by means of an interpreter, and when a large number had gathered, surprised and startled them by a variety of sleight of hand tricks; then assuming a fierce look he told them he could burn the earth if he so desired and to prove it, he would set the ground on fire. Now the land of Punta Arenas is covered to a considerable depth with white sand. While Kellar had been mystifying the natives, his assistant had mixed some chlorate of potash and white sugar in equal parts and filled a deep hole in the sand with it, without attracting attention.'* Kellar had only to thrust his wand into the ground – having carefully dipped it in sulphuric acid beforehand – and a huge column of flame appeared as he roared the words: 'Burn, O Earth!'

Víctor devoured all 212 pages that very night, arriving breathless, and a devoted admirer, at the final paragraph in which Kellar's satanic alter ego took his leave: *'Having thus briefly sketched the more or less supernatural and decidedly checkered career of my great master, I, his "familiar", and in this instance his scribe, take leave of him and my polite readers for the time being. We shall meet again, however, if my readers are by any means interested in what I have set down. Wizards and sorcerers are immortal, and their fame, at any rate, lives after them. The Magician, like the King, lives for ever.'*

Patagonia, Australia, Mexico, the South Seas, Calcutta, boats and trains, natives, aristocrats, castaways and soldiers. Of course Kellar's life was fascinating. As was his tale, even if it was clearly embroidered by an overheated imagination and an undeniable passion for self-promotion. Kellar had journeyed to places untouched by man, had frequented legendary sailors, and distant tribes, and he had embellished his story with passionate descriptions of flora and fauna, anthropological commentary, weather reports about the cold in the Suez Canal. He even claimed that, all the way from Singapore in late August 1883, he had heard the explosion of the volcano Krakatoa, which sundered the island in two, covering the Java Sea and the southern part of the China Sea in a thick layer of ash.

However, none of these adventures explained why the book should have fired Peter Grouse – an eminently pragmatic man, from Galván's description of him – with such passion that he left his room, by now a thriving workshop, and boarded a ship for America. On the contrary, it seems clear that he was persuaded to do so by three short passages in the book, three passing comments to which no other reader would have attached the least importance. The first appears on page 131: 'On the 9th of December 1878, under the management of the Redpath Lyceum Bureau, my master opened at Horticultural Hall, in Boston. One of his attractions at this time was the famous automaton, Psycho, and the entertainment he gave was one of great excellence.' Full stop. The passage goes on to talk about Kellar's financial difficulties at the time: there is no other reference to Psycho in the book. It is easy to imagine Grouse suspiciously reading on until he came to an extract from a review which appeared in the *Natal Mercury* in Durban dated 21 June 1881: 'We have at Mr Kellar's in perfection all the outstanding automata, which Maskelyne has made himself famous with.' And if that were not enough to pique Grouse's interest, on page 200, there is a mention of 'an unprecedented run of 323 consecutive performances' at the Egyptian Hall, with the singular difference that it referred not to the London theatre, but to one in Philadelphia.

Grouse would doubtless have found the rest of the book boring, irritating and, most of all, useless. A consummate braggart, Kellar missed no opportunity to mention the astonishment provoked by his devices – at no point does he refer to them as 'tricks' – but he never bothered to give any details about their workings. There was nothing here to steal, to improve on. In fact, there was little point in trying since, of all the illusions mentioned in the book, there was not one that could reasonably be considered original. They were all facsimiles of classics performed by the magicians of the Golden Age. And of course Grouse would have cared little for the rapturous descriptions of Kellar's travels, and his sententious opinions on matters as diverse as the reform of the penal system, the beauty of the women of Ceylon or the subhuman nature of the indigenous peoples of New Zealand. He would undoubtedly have found Kellar exasperating, though he may have held a certain admiration for the man's capacity to reinvent himself whenever he encountered a difficulty. The references to Maskelyne, however, made him suspicious. Doubtless when he finished the book, Grouse did not close his eyes, as Víctor did, revelling in the glorious exoticism; instead he immediately turned to the contents page to find and reread the one brief chapter which described Kellar's performances in Europe, entitled 'Before Her Majesty'. At first reading, he had paid the chapter little heed since it seemed to have been included in the book purely because of the immense pride the magician felt at having performed for the Queen of England at Balmoral Castle. Rereading the chapter carefully, Grouse found other grounds for suspicion: Kellar gave an account of a glorious arrival at Portsmouth, bragged of a successful run in Edinburgh, mentioned a tour of 'most of the cities and large towns of the United Kingdom', mentioned Brighton and Cambridge, but London was remarkable only for its absence.

This was impossible. Grouse had reason to know better than anyone how jealously Maskelyne guarded his secrets. There were only two possible explanations as to how another magician, one famous enough to have spent years touring the world, could have used exact replicas of Maskelyne's automata. Either he was a remarkable thief, or he had struck a deal with Maskelyne for the use of his patents. The fact that Kellar had never performed in London tended to suggest the latter: I will grant you the right to use my machines, but on no account should you set foot in my territory. Both possibilities aroused Grouse's curiosity, and justified a visit to Kellar. If the man were a thief, measuring up to him would provide a challenge that made it worth leaving his self-imposed seclusion. And if Kellar had bought the right to use the patents, he might be persuaded to make another investment since, having checked the dates, it was clear that the American version of Psycho did not include Grouse's enhancements. Could he manage to be paid twice for the same illusion? Now that *would* be magic. Like stealing the same wallet twice and finding it full again.

Even Though You Cannot See Me

Viktor. Or is it *Vikter*? *Vikter Lousa*. Maybe *Loussa*. He pronounced his name with an English accent, stressing each syllable, speaking slowly and in a low voice – not in case someone might hear him and think he was mad but so that he could draw out this blissful feeling, something that existed only in his mind and yet filled him with wonder. He was alone in the dressing room, but he could still hear the echo of the applause, the joy with which the technical team had congratulated him after the performance, the respectful tone of the four journalists who had asked to attend, the flashes of the photographers' cameras. Galván had been the last to take his leave, pleading that his health would not permit him to stay up all night. Though Víctor enjoyed the solitude and the silence of the dressing room, he was sorry that Galván was not there now so he could talk to him, so he could finally find a way to express his gratitude for everything he owed him. Mario Galván and Vikter Loussa.

As his lips formed his name for the last time, he stared at his reflection in the mirror, like a goldfish mouthing the water in a fishbowl. He took a deep breath. The success of his London debut meant a lot to him. It was not his ultimate goal, but it was the frontier to a country where he had long dreamed of planting his flag so he could say: 'I have come this far. My name is Víctor Losa. Or Vikter Loussa, you decide.'

And all this for a shadow, for a dream, something he could not put a name to. All this so that, for an instant, he might recapture the moment when Galván, drawing on the past in order to speak of the future, had first shown him the techniques of Professor Pepper, warning Víctor that there was, of course, no proof that the man was a genuine professor, although in this case the surname seemed to be genuine.

Víctor's reaction the first time Galván mentioned Pepper could hardly have been less enthusiastic. The maestro had presented him with a metal box and told him to look through the two holes cut into the lid. Inside, Víctor could vaguely make out a theatrical scene with a crude backdrop of painted trees. When Galván manipulated the side opening to let in more light, a number of blurred shadows were projected against the backcloth. Víctor could see the expectant look in Galván's eyes, but all he could think to say was:

'It's a cute toy.'

'Toy?' Galván blustered indignantly. 'A toy? Pepper had only to look into this box for a few seconds to invent one of the most brilliant illusions in the history of magic.'

The maestro grabbed the box from the table and turned on his heels to go. Víctor quickly asked how it worked, feigning a curiosity he did not feel. Galván, without even turning back to look at him, brusquely interrupted.

'You can go now. I'll see you at four o'clock tomorrow at the Liceo.'

They knew each other so well by this stage in their relationship that a snub from the maestro upset Víctor more than any rebuke. Víctor made sure that he arrived at the theatre promptly the following day, and he feared the worst when he was met in the entrance by an usherette who showed him to the stalls, explaining that Galván had phoned to say he was running a little late. He made his way to the front row and sat down. While he waited, he contemplated the dimly lit set and the orchestra pit, which was covered by a black tarpaulin. There followed three or four minutes of utter silence. Suddenly, there came the rasp of a lighter and Víctor, accustomed to this calling card, glanced around the theatre.

'Mario! Where are you? I can't see you.'

'I'm here.' Galván's voice seemed to be coming from the stage, but there was no one there. 'I am here, but you cannot see me.'

There was a breath and a puff of smoke appeared on the stage. Something more ethereal than smoke. Mist perhaps. He could not see a trace of Galván's face, his hands, his cigarette.

171

'But you will see me,' the voice announced after another puff of smoke. 'You will see me, although I am not here.'

Suddenly an apparition of the maestro was floating on the stage. A ghost. There was no other word for it. The figure looked exactly like Galván, it moved like him, but it was transparent. Or translucent. It did not have the murkiness of a shadow. Víctor got to his feet and took a few steps towards the stage. As he drew closer, his brain furiously scrabbled to find an explanation. Ghost. Projection. Hologram. He was convinced that if he reached out to touch the figure it would disperse through his fingers.

'I said see,' Galván warned, 'I said nothing about touching. Don't come any closer. Though if you did, you would not catch me.'

The figure of Galván moved away each time Víctor took a step forward as though mirroring his actions. Then it began to move around the stage with such a natural motion that it was even more difficult to understand or sense the nature of this intangible body.

'And even if you did manage to catch me, it would not do you much good,' the voice went on. 'For you will see, I can be in several places at once.'

At that point, the figure disappeared behind the backcloth, or rather across the backcloth, moving through it as though it were made of water. Víctor was speechless. He had only a moment to think before the figure reappeared at the front of the stage, as though out of thin air, and moved towards him accompanied by a strident, mock-imperious monologue:

'Pure science, ladies and gentlemen. The only marvels you will see here are those the human mind is capable of creating when it understands the laws of physics, mechanics and optics.'

Víctor recognised this clumsy imitation of Maskelyne and smiled. Galván was inviting him to play the role of Peter Grouse. There was no need. He was desperate to work out how this miracle was performed.

'Not another step, Víctor,' the maestro commanded again. 'For years now, I have been waiting for you to bring me a story. I'm still waiting. Go home. If you can bring me a story next Tuesday, I will tell you Pepper's secret in exchange. If you can't, don't bother coming.'

The ghostly apparition vanished as suddenly as it had appeared. Víctor turned and walked down the centre aisle. As he left the theatre, he formulated the words that he would say so many times in the years that followed. The first words of a long story: 'My father died when I was seven years old. Although he had never smoked a day in his life, it was nicotine that killed him. Ants might have had something to do with it but, as we shall see later, it could truthfully be claimed that it was in self-defence.'

He suddenly remembered his second lesson with Galván, when the maestro had made him recount in the third person the death of his father, one Martín Losa, after having drawn from him, as he stood naked and embarrassed, the notes to a lullaby which over time had become embedded in his throat. Once again, as on that occasion, the words seemed to sweep away the dead leaves that choked up his life, the small trickle of truth that freed him, only now it wasn't a trickle but a wild and roaring torrent. He was free to make up anything he wanted. Or rather, he was duty bound to make the most of this freedom.

As soon as he got home, he wrote down the first words and went on: 'I saw his body lying on the floor and didn't understand what had happened. I couldn't even understand what it meant to die. I thought my father was playing a game.' Martín Losa had become a figment, an alibi, something as intangible as the shadowy figure he had just seen projected on the stage. Víctor began to tell himself a story which was not precisely his own, since it included events he had never witnessed, but one which was more real than the factual account, because each of the details he invented had something to do with his longings, his fears and his desires, with what might have happened but never did, with what perhaps should have happened. The portrait of Martín Losa in his mind was more complete, more rounded, more distinct and truthful than the vague sketch offered him by memory. As he wrote, he constantly thought about the plume of smoke with which Galván had announced his presence on the stage at the Liceo that afternoon. Ethereal and yet much more real than some of the things he was currently writing down: the nicotine vapour that had killed his father, his puzzlement when he had found him lying on the ground, even the stabbing pain he still felt after all these years

173

whenever he remembered that day. All now seemed evanescent, as though they had dissipated with time, as though only by crystallising them into words could he bring them back. He spent hours writing, without stopping to erase or correct a single word, without knowing where this story would take him, wandering the no man's land that exists between imagination and memory, jotting down all the scenarios that came into his head, in which Martín died and came back to life in impossible but conceivable ways, while the smoke seemed to breathe life into wondrous figures and he, Víctor Losa, as both child and man, as actor, spectator and narrator, created, correcting time's blunders, playing hide-and-seek with the truth. At no point did he stop to think of the practical uses of this story, of the obstacles he would come up against when he performed it onstage. He went on writing until it was finished and then slept like a baby.

The following morning, he sat down a little apprehensively and stared at the pages, as though he had been drunk and only vaguely remembered writing them. After he had read through, he felt ambivalent. It was a story. A good story. Not even the most demanding reader, as Galván would no doubt prove to be, could deny that this somewhat confused and repetitive story, full of inconsistencies, had a ring of truth to it, a leisurely but powerful voice which both carried the reader forward, and yet made him want to linger over every word, to savour every phrase. And, having finished, to close his eyes, to allow the imagination to fix all these events in his mind.

And yet, to Víctor, it seemed useless. Not even the most experienced stage director, not even Galván himself with all his knowledge, could transform this into a magic show. Everything was insubstantial, almost invisible. The story existed only in his mind – or with luck in the mind of whoever was reading it. There was no means of staging it, of giving it form.

He put the sheets of paper into a red file, consoling himself with the thought that at least Galván had not asked him to come up with a list of tricks or a scenario for a show, only a story. And this, at least, he had done.

The following Tuesday, the maestro took the file, sat in his usual chair, laid the pages under the narrow beam from the spotlight, and read the story from start to finish. He turned the pages without a word. He did not speak, or wink, click his tongue or clear his throat, he did nothing that might indicate what he was thinking. When he had finished, he pushed the pages to one side, bent down and began to fiddle with something under the table. Víctor realised that he must have liked it only when Galván reappeared holding the metal box that had started their argument. Though eager to hear what Galván thought about what he had read, he assumed that the maestro was finally going to explain Pepper's techniques, so he made himself comfortable.

Pepper and Dircks. Alone in the dressing room, Víctor removed the top from the jar of cold cream he used to take off his make-up, put a dab in the middle of his forehead and started spreading it with a circular motion. He had been dreaming about his London debut for months now. In magic, in the great magic that Galván had taught him to love, all roads led to London, Maskelyne, Cooke and Grouse, Pepper and Dircks.

Henry Dircks was an aficionado of magic. One afternoon, some time during the 1850s, he had stopped as he was leaving a London shop to admire something in the window. It was closing time. Just at that moment, the lights inside the shop were turned off and Dircks saw himself reflected in the glass. Or rather half a reflection. He seemed to float among the objects in the window display. It was, in a word, phantasmagorical.

Dircks immediately wondered what would happen if a sheet of glass such as this were placed on a stage with the same kind of lighting that had just caused an ethereal image of his body to appear on the shop window.

When he got home, he extracted one of the small panes of glass from the dining-room door and began to experiment. He took a small box in which he usually kept his pipe-cleaning tools, emptied it and saw to his relief that the dimensions would work. He placed the piece of glass in the centre, then rummaged in his pockets and took out the first thing he found: his house key. He put this inside the box a few centimetres from the piece of glass. Now he needed a candle, which he lit and brought over to the box. He noticed that if he held the candle behind the piece of glass, nothing happened. But if he held it in front, meaning he used it to light up the key, an image was immediately reflected on the glass. Even more interesting: if he moved the key around in the box, the reflection seemed to move closer and farther away as though it had a life of its own. A floating, tremulous life. Phantasmagorical. Perfect.

He was euphoric now; he thought perhaps he should go to bed immediately so he could get up early and rush out to the patent office. But then he realised there was an obstacle to his brilliant invention.

If he installed a sheet of glass onstage with an actor or a magician behind it then shone a light, the image would be projected on to the glass, but being lit up, the actor would also be visible to the audience.

He had to hide the key. In other words, he had to conceal the actor. Dircks took out a handkerchief and folded it clumsily to create a screen, something that would hide the key. He made several attempts but the problem was that, if he covered it too much, he could not illuminate it. In the end, he almost succeeded, but to do so he had to hold the candle almost directly under the screen. After a short while, the inside of the box was full of wax and both the handkerchief and Dircks' finger were singed. The best thing to do, he decided, was to leave it until tomorrow.

Two years later, the box was bigger and more sophisticated and included a number of technical improvements. Dircks had cut a piece of sheet brass to simulate an actual stage on which he had painted a backdrop of forest. Now, instead of the key, there was a silhouette covered with a hood. The major improvement was that now there was no need for a candle to provide the lighting. With the cover on, Dircks could manipulate two slits at the sides to allow daylight in at the perfect angle so that it illuminated the figure creating a reflection on the glass. To see the illusion, one simply had to bring the box up to one's face and peer through two holes at the front, where the audience would be if this were a theatre.

It was a charming toy, but it served no purpose. All the effort expended on regulating the component parts, the angle of light, down to the last millimetre, was doomed to failure when he tried to adapt this concept to the realities of a theatre. The audience might be prepared to accept the presence of the screen, but they could hardly fail to notice the sheet of glass for the simple reason that they would see themselves reflected in it. An illusion that works only when no one can see it was hardly much of an invention.

Several years were to pass before fate offered Dircks what, at that moment, seemed to be the solution to his problem. One day, towards the end of 1859, he went to the theatre to see a one-act play by Charles Dickens called *The Haunted Man*, which featured a ghost. The actor playing the ghost crawled from the wings and hid behind a sofa, which did not even hide him completely, and then suddenly stood up. Dircks immediately looked around to gauge the audience's reaction. Sitting in the upper circle, he had a full view of the theatre and saw that the appearance of the ghost provoked more laughter than it did fear. Suddenly, the solution struck him with dazzling clarity. Raise the audience! It was as simple as it was brilliant! Raising the seats above the level of the stage solved two problems: the actor would still stand in front of the sheet of glass but now there was no need for a screen since he was hidden beneath the raised platform. And if the sheet of glass was angled correctly, the audience would not see their own reflections.

Dircks left the theatre halfway through the performance and rushed home, took the metal box and some tool from his trunk and made the only change necessary: two new holes higher up, in the lid. Since it was dark, he had to resort to candles to test his changes, and although the effect was not as good as it was in daylight, he was satisfied nonetheless. He was so excited at having solved the problem that he did not get a wink of sleep. When dawn broke he was still sitting with the box in his hands, ready to check his results again in the light of day. Then, without even changing his clothes, he headed off to the patent office.

He had solved the problem, but in order to put it into practice he would need the co-operation of a London theatre owner. He visited every impresario in the city, and received a condescending pat on the back for his pains, or an outright refusal. One impresario asked whether he would leave the box with him for a day or two to think about it, but Dircks refused, fearful that after years of effort someone might steal his idea. But in most cases he did not even manage to pique their interest. Rebuild the theatre? Spend a fortune putting the whole audience on a raised platform and lose a goodly number of seats? Was the man mad?

He almost came round to their point of view. Perhaps the whole thing *was* madness. It was then that he consulted Professor Pepper. Dircks knew the professor was famous for his knowledge of optics and decided to show him his invention. Pepper did not even listen to his explanations, but asked him to open the box, which Dircks did. After all, he had nothing to lose.

'Would it not be better to lower the actor rather than raise the audience?' Pepper asked. 'It would at least be less costly.'

'Lower the actor? And put him where exactly?'

'I don't know. Many theatres have an orchestra pit below the stalls.'

'But ...'

Dircks could not conjure an image of what the professor was proposing. In fact, until the last moment, he assumed that Pepper was mistaken, or was perhaps making fun of him. It did not take a sophisticated knowledge of optics to realise that if the actor was no longer on the same level as the sheet of glass, it could not capture his reflection. He voiced these doubts and only began to believe Pepper was serious when the latter replied:

'Shall we say a fifty per cent share of takings?'

'Of course. Supposing it's possible ...'

'With your permission ...'

Pepper pulled the pane of glass out of the box with a jerk. Dircks could not suppress a whimper as he next removed the screen, took out the tin man and handed it to him. The professor held the glass at shoulder height and said:

'Put the figure in front of the box. Good, now lower it. A little more, a little more ... another inch ... perfect. Don't look at me, look at the glass. Can you see a reflection?'

'No.' Dircks shook his head. He was infuriated by the patronising tone Pepper adopted when addressing him, as though he had to be forgiven for his ignorance of certain fundamental laws.

'And now?'

Dircks was dumbfounded. The tin man's reflection suddenly floated in the air: semi-transparent, tremulous, intangible. Phantasmagorical, just as he had always imagined it.

Without saying a word, he looked at the pane of glass and suddenly understood what had happened: almost imperceptibly, Pepper had tilted the top of the pane forward. It was a moment of explosive joy, a moment that made up for all the years of madness and frustration. And yet Dircks was angry with himself that he had not been able to think of this solution which, now that he had seen it, seemed so simple as to be infantile.

'An angle of forty-five degrees,' Pepper explained. 'Precisely. Otherwise it would not work. There are a number of problems we shall need to resolve,' he added, and began to enumerate them, as though they had already agreed to perform the illusion. 'The sheet of glass must be brought forward to the edge of the stage. There cannot be even a speck of dust on it. The actor,' he warned, reaching out to correct the position of Dircks' hand, 'has to be on a platform at precisely the same angle as the glass so that the reflection appears to be vertical. He can stand on a rolling platform that can be pushed to make it appear as if he is moving. It will not be very comfortable for him. There will have to be a black half-roof over the orchestra pit so that the audience does not see the glow of the light. And for it to work at life size, we will require spotlights so powerful they will make the pit hellishly hot. Aside from that, I can see no problems making it work.'

London, Pepper and Dircks. Maskelyne, Cooke and Grouse. Galván and Losa. Or *Loussa*. As he wiped the last of the make-up from his face, Víctor smiled distractedly at his reflection in the mirror. More than anything, he wished the maestro were here with him now. He still remembered the precise moment when Mario, after telling him about the meeting between Pepper and Dircks, had hidden the metal box under the table once more.

'Pepper found a way to resolve these problems, only to encounter two more which were just as serious. First and foremost, at the time, no one made sheets of glass more than five feet wide, which meant that the ghost's movements were extremely limited,' Galván explained. 'There was another problem. If the ghost was to interact with the other actors on stage he would have to speak and the audience would realise that his voice was not coming from the stage. For this reason, though the illusion was a relative success and its inventors made a sizeable living from it for a time, in the end it fell victim to its limitations. The ghost could only appear in dramatic, climactic moments, but over time this was not enough.'

By now, Víctor knew all too well that Galván's speeches were invariably intended to be edifying. Still embarrassed that he had initially been so dismissive of Dircks' box, he tried to second-guess the obvious moral of the story.

'Microphones,' he said.

'Exactly, Víctor, microphones. Nowadays it doesn't matter where a voice is coming from. And it is the easiest thing in the world to find someone who can make a sheet of glass that would span a whole stage. The one problem is, we only have three months.'

'Three months? Are you mad? That's not even time ...'

'This is a masterpiece,' Galván interrupted him, picking up his pages and placing them under the spotlight once again. 'I'm not going to allow your doubts to get in the way of making it possible.'

'Wait, wait.' These were the first real words of praise Víctor had received from Galván. He would have liked to have the time to savour them. 'Wait. Supposing you're right. Suppose I am capable of learning this story by heart, of reciting it on stage for, I don't know, let's say an hour and a half. That's a lot of supposing, but right now I'll let it go. What about the rest?'

'The rest of what?'

'My father, for example. We know how to project his image on to the stage, but someone ...'

'Don't worry about that. I'll be your father.'

Víctor said nothing. For the first time he began to think it might be possible, especially if they worked together.

'But ... what I've written, it's lunacy. Read it again and you'll see. I've got planets orbiting in the palm of my hand, oranges appearing out of thin air, jets of water spilling from nowhere ...' He suddenly stopped. Galván was staring at him, grinning like a lunatic and gesturing for him to go on. 'The Black Art,' Víctor said suddenly. He looked down at the black floor and said it again as though he needed to be sure. 'The Black Art.'

'You have just crossed the line of fire,' said Galván. 'Welcome. I guarantee you won't get burned. It's so simple ... A sheet of glass across the stage. With not a speck of dust on it. Tilted at a forty-five-degree angle so it reflects my image. I am in the pit, no one can see me. I am your father. Or rather, my reflection is your father's ghost. You are behind the sheet of glass. There is an ant farm at your feet. The rest of the stage looks completely empty. An assistant dressed entirely in black moves around the stage, revealing things at precisely the right moment so it seems as though they appear by magic.'

'But ... what's the hurry? Three months isn't much time.'

'Or it's a lot of time, depending on who you ask. I'm a sick man. It's only natural that I'm in a hurry. Besides, I want to spend my time setting up a museum, remember?' Galván bent down again and lifted the metal box. 'There are a few precious things I want to exhibit. And for that, I need you to be a success. If you are, you'll make a lot of money. And my fifteen per cent will go a long way to financing the museum.'

'We haven't even got a name.'

'What do you think about *Espectros*?'

Víctor started putting moisturiser on his face. The idea of him wearing white make-up to stand out against the back backcloth had also been Galván's.

'*Espectros*,' he said to the mirror. 'Spectres.'

At first it hadn't seemed much of a name. He had not really felt comfortable with it since the premiere in Barcelona when the critic from *La Vanguardia* headed his review with the eloquent pun *Espectracular!* The opening night took place in Barcelona, of course. His mother sitting in the front row. How he missed his mother. Madrid, Valencia, Bilbao, Seville. Sold out. 'Never have magic and theatre been so perfectly combined,' someone had written. Víctor could not remember who, or where. The show had toured every provincial capital in Spain, every major theatre festival. And two years later, just as Víctor was beginning to tire of it, when he barely found any wonder in the routine, Galván had asked him:

'Do you think you could do it in English?'

181

Spectres. London. Before that, Berlin, Paris, Amsterdam, Oslo and Milan. Theatre festivals: Edinburgh, Avignon. Two years touring before finally coming to London. Maskelyne, Cooke and Grouse. Dircks and Pepper. Galván and Losa. *Vikter Loussa*. He lit a cigarette and blew a puff of smoke towards the mirror. Martín Losa and his son Víctor. Suddenly he felt as though this happy nostalgia was poisoning his blood. He needed fresh air. He knew that when he went outside he would run into the stragglers who hung around talking about the show. He knew that somewhere among them would be a woman waiting for him. It was one of the perks of an international tour. Someone would always come up to him, usually under the pretext of asking for an autograph, or would bump into him accidentally on purpose while they pretended to read the poster for the show. Víctor left the dressing room thinking that tonight he would rather be alone. Go on floating through the mists of time. Spend a few hours without having to say a word. His throat was dry, and he was all too aware of the irony. While Galván sweated in the pit to give life to his father's ghost and the assistant contorted himself, weaving through the darkness and making wonders appear, all he had to do to bring the show together was talk, endlessly, ceaselessly. Víctor Losa; the man who did not believe in words.

23°C

He brings his face close so he can see the screen and the thermostat controls properly and selects the temperature: 23 degrees. What a relief. He has just made his first decision. It is what Galván has said to him a thousand times over the past few days. It is what his own mind tells him constantly, though he isn't listening: you have to stop thinking about the problem and start focusing all your energy on the solution. Solutions, plural. But not too many. This is the first one. Twenty-three degrees all year round. He will never have to touch the thermostat again. What else? One solution for each problem. Something simple, something routine, something that does not force him to spend the rest of his life worrying about the small things.

He moves through the apartment. Energetic, almost happy. He goes into the bathroom. He doesn't need all these potions and concoctions. A neutral shower gel. Something that's both body-wash and shampoo. Towels. Fresh towels once a week. The laundry service. He doesn't have to worry about money. Or does he? He has earned much more than he can ever possibly spend, especially now that his life is about to get smaller. But it's no use to him sitting in the bank. Of course, there are specially adapted ATMs But this is not the kind of solution he's looking for. He needs to have money at home. A lot of money. What else?

He goes into the bedroom. What is he going to do with Lauren Bacall? Leave her there, hanging on the wall even though he can't see her? Dream about her at night? His guardian angel, a sweet companion. The bed. Who is going to make the bed? He goes into the living room. He sees the television and it almost makes him laugh. He keeps walking. Eating, dressing, sleeping, a basic level of hygiene. Surely there must be something else. Surely he must be forgetting something. He goes into the workshop. The museum. The gift. He doesn't even know what to call it. He has spent years postponing the decision of what to do with all these props and automata. They were supposed to be a gift for Galván's museum, but the idea no longer makes any sense. The museum will never be anything more than a project. All Galván thinks about now is dying. Víctor fumbles in the air for the wires that hold up Harry Kellar's levitation table. Eighty-five wires chemically treated so as not to stand out against the black backcloth, suspended from the ceiling by a complex system of counterweights to make sure the table is always horizontal and does not tilt as it rises into the air. And a single lever to activate it. A work of art that no one has been able to improve on in a hundred years. Kellar stole the idea from Maskelyne, but improved on it. Having hovered some six feet above the stage for a few minutes, it would rise to ghostly strains played by the orchestra and move through the air. Through the air. God, the bastard was ambitious! He even floated over the heads of the audience.

He lets go of the cables and wipes the dust from his fingers. This is no time to think about the past. He needs to get out of this room, to go on thinking about solutions, yet he lingers. Everything in this place touches him. Recently he has begun to mistrust things. It is as though they are conspiring against him. He can almost hear them whispering behind his back, plotting to disappear together. Sometimes, he creeps through the apartment with extraordinary care, and not because he is afraid of bumping into something, quite the reverse: he is afraid that one day everything will disappear, and no matter which way he turns, all he will find is a vacuum.

He opens the Proteus Cabinet and sits down. Perhaps this is one possible solution: to slide back the mirror and disappear. Become a spirit. Cross the frontier. Play the lead in this disappearance rather than the victim. Tell the world and all the things in it: 'There you stay.' But there is only one frontier: that which separates what exists from what no longer exists.

A Just Man

Galván was touched to think of Grouse dusting off the leather case before slipping his well-oiled picklocks and his copies of *Modern Magic* and *A Magician's Tour* inside. He imagined him standing on the poop deck of the ship taking him to America, dreaming perhaps that the line traced by the ship's wake might at some point cross those of Maskelyne and Kellar to create a symbolic triangle. He found it moving to think of Grouse arriving at the port of New York alone, bewildered by his ignorance of the New World, perhaps astonished by his own daring, and above all obsessed with the idea of meeting Kellar. With this in mind, when he took the train to Philadelphia, not even waiting to get to the city, he immediately struck up a conversation with his fellow travellers to try to ascertain the address of the Egyptian Hall. The first three people he asked had never heard of the place. The fourth recognised the name but seemed to remember that it had closed some years earlier.

The first few days in the city were enough to dispel Grouse's doubts about the possibility of running into Kellar. Given the magician's famous penchant for turning his every move into a public performance, it is hardly surprising that each morning Grouse found some mention of him in the newspapers over breakfast: a gala benefit, a celebrated performance in his home town of Erie; a very public reunion with the Fakir of Ava, the magician to whom he owed his early years of training ... Anything and everything was worthy of appearing in the papers. Fortunately, Kellar seemed inclined to rest for a while after his travels, or at the very least to limit his trips to Boston and Philadelphia. Grouse had only to do what he did best: wait, and prepare for the encounter.

In the meantime, there was much to do. The corner of page 198 of his copy of *A Magician's Tour* was turned down, marking the passage where Kellar recounted his appearance before the Seybert Commission. In a few clumsy sentences the magician gave a vague and incomplete account of the circumstances surrounding the establishment of this 'spiritualists tribunal'. On the other hand he spent several pages describing his appearances before the commissioners and the ease with which he left them open mouthed. Perhaps in search of some credibility which even he seemed to doubt, he announced that the commission was about to publish a final report confirming Kellar's testimony and putting an end to the spiritualists' claims once and for all. Not content with this, Kellar went on to give an account of one of his most brilliant performances, at which the victim was one Edwin Booth, a famous actor of the day, and which was witnessed by Horace Howard Furness, a member of the commission. Apparently, the magician had made fun of Booth using his own particular version of the Proteus Cabinet. He had closed himself into it with the actor for only a few seconds, during which time, to the actor's astonishment, his hat was transferred to the magician's head, and vice versa; then mysterious hands appeared from the aperture in the cabinet and threw a tambourine at the great tragedian. When the cabinet doors opened, Furness pestered the actor with questions about what he had seen and heard while he was inside and, more particularly, whether it was possible this had been the work of spirits. Booth replied, 'I think that it is the devil!' though he had to repeat himself and finally had to shout into Furness's ear trumpet since the man was profoundly deaf.

Grouse did not need to investigate the Proteus Cabinet; he knew the history of the illusion and its successful variations. The original had been of such simplicity that it commanded respect. A seemingly ordinary wooden wardrobe, seven to eight feet in height by four or five feet square, supported on short legs, so as to exclude the idea of any communication with the floor or a trapdoor, and two folding doors. Inside, it was covered in wallpaper, like most domestic wardrobes of the period, and in the centre there was a narrow pillar from which hung a small oil lamp so that the audience could see inside.

The trick was based on the same principle Maskelyne used to

display a decapitated Cooke in the Egyptian Hall. Two movable mirrors mounted on hinges were fixed to the back corners. When closed, they met at the central column and reflected the sides of the cabinet, creating the illusion that the cabinet was empty since the audience assumed they could see the back. The magician's assistant would hide behind the mirrors before the trick, and the magician would then open the doors to show the audience that it was apparently empty. As soon as the doors were closed, the assistant would push the mirrors back against the sides of the cabinet, where they disappeared since the backs of the mirrors were lined with the same wallpaper as the rest of the wardrobe. When the magician opened the cabinet, the assistant would appear to the astonished gasps of the audience. To prove that he was flesh and blood, he would even climb out and walk around the stage.

Over time, the appearance of the cabinet changed somewhat to adapt to the various different scenarios magicians used. Maskelyne himself had been responsible for some of the most important enhancements. But it was not the magicians but the spiritualists who discovered the best use for it: they replaced the two mirrors with a single mirror set into the back corner, which left considerably more room inside the cabinet. No one made better use of this improvement than the Davenport Brothers. A member of the public was invited to step inside with one of the brothers, who had been tied up with ropes to the volunteer's satisfaction. The other brother remained onstage and entertained the audience with a speech about the electrical transmutation of spirits. Meanwhile, inside the cabinet, disembodied hands played all manner of tricks on the hapless volunteer: played a flute in his ear, placed wigs and hats on his head, sprinkled him with flour, whatever might provoke the surprise and astonishment of the audience when they saw him re-emerge, faced flushed, from the cabinet. As if this were not enough, from time to time a ghostly hand would appear through the aperture in the centre of the cabinet ringing a bell.

Every magician understood the principles behind the Proteus Cabinet and appreciated it for the range of illusions it afforded in spite of its simplicity. Even a writer as dull witted as Hoffmann had been able to describe it in no more than thirty-five lines together with a simple diagram. It clearly did not matter to Kellar that the illusion was well known, since he mentioned it at least thirty times in his memoir. He even noted that he had a new one made by local craftsmen in every city he visited so as not to have to transport it with him. He never explained precisely what he used it for, nor did he reveal how the illusion worked.

But what intrigued Peter Grouse was the mention of the Seybert Commission, whose formation and subsequent investigations had not been acknowledged by the London press and therefore had not come to his attention. A group of university scholars assembled to give an opinion on whether spirits could be said to exist and what truth there was to the claims of those who purported to be able to communicate with them. Sixty thousand dollars to fund such an undertaking? Because this, in truth, was the real focus of his interest: that someone should have donated such a sum to study phenomena which any aficionado of magic could explain.

Grouse decided to go directly to the source. Although Kellar maintained that the commission had not yet published a final report on their investigations, Grouse also knew that the magician was not exactly scrupulous when it came to reporting such matters. Besides, almost four years had passed since *A Magician's Tour* was first published. Though Grouse suspected that the true goal of the commission was to spend Seybert's money on travel and lavish meals, it was nonetheless possible that it had since published something to justify its activities. He found his answer on his first visit to the university, and he did not even have to steal it; in fact, he had only to ask. The eagerness with which the librarian pressed a copy of the preliminary report on him made it clear the institution was proud of its role in something that he considered to be arrant nonsense.

He immediately set about reading it. Like Galván and Víctor more than a century later, in fact like anyone with more than a passing knowledge of the history of magic, the more he read, the more astonished he became. Nor was it a quick read. He had to spend four mornings at the library in order to wade through the 150 pages of the report. However, in spite of his reading difficulties, he too reached the obvious conclusion: the members of the commission, honest but credulous men, had not encountered a single spiritualist capable of dressing up his claims with even a modicum of craftsmanship. He was not surprised that the commission had been bowled over by Kellar's skill after so many third-rate spiritualists. The report only truly aroused his interest when he came to Furness's appendices. Although in the main body of the report, Reverend Fullerton had endeavoured to maintain a strait-laced neutrality, Furness seemed intent on writing an adventure novel. He recounted his experiences in the first person, amused himself by detailing the circumstances of each disastrous encounter and described these self-professed mediums with biting sarcasm. More importantly, he seemed to bring to the task a sort of vengeful vitality, a violent scepticism and moral rage, as though he had concluded that the very idea of the existence of spirits was an insult to his intelligence. Peter Grouse was sufficiently acquainted with the human condition to realise that it was precisely the reverse. Furness's rage at being duped could only be explained by his desperate need to believe. This was why he had continued to pursue his investigations, outside the aegis of the commission. His sarcasm concealed a deep, fervent, frustrated desire to happen on the exception, that one, perhaps unique, encounter that would allow him to finally let go, to exclaim: 'They really do exist!'

Could he use this to his advantage? Could Grouse use Furness's zeal, his indignation, to somehow help in his own machinations against Kellar? In other words, could he reawaken the commission's interest and profit from its members' gullibility?

He had to wait only two days to find out. That morning the newspaper announced 'Harry Kellar's triumphant return to the Philadelphia Opera House'. By dawn, the city was strewn with flyers advertising *KELLAR'S STARTLING WONDERS* and depicting the magician surrounded by goblins, demons and skeletons gesturing dramatically towards the dark interior of a wooden cabinet. Grouse made sure to get a front-row seat for the first night and had to admit that the show was first class, as long as he was prepared to ignore the integrity of the performer. Kellar effortlessly performed the finest illusions from around the world; the only problem was that none was his own invention. Zero. Not one. His only real addition was the introduction of magnets, clips and glues which he needed to perform the basic sleights of hand any other magician could perform without any help. So Grouse sat, silently recalling the names of the genuine inventor of each trick, grateful that at least Kellar's tone and his attitude onstage were not as arrogant as those of Maskelyne. By the end of the performance, his only concern was financial. By now he understood that Kellar would not be prepared to pay for a new trick. He clearly would not give a damn about improving his version of Psycho. No one knew better than Grouse how difficult it was to sell something to someone who was prepared to steal it.

But he had not made such a long and costly journey to give up at the first hurdle. Early the next morning, he sent three anonymous telegrams, all with the same wording: 'Henry Seybert requests your presence tonight at the Park Street Opera House.' Two were addressed to the editors of *Banner of Light* in Boston and *Mind and Matter* in Philadelphia, magazines which, for years, had been engaged in a bitter campaign not only against the Seybert Commission but against anyone who purported to unmask the spiritualists. The third telegram he sent to the University of Pennsylvania, addressed to Horace Howard Furness. All the recipients believed that Kellar himself had issued the invitations, undoubtedly another piece of blatant self-promotion. The magazines duly dispatched their editors in the hope of catching the magician making some mistake they could use against him. Furness showed up as requested simply to be entertained and, perhaps, out of gratitude for Kellar's honesty.

The brilliance of Peter Grouse's plan was its apparent simplicity: at some point during the performance he would make something unexpected happen in the cabinet, something for which even Kellar would have no explanation. If those he had invited were in attendance, the magazines would give the event considerable coverage and the commission would be forced to intervene. This would bring Kellar new fame, something the magician would make every effort to turn to his financial advantage. And by subsequently revealing the secret of the illusion, Grouse would ensure that he too was amply rewarded. He realised, however, that to pull it off would require considerable skill, sang-froid and an ability to improvise. So, as soon as he had sent the telegrams, and although there were twelve hours before the show started, he set off for the theatre with his picklocks. Once inside, he spent no time examining the replicas of the automata or studying the marked cards and various mechanical devices Kellar used to make up for his lack of dexterity. Instead, he headed directly for the cabinet and, seeing that it was locked, could not help but smile. Did Kellar truly think this would protect the secrets he had had no compunction about stealing? Because to judge from its size, the cabinet was an exact copy of the one used by the Davenport Brothers. He quickly forced the lock, taking care not to damage it. The first part of the plan entailed hiding in the cabinet without anyone noticing – at least not until after the performance had started. He examined every inch of the interior. Sliding back the mirror, he found a nail from which hung a black canvas bag. He took it down and checked the contents: a cowbell, a folded hood, a small bag of flour, a stick of white chalk and a tiny pair of shears with blades so sharp they could cut through sheet metal. Kellar clearly did not do things by halves: when he asked his volunteers to tie him up, he did not give them ordinary rope, but ship's cable. He had once allowed his wrists to be bound with chains.

Grouse put everything back in the bag and hung it on the nail. Then, he stepped into the cabinet, pressed himself into the corner and slid back the mirror. In the darkness, he opened his eyes and felt about him, calculating the size of the space. Though it would be tight, two people could fit in here, as long as the other was as thin as he was. This was all he needed to know. Now he could spend the remainder of his free time making a note of Kellar's other mechanical secrets. And he could do what he most enjoyed: anticipate, run through in his mind every eventuality, every possible reaction, both of Kellar and of the witnesses he had invited. Memorise the score so he felt confident to improvise if he needed to.

Though he left the doors open, he spent a lot of time inside the cabinet, as though familiarising himself with it would make him more comfortable. He even sat inside while he ate the bread and sausages he had brought with him. In the early afternoon, a sudden hubbub alerted him to the fact that Kellar's assistants had arrived to prepare for the evening's performance. He savoured the last fresh air he would taste for quite some time, closed the doors from inside, pressed himself into the corner and slid back the mirror.

Then he dipped his hand into the canvas bag and took out the stick of chalk. This, he knew, was the first thing he would need. Instinctively, he rummaged for the shears too. Though the cabinet required no preparation before the show, there was no way of telling whether someone might decide to pop their head inside.

He spent two hours standing in the darkness, shifting his weight from one foot to the other to relax his muscles and breathing shallowly so as not to give himself away. From the noises outside, he kept track of the assistants' progress, heard Kellar arrive with a roar of last-minute orders and instructions, listened as the audience filed in and took their seats, their applause as the curtain went up and, somewhat distantly, the magician's opening speech, full of bluster and clichés about modern science. He listened attentively until Kellar mentioned the cabinet and, steeling himself for what was about to happen, pressed himself into the far corner of his hiding place. Just then, the cabinet was pushed towards the stage, and someone swiftly opened the doors, slipped inside, and slid back the mirror. It was Eva, Kellar's petite wife, who acted as his assistant for almost all of his illusions. As though his own presence was the most natural thing in the world, Grouse brought his finger to his lips to silence her and gestured to the space next to him. Perplexed, Eva hesitated for a moment, but then saw there was nothing for it but to do as he suggested. By now, the cabinet had been wheeled onstage by two assistants and she could not risk any part of her body being visible when Kellar threw open the doors. Nor could she say anything without alerting the audience to her presence.

Oblivious to what was happening inside the cabinet, the magician, as always, called for two volunteers from the audience. The editors of *Banner of Light* and *Mind and Matter* immediately jumped to their feet. As they made their way to the stage, Kellar announced that what they were about to witness was the fruit of his ingenuity, of his mastery of molecular transformation, blah, blah, blah.

He opened the doors and asked the volunteers to examine the cabinet and tell the audience of any irregularity they encountered. The volunteers eagerly examined it in minute detail and were forced to admit that it was just an ordinary wooden wardrobe.

'Very well,' the magician said with heavy irony. 'Well, it can't hurt to make sure. And since we know that the spirits like to communicate by writing on slates, let's give them an opportunity to do so.' He showed a slate to the volunteers to confirm that it was blank. Then he set it down on the floor of the cabinet, closed the doors and rapped on them with his knuckles. 'As you can see, it's made of solid wood.'

The knocking was a signal to Eva that she could get to work. Grouse slid back the mirror and grabbed the slate. Eva tried to stop him and, in the scuffle that followed, she gave a sort of grunt. Kellar thought that his wife had had some minor accident, but immediately recovered his composure, making a quick joke and still mentally counting off the twelve seconds he usually gave Eva to write the message.

When he opened the doors, the slate was on the floor where he expected it to be. Normally, he would hand it to one of the volunteers without even looking at it so that they could read the message aloud, which was invariably the same: 'Enough with the spirits, Kellar, show us the science.' But on this occasion, alerted by the curious sounds, he glanced at the slate before handing it over. 'Summon Mr Furness. We have a message for him.' Kellar had no choice but to accept the situation and allow the volunteers to read out the message.

Furness was not at all surprised to be called onstage. After all, if Kellar had sent the invitation it was logical that he should try to take advantage of his presence. The magician greeted the investigator and, as he looked at him quizzically, informed the audience that Furness was an eminent scholar, famous for debunking fraudulent spiritualists. He offered Furness the opportunity to examine the cabinet, which the professor did somewhat carelessly since he assumed he would find nothing. Then, he invited him to step inside and close the doors. This was the moment when Eva usually pulled the hood over the volunteer's head and sprinkled him with flour, skilfully using only one hand since she needed the other to ring the bell for the audience to hear. But Grouse prevented her getting to the black bag, pressing her back into the corner with one arm so she could not move.

'Horace, it's Henry Seybert. Though you cannot see me, I am here,' Grouse said, disguising his voice.

'Furness, let my husband know there is someone in here with me,' whispered Eva.

Neither had reckoned on the professor being quite so deaf. For several seconds nothing happened. Outside, Kellar realised that something strange was going on when he did not hear the bell ringing. A moment later he opened the doors and found Furness standing there, with no hood on his head and no trace of flour. Forced once more to improvise, the magician turned to the audience and said:

'Well, well, it seems the presence of our illustrious guest has frightened the spirits themselves.'

One or two spectators laughed, but most shifted uneasily in their seats. A magician's worst nightmare is not when an illusion goes wrong, it is when it does not go at all. When nothing happens for several moments. The audience's suspension of disbelief depends on the magician's ability to explain what is happening, to interpret each event before the next one occurs. Any break in this fragile narrative thread can ruin that rapport. There was no booing, but coughing and whispering indicated that the audience's uneasiness was spreading. Kellar did what any magician with a minimum of experience would do under the circumstances: he ploughed on, trusting in his ability to improvise.

'Let's try it again, but perhaps this time I shall go in with him.'

He asked Furness to bind his hands and had the two volunteers check the knots. Then, he invited the investigator to step into the cabinet with him. As soon as the doors were closed, Kellar whispered, 'What the devil is going on, Eva?'

Almost blindly, Grouse reached out and put the hood over Furness's head and tipped the bag of flour over him. His other hand was still covering Eva's mouth, but she bit him and managed to free herself. Grouse could not suppress a cry but he managed to ward off her blows as she tried to grab the shears from him. As they struggled he felt the blades snap closed on something hard and thick. The blades fell to the floor of the cabinet with a clang. Even Furness, through his deafness, heard the howl that suddenly rang out, startling the volunteers, who were standing outside the cabinet, and Kellar's assistants waiting in the wings, the entire audience and possibly those walking past the theatre.

Kellar brutally pushed the mirror closed, opened one of the doors and leapt out on to the stage, blinking against the light. He had no idea what he was about to say. In their confusion, some of the audience burst out laughing: logically, they had expected him to emerge with his hands untied. The magician managed to play on their expectations. Slowly and deliberately he opened the other door and asked Furness to step out. There was a gasp, followed by thunderous applause – the trick was even better than they had expected: without untying his hands Kellar had managed to place a hood over Furness's head and cover him in flour. The magician bowed deeply, then turned to the audience:

'All that remains is for Dr Furness, who is renowned for his honesty in such matters, to tell us whether he sensed the presence of a spiritual force inside the cabinet.' Kellar turned to the journalists. 'Take off the hood.'

Furness, shaking his head in puzzlement, asked Kellar to repeat the question. Then he turned to the audience and said:

'I felt a force, certainly, but it did not feel very spiritual.'

'In that case, I can ask only that my assistants remove the cabinet,' Kellar gestured for them to do so as quickly as possible, 'and carefully guard its secrets.'

Hearing these last words, the assistants knew what was being asked of them. As soon as the cabinet was out of sight of the public, they opened the doors. Inside, they found Eva Kellar in hysterics. Though clutching her hands to her belly and doubled over in pain, she was still kicking out at Peter Grouse, who was virtually turning somersaults to avoid the blows. The assistants joined in but Grouse tried to ward them off, shouting that they should forget about him and take care of Eva, who had suffered a serious cut.

They helped Eva out and locked the intruder in the cabinet while one of the assistants took her to the nearest hospital, fearing she might bleed to death. The other stood guard over the cabinet, awaiting Kellar's instructions. Sitting in the darkness, Grouse patted himself and withdrew the small, wet object stuck to his left buttock. He did not need any light; his sense of touch immediately recognised the skin, the nail, the blood, and he knew that it was part of Eva Kellar's thumb.

Kellar concluded the performance with four hurried illusions, dispatched the audience and marched into the wings incensed, threatening to strangle his wife and demanding an explanation for this sudden fit of incompetence. The assistant attempted to explain what had happened but the magician interrupted him, demanding details, which finger, which hand, what weapon, which hospital, how and with whom. Then there was an uncomfortable silence. Grouse pressed his ear to the door of the cabinet, trying to work out what was happening outside. He heard only a murmur, a whispered conversation, words exchanged that undoubtedly concerned him. He heard footsteps retreating and then, from the door, Kellar's last instructions to his assistant:

'The same hand, all right? The same finger. Exactly the same part. Not an inch more. Then take him to the hospital. Let nobody say I am not a just man.'

When the doors finally opened, Peter Grouse knew what awaited him and could see no way of avoiding it.

Music for the Spirits

He remembers the cold, but he cannot quite remember what city they were in. It was fifteen years ago. Names come back to him: Dresden, Oslo, Vancouver. Nor can he remember what they were celebrating: a good review, perhaps, though they never paid the critics much heed; or perhaps the however many hundred performances of *Espectros*. Whatever the case, it was the early hours of the morning and they were on their way back to the hotel. They walked with their hands in their pockets and the collars of their coats turned up. He thinks he can remember that the pavement glittered with frost and, if he concentrates, he can see, can almost feel, their misty breath. They had been walking in silence for some time, their elation giving way to a quiet sense of satisfaction.

Galván was telling him that if he thought he had made it to the other side of the line of fire, he was mistaken; that he should not let himself be blinded by praise; that to rest on his laurels would be to run a terrible risk. Víctor listened politely; the speech fondly reminded him of Galván's lectures long ago, but he did not really take notice until – as usually happened in these lectures – Galván's vague moralising resolved itself into a specific conclusion: he needed to come up with a new show. Something bigger, more ambitious. He had to come back across the line of fire so that he could pass through it again, or better still, dance amid the flames until he was burned. He had to take up the baton passed on by the great magicians of yesteryear and, in doing so, pay tribute to them. And one more thing: he would have to do it alone.

Víctor stopped walking and Galván stopped and stood next to him. This, he remembers. The silence gradually absorbed the echo of their footfalls. The maestro looked him in the eye and told him he was not abandoning him. He still believed in him, believed in his ideas and in his ability to execute them to the most exacting standard. He was sure the new show would be a triumph and it was because of this that he had to take a step back. He cut short Víctor's protests, promising he would help him devise the new show and support him in the workshop, that he would be with him through rehearsals and was even prepared to direct the Barcelona premiere. And he was not about to give up his fifteen per cent, he said jokingly. But when it came to going on tour, he would stay at home. 'Look at me, Víctor, I'm too old for this. I can't keep travelling halfway around the world with holes in my lungs.'

It had been difficult for Víctor to get used to working without Galván. His missed his company on tour, and his advice after the obligatory rehearsals when he arrived in each new theatre. But most of all he missed the maestro's presence in the moment just before his first performance in each new town. Standing in the middle of the stage, waiting for the curtain to go up, he felt a terrible emptiness in the pit of his stomach, a mental weakness which he could only rise above by constantly repeating the first words he would say when the curtain rose: 'My father died when I was seven years old.' He had said the words so often now that they no longer reminded him of death; quite the reverse, they were like a rebirth. Something magical about to begin. And a second later he forgot about the maestro and did not think of him again until the time came to leave the stage and, waiting in the wings, listening to the roar of the applause, he thought of Galván and murmured: 'This is my tribute to you.'

In following his advice to pay homage to the greats, Víctor ensured that he numbered Galván among them. The maestro was the bridge, the invisible thread that made it possible, during the two hours of uninterrupted performance, to move effortlessly between the nineteenth century and the present, between wonder and admiration, between the 'it's not possible' and the 'yet it is'. Furthermore, Galván's name still appeared next to his on the posters and the programme. Víctor had not forgotten how much Galván had contributed to the text, not only through his initial comments but more importantly when the two of them had sat down together in the workshop and begun turning this idea for a show into a script that could be performed. He still had the text in a drawer somewhere, in a red folder with the word MORTAL written on the cover, for that was the name of his new show.

There is no point looking for it now since to read it he would have to hold the pages two inches from his face, cover his left eye and trust his right eye to work properly for several minutes, something it has not done in the past two weeks. Besides, he is sure he can recite it from memory. In Spanish and English. He performed it in theatres the world over for five years. It is like a favourite song not heard for some time. He says the first words aloud, convinced that he has only to throw open the floodgates of memory and the rest of the words will fall into place:

'My father died when I was seven years old. One day, I came home and found him lying dead on the floor. His body was there but he was no longer inside. Simple as that. Or not so simple. I remember there was music playing. The same music that is playing now.'

At this point, the *andante* from Bach's first violin concerto would begin to play. Víctor would fall silent, allowing the tremulous chords to spill out over the audience. He even remembers how long he had to pause: eight bars, almost thirty seconds in most versions at standard tempo. During rehearsals, Galván had thought it was too slow, but in performance, with the musicians in one corner of the stage and Víctor standing alone in the spotlight, it was dramatic, all eyes were fixed on him.

No one is looking at him now, no one but the ghosts of the past. Four ants are crawling across the surface of the terrarium but, unless some evolutionary mutation has produced a miracle, they cannot hear him. He is alone here on the terrace, leaning on the railings and through force of habit his tone is slightly dramatic, his voice is barely audible:

'My father loved music. At home, there was always music playing. Once, when we were going out, I asked him why he was leaving the music on and he said, "For the spirits." My father was a scientist. I doubt he believed in spirits.'

Science and magic. It had been Galván's idea to mention Martín's profession. Before he goes on, Víctor throws his arms wide as he used to do onstage, indicating the void.

'I don't give them much credence myself. And yet, a long time ago, magic not only gave me hope they might exist, it seemed to offer the possibility of seeing them, of communicating with them. Today, I realise that all that exists is what we can see.'

At this point, the music would drop to an almost inaudible pianissimo so the audience could hear the creak of wood as the cabinet appeared from the back of the stage without anyone seeming to push it.

'A hundred years ago, a cabinet just like this toured the world, leaving astonishment in its wake. Inside was a mirror, an ordinary pane of glass whose reflection ...'

Víctor stops, thinks for a second, then begins again, '... a mirror, a pane of ordinary glass whose reflection ... No, a pane of glass, whose ...'

He thumps the railing and curses. There is no sense in carrying on. A single hesitation, a single misplaced word, has shattered his confidence. The echo lingers in his mind not of his own voice, but of Galván's during the first rehearsals: 'Fluidly, Víctor, fluidly. Think about water. All you need to do is let it flow.'

And he was water. Rushing water. For two whole hours he unleashed wild torrents only to have them ebb and then evaporate to the amazement of the audience. Galván had told him to be ambitious, and from the start, he had done just that. A chamber orchestra onstage. A battery of technical resources which had taken them two years of preparation in the workshop, he and Galván working side by side, to create precise replicas of nine-teenth-century props and mechanisms.

It was a brilliant idea. It seemed to be simply a matter of recreating the finest moments of the golden age of magic. Onstage, Víctor practised every variation of the Davenport cabinet; he presented exact copies of Maskelyne's automata; performed con-juring tricks using the methods of the great innovator Jean Eugène Robert-Houdin; sawed a woman in half using the techniques of Horace Goldin; floated above the audience as Kellar had done; decapitated his assistant on a table exactly like the one Stodare had used; became invisible like Tobin; at the climax of the act, he had a member of the audience fire a gun at him and caught the bullet in mid-air, uttering the very words used by William

Robinson, who died onstage the day the trick went wrong. This was the list of great moments which he and Galván had agreed upon in long discussions during which the maestro refused even to allow Houdini's name to be uttered.

Each time Víctor opened a performance, Martín Losa's death served as a hinge to open a new door. Again and again, the tale returned to spirits, to the conflict between science and magic, moving it forward, giving it narrative drive, ensuring that the show did not simply become a succession of illusions. But the brilliance of the idea was that it only appeared to pay homage. Onstage, Víctor presented illusion after illusion, never forgetting to mention the name of the person who had invented it, the person who first performed it. Then he revealed the secret of the illusion. Not only did he tell the audience the mechanisms which made the illusion possible, he invited them onstage to see for themselves and then take it apart. The mirror that had served to hide the body of the decapitated man was smashed to smithereens, a pair of shears cut through the cables that had made possible the mysterious levitation.

And then he performed the illusion again. The audience spent two hours going from pillar to post, first watching in fascination as a historic trick was performed, then dazzled as the working of the trick was revealed to them only to be enraptured when the illusion was repeated without any possible explanation for how it was done.

Just when it seemed that Víctor could not possibly pull another trick from his metaphorical hat, the string quartet began to play the first notes of *Mumuki*, slow and disjointed as the sound of an approaching storm. Víctor would walk to the front of the stage and recite the valedictory:

'There are no spirits. All things come to an end. Life is a fleck of gold glimpsed in the lode. Some day, someone comes and finds our body deserted.' At that moment, with exquisite slowness, he collapsed onstage saying: 'And we disappear.'

And he disappeared. The quartet unleashed the violent storm that is *Mumuki*, pure Piazzolla, profane tango, and the audience would sit, dumbfounded, as the music played on, three, five, six minutes as the measures spilled out and the magician did not reappear. Only after the last bar, when silence fell on the hushed theatre, did some of them realise that Víctor was not coming back, and they began to clap, and applause spread like contagion through the theatre.

It always worked. The clapping, the stamping, the rhythmic beating on the seats; it was not simply a testament to their appreciation, or even their gratitude for the marvels they had witnessed, it was a refusal to accept that this journey, which some felt during the performance might go on for ever, was over. It was a demand for Víctor's return, as though only his reappearance on the stage could restore them to normality, the blind, unthinking humdrum life they had willingly relinquished when the show began on condition that it be restored to them at the end. More than once, Víctor felt tempted to reappear, to bask in the applause, but he never did so. He always stayed in the wings, paradoxically happy but alone, thinking of Galván and denying his audience the thought of a return after the end.

Standing on the terrace, he now says the last words aloud: 'And we disappear.'

Before, Now, After

He's annoying you, Víctor, admit it. You only opened the door, only let him in, because you thought it would be the quickest way to get rid of him, but the conversation has gone on for more than two hours now and there is no end in sight. You are sick of his questions, irritated by his patronising tone; above all you are tired of the pauses, the scratch of pen on paper that follows your answers. Sometimes it is rapid, as though he is merely ticking a box, turning your answer into 'yes' or 'no' on a questionnaire. At other times, though the short strokes of the pen sound like a stenographer eager not to waste time, he seems to be writing long sentences you know nothing about. You know this is a standard questionnaire: yes or no; none, a little, some, enough, a lot, too much; never, daily, weekly, monthly, annually. But now and then there seems to be a box for observations over which the social worker lingers. You want to ask him what the hell he's writing, but you say nothing. You've decided to confine yourself to short answers and pretend to be completely uninterested in this interview and its consequences.

He asks whether you have any family, and you say no. Friends? No. Acquaintances? No. There has to be someone. You raise your eyebrows in a gesture of mild irritation, as though this might force him to move on to the next question. But he insists: nobody? He glances down at his paperwork and mentions Mario Galván. He tells you it was Galván who called ONCE in light of your circumstances. This irritates you too, this carefulness with language, the euphemistic way he refers to your blindness as a visual impairment concomitant with atrophy of the optic nerve. Of both nerves. Galván? Oh, yes, my old teacher. But we don't see each other any more. You can't help but smile when you use the verb 'to see', a fact he quickly jots down. You don't tell him that, since his last visit, Galván has been calling you. That would mean giving him an explanation that corresponds to the boxes on his questionnaire: initially, several times a day; now, never. We don't talk any more. You have every right not to tell him you've disconnected the phone. Everyone has their secrets.

It's possible this man thinks you are the most disagreeable person on the face of the earth, though from his tone it seems more likely that he pities you. You know: your circumstances. He may also think you're stupid. Slow witted. Because given your obvious intention to get this over with as quickly as possible, you linger every time he asks you to clarify something. Come on, Víctor, it's not hard. All he wants to know is whether you take the bus, whether you manage to shower, cook for yourself, cope with the housework, go out from time to time. Stuff like that. But on the questionnaire, there are three boxes for each of these questions. The first marked 'Before'; the second 'Now'. Before you lost your sight: yes or no, a little or a lot, daily, weekly. Now that you're blind: no, no, nothing, never. You understand him, don't you? What's your problem? Box number three? This is marked 'Prospects'. It's just a name so the box fits the questionnaire. What it really means is: 'Prospects with regard to rehabilitation'. Bluntly: before, now, after. Afterwards, in the future. Will you need to be able to take the bus? Or to take a more concrete example: will you want to eat? Everyone needs to eat, Víctor. They'll teach you, but you have to do your bit. Get a move on and answer the questions, because he hasn't told you yet, but after this section, there's a general section with lots of white boxes with titles such as 'Attitude'. You know, Attitude with regard to rehabilitation. He needs to decide whether you demonstrate hope, denial, euphoria, urgency, indifference or fear. And he doesn't know what to put because every time he uses the word 'before', you take refuge in silence as though decades have passed, as though to remember what you did when you were blessed with the gift of sight, you have to cross over to some previous life. And every time he uses the word 'now', you freeze, as if the word is absurd, a meaningless sound to which your only response is an echo: now? You mean, now, now? And, naturally, with every passing second, the word now means something different. Now, Víctor, the present, Jesus! Today. Have you taken a bus? Did you shower and dress yourself? When he leaves will you be able to make a decent meal? Don't just sit there looking bewildered, say no. Now, no. Today, no. In the present, not, nothing, never.

He's a nice man, Víctor. Admit it. He's not pressuring you, he's trying not to make this any more painful than it has to be. Sometimes, he's a little too persistent, but he's only doing his job. OK, you don't like his manner, he irritates you; when he's not making notes, when he looks at you, waiting for you to answer, he constantly clicks his plastic ballpoint. Click, click, click, click. The unbearable sound of the little spring creeps into your ears, travels along the dead roads of your nervous system. You are about to reach out and rip the pen from his hands. You have lots of reasons to forgive him. Because this situation isn't easy for anyone and he has as much right to be nervous as you do. Because in all probability he's not aware that he's doing it; he's too busy studying your face, finding some word that sums up your attitude. And because he has only just met you. He knows nothing about your life. He doesn't know that the sound of him clicking his pen is precisely what makes it impossible for you to travel in time, it is what anchors you to the last moment you want to think of right now.

Take a leap into the future, Víctor. Or just a little step. Ten minutes, fifteen, nothing much. At some point this interview will be over. The man will gather his paperwork, put it in the folder he was hugging to his chest as he arrived, the yellow folder you could barely make out, he will put his pen back in his pocket, get to his feet and, before he says goodbye, he may pretend to smooth the creases in his trousers so he can dry his hands, because he is sweating just as much as you are. And though he will tell you it's not necessary, you will insist on walking him to the door and you'll pretend not to be conscious of the fact that, as he walks behind you, he is watching the way you brush the walls with your fingertips, the slight deviation in your steps, the way your fingers hesitate before they find the handle and open the door. You'll say your goodbyes, exchange awkward, interminable small talk about the heat, the rain, and eventually he will say what you expect him to say:

205

'We'll be in touch.'

We, plural. You won't ask who: ONCE? Social Security? Who knows. Someone will call you. Maybe you should reconnect the phone. 'When?' you'll ask. And you'll realise that it took you too long to ask, because before you hear his voice you will hear his footsteps stop on the stairs, hear him clear his throat as people do before answering an awkward question:

'I can't really say, there's a long waiting list. It's usually within the year.'

'Oh.'

This is what you will say: 'Oh.' Then you will close the door. And the social worker will be relieved that you have finally said something laden with meaning, a single word by which he suddenly grasps the before, the now, and can fill in all the little boxes relating to after.

Emptiness

Every journey, every voyage, imposes a suspension of time during which the armies of the past and future sharpen the swords they use in their permanent duel. Aboard the boat that brought Peter Grouse back to London, memory and imagination squared off in an unequal battle. Memory, though benefiting from superior forces and more effective weapons, stood to lose everything. For Grouse found it both difficult and unrewarding to recount precisely what took place during his last days in Philadelphia.

He records that he was held down by four thugs who gave him a good beating and threatened to cut off his entire thumb unless he stopped struggling. He records the feeling of cold steel against his skin. The sweat on the arms of the men who held him down, the noise of frantic breathing, the curses. He even records the moment when he took a deep breath and closed his eyes so that at least he might be spared the sight of the blood. But he says nothing about the pain. Nor the sound, the inescapable crunch of bone and cartilage. Memory cast a blessed veil over the time he spent in the hospital, where he was dumped at the door by the four men. The sutures. The smell of flesh burning as it was cauterised. Even the days that followed, spent in bed in his lodging house, waiting for the infection and the fever to subside, not daring to sleep for fear that even a slight movement might drag his thumb across the sheets.

When, eventually, the fever passed, he made the sort of false account of losses we invariably make to console ourselves with what remains. He had come through with his life, and by the merest chance, with his right hand unscathed. He could use the tools of his profession as effortlessly as he had before. Of both his professions: picklocks, of course, but also pencils and tools for designing and constructing illusions. And though he lamented the loss of half his left thumb, he suspected that the remaining part could still fulfil the basic functions required of it: holding, pinching, pushing. But it would be weeks, perhaps months, before that was possible. Grouse was in no doubt that, as he had been told when he was given first aid, the skin of the stump would eventually scar and, with time, would become hard and insensible. But until that happened, the slightest touch was enough to send a shudder like an electrical shock all the way from his hand to his feet. Washing, dressing, eating, all the day-to-day activities could trigger excruciating pain which he could avoid only by keeping his left hand behind his back, as though it had been not his thumb but his wrist which had been severed. Moreover, the wound, which was still tender and raw, leaked pus continually, forcing him to change the dressing several times a day, something he could do only by biting his lip, distracting his attention with self-inflicted and hence manageable pain.

Aside from the physical consequences, his trip to Philadelphia had been a disaster. Grouse cursed the moment when he had had the absurd idea of trying to profit from a plan so foolish and ill conceived it hardly warranted the name. Force the Seybert Commission to reconvene? During his time in hospital, he did not even read the accounts in the local newspapers of his misguided involvement in Kellar's show. However, he assumed that not even the elderly, stone-deaf Furness could have attributed Eva's howl of pain to the work of spirits. As for the reporters from the spiritualist magazines, at most they would take advantage of the circumstances to make fun of the magician's ineptitude, to settle the score for the many insults he had directed at them over the years. There was no way to turn a penny out of the fiasco.

Grouse returned to London ruined and sadly condemned to forget his forays into the world of magic, going back, for some time at least, to his profession as a common thief. In fact, he might well have started aboard ship, since the frequency with which he was presented with the opportunity to plunder cabins, bags, wallets and pockets was almost insulting. Only the fear that he would have to use his left hand held him back. The humidity aboard softened the skin of the wound, preventing it from scarring, so that by the third day out, he did not even need to bump it accidentally to feel the pain. It throbbed constantly as though the blood coursing through him were chafing at the wound from inside.

It was the pain which prevented him from wallowing in the memory of the past few days. He needed to find something to protect the stump as soon as possible. It was child's play to get his hands on a piece of balsa wood, a hacksaw, sandpaper and a chisel. He fashioned a hood, hollowed it out and sanded it until the interior was completely smooth. The real problem was calculating the correct size and width. For the protective cover to work it had to fit snugly against the base of his thumb, or at least neatly over the severed digit so that it didn't chafe the sensitive skin. It took a week of agonising trial and error, but eventually he managed to create what he wanted, a cover that was both comfortable and aesthetically pleasing. At last he could reach for the fork at dinner without worrying about seeing stars, at last he could put his hand in a pocket, his own or someone else's, without fear of his hand spasming. Though it mattered little to him, the prosthesis was rather attractive. From a distance, his thumb was once again the correct size, and the colour of the wood, closely matching that of his skin, gave a fleeting impression of normality.

More importantly, between the tip and the point where the thumb had been severed, there was an empty space. Empty. This was the word that tipped the battle in favour of imagination. Something empty can be filled. A neatly folded silk handkerchief would fit in there; scraps of paper bearing mysterious messages, small coins, rings ... Of course, he would need time to perfect a means of using this new invention; when and how the cover could be filled and emptied. But he had the essential, something every magician through the ages would like to have invented: an empty space, undetectable, and always to hand, or more precisely, to thumb.

Most importantly, it was universal. One did not need to lose half a thumb, it could be adapted to any size, and still leave an empty space, like the space that invariably exists between the toes and the end of a shoe. Moreover: a magician who had covered his thumb with this device could show his hands to the audience without worrying, as long as he kept them moving. Arms outstretched, Grouse brought both hands to eye level and shook them like someone who has just washed their hands. He realised at that moment that sight is slower than the mind. We know we are seeing the nails, the knuckles, the hairs, but what we see, what we actually see, is simply the movement of the hand. Ever the perfectionist, Grouse went on working on the prosthesis, creating a bas-relief in the shape of a nail and a number of grooves simulating the wrinkles around the joint. Now he needed only a powder compact, something he stole from one of the ladies aboard the following day. He covered the wood with a fine layer of make-up which further blurred the difference in texture between flesh and wood. There was one final detail which he could not address until they arrived back at port: patenting his invention. Because, unless he was much mistaken, generations of magicians would make use of such prostheses for decades, perhaps centuries, to come. And it was only fair that, just as he had suffered the consequences of his actions, so should he reap the rewards.

The Besieged City

He always believed there would be one last instant of light. One last useless flicker, like the white dot that lingers when you turn off an old television set. Until recently, he toyed with the idea of carrying something around with him, some gift for his eyes, something worthy of being the last thing he ever saw, a safe-conduct into the world of shadows. He has given up that idea now; no single object in itself has such value. Now he feels that the moment is approaching and he knows exactly what he wants to do.

He draws up a chair to the wardrobe in his bedroom, takes his shoes off, climbs on the chair and opens the trapdoor to the loft space. He feels around, his arms sweeping the space, bringing obstacles raining down on him: blankets and pillows, a rug that stinks of mothballs, old metal cases he has never bothered to open and which, from the racket they make as they fall, might be full of nut and bolts, or tools maybe. He pushes two large bags of clothes back into a corner and, standing on tiptoe, almost crawling into the attic himself, feels his fingers touch the wooden box that once belonged to his father. He drags it towards the edge until he can get a grip on it then jumps down from the chair, clutching the box to him as though it contains a parachute.

He goes into the living room, sits on the floor next to the hi-fi system and opens the box. At first, he tries to search it by touch alone, pushing aside things he recognises immediately: his father's favourite ties, a handful of photos, a pair of gold cufflinks. He has never dared wear cufflinks. He turns the box over, tipping the contents on to his lap. He carries on sorting through the objects until he hears the sound he has been waiting for: a cassette tape.

He gets up on his knees, crawls over to the stereo and puts it on. Immediately he hears background music, the sound of someone coughing, but Víctor reaches out, finds the controls and manages to rewind the tape to the beginning. In the beginning is silence.

For several seconds all he can hear is the sound of the cassette player. Then, whistling. Over the years he learned the little tune by heart in case he heard it in the street, on a record, on the radio. So he would finally know what the hell his father was whistling just before he died. He never heard it again. Besides, it is only a brief snatch of music, and perhaps Martín Losa was improvising while he was setting out his tools on his workbench: in the background there are three metallic clangs, two hollow thuds as of something plastic, the sound of paper rustling, a ballpoint pen clicking, up and down, up and down. It was one of Martín's tics. Click, click, click. The Parker pen he was never without. Víctor's fingers have just found it at the bottom of the box.

He makes himself comfortable, leans his head back against the wall and closes his eyes. Anyone would do the same in order to concentrate, to listen more attentively, but this small, impulsive action, this miracle which for most people means closing themselves off from the world, is fraught in his case with a terrible contradiction. Because Víctor is closing his eyes so he can see. The workbench, Martín's thumb clicking away, the arrow logo on the Parker pen. He wants to trace a path through this labyrinth in which he has been lost for weeks, perhaps for years; reach back through these sounds to the moment his father died and see it for the first time. Imagine it, since he has no other way of seeing it now.

He knows that soon he will hear the radio come on in the background. The volume is so low that it is impossible to decipher most of the words spoken by the female announcer. There was a time, though he has played it over and over, when all he could make out was the station jingle – Radio 2 – the name of the programme – *Contrapunto* – and two other names, Saint-Saëns and Stoltzman. And the two instruments mentioned, clarinet and piano, though this is hardly necessary since he recognises them immediately once the music begins to play. It is playing now. There has been no sound from his father for some time. Just the creaking of his chair, and the pen clicking, slightly exaggerated now, as though Martín is trying to follow the languid rhythm of the first movement. He clearly likes the sonata since he suddenly turns up the volume and the music now takes the foreground. Víctor can see his father's hand, the precision with which he touches the volume control using thumb and forefinger. He hums along to the melody. He has always found it graceful, beautiful even, but he has never really paid much attention to it, as though unwilling to think of it as anything other than background music.

After a brief silence, the second movement begins. *Allegro animato*, though the controlled performance keeps both the joy and the liveliness in check. Víctor turns the volume all the way up now, not so that he can hear the music more clearly, but the reverse: there is a click in the background and if the assumptions he made all those years ago are correct, he knows that it is not the pen, but a switch. The switch that operates the heater. His mother had the good grace to get rid of it, or perhaps the police or the forensics team kept it, the weapon in this act of criminal stupidity. And yet, Víctor remembers the device, he knows it was not a standard piece but his father's brilliant solution to a lack of equipment when setting up a home laboratory; it is a bottle warmer. It has a Mickey Mouse sticker on the front.

Rewind, darling, rewind. Listen to it again and experience the surprise. You wanted to see everything for the first time, didn't you? Well, there you have it. Click: death. Or the prologue to death; the means by which it came about. And who is your father calling to now? Come here, he says. Come on, you stupid thing, I'm not going to hurt you. You can see it, can't you? His right hand holds the tweezers, dipping them into a test tube to take out an ant. And his left hand? See it with your eyes closed, see it hover in the air, the slight, stupid motion, the quiver of the jar of liquid nicotine.

Stop now. Stop the tape, stop time and think. You have done it a thousand times because this is the point when you hear a sound you cannot understand. It is a vibration. Or rather two vibrations, one after the other. You used to think it was a buzzer; if such things had existed back then, you might have thought it was a mobile phone vibrating.

Keep thinking about this sound, concentrate on what you cannot understand, pay no attention to those sounds that you unfortunately know all too well, the dull, soft, almost inaudible thud of the plastic jar coming into contact with the bottle warmer. There is nothing to be done now. There are eight seconds left. There will be three more vibrations and a cough that would sound faintly ridiculous if you did not know what it meant. Experience the surprise again, if you like, the paradox between what you can see and what you are hearing. A man is dying, Víctor. He is foaming at the mouth, doubled up in pain, his body spasms so violently that he will wind up on the floor in a preposterous, undignified position, the same position that, half an hour later, you will think is a poor imitation of a cockroach, a man is spitting out his soul, dying without even exercising his right to one last breath, and all you can hear is a slight cough, the creak of wood as the chair tips over, the metallic ping of the tweezers as they fall to the floor and, were it not for the radio, were it not for chance, which has scored your father's death to a soundtrack that is *allegro animato*, you would hear the only truly revealing sound: silence, Víctor. The silence of death.

But you are not thinking about that, you are thinking about the only question you have never voiced, the one thing about this recording that you have never dared to incorporate into the fiction of your shows. Something you have never even dared to ask your mother. Admit it, damn it, at least admit that this question has haunted your every nightmare, troubled the darkest moments of a life that, only two months ago, you wanted to contemplate from the viewpoint of happiness. Be a man, Víctor. Put the question into words. Why did Martín record his own death? And more specifically: did he know he was going to die? Now that you can formulate the words, can accept their exactness, use them as they are meant to be used, you can ask the question that truly terrifies you: did he kill himself? Did Martín Losa kill himself?

The answer lies in the strange vibration, though you will never know it. No one can ever say you did not try. You listened to it until it bored you. You came up with every possible conjecture. The only thing you failed to do was ask the right person. If you had given the recording to any of your father's colleagues, to any of his friends at the university, you'd have known that your father's last wish was to prove you right. To demonstrate that you had been right all along. To leave proof. The vibration is made by certain ants, and it is so common that it even has a name. It is called stridulation. Most species have a hard patch in the upper section of the abdomen, which looks like a scraper. In extreme circumstances, when faced with imminent danger or an unexpected source of food, they move their waist so that this patch rubs against a ridged section of the lower abdomen. This is what you can hear, amplified a hundred times, since your father was holding the ant with tweezers right in front of the microphone, possibly squeezing hard enough to kill it. He did what he needed to do in order to record the sound, so that later that day, or the following Saturday – the first of many he would not live to see – he would be able to say: here, listen to this, this is the sound you've been longing to hear. And if his left hand did something it shouldn't have, if it shook the little jar, took off the lid and placed it in the warmer, perhaps it was because Martín was trying to imagine your face when he told you, your smile when you realised that, between those four glass walls, the thing you most desired to hear did occur from time to time: a muted sound but one filled with meaning.

Is buzzing a language? Would it have been enough for you? Ants don't have ears, but stridulation is transmitted through the ground and ants detect the surface vibrations in their legs and their bodies. And they run away. Or they rush to eat. Or they look for a safe place for the queen. It would have done you good to know this, to be free of your doubts once and for all, to see with your eyes closed that your father was not thinking about dying, he was thinking about you, about the Saturdays you spent together, about you stubbornly going round and round the ant farm, ear pressed to the glass. You would finally be able to stop the tape, rip it out, burn it, forget about it for ever and not, as you are about to do, as you are doing now, rush headlong into the six seconds of silence that follow your father's death. Then three notes on a piano, the same note played three times. This is the beginning of the third movement. *Lento*. This is how it is described, slow and deadly. With the fourth chord comes the mournful voice of the clarinet, a moment you have always found heartbreaking. It is easy to believe that your father must have chosen the music, chosen this moment, the perfect funeral march. There was a time when it fuelled your suspicions. But this is not the sound of death knocking, Víctor. It is simply light bidding you farewell. The last moment has come and gone, Víctor, and you had your eyes closed. And your face is wet with tears.

Are you ready? You have one last task. You can see nothing, but you can do it if you pretend for a moment that you can see a flicker, a ray of light fashioned from memory. Crawl, if you have to. Feel your way across the floor. Pick it all up, the photos, the plastic finger, the Parker pen, the tie, the cufflinks. That thing rolling away is the piece of amber your father proudly showed you. Put everything back in the box, find the stepladder, climb up to the attic and put it back. Hurry now, don't stop. You know you can't afford to. After today, you will stumble at every step; the table, the chairs, the doors, every object in the apartment is lying in wait to trip you up when you go astray. These things you can survive, but nothing can protect you from stumbling into the past.

And don't forget to turn off the tape and take it out. Or maybe not. Let it run, what does it matter? The footsteps you hear now are your mother's. You can also hear her voice: 'Martín? Martín!' This is the last thing on the tape; after that comes silence. Do you remember? You were still out on the landing. No one stopped the tape. Until the following day, no one noticed that your father had turned the tape recorder on. The tape simply ran out. And you were lucky that it stopped at that moment. If it hadn't you would hear your own footsteps, the footsteps of a seven-year-old boy, your laugh when you found your father's body lying on the floor, your surprise to see he was not moving, you would hear the word 'cockroach' and the past would bury you like an avalanche. It's better that you do not hear any more. Or that you learn to interpret any sound, whether it be the sigh of a clarinet or a buzzing you cannot understand, as an echo of the army of the future that is preparing to lay siege to your city.

part two

To see, I do not only have my eyes
To see, I have beside me something like an angel
That says to me, slowly, this or that,
Here or there, above or lower down

HÉCTOR VIEL TEMPERLEY

One Year

He connects the phone only for a few hours on Monday mornings so he can answer when the supermarket calls. He doesn't need to talk to anyone. He doesn't want to change his gas supplier, he doesn't want a flat-rate contract, and if someone called with a survey all he could tell them would be no, never, nothing. This is why, at seven o'clock in the evening, when he hears the first ring, Víctor curses himself for forgetting to disconnect the phone that morning.

He picks up the receiver and brings it to his ear, but does not say anything.

'Hello? Hello? Anyone there?'

Víctor is about to hang up when he hears his name.

'Víctor Losa?'

It sounds strange, his name on a woman's lips. He wants her to go on. He wants to be able to listen to her without having to say a single word.

'Is that Víctor Losa?'

'Yes.'

This is as much as he is prepared to concede: a monosyllable, the minimal possible confirmation, though all she hears is the phlegmatic timbre of a throat scarcely used. The woman introduces herself: Alicia. Just Alicia, no surname. She tells him she is calling from ONCE, though she does not use the acronym but gives the full name: Organización Nacional de Ciegos de España. She tells him she is to be his Rehabilitation Technician. Víctor can hear the capital letters in her voice. He finds the job title amusing, as though blindness were an addiction from which he might be rescued. Alicia offers her apologies that he has had to wait a whole year, tells him what a tremendous pleasure it will be to begin working with him and asks whether he has any free time tomorrow so she can visit and make initial contact. These are the words she uses: initial contact. Víctor listens as though this were someone else's conversation, a recording. Initial contact. Like the spark between electrical poles, he thinks. Or between neurons. Contact. He says yes. A very useful thing, this monosyllable. So far, he has said nothing else. An awkward silence follows. Perhaps she is hoping for something more enthusiastic, less passive, something more akin to a conversation. Eventually, in a strangled voice, she asks whether 9 a.m. would be convenient. Yes.

Víctor hangs up, stands next to the telephone, then takes a step back and says: 'A year.' His head jerks round like a wary bird's, as though the voice he has just heard was not his but someone else's. He frowns. He is not thinking about the darkness, the depression, the seclusion, about the constant fear, the bruises, the dozens of times he has burned himself, hurt himself during that year. He is not thinking about the loneliness, the unremitting exhaustion that has made it possible for him to get through it, as though only by doing as little as possible, keeping his body lifeless and his mind anaesthetised, can he forget the pain of not seeing.

One year without sex. This is exactly what he is thinking. He has only just realised the fact, and cannot quite believe it. As though the terrible pain of all the things he has been forced to give up has prevented him from noticing this one.

He says her name aloud: Alicia. He can find no way to sink his teeth into it. He closes his eyes and tries to imagine her. He still does this. Even after a year, he still closes his eyes. The first thing he sees is a pair of lips. Nothing remarkable about them: just lips. He raises his hand and allows it to hover in the air. Mmmm, he thinks. This is the sound inside his head: mmmm. It is as though, over the past year, the eagle inside his brain has devoured every vestige of articulated speech. He presses his tongue against his palate, as though he has just eaten his first late-season cherry.

He goes back to the phone and calls directory enquiries. Three times he dials the wrong number, but the fourth time a woman answers, young, to judge by her voice. He asks her for the number of an agency.

'I'm afraid agency on its own is too general a term,' the operator

222

says after a brief silence. 'Could you be more specific . . .?'

'An escort agency.'

'An escort agency,' the woman repeats, her tone absolutely neutral. 'In Barcelona city?'

'Yes.'

'Let's see . . .' A smile flits back and forth across the telephone line. It is as if both of them have decided to behave as though he has asked for information about a china shop. 'Let's try under massage parlour . . . ay, there are a lot of listings. Do you have any preferences? Sorry, I mean about the area?'

'Whichever one offers home visits.'

'Home visits . . . there're quite a few.'

'How about in the centre of town?'

'OK, have you got a pen . . .'

'Just a minute,' Víctor interrupts. 'If you don't mind, could you just read the number twice. And very slowly, please. It's just . . . I don't have anything to write with.'

'No problem, sir.'

The operator repeats an 803 number twice. Víctor thanks her and hangs up, repeating the number aloud to himself, then tries to dial it immediately. Though he can easily imagine the keypad – 1 at the top right corner, 0 at the bottom – his fingers seem unable to follow through. He strokes the keys as though reading a text in Braille. Several times he dials the wrong number. Eventually he gets through to the massage parlour and asks for a home visit. This is his first time, but he finds it no more difficult than he does ordering peanuts from the supermarket. Without any shame, or guilt, or embarrassment. He is asked to repeat his address then asked at what time he would like the appointment.

'Now,' he answers.

'Now . . . I have Irina available.'

'Irina.' Víctor repeats the word, as though it were a brand name. 'Irina. That's fine.'

Irina

As she walks, she thinks that it's a strange time for an appointment. It's only just after 7.30 p.m. She has been doing this for two years now and it still seems strange to her that there are so many men who want to fuck in the middle of the afternoon or early evening and who are prepared to pay for it. She puts it down to a statistical anomaly. Maybe it's just that all the strange guys pick her? Not that she's complaining: the timing suits her, it means she can drop her son Darius off with a neighbour and save on a babysitter. Though money isn't a problem. She makes a good living.

She takes a piece of paper from her bag and checks that she has the right address. She presses the button on the intercom and is not surprised when the door immediately buzzes to let her in. It makes sense. They're always waiting for her.

She is sorry to see there's no lift, not so much because she has to climb six floors as because there's no mirror so she can touch up her make-up. Just as she arrives on the top-floor landing, the light in the stairwell goes out. A tiny indicator light, a red dot in the darkness, makes it possible to tell where the switch is. She steps towards it, her arm out, feeling her way. Her fingers are only inches away now. She stretches out her hand.

'Don't turn it on.'

The voice is barely a whisper, but it carries the weight of authority. So much so that she obeys, draws her hand away. But it is a friendly voice. In spite of her apprehension, Irina does not think of running, she is not afraid that the owner of this voice might harm her in any way. A sixth sense tells her if she takes another step, she will come to the door, that the door is ajar and that he is behind. Whoever he may be. There is no light on inside the apartment either. She says nothing. Waits for instructions, but what comes is a question.

'Irina?'

She hesitates before answering. Now she feels something like a threat. Here, whispering in the darkness, the name is charged with intimacy. As though she were standing in front of a mirror, she stands up straight, smoothes the creases from her dress, brushes away the wisp of hair that has fallen across her face. The questions sounds like an examination. As though today she will be judged not by eyes looking her up and down, or by a hand stroking her body as a way of a greeting, but by something as arbitrary as her name.

'Yes,' she says, 'I'm Irina.'

The name sounds different in her mouth. The first 'I' is longer, almost liquid. The rest sombre. Irina, a Romanian whore. He is smelling her. She thinks he is smelling her.

'Come in,' the voice says, still serious though a little farther away, as though the owner has moved away slightly, or turned his back.

Irina takes a step forward, her arm out, and touches the door, which yields to the pressure without a sad whimper of its hinges. Another step. She is inside the apartment. Without realising it, she has closed her eyes, as children do when they're hiding in the dark. She leans back against the door, pushing it slowly until it closes. She opens her eyes. There doesn't seem to be a single light on in the apartment, nothing but the dying embers of evening, barely enough to make out the dimensions of the hall and the corridor down which the man disappears. She follows him and, as she turns the corner, sees him for the first time, from behind. He is naked, barefoot. He walks down the hallway with his back very straight, the reach of his arms a little wider than his body. Short steps. He brushes the wall with his fingers as he walks. Without turning, the man says:

'My name is Víctor, Irina.' She says nothing. What could she say? Pleased to meet you? 'Your money,' he says as he comes to the end of the corridor.

Once in the living room, he holds out his hand, waving it so she can see it is empty. He makes a fist, brings it up behind his neck, then opens his hand again to show her a hundred-euro note. As though he has plucked it from his ear or from behind his neck: a child's magic trick. Without lowering his hand, Víctor rubs the banknote between thumb and forefinger, fanning it out so she can see that in fact there are three of them, two hundreds and a fifty. He sets them on the living-room table and carries on walking. At the door to a room, he stops, opens it and goes inside without turning on the light.

Irina stands next to the table. She does a quick calculation. It is €20 too much, but in this situation nobody expects you to give them change. She is about to say thank you. Not for the tip, but for sparing her from having to ask for the money up front. She puts the notes in her purse and, as though doing so signals the beginning of her professional assignment, she slips off her shoes. She puts her bag on a chair, places her shoes under the table. She opens the zip that runs down one side of her dress, pushes the straps off her shoulders and lets it fall to the floor. Quickly, in a single movement, as though removing an outer shell. Her bra is expensive but elegant, a hint of lace supporting her breasts. She takes it off too. Slowly she goes into the bedroom; she feels extraordinarily relaxed as though she were not approaching this vast white bed to do her job, but to get some sleep. He is lying face down in the middle. Irina lies down next to him and places her hand on his back. She doesn't speak. On the contrary, she is grateful to Víctor for his silence, she almost holds her breath in support. She is waiting for him to turn over. Perhaps then she will know the reason for the strange, shadowy welcome – some embarrassing deformity, a harelip, an old scar, the ravages of smallpox.

Víctor turns over. He raises his hand as though to caress her, but leaves it hovering, suspended, hesitant. Irina looks at his beard and it reminds her of a rabbi, a tramp, a castaway. She thinks he is trying not to look at her because his eyes barely graze her, as though something, something she cannot see, a few inches from her face, demands Víctor's attention.

'Víctar,' she says, trying to pronounce the name properly. 'Víctar.' She fails again.

She does not know what to think of this man, but she feels that she can trust him. She dismisses curiosity, it is a bad investment. She isn't being paid to ask questions. Or perhaps she is, she doesn't know yet. Time to act, she thinks. Too much talking. But it is he who acts. His arms, like his voice, are warm and powerful. With no apparent effort, Víctor turns her on her side and hugs her from behind. Then he is still. They lie like this for some minutes, like two spoons forgotten at the back of a drawer. He buries his face in her neck, his nose in her hair. Now he really is smelling her. Maybe that's all there is to it, thinks Irina. Maybe nothing is going to happen. She's heard of punters who only want someone to hold while they sleep, a hug, or a chat. She wouldn't mind.

This is clearly not the case with him, though. Irina quickly feels this between her legs, or more accurately between her buttocks, because it is here that Víctor slowly presses his erection, playful at first, almost tender, but then insistent, brusque. She should have expected it: no one asks for someone to come round at seven o'clock to take a nap. It's better this way. Whatever is going to happen, let it happen quickly. Víctor slides one hand across her hip. Covers her belly with his other hand. He enters her. Irina cannot see his face. She slips a hand down between her legs and finds that Víctor has put on a condom, though she does not know how or when. She has only a moment to think about how strange this man's hands are, the mysteriousness of his gestures. Well, she too has her tricks. She cups his testicles with her hand, not clutching, not even stroking them, simply lifting them slightly. A lot of men like this, but that is not why she is doing it. She does it so they come quickly. But it is not going to be so easy. Víctor moves her hand away and, for the first time since he penetrated her, he speaks:

'No.'

This is all he says, speaking in a low voice but so close to Irina's ear that she begins to realise how together they are, and though she tries to perform another trick to bring him off quickly, moving her pelvis in long, slow, distinct thrusts, he places his left hand firmly on her hip to stop her. His right hand under her body is folded back against her breasts, though he barely touches them, as though he wants only to cover them lest someone should see. Irina knows she is literally in his hands, that nothing that happens from this point forward will be determined by her. Víctor moves his lips along her spine; from time to time he holds a piece of skin between his teeth, although he does not bite; it is as though he is keeping time, following the same rhythm she can feel in the steady pulse of his penis. It's only blood, thinks Irina, blood pulsing to the beat of his heart. Yet it beats with the cold, clinical precision of a metronome. Almost without realising it, Irina makes the mistake of echoing this pulse in the muscles of her vagina, the way an audience's feet sometimes tap to the rhythm of an orchestra. Other men have tried to bring her to orgasm, generally thrusting into her brutally as though this role reversal were the mark of a real man: the ability to make a whore come. This, Irina thinks, is not why she is here. It is important to know where she is and why.

She decides that she has had enough and fakes an orgasm. Or rather, she starts to fake it. Without overacting, without crying out, without pretending to shudder. She breathes heavily and purrs. Another mistake. Without moving his arm, Víctor pivots his hip, turns his body slightly and both of them are now lying on their backs: her on top, him below. Him inside her.

A lot of men have struggled to impress her with all sorts of gymnastic, sometimes impossible, positions which they've dreamt of or read about in a book. Nothing as simple as this, which Irina finds comical, naive, a little clumsy. Here they both are, staring at the ceiling. And this guy is so thin that if she moves, she might crush him. She quickly realises there is a reason for the move: it allows his hands greater freedom. With the fingers of his right hand he grasps her nipple. He does not rub it or press it or pinch it: he simply holds it firmly between his fingertips, perhaps pulls at it gently. With the fourth finger of his left hand he finds her clitoris.

Now it is Irina who says no. Or wants to say it. She thinks it three times, four, and bites her lip. Víctor moves inside her slowly. In and out. Irina tries to avoid it, clamps her vagina around his finger, trying to suck him in, to stop him, she wants him to stop, she clenches her thighs too, and her teeth. She is not going to let herself go, she doesn't want to go. She thinks about Darius. It is a way of bringing herself back to reality. She plants her feet firmly on the bed, tenses her back, jerks her hips and manages to break free of Víctor's embrace; then she straddles him, her back to him and rides him hard and fast. She wants him to come. She needs him to come. She wants him to feel his heart heave into his mouth. They call it professional ethics: nothing to do with desire. After all, he has paid already, and given her a tip. Up and down, up and down. Like a frog, like a crazed kangaroo, she bucks and bucks on him, cursing his staying power until a pulsing jet from his glans tells her she has achieved her aim. She stops abruptly, still pressed against Víctor, surprised by the heat of the cum she feels inundating her in spite of the condom.

With a gentle movement, Víctor pulls out of her and, with a quick flick of his fingers, peels off the condom. Irina begins to understand. Or perhaps she does not understand, but she senses: from Víctor's movements, his deftness, the things this man does with his hands. A magician's hands. Still lying on his back, his voice somewhat drowsy, Víctor says goodbye.

'Thanks, Irina. I'll call you again. Your money is in the hall.'

'No. You are paying me already.' She is flustered, angry that she cannot conjugate verbs in this language she can barely pronounce. 'You have paid me already,' she corrects herself in a murmur.

'No,' Víctor says. 'It's on the dresser in the hall. You know the word "dresser"? In the hall.'

From the bedroom door, Irina manages to make out the rumpled bed, the damp stains on the sheets, the man half asleep. There is something familiar about the image, something domestic which unsettles her. She goes into the living room, dresses and puts on her shoes. She thinks about what she will make for dinner. Chicken. Grilled chicken for Darius, grilled chicken for Irina and then bed. She is exhausted and a little sore. She opens her purse and takes out the three banknotes. But they are not banknotes, they are blank pieces of paper. It's not possible. She saw them with her own eyes, she could swear she counted them. A magician's hands, she thinks again. On top of the dresser she finds €300 in fifty-euro notes, held together by the pen clip shaped like an arrow. The pen looks old, though not necessarily valuable. She holds the money in one hand and, with the other, she clicks the top. Several times. Click, click, click. She puts back one note and keeps the others, still staring at the Parker pen. She has never stolen anything in her life. She's not a thief, she's a whore. And she doesn't need it.

'Not the pen,' Víctor's voice warns, just in case. 'It belonged to my father.'

Irina suddenly feels an urgent need to be out of there. To be free of the shadowy scrutiny of this voice. She sets down the pen, turns and goes. The first thing she does as she leaves is hit the light switch on the landing, as though turning it on were some small act of revenge for she knows not what.

Ants

Víctor wakes with a start, a powerful prickling in his right arm. He has heard somewhere that this is the first sign of a heart attack. Or is that the left arm? He sits up, puts his feet on the floor. It is an intense feeling running all the way from his elbow to his fingers, but it is only superficial. And it seems to be contagious, because when he brings his other hand up to scratch the itch, he feels a tingling all along his left arm. He cannot work out what it is, this prickling that is making his skin crawl; then he realises that it is literally crawling, an army of ants is marching across the sheets and up his arm, blindly drawn by the fructose in his semen, scavenging for dried specks on his fingers. He gets to his feet and stands there for a moment or two until he notices the same pins and needles in his right leg. First on his toes, his instep, around his ankle, then up his shin, as though an assault brigade is marching across his body to rescue the companions trapped on his arm.

He imagines how the feat began, the first ant, lost or perhaps curious, had discovered the source of food in the middle of the night, or perhaps at dawn, he doesn't know, cannot tell how long the banquet has been going on. The first ant, rather than eating its fill, rushed back to the ant farm, conveying the news of its discovery to another, who passed it on to another and another, until hundreds, perhaps thousands, of ants became aware of the location and the biochemical composition of the spilled liquid. He imagines the hysteria that ensued in Martín Losa's ant farm, the subterranean excitement unleashed, the collective voice announcing the presence of massive quantities of protein, amino acids, chlorides, phosphorus, lactic, citric and ascorbic acids, carbon dioxide,

231

acid phosphatase, hyaluronidase, phosphorylcholine, prostaglandin and fibrinolysin.

Each of these ants carries a message in its antennae for Víctor. They are telling him who he is. Not just his semen, his whole being, every firing of his confused neurons. The one and only specific combination of chemical elements that make him who he is rather than anyone else, even if he wouldn't recognise himself. It is written. His likeness is written on the sheets, across the floor, a moving trail blacker than any ink running from the bed to the formicarium, coming and going, a living, shifting, indecipherable calligraphy.

Now he begins to walk and he laughs, realising that he has never walked with such self-assurance, even when he could see, perhaps because his feet no long claim to take him anywhere, they are simply walking, or more accurately pacing, crushing this army, annihilating it with a precision a sighted person might envy. He moves like a tightrope walker, leaving almost no space between his steps, and not because he is afraid of falling, but because he is determined to give no quarter in this carnage. He places his foot on the floor and, exerting no pressure, waits until he can feel the ants tickling, then puts all his weight on his foot and turns, then takes another short step, until finally he reaches the ant farm; he knows that he has reached it from the swarming chaos. He lifts his knee, climbs over the glass on to the soil and tramples it furiously until he is exhausted.

He thinks about Martín Losa. He thinks about the irony: his father had never been able to show him the queen. But right now several drones are probably busy moving her, only he cannot see it. Obviously things are not the same now. Generations have passed by, secret, silent, blind, mute, capable of surviving on what scant minerals they can get from rainwater, plus the meagre crumbs that have fallen on the surface of the ant farm from time to time. If this were Saturday morning, if you were still a child stubbornly pressing your ear to the glass, you would hear a faint buzzing, a perfect example of collective stridulation, a dance in the darkness, the glandular secretions with which they congratulate each other for having survived, for never giving up on the hope that some day, if only through carelessness, someone would once more leave food within reach. Go on stamping, but don't forget that it is pointless. At the very moment you began this carnage, nature devoted itself to life; for every stamp it lays an egg where it cannot be reached.

Naked, he tramples the soil for more than fifteen minutes without for a moment feeling disgust or grief or rage, his mind possessed by a single idea. This is who I am, he is thinking. This is me, my feet carried me here, this is what I am doing. Trampling ants. I am a blind man who tramples ants.

The commotion beneath his feet begins to subside and Víctor stops for a moment. Alicia is coming. Was her name Alicia? They agreed on 9 a.m. He has no idea what time it is. It must be early, the sun does not feel very hot. He walks to the bathroom, turns on the radio and stands there, holding it, until the presenter announces it is twenty past seven. He gets into the shower. He scrubs himself with a sponge as though trying to wash away all the darkness that has built up on his skin over the past year. He rubs his feet gently. He sniffs himself. He can smell no trace of Irina. Irina smelled clean. He soaps and rinses himself three times. When he gets out, he tries to shave. The last time he tried, several months ago now, he cut himself so often that he decided not to try again. His beard is long, thick and unkempt and the blade is old. He is ripping out hair rather than shaving it off; after the fifth stroke, he gives up. The radio announces there is a little more than half an hour left before Alicia arrives and he still needs to get dressed. Maybe he should wear shoes today, but he has no idea where his shoes might be.

'Al Dente'

A month ago, when they assigned her the case, Alicia cut out a photograph of Víctor Losa and stuck it on her fridge. The image is so familiar to her now that she can recreate it with her eyes closed. Ears slightly lopsided, though that might just be the photo. Large, white, even teeth. It's hardly surprising that he opens his mouth wide when he smiles. A dimple in the left cheek. Perfectly clean shaven. She imagined Víctor puffing out his cheeks as he shaved so as not to miss a single hair. If they were friends, she would smooth his unruly eyebrows with her finger. If she had to choose a place to kiss him, she would choose his cheekbones. Or take his face in her hands and kiss his forehead. What a shame, she would say, what a shame. So handsome. And the finest magician in the world. What a fuck-up, Víctor Losa.

But they are not friends. And Víctor is not a photo; he is a man. A man with a problem. This is what she thinks as she cycles up Mayor de Gracia, weaving between double-parked cars. 'We're not friends. I'm not his mother or his girlfriend or his sister. Nothing personal.' She has a job to do. She has had time to examine thoroughly the theoretical material and her preparatory coursework from ONCE, and to immerse herself in the specific details of this case. She knows more about Leber's syndrome than most doctors. She is prepared.

She is glad her client is a magician. An artist, someone with imagination, a noble spirit. Alicia believes in such things. Besides, a magician hardly needs his eyesight to work. At least, that is what she supposes, she has never done so much as a card trick in her life, but she is fairly sure there are tons of tricks you can do without having to look. It just so happens that many of the qualities

234

essential to being a good magician are useful in rehabilitating someone who is blind: a good short-term memory, a keen sense of touch, a well-developed routine, perfectionism, responsiveness to training. She knows Víctor has not worked since he lost his sight, or at least she has not been able to find any indication of recent performances. The most recent reference on the internet is his triumph at the Lisbon International Festival a little more than a year ago. ONCE received the notification about his blindness about two months later. Well, it would hardly be surprising if he is depressed. Almost everyone goes through that phase. One day at a time.

It's good to have a goal, a distant but realistic objective. She imagines Víctor onstage, taking a bow as the audience applauds, perhaps giving her a wink, some secret sign of gratitude. She can see herself sitting in the front row, applauding wildly, for this triumph is her triumph. And while she is imagining, she sees herself standing next to Víctor, sharing the applause, dressed as a magician's assistant: silver lamé, sequins, stilettos, who knows, maybe a platinum-blonde wig. It would be fun.

Víctor being sort of famous is an advantage. It's as though she has known him for a long time. She has been able to read articles about him on the internet, biographies, a few reviews, most of them full of superlatives, a couple of interviews. In one magazine there was a questionnaire, a series of short questions and answers, next to which she wrote her own comments before sticking it on the fridge by the photo:

Your greatest strength: constancy *(like me!)*
Your greatest weakness: stubbornness *(isn't that the same thing?)*
Where would you most like to live: Lisbon in winter, Amsterdam in spring, London in summer, Malespina in autumn *(I've only been to London!)*
A secret wish: to be someone else *(?)*
If you weren't a magician, what would you be: a typist *(?)*
Favourite film: To Have and Have Not *(Find D VD)*
Favourite song: If, the version by Louis Armstrong *(Louis Armstrong? what a bore)*
You couldn't live without ... oxygen?

The world would be perfect if . . . it were an idea
The worst thing that could happen to you: if nothing happened to me
How would you like to die: alive *(Ha ha!)*
Favourite drink: water
Favourite food: Black pudding *(disgusting!)*
How do you like your women: 'al dente'

'Al dente'? Young, like her? Long in the tooth? If Alicia is thinking about this detail in the questionnaire as she pedals, it is because every possible meaning points to her. This is how she feels: ready, right on the cusp between the moment when something crucial is about to happen and the fearful moment when, if nothing has happened, it will be too late.

Alicia is twenty-nine. 'Al dente'. Better to put it that way.

She did not count on the terrible heat, did not remember that the slope of Calle Mayor de Gracia was so steep. As she turns the corner into the Plaza de Lesseps, a few drops of sweat drip from her armpits, trickle over her breasts and come to rest in her navel. Two blocks farther on, she turns right and coasts downhill. She straightens her back a little, freewheels, spreads her elbows wide so that the breeze can creep under her shirt and cool her torso. When she arrives at Víctor's doorway, she sees her reflection in the glass, ruffles her fringe a little and, almost without thinking, slips her hand behind her and tugs at the elastic of her panties. She pushes the button on the intercom. As she waits for a reply, she slips her left hand into the neck of her blouse, runs a fingertip over her right armpit. She brings the finger to her nose and sniffs. Not too bad.

Someone answers the intercom, but all she can hear is a crackle. Eventually, she hears a tinny voice:

'Who is it?'

'Alicia.'

'Alicia who?'

Is he joking? She checks her watch. They have an appointment, today, here, now. It was arranged only yesterday, so there can't be any mistake. How many Alicias does this man know? She could give her surname: Alonso. She could say: 'Your Rehabilitation

Technician,' but she doesn't like the title. At ONCE everyone uses the initials, but 'Your RT' would sound weird. She would feel more comfortable saying 'Your guide dog.' She is still trying to think of a reply when she hears the buzzer. She pushes the door and is relieved to find there is more than enough room to leave her bike in the hall.

She notices that there is no lift. She counts six paces to the flight of three steps in the middle of the entrance hall. On her right are the letterboxes: Víctor Losa, Top Floor 2, is the last box in the row, so easy for a blind person to find. It is also so jam-packed it would be impossible to slip even a postcard into it. A bad sign: clearly Víctor has not checked his post for some time, and he doesn't have anyone to do it for him. The social worker's report mentioned he lived alone.

She smiles. Alicia's smiles involve her whole body; she raises her shoulders, clenches her stomach and her buttocks, narrows her eyes, even contracts her fingers and toes a little. She has been waiting for this moment for a year and a half. This is the first case for which she will have complete responsibility, though she has already been involved in other cases, acting as assistant to a more senior technician. Her lack of experience does not worry her. She knows she is ready for this. Before training at ONCE, she studied psychology. She is capable of putting herself in someone else's place, however dark that place might be. This she firmly believes.

She closes her eyes. During the training course, they did exercises like this. One student would take the role of the blind person, the other the role of the technician, with two others observing. She was always the best. Especially when it was her turn to play the blind person. Everyone said so. The last course was eight months ago, but she has been practising regularly since then. There is very little she doesn't know how to do without looking. She's better at being blind than most blind people. She can shower, pick out an outfit with the right combination of colours and textures, dress herself and even put on her make-up without looking. She can cook and eat with perfect poise. A lot of blind people, even those with years of experience, never get beyond microwaving ready meals and eating without even setting the table. The perfect dessert is an apple.

She walks blindly to the foot of the stairs, then turns and opens her eyes to contemplate the entrance hall one last time. Makes sure there is no obstacle she has overlooked. Soon, perhaps even tomorrow morning, Víctor Losa will be able to find his way around this hall without stumbling. Collect his post. And go outside. Conquer the world. It'll be fine, she is sure of that. It has to be fine. For Víctor, and for her.

She makes a mental note of things as she climbs the stairs. One hundred and twenty-three steps, about three feet wide from wall to banister. She is about to ring the doorbell but notices that the door is already ajar. She has only to push gently and it swings open on to the dark hallway where Víctor is waiting, leaning slightly, legs apart, arms a little outstretched. It's difficult to tell whether he is trying to greet her or block her path. Though he is wearing dark clothes, he is so thin he looks almost transparent. It is difficult to tear her eyes away from his bare white feet. Alicia tries to concentrate on his face. In her imagination, the photograph suddenly falls from the door of her fridge, tracing spirals in the air as it drops to the floor, the victim of a sudden autumn squall.

She had been expecting the stooped shoulders, the depression, the outstretched hands – pleading, open, yet tense. She had prepared herself for the anger, the stiff neck, the clenched teeth. She had imagined the resignation, the passive resistance. But never did she imagine all these things would be mixed together in the expression of this shell of a man. If she really wants to put herself in his place, she will have to multiply herself and become several different people. Or more accurately, break herself into pieces as he has. Theories she has learned come rushing back, paragraphs highlighted with different colours in her notes. The Chloden Phases, the Tuttle Stages: Trauma; Shock and Denial; Mourning and Withdrawal; Succumbing and Depression . . . These are words, not tools. They will be of no use to her.

Alicia pricks up her ears in the hope that there is someone else in the apartment. It would be good to know this man is not alone. Or at least not as terribly alone as he seems. If she were to hug him, she thinks, he would crumble in her fingers like a dead leaf. Even looking at him frightens her. What now? Should she touch him? Kiss him on the cheek as she would anyone else? There is a protocol for this first meeting, one that Alicia knows by heart. First chat a little to evaluate the needs and expectations of the patient with regard to the process of rehabilitation. The social worker's report was not forthcoming on the subject. Then, a series of simple tests to evaluate motor skills, sense of touch, direction and balance. But none of this is going to happen unless she manages to nudge time, which seems to have stood still, here in the half-light of the hallway. Do something, thinks Alicia. Or say something. Better still, get to work.

'Are you alone?'

What a pathetic question. Víctor nods but says nothing.

'Can I come in?'

'Of course,' says Víctor.

His voice sounds as though he is talking through a pipe filled with cobwebs. Even he seems shocked by the sound and clears his throat. Alicia takes three steps towards him. She talks as she walks so that her proximity will not startle Víctor. He stands there, holding one arm out for Alicia to take.

'Actually, it's better if we do it the other way round. You grab mine.' Víctor still does not move, as though he has no idea where she is, still less where to grab her. 'Here. I'm standing in front of you with my back to you. You're going to take my right arm just above the elbow with your left hand. Thumb turned out,' she adjusts his hand as she talks, 'fingers turned in. Perfect. Now we can walk.'

She takes a few steps and he moves in tow behind her. Víctor has seen blind people in the street walking like this, hanging on to a guide, but he never stopped to consider how practical the position is. He immediately feels safe. A whole world has opened at his feet where before there was only an abyss. Right now he wants to kidnap Alicia, attach himself to her and go on walking. He doesn't need her to walk around the apartment: this is something a year of bruises has managed to sort out.

As they walk down the hallway, she gives him a few instructions. He needs to squeeze her arm just enough to hold on, but not too tight. Adjust his stride to hers to maintain the distance: if he comes too close he'll trip over her heels. And if he lags behind, he'll end up pulling her back or, worse, end up walking stooped. The most important thing is that he trust her.

To Alicia, it is almost a game. She has done this a hundred times during her training. She knows how the system works. All it requires is that both parties keep their arms in the correct position at all times so that every time she changes direction, he automatically turns with her. They could go round the world like this. All that needs to happen is for Víctor to walk more naturally. And not hang on so tight. Her elbow is beginning to hurt. They all hang on tightly at first, as though fate has just thrown them a lifeline.

In spite of the huge floor-to-ceiling bookshelves that line the wall on the right side, the hallway itself is very wide, narrowing only when they come to the dresser.

'We're not going to fit through here,' Alicia announces. 'Imagine we're in the street and I need you to walk behind me. It doesn't happen very often, only when the pavement is narrow for some reason, if there's a group of people coming towards us, or someone is walking a dog, or there's scaffolding maybe. I move my arm like this,' she explains, moving her elbow behind her back, 'and you move with it so that you're right behind me. That way we take up half as much space.'

The slight shift in the position of Alicia's elbow has brought Víctor directly behind her. They move effortlessly around the dresser and continue on as though performing a piece of choreography they know by heart. A drop falls from Alicia's arm on to Víctor's hand. He moves a little closer. She does smell of sweat, but it's not unpleasant. Immediately he trips over her heels and ends up with his nose between her shoulder blades.

'You see? You forgot to keep your distance. Let's try again.'

'OK.'

A shudder runs down Alicia's back. The voice sounded too close, like heavy breathing in her ear.

They start walking again. For the first time in more than a year, Víctor feels time move with him. Even if it is backwards. Galván's voice, old and distant, echoes in his memory. This is a pack of cards. This is how you pick it up. Don't look at your hands. Don't smile. Tell me a story. Don't ask how it's done. Hold my arm. Keep your distance. Trust me. It has been years since someone gave him instructions. All he needs now is a light, a meagre spotlight set into the ceiling of his brain, a small grimy window deep in his neurons, something that would allow him to sense Alicia's face if nothing else. Or her hands.

When they come to the living room, she manoeuvres Víctor so that he is leaning against the table, takes a chair and slides it against the back of his knees, as a maître d' might in a restaurant. She needs to stall for time. She takes a step back to look at him. She feels as though she is working with two different men simultaneously. One holding her elbow with exquisite gentleness, following her instructions to the letter; the other whispering suddenly into her ear and sniffing her like a cat. She stares at him and for the first time notices something so incongruous that, in other circumstances, it would be funny: Víctor is wearing glasses. The lenses are spotless as though he conscientiously cleaned them that morning. Alicia remembers that the previous reports clearly stated that Víctor's sight had been devastated by the effects of Leber's syndrome, and he had been left with absolutely no trace of vision. What could this mean? Why would someone who is completely blind continue to wear glasses which, to judge by the thickness of the lenses, could only have been used to correct an earlier minor myopia. And how did he manage to clean them so perfectly? She continues to study his face, or more precisely, what little of it can be seen under the thick, unkempt beard, one which, over the months, has extended in every direction so that it partly covers his cheekbones, emphasising the dark purple circles under his eyes. The paleness of his skin is telling: it has been months since this man left his apartment. His face looks like a thin sheet of glass on which someone has sketched blue veins. She wishes they were two or three weeks farther on in this process. 'It's such a shame, Víctor,' she'd say, 'you used to be so good looking. Now you look like a member of the Taliban.' But at this moment she is staring at the straggly hairs on his neck, the cuts on his face, the three spots of dried blood, and she realises that Víctor tried to shave this morning. Once again she recognises the same duality: the combination of slovenliness and affectation, resignation and rebellion. She doesn't know how to deal with this man.

From her bag, she takes a notebook and wooden case.

'Are you comfortable?' she asks as she opens the box. 'To begin with, we're going to test your sense of touch. I'm going to give you a series of simple geometric shapes and you have to recognise them by touch.'

Víctor feels the first shape and says:

'A square.'

'Check to make sure all the sides are equal . . .'

'A rectangle,' Víctor corrects himself, running the tips of his thumb and forefinger around the object.

'Excellent. And this one?'

Triangle, square, semicircle, circle. He correctly identifies each one within seconds. The rhombus takes a little longer. But the deftness with which he handles the pieces is remarkable. Under such circumstances, she would expect him to frown, look at his hands, even though he cannot see anything. But Víctor's fingers seem to respond to the objects instinctively. Alicia decides the magician in him is still alive and congratulates herself. On the other hand, the way Víctor stares at her makes her uneasy. Well, stares in a manner of speaking, as he cannot actually see her. Though he seems to be trying hard to do just that.

'Now let's try indirect touch,' she says as Víctor hands back the rhombus. 'You can use your left hand to hold the shape in place on the table, but without feeling the contours. With your right, take this stick I'm giving you. That's right, like that. You have to trace the outline of the shape with the tip of the stick and tell me if you recognise it.'

Like a small child absorbed in a task, Víctor correctly identifies the first shape as a triangle.

'Rectangle,' he says, tracing the second shape. 'No, square. Rectangle. Wait a minute, rhombus.'

He drops the stick and the shape. Sighs. Tries to start again but accidentally knocks the stick off the table. He thumps the table. Alicia jots something in her notebook.

'What are you writing?'

'I'm just making a note of the excellent results we're getting.'

She is lying. She has just written: 'Not good at dealing with frustration.' She gathers up the objects, puts them in a pile in front of him and gives him a wooden block with the dimensions of each shape carved into it.

'Now I want you to help me put them away. Could you put each piece in the right place?'

Víctor works slowly, but surely. When he is finished, he pushes away the wooden case and sits in silence, as though gathering enough patience to deal with the next task. Once again, Alicia recognises a duality: an eagerness and determination to do things properly but scorn for what he has achieved. Gently, as though afraid to break Víctor's concentration, she pushes the block towards him again and asks:

'Could you tell me what shape it is?'

Víctor traces the outline with a finger. He gives a faint smile, one corner of his mouth barely moving.

'A teddy bear?'

'Excellent,' she says with exaggerated enthusiasm, like someone encouraging a child to scrawl his first letters. 'You'll notice that there are a number of holes around the edge. I want you to take this lace and thread it through the holes as if you were lacing up a shoe ...'

'You want me to tie a bow?'

'You don't have to, unless you want to earn yourself an extra point ...'

Perhaps humour will bring him out of his silence. Víctor hands her back the base, the string neatly threaded through the holes and tied in a perfectly symmetrical bow.

'Amazing. Now I'm going to give you ...'

'How long is this going to go on?'

Finally, an opening, a chink of insecurity, or maybe irritation. It doesn't matter. Next she needs to give him a shirt to see whether he is able to fold it properly. Then take out the samples she has in her bag and hand them to him one by one so that he can smell them and see whether he can guess what is inside. Alicia calmly puts the shape block in its case and places her hand on Víctor's shoulder.

'Let's leave the tests for later,' she says. 'I think maybe we should talk a bit first.'

'I'm all ears,' Víctor replies.

And he stares at the ceiling, so to speak. His face turned upward, his mouth half open. He looks as though he is merely imitating a blind man.

So Let's Talk

He has three pairs of jeans, eight pairs of white boxer shorts, eight black short-sleeved shirts and eight identical shirts with long sleeves, which he wears depending on the weather. The temperature in the apartment, day and night, is set at 23 degrees. He always gets undressed in the bathroom, next to a laundry basket into which he puts his dirty clothes. First thing every Monday someone from the launderette comes to pick them up and brings the clothes back washed and ironed in the afternoon. When the package arrives, he takes it into the bedroom and, on top of the chest of drawers, sets out the boxer shorts, the trousers, the shirts, in piles next to one another. He always puts his clothes on in the same order. Alicia, thinking she can see another opportunity, asks: what about socks? Shoes? Víctor tells her he has no need for them. What do you mean, what about when you go out? I don't go out. But . . . But, Víctor . . .

Alicia bites her tongue. They have only just started talking and she does not want to make him defensive. Besides, she doesn't know what to say. Because he's not complaining. Víctor is not saying that he can't go out, that he's afraid to try, that he wants to but doesn't know how. He is saying he doesn't go out. Full stop. He turns his face towards her again as though it is obvious that she needs to move on to the next question.

What about eating? Simple: open the fridge, take out the sliced bread, the ham wrapped in tinfoil, the cheese slices. It's not hard to work out which is which, since there's nothing else in the fridge. He makes a sandwich and eats it, standing in the kitchen. And if he's really hungry? Another sandwich. What about dinner? Another sandwich. Every day? Yes, every day. For a year. Always cold? Always cold. What about breakfast? Fruit. Grapes, when they're in season. Apples. Bananas sometimes. Nothing to heat up, nothing to wash. What if he wants a snack? Peanuts. If she's interested he drinks water. Straight from the tap. Every answer is accompanied by a telling shrug of the shoulders: this is how it is.

Alicia doesn't know what to write in her notebook. Her task is to help this man with his dark life, his dark home, his dark voice, his pale skin. But what if Víctor does not need anything? She mentally runs through the points, the advice her instructors gave her, the stories she has heard other technicians tell. Denial is common in the early stages. A lot of people refuse to accept that they have lost their sight. They constantly change the subject, postpone making decisions and learning to cope, focus on secondary problems to avoid thinking about the real problem; some even go so far as to invent other ailments which require attention. But this is not the case with Víctor. Quite the opposite; rather than refusing to accept his blindness, he seems to have embraced it as though it defines him: yes, I am blind. Yes, I deal with the consequences. Yes, I get by. This is who I am now.

She had expected to find a ruined village crippled by need and instead has found a fortress besieged by loneliness. She looks for a single crack, some weak point through which she might sneak her Trojan horse of resources. She came prepared to put herself in his place, but that place is so cramped that she can make space for herself only if she pushes and jostles. Unless she can think of the right question. Unless Víctor finds himself forced to admit that he needs her. She goes on with her questions.

The bed? In summer, nothing but a fitted sheet. In winter, a duvet. The launderette takes care of them.

Let's move on. How does he manage to do the shopping? By telephone. He doesn't even need to phone the supermarket; they phone him to confirm that his order is the same as usual. Ham, cheese, bread. Fruit, whatever they've got. What about paying? Víctor tells her to go into the hall and look in the dresser drawer. Alicia opens it and quickly shuts it as though there were cockroaches inside. Or the spoils from an armed robbery, because that is what it looks like. Coming back to the table she fights the urge to calculate the value of the notes she saw: thousands, maybe tens of thousands, of euros. She asks whether at least he is able to tell the notes apart and Víctor replies there's no need. If she had checked, she would have noticed that they were all fifty-euro notes. What about change? There's never any change. Whatever is left over is the tip, to cover small favours such as taking down the rubbish. Or waiting until he puts everything in the fridge and taking away the plastic bags. So, the rubbish is taken out only once a week? Of course. After all, there's not much of it. A banana skin from time to time.

The ideal blind person is one who, while waiting for ONCE to come and help, and during the first rehabilitation sessions, manages to make a little progress and, above all, is aware of the progress he makes. The technical term is 'perceived self-efficacy'. The blind person realises that he is able to make progress through effort and this generates expectations that will encourage him to go on learning. Ideally, such expectations are confined to the realms of the possible so as to avoid disappointments. It is not a matter of becoming who one was before, but of becoming someone else. Someone more or less functional. Adapted. Rehabilitated. Alicia thinks Víctor got lost somewhere along the way, like a snake that has feverishly rubbed up against reality to shed its old skin but cannot find a means to cover itself with a new one and therefore decides to hide away under a rock. If Alicia stepped out on to the terrace, if she saw Martín Losa's ant farm and learned the story behind it, she would realise that the comparison is mistaken. That she has chosen the wrong creature. That words will never take her to the dark corner where Víctor is hiding, because ants have no ears. To draw him out, she needs antennae. Antennae and a pheromone trail. And centuries of patience.

She asks him whether she can use the bathroom. It is an excuse to nose around: a neutral shower gel on the shelf, good for washing body and hair every day. A toothbrush and a tube of toothpaste on the washbasin and next to them a nail file. Perhaps his supermarket order includes a new toothbrush from time to time, because although the bristles on this one are slightly worn, it is still serviceable. A razor clogged with a few stray hairs. A roll of toilet paper on top of the cistern and, on the floor, a recently opened twenty-four-roll pack. There is no hand towel, but there is a bath towel, hanging from the shower screen. Alicia goes over, brings it close to her face. It smells clean. Hardly surprising; today is Tuesday, the launderette delivered yesterday. Her nose still pressed against the damp cotton, she closes her eyes and pictures Víctor. She sees him naked, his skin chalk pale, the water beading on it. Skinny as a rail. She sees him turn off the tap, take down the towel and dry himself, walk naked and barefoot back to his bedroom, fingertips running along the walls. Alicia trembles. She had to see this ghost to understand completely.

She goes back and finds him exactly as she left him. She asks him something, anything that will make him go on talking, but she has stopped paying attention, stopped taking notes. He is sitting so close that she can smell his breath and, taking advantage of the fact that he is blind, even count the hairs sprouting from his ears. She need only stretch out her hand and she could follow the dark blue tracery of the vein beneath the pale skin of his forearm. She could feel his bones, the gaunt flesh, but not even this would chase away the thought that she is staring at a ghost: Víctor Losa, the finest magician in the world, the man who likes his women 'al dente', is dead. What remains, what is here before her very eyes, is the last vestige of his spirit, the remnants of a time long gone. A ghost. And the worst thing is, he knows it.

'I think we'll leave it there for today,' she says suddenly. Not that she is giving up. She needs a little distance, needs to go home and go over her notes, to prepare a strategy. 'We're both exhausted. I'll come at the same time tomorrow, if that's OK with you,' she says, getting to her feet. 'I'll programme my number into your phone just in case.'

The phone is a Telefónica DOMOuno with large, well-spaced keys and additional buttons for memory and redial functions. It's perfect. Alicia knows these things. She knows which phone models suit blind people. And when they're not suitable, she knows how to customise them using DYMO labels. Shit, she knows a lot. She has studied everything there is to know about helping blind people improve their quality of life. It's her job. But nobody ever said anything to her about ghosts.

She enters her home phone number. Thinks perhaps it would have been better to leave her mobile number, then dismisses the idea. That time will come and she's in no hurry to become too intimate. This is something else the training courses do not deal with: in less than two hours she has exchanged sweat with this stranger, she bears the imprint of his fingers on her elbow, has felt the warm haze of his voice, has even seen him walking naked, barefoot, wet from the shower. Admittedly, this happened only in her imagination, but ... can there be anything more intimate than imagination?

'If you need me, all you have to do is press "1" and hold,' she tells him. She slings her bag over her shoulder. 'In any case, one of these days, maybe even tomorrow morning, I'll show you how to dial any number you like. It's easy.'

Víctor has his back to her. He hasn't moved. Alicia wants to leave.

'Víctor,' she calls, her voice weak and exhausted. 'I'd like you to show me to the door.'

He hasn't forgotten this lesson and matches his steps exactly to hers, but this time, rather than gripping her elbow, his hand barely grazes it, as though intent on confirming her suspicion that he is a phantasmagoria. The ultimate question, the one that might finally break down Víctor's defences, the wall he has built around himself, occurs to her as she opens the door.

'And what happens when the money runs out?'

He doesn't answer. Leaning against the door frame, ready to close the door as soon as she leaves, he shrugs his shoulders and sighs.

'Look, Víctor ...'

She knows she shouldn't push him. She does not want her words to force him to retreat even a millimetre farther into his lair. Quite the reverse, she wants to lure him out, to tempt him with something that might make him want to poke his snout outside. She tells him of genuine wonders: a French photographer who lost his sight in an accident but still managed to go on working, specialising in night-time scenes, spectacular full moons that now hang in galleries; a woman who spent months crying because she would never see her newborn son's smile again, until the baby chuckled next to her ear, a giggle so contagious she laughed and laughed, tracing the child's lips with her fingers: her rehabilitation began the following day. The last case she was involved with was that of a sous-chef whose blindness was caused by macular degeneration. He went through hell, but now is about to open his own restaurant. There are many cases. If he is prepared to come to the group sessions at ONCE, he can meet these people himself.

He shouldn't worry, she tells him. He has all the time in the world. Nobody is expecting miracles, or even radical changes. Just a series of small steps. A gradual evolution.

She is careful not to reproach him. On the contrary, she congratulates him on the extraordinary progress he has managed to make with no help. Tells him he deserves a lot of credit for being able to feed and dress himself. It's an important step. In fact ... Alicia pauses as though she needs to catch her breath, because she has been talking non-stop for several minutes now. She makes the most of this short silence to consider him again. Even if he genuinely wants to carry on as he is, never going out, never speaking to anyone, there are still things she can help him with. She decides not to mention the deplorable state of his beard, or his toenails, which are so long they would pose a serious problem if Víctor did decide to put on his shoes. But there are lots of things, she tells him, there's a whole world within his grasp. Damn it, there's pretty much nothing he can't do if he is prepared to accept her help. That's what she's here for, to put herself in his place, to grope with him through the darkness and guide him back to the light. At this point Alicia recites a long list of of activities, including going to the cinema, to the beach, the theatre, to restaurants, hobbies of every kind, holidays, social events. But Víctor's posture is telling: he is still standing with one hand on the door as though waiting for a pause so he can say goodbye and close it. It is obvious that, if he seems attentive, if he appears to be listening to her, it is only out of politeness, the way he might put up with some idiot selling encyclopaedias. Alicia realises this and hurries on, she knows she doesn't have much time.

'It's up to you,' she sums up. 'But you have only two options. You can either take control of your life, or you can hole up here and disappear from the world, like Houdini.'

What a brilliant example. She feels proud of herself.

'You're right.' Víctor cuts her short. 'We're both exhausted.'

And he gently closes the door. Alicia starts down the stairs, but after only a few steps, she gives in to the weakness in her legs and sits down. She needs a few minutes to take stock. Her blouse is soaked with sweat. She wraps her arms around herself as though she might console herself with a hug. She feels awkward. If she were not sitting alone in the dark, she would swear there was someone behind her.

If she felt 'al dente' when she arrived, she is definitely overcooked by now. She finds it difficult to pinpoint why she feels she has failed. After all, for a first day, she could say that Victor has made some progress. And she did not even have to fight. Perhaps that is the problem. She arrived armed for battle, with a whole army of gambits ready to be deployed, ready to lay siege to Victor's fortress, only to find the city burned to the ground and the sole surviving inhabitant, a ghost, entrenched behind a wall.

She sighs, grabs the banister and hauls herself to her feet, then glances back up the stairs and says: 'That bastard isn't going to make it easy for me.' She hears a slight crack, as though Victor has been standing behind the door all this time and has only now decided to close it. Alicia pictures him, his ear pressed to the door, motionless, silent. Sniffing the air. By the time she gets down to the entrance, she barely has the strength to lug her bicycle out through the front door. Her lips pressed tight, she shakes her head as she leaves.

Upstairs, Víctor rushes down the hall with astonishing speed, gets to the telephone, lifts the receiver and presses '1'.

The Wellspring

Alicia stands in front of the bookshelf, head tilted to one side so she can read the spines. The idea of going back through her university books, reading up on theory, is something she can hardly bring herself to think about right now. But her indignation is stronger than her weariness. She cannot be so naive. She cannot show up at Víctor's apartment tomorrow the way she did today, with nothing to protect her but her conviction that everything will turn out for the best. She needs to be better prepared. Someone, somewhere, must have described the place where this man is holed up, and how to reach him. Because no man is an island. And anyone who tries to be is forgetting that, at best, he is part of an archipelago. There is an established itinerary for reaching all the places men will hide. If Alicia did not believe that, she would give up her job today.

The blinking of the answering machine catches her attention. She's been out of the house for only two hours and has six missed calls. Strange. She sits down, presses play and immediately recognises Víctor's voice.

'Look ... *[A sigh, a long pause then, in a single breath]* Look, Alicia. I'm not stupid, I know everyone says "look" when they mean "listen", but let's see if you get this. I don't like it when you say "look, Víctor". I don't know, it's like shaking the stump of a one-armed man. It's in poor taste, if you want to know the truth. But that's not why I'm calling you. I'm phoning to ask you not to make predictions. It's a long story and, since you're so keen for us to sit down and talk, maybe I'll even tell it to you one day. The thing is, I don't like predictions. It messes me up when they come true. Maybe I am a bastard, but at least I have an excuse. And all right, maybe I'm not making things easy for you. You'd know, you said it. And while we're at it [*The voice, which sounded perfectly calm in spite of the complaints, breaks here*], while we're at it, I'd like you to know that I don't give a fuck about all the smiling babies in the world . . . or about full moons, especially full moons, because I had a couple in my eyes, full moons blinded me, and beaches, I don't care about beaches, sunsets and sea horizons. I can't remember what else you mentioned, but it doesn't matter, because I don't give a toss about all that picture-postcard bullshit. Don't get me wrong, I'm really glad about all the progress your poor little blind people have made, honestly. I'm really happy for them. [*A beep indicates that the minute available for a message has elapsed. Alicia slumps back against the chair. She now suspects all six calls are from Víctor, whose voice rings out again*] Like I was saying, I'm happy for them. I hope your photographer gets to show his moon shots in every gallery on earth and your chef manages to prepare the menu every day without cutting off his fingers, but the truth is I just don't give a shit. With all due respect, of course. There you are telling me about all the things I can do, when the only thing I want to do is see. I don't know if you get the distinction, Alicia. *See*, Alicia. Ask your little chef to open a pod of fresh peas. Ask him, and watch his face as he's doing it. I'm sure he's capable of doing it, and of shelling the peas. I'm sure he could boil them or fry them or do whatever it is you've taught him to do. But what I want to do is see them. I assume you've shelled peas at some point in your life. There they are, inside, protected, then suddenly, along you come and crack, you squeeze the pod with your fingers and the peas exist. It's a fucking miracle! A miracle of light, which until that very moment had never entered that place, but the moment your fingers split the pod, the light pours in and the peas start to quiver if you move your hand, even a little, they tremble as though their lives depend on the filament on which they are suspended, a minuscule thread almost impossible to see, but you can see it, you can fucking see it . . . [*These last words are rushed, as though Víctor has been counting the seconds, and doesn't want the beep to cut him off in mid-sentence*] Where was I? Oh yes, peas. And eyes. Well, the brain actually. The neurologist explained the whole thing to me. It's the brain that actually sees the light, sees the peas, sees the quivering. The only problem is that in the middle there's a nerve, get it? Looking is a nervous tic. And it's one I've lost. *[A few seconds of silence, three deep breaths as though Víctor is doing his utmost not to lose control]* Anyway. Let me give you another example of the verb to see. You're in a car, and you see a hand. There's a man on the pavement, he has his back to you, he's talking on the telephone, you rush past and all you see is the hand holding his mobile phone to his ear. What am I saying? Not even the whole hand, you see his knuckles and you keep on driving and you imagine the hand lighting a cigarette and days later or years later, that hand is beating eggs to make an omelette in your imagination, or in your brain to be precise, it points to tell you where to look or holds a gun and aims it at you, or takes a thorn out of your back, because it's your lover's hand, or your enemy's hand, light, light made it possible for it to exist in your brain with absolute freedom. Your gaze, Alicia. A completely involuntary action that illuminates life. When that doesn't happen, when an atrophied nerve turns out that light, all you have are memories. Nostalgia, which kills imagination. Oh, don't tell me, things can evolve. One little step, then another. Everyone loves to think that we evolve towards a perfect state. But that's bullshit. What we call evolution is decay. Latin decayed to become Spanish which decayed to become the thing we speak today, which doesn't even have a name. Things that are perfect are born perfect, they don't need to evolve. Like a spoon. *[Another beep. Message number four. Alicia is counting them]* Just so you know, I don't care that I get cut off every minute. Make yourself comfortable, because what I've got to say to you I'm going to say however many messages it takes. You tell me I shouldn't give up, I should be strong, I should face adversity head on, all that kind of thing. I get the impression you're keen on films. Speaking of films, I suggest you get a DVD of *To Have and Have Not*. You're probably too young to have seen it. Put it on, then close your eyes. When Lauren Bacall asks "Anybody got a match?" open them and watch. And think about ... Don't bother, it doesn't matter. You won't get it. You know what I really miss? Sorry for changing the subject but anyway ... You know what I would pay anything to see again? A shadow. A fucking shadow! I bet that didn't occur to you, did it? It's the light you don't see. And the brain understands that! Straight off! In a millionth of a second. That stretch of wall you can't see, your brain immediately tells you, that patch of negative light, that dark area in the shape of a tree when you can't see a tree anywhere, means that the wall is here and the light is coming from behind it, it means the tree is there too. All that from a shadow! *[Penultimate beep. Alicia is sitting rigid in her chair. If Víctor was trying to insult her, he's made a mistake. Because she is going to rewind this tape and play it over and over, listen to it until the words start to sketch out the map she has been searching for. Right now, she knows where she needs to start: enthusiasm. She has to find some way of focusing all the power, the energy that Víctor is spitting and sputtering into his calls and turn it to his advantage]* OK, that's it. There's just one more thing. Don't ever ask me to have faith again. Faith in you, faith in rehabilitation. Jesus Christ, what an awful word. Just hearing it pisses me off. Faith is people believing without having seen. I've seen lots of things and I believe in them. And don't tell me there's hope. Hope takes up a lot of space and my world is small and fragile. It's pathetic and bitter. It's wretched, if you prefer. I just need you to know that, since you're so determined to be a part of it. A world so narrow that the minute you try to turn round you trip over something. Oh, and if you ever say you only want to put yourself in my place again, I'll staple your eyelids shut. That is my place. *[Abruptly the line goes dead and Alicia, surprised that Víctor didn't use up the whole minute, gets up and goes over to the machine. As she does so, there is another beep and she hears the same voice, much calmer now]* I forgot one thing. Never mention Houdini again. Or if you have to, do your homework first. Houdini didn't disappear. I'm sure you've heard all the stories. Drowned in the Hudson river, suffocated in a trunk ... None of that, please. He was crude, flashy, always boasting about how he could take a punch to the stomach. And his abs must have been strong because, after every show, he'd try to get members of the audience to punch him, made a fortune on bets that no one could knock him down. But one day, he was caught unawares. It was after a performance, people were having drinks in the dressing room and some bastard punched him right in the stomach when he wasn't expecting it. Bye, bye, Houdini. Oh, and I'm sorry for that thing about stapling your eyes shut. I know it sounded aggressive. Maybe your prediction is coming true after all. Anyway, I'm sorry. See you tomorrow.'

The silence that follows is a relief, like someone shutting off an engine. Well, at least now she knows what she's up against. Don't say this, don't mention that ... She's clearly landed herself a grouch. History is full of whining blind people, some of them famous. It's one of the many possible reactions described by psychologists. What can you do?

All her efforts to come up with a theory, an inference from her notes, something that might help her deal with this situation, now crystallize in one name: Frijda. N. H. Frijda. She can't remember what the initials stand for. She goes back and stands in front of her books, racking her brains for the title of a book she hasn't read since she was at university. It was *The Laws of Emotion* or something like that. And there was a chapter in it called 'The law of hedonic asymmetry'. A horrible phrase, she thinks. Alicia smiles. She is trying to remember Frijda's exact words. 'Pleasure is always contingent upon change and disappears with continuous satisfaction. Pain may persist under persisting adverse conditions.' Something like that. She remembers how the idea fascinated her when she first read it. If the waters of perpetual happiness flowed from a wellspring, we would quickly stop drinking from it. On the other hand, we can bathe our wounds for all eternity in the fetid wellspring of pain. Time heals no wounds; it only makes them deeper, darker.

It is not much of a step forward. She can hardly show up tomorrow morning and say to Víctor: 'I know what's happening to you. You're a victim of the law of hedonic asymmetry as set out by someone named Frijda.' Now that she has witnessed his predilection for irony, she can easily imagine what he would say: 'No, dear, no. What's happening to me is that I've gone blind.' But to put a name to a thing helps a little. No matter how horrible the name. Or the thing. This is what Alicia believes.

The Gallery of Famous Blind People: I

Claude Monet is one of the most prominent figures in the Gallery of Famous Blind People; a small, exclusive gallery in the afterlife to which, down the centuries, a number of great men have been admitted to receive eternal restitution for their blindness. It hardly matters in which period they lived, because here, a place that exists only in Alicia's mind, everyone wears timeless clothing and recounts, without the least trace of bitterness, the details of their agonies in this world.

However, although no one ever mentions it, Monet's presence here makes many of them uneasy. First and foremost because of his habit (unconscious, it must be said in his defence) of squinting as he paints, as though he still can't see properly, or is irritated by the lighting conditions. No one here likes to be reminded that they are blind, or rather that they used to be. Because one of the advantages of the Gallery of Famous Blind People is that, simply by stepping inside, a person automatically recovers his sight. This, incidentally, leads to a number of people comparing grievances, a case in point being Ella Fitzgerald, who goes around in a wheel-chair, legs amputated, bitching (not unreasonably): 'All things considered, I'd rather they'd left me blind and given me back my legs. Or cured my diabetes, since that's what caused the problem in the first place.'

This tic Monet has of constantly squinting irritates a lot of people. There is abundant light in the gallery. This is why Ray Charles always wears his sunglasses. Furthermore, there's always more than one volunteer who would be happy to remind Monet that, technically, he doesn't qualify as being blind. Or at least not completely blind. The artist grumpily defends himself: 'So you're saying three operations aren't enough for you? Well?' And he goes on painting. If they really think he doesn't belong here, let them throw him out. Maybe he wasn't completely blind but there is more than enough proof of the catastrophic effects the loss of sight had on his life. In letters to friends, he always reserved a paragraph to describe his constant dread that he would no longer be able to paint. And he finds it funny that it is always the musicians who complain about whether or not he should be allowed in. What do they know? They can bitch all they like – their blindness didn't do them any harm. On the contrary, a lot of them wouldn't even have become musicians if it weren't for their parents desperately trying to compensate for their blindness by giving them special favours. Private music teachers, for example. Now if Beethoven wanted to chuck him out, or criticise him, that might be different. But ... blind musicians? They should get on with their playing and leave him in peace. He has got more right to be in this gallery than any of them: you can dictate a score, you can't dictate a painting.

Besides, if he's grumbling it's because he always was a whiner. Nobody really wants to throw him out. Monet devoted the greater part of his life to cultivating opium because in his day it was thought to be a cure for cataracts. As we've already pointed out, no one here suffers from cataracts or any other visual impairment. But a little opium never goes amiss when certain memories start to nag. Or old vices, as with good old Ray Charles. Or when Bach starts to bore them rigid with his endless fugues and counter-fugues. Will Víctor have enough of a sense of humour to understand this story?

Opening and Closing

'And now I want you all to imagine your body is full of hinges.' Although Alicia has been taking biodance classes with Viviana Szpunberg for more than four years, she is still surprised by the grating tone of her deep voice, as though her vocal cords were intended to be played with a bow. 'Forget everything we've talked about and imagine that your body is full of hinges. Today we're going to work on the concept of opening and closing. With the whole body. The whole body, remember.'

It all started with a leaflet picked up in a bar late at night, and even now she doesn't know why she chose biodance rather than ju-jitsu, Pilates, belly-dancing or kundalini yoga. Curiosity, maybe. And the desire to do something with her body. Express herself. At the beginning of each session, they all sit on the floor in the lotus position and tell each other how their week has been. Just twenty minutes; nothing too detailed. Just something to ease their burden. Alicia manages not to say anything that might compromise her too much and listens carefully to what everyone else says, though without ever becoming too involved. Then Viviana puts on some music and gives instructions: today, we are going to explore the limits of our body; today, the sense of balance; today, the ability to go beyond; today, the need for the other. That kind of thing. It's not dancing exactly, since everyone does whatever they like, they're not even expected to move to the rhythm of the music. All Viviana asks for is total commitment. The first year, Alicia felt so self-conscious that for several sessions she barely moved at all, apart from rocking slightly so no one could accuse her of not taking part. She watched Viviana, expecting her to give instructions, something that would tell her exactly what she should do. As though some invisible jury – or one that was ever present in the watchful eyes of Viviana, someone Alicia still did not know how to refer to: teacher, therapist, guru – were judging her. It's not a dance competition, Viviana used to say. Do whatever you feel, it doesn't matter if it's awkward, just move, allow your bodies to speak. Getting used to it, and a couple of private conversations with Viviana, put an end to her awkwardness. The second year was a liberation. She participated in every session with genuine passion; pouring out – in addition to pints of sweat – everything about her day-to-day existence that words could not express. From that moment, she turned biodance into a more constructive, more complete experience. Now, the very idea of missing a session is unthinkable. That is not to say that every Tuesday goes perfectly. Sometimes her body has only hateful things to express, but that doesn't matter. It's all part of the therapy. And when it does happen, she has no problem throwing herself against a wall or crawling across the floor like a black beetle, to the astonishment of the neophytes who join every year.

Today she tells everyone that she's happy because she has her first blind person. She doesn't need to say any more. They know she has been waiting for months. She doesn't talk about the problems. When they've finished speaking, Viviana asks them to get to their feet and puts on some music. The music is always a single melody repeated for the whole session. It's part of the ritual. On the third or fourth repeat, Alicia forgets the music, or rather, she becomes a part of it, so much so that the melody and rhythm become part of her body, tracing a spiral around her and protecting her from the gaze of others, from embarrassment. Today, the music is a playful clarinet. Jewish music, thinks Alicia. She remembers having heard melodies like this in a film, a troupe of musicians, maybe playing at a wedding. Or maybe they were Gypsies. Whatever, it seems more appropriate to a march than a dance: it's a two-step, almost a hymn.

Alicia starts with the obvious, the hands. Open and close, she splays her fingers wide as though she wants to project them, detach them from herself. Then she closes them tightly, not caring that her nails are digging into her palms. Little by little, she brings other parts of her body into play. She spreads her shoulders, slowly stretching her arms behind her until her hands touch behind her back, then folds them back across her chest, curling her torso into a ball. This is just a warm-up. She has not even begun. She is still thinking about what she is going to do. Viviana calls this self-awareness. Don't think. We're not here to think, she tells them, we're here to express ourselves. Suddenly, she thinks of her toes; these can be opened and closed too, though as she does this, it becomes difficult to maintain her balance as she wheels around the room. She always spins, sometimes simply on the spot, sometimes hugging the walls, sometimes circling the other dancers. It is part of the process that allows her to put everything out of her mind, the music, time, the world. Now she is opening and closing her navel without even realising it, her abdominal muscles contracting and relaxing as she breathes deeply. And suddenly she realises that air is the key that can open and close all the doors in her body; she opens her lungs, really opens them, and an explosion of air comes from her mouth, which has also just opened and closed, because now every muscle in her body seems to be following some predetermined pattern, though clearly not one she has made. She can open and close several parts of her body simultaneously. Her attempt to bend her knees and ankles at the same time almost sends her sprawling to the floor, but she catches herself in time because the dance, the spiral she is tracing, saves her. She feels like an astronaut, spinning in zero gravity, and at precisely that moment, she makes her first leap. Though seen from without, jumping might not seem like opening and closing; every time Alicia launches herself into the air, hurling herself forward, she feels her whole life opening up only to close around her again as the soles of her feet strike the floor. By the fourth leap, she feels as though some mysterious hand is compelling her to fly, and although it is only a fleeting impression, she jumps so wildly that she has time to open and close every possible muscle before she lands again. Her groin takes the force of the blow and Alicia contracts her vagina. The vagina, she thinks, I forgot about the vagina. She goes on spinning, opening and closing it continually. It's easy. Like trying to hold it in when she needs to pee. And then Viviana's voice roars over the music: 'I said your whole body, damn it. You don't think your eyes are part of your body? Alicia, you should know this better than anyone.' She opens them wide, so her face looks almost comical, like an actress in a silent film. At this moment, she cannot help but think of Víctor, the ghost of Víctor, with his eyes open on nothing, and the dance is over. She stops, frozen in the middle of the room. The magic has melted away. Besides, she really needs to pee now. It doesn't matter: the session is almost over. They'll do a few relaxation exercises and then everyone will head home. No one talks. They should think about the meaning of everything they've done, Viviana always says to them, telling them to take deep breaths. And everything they didn't do. Especially the things they didn't do.

As they are leaving, she gives each of them a piece of paper with the details of today's music: *Lustige Hasidim*, Alicia reads. Margot Leverett and the Klezmer Mountain Boys. She might buy this one. Sometimes, Viviana makes a little comment: you were magnificent today, Ali. Pity about the end. Thanks, Vivi. Alicia says her good-byes and goes out into the street with the peaceful, contented weakness that comes with physical exercise. Your life is good, Alicia.

There Is Not A Place

As she starts up the hill at Mayor de Gracia, Alicia lifts her bottom off the bicycle seat so she can lean her whole weight on the pedals. She cycles with such fury that she arrives ten minutes early, though she doesn't realise this since she has not looked at her watch. Even Víctor's cheerful tone as he greets her over the intercom does nothing to mollify her. She drags her bicycle into the entrance, banging her foot against one of the pedals, then drops it with a crash and dashes up the stairs as fast as she can, still muttering to herself. When she gets to the top, she finds the door ajar, as it was yesterday, and senses Víctor's presence on the other side. She is about to push the door and walk in, but then she takes a step back and decides to have done with these ambushes once and for all. She reaches out her hand, closes the door, and rings the bell. She waits for two or three seconds, then rings again, keeping her finger on the bell until he opens the door.

'Look, Víctor,' she says almost before she sees him. 'Sorry ... Look, listen, do whatever the hell you want. I'm paid to come here to help you as best I can. Maybe I don't have much experience, but I've spent a lot of time and effort preparing for this. This is my job. It's what I do. And I'm good at it. If you don't want to carry on, fine. Call ONCE, tell them you don't want me to come any more and I'll take my act elsewhere. In the meantime ...'

'There's a problem with that ...' Víctor interrupts her. He seems different. His voice is light, delicate. 'I don't know how to use the phone, and even if I did, I'm not sure I'd be able to dial the number. But we're going to sort that out today, aren't we?'

He reaches out his hand at precisely the height of Alicia's elbow, and with his other hand, he gestures for her to come in. The

263

difference in his voice makes her heave a sigh of relief, but she does not drop her guard.

'You've been shut up in here for a year, haven't you? And I don't suppose you spend most of your time lying in bed. Every now and then you go to the kitchen or the bathroom. In fact, you've just come to the door and you obviously didn't bump into anything. So maybe, for the moment, you don't need a guide while we're in the apartment. When the day comes that you want to go out, I'll be happy to lend you my elbow. You can have my whole arm. But right now I need to know if you can walk in a straight line by yourself.'

Víctor shrugs his shoulders and walks up and down the hall. As he comes back for the third time, Alicia finds herself obliged to correct him.

'Without touching the wall.'

'Am I touching it?'

'With your right hand. Obviously if you need to touch it, the most logical thing would be to put your arm out in front of you. That way you won't bump into anything. For example, you'll notice the dresser before you reach it. Bring your fingers together,' she tells him as Víctor keeps walking. 'Perfect. And you can bend them a little. You don't need to touch the wall with your whole hand. The back of your little finger is enough. It's the one part of your hand where it doesn't matter too much if you prick it or burn it.'

When he gets to the end of the hallway, she asks him to turn around and walk back, this time without using his hands. After three steps, his right shoulder grazes the wall. Without saying anything, Alicia puts her hand on the small of his back and pushes gently to centre him. Víctor takes six steps with apparent confidence, walking so quickly that Alicia has to intervene so he won't smash his face against the wall. He stands motionless and sighs, then waves his hands around. He needs to touch something.

'It's all right,' she reassures him. She would like to stroke his back, to soothe him. 'It might seem easy, but no one can walk in a straight line with their eyes closed. We have an image of our body that is symmetrical, one that doesn't conform to reality,' she explains. For the first time she feels comfortable. She could recite whole pages about balance and orientation from her notes. 'We all have one leg shorter than the other, or we favour one foot, or tilt one hip without realising it. It's something we generally don't notice because our sight corrects the imbalance. You have a tendency to veer to the right. It's important that you know that and learn to correct it.'

They practise for twenty minutes, until Víctor finally manages to negotiate the length of the hallway without swerving. When he gets to the end, he turns around, takes a couple of seconds to ensure he is centred, then runs to the other end of the hall where Alicia is waiting, biting her lip so as not to shout out a warning when his hip comes within an inch of the dresser. She has to stop his body with her own. Something very much like an embrace.

'You're crazy,' she says.

'I call it the kamikaze method.'

'Well, I call it stupid, but I'm not going to tell you not to do it. After all, it's your head that you're going to split open. In any case, I can teach you to protect yourself.'

'From what?'

'From everything. From bumping into things. And don't tell me you don't need me to. Right now, I decide what you need and what you don't. Raise your left hand. Now bend your elbow as though you want to grab your right shoulder.'

Rhythm, thinks Alicia. That's what is missing. If yesterday it felt as though she had stepped into a cage where time stood still, today everything seems to be passing in a flash. She gives orders and he complies. Does his utmost to comply. Manages to do so with unexpected skill. He is prepared to do each task as many times as necessary. It works.

'Don't stick your elbow out so far. And move your hand away from your shoulder slightly.' She continues to give instructions. 'Palm turned out. Stretch out your fingers and bring them together. That's it. Good, now relax your hand a little. Perfect. Now the other arm. Bring your right hand over to your left thigh, but don't actually touch it. The idea is that your arms create a sort of protective barrier. The left arm protects your top half, the right arm protects the bottom.'

'And I look like I'm doing karate.'

'Not exactly,' Alicia says, though she cannot suppress a smile. 'More like a footballer in the wall when someone is about to take a free kick.'

Or a blind person who doesn't even know what he's protecting himself from, she thinks.

'And what use is all this?'

Carefully, making sure she makes no sound, Alicia picks up a chair and sets it between them.

'Come towards me slowly,' she says. At his second step, Víctor bumps into the chair. 'I'll let you work out for yourself where that would have hit you if you hadn't had your arms in front of you. Depending on where you are, you might need to bring your left hand up to protect your face. But we'll come to that later.'

We'll come to that. Perhaps deciding when the time is right for something is the most important aspect of her profession. Víctor's attitude makes it seem as though he could be taken out into the world right now. But she only has to look at him to see how the awkward gestures he has just learned barely protect him from the air to realise it is too soon. To stumble at this point, to fall or take a painful knock, might have drastic consequences for the whole process. She has managed to run a thread right into his lair, now she has slowly to draw Víctor out. But the thread is made of flimsy materials: trust, desire, panic, need. With the slightest jolt, it could snap.

Víctor is still standing with his arms in the defensive position.

'You can put your arms down now,' she says. 'Relax. Now, for this next bit, we'll need more space.'

Quickly, fearful that this interruption might break the spell, she pushes the dining table and chairs into one corner of the living room and the sofa into another. Then she guides Víctor to the centre.

'Do you know where the door to this room is?'

'There,' Víctor answers, jerking his thumb over his shoulder.

'There is not a place. It's no good to me. Is it in front of you or behind?'

'Behind me.'

'Exactly. What's in front of you?'

'The wall. Well, the bookshelves. And you.'

'That's right. I've moved the furniture. Now the table is on your right and the sofa is on your left. Turn around. I mean, turn and face the other way.' Víctor does so and stands with his back to her. 'What's in front of you?'

'My bedroom.'

'And behind?'

'You.' A long pause. 'OK, the bookshelves.'

'To your left?'

'The table, and the sofa is on my right.'

'Very good. Make a quarter-turn to your left, please. Try to turn without moving from that spot. Where's the door to your bedroom?'

'There. Sorry, I mean to my right.'

Víctor answers confidently, without stopping to think, though he seems puzzled, as though he thinks this is a waste of time. Alicia knows that it is still too soon, that she will have to confuse him a little more before his sense of direction deserts him. For fifteen minutes, she has him spin around in the middle of the room like a top, but every time he is able to identify correctly the cardinal points of his apartment.

'Now I need you to pay careful attention,' she tells him. 'I've taken a pen from the dresser. I'm going to drop it on the floor and I want you to tell me where it lands. Or rather, I want you indicate where you think it's landed.'

'No.'

'What?' This is the first time he has refused. Maybe he didn't hear her correctly.

'Not that pen, no. You can use anything else.'

'Oh . . .' Alicia stares at the Parker pen. 'I'm sorry. I didn't realise it was so valuable.'

'It was my father's.'

Rhythm, Alicia, don't stop now. No questions.

'OK. We'll use a coin.'

She takes one from her pocket and throws it a few inches in front of Víctor. He stands for a moment, as though sniffing the air, then points to the right place. Alicia goes over and, as she bends down to pick it up, she cannot help but stare at Víctor's toenails again. The day she teaches him to cut them, or rather the day she gives him a reason to want to cut them, will be a major victory. Maybe by that point it won't be a problem, asking him what happened to his father, or why he's so alone. Maybe she will tell him stories about the Gallery of Famous Blind People so they can laugh together. But right now she has a different battle to fight.

At every attempt, Víctor gets it right. He even draws in his neck when she tosses the coin over his head so it will land behind him. As though the air anticipated its route and alerted him to dodge it. Alicia decides to vary the test. Now, Víctor has not only to identify where the coin has landed, but also to bend down and try to pick it up. Although he still gets it right most of the time, once in a while his fingers brush the floor an inch or two from the coin without finding it. So Alicia teaches him to feel for things. There is even a specific technique for this which entails squatting down, reaching out and feeling, first around the feet, working from the outside in first, and then the other way, then working in a line parallel to the first, over and back, first with the knuckles, then with the fingertips, first horizontally, then vertically, reaching out, picking up, fumbling, stretching, bending. As Alicia instructs him, Víctor repeats the movements over and over, and if he shows the least sign of getting tired, she encourages him: 'Imagine it's a knife or a thumbtack,' she says. 'You can't just leave it there, especially since you never wear shoes.' Víctor concentrates. He is enjoying this. And not simply because he is obviously making progress, not because each time it is easier for him to find the coin – who cares about the coin? – but because in the thirty minutes he has spent pawing the floor, he has ceased to be a ghost. He fumbles, gropes, picks up, notes the dust, feels his calves cramp from constantly getting up and bending down, notices the sweat beginning to pool at the back of his neck, and he realises that his skin is drawing a frontier between his body and the void. He is here, the floor is there. Alicia is right: there is not a place. It is a void, it is nothingness. The coin is nothing and it falls on to the nothingness that is the floor with a sound that means nothing, but Víctor is here and he is something: he is the man who is searching, the blind man who feels around, finds the coin.

Though she hasn't forgotten yesterday's session, nor Víctor's tone of voice on her answering machine, Alicia is happy. There is not a trace left of the anger she felt when she arrived. It is a reflexive, groundless happiness. And this is just the start. She looks at Victor and, though he seems more than happy to keep on practising, she senses his tiredness in the way his shoulders slump.

'Good. Congratulations,' she says to him. 'You're doing really well. As a reward, you get to sit down now.'

She sets a chair in front of the telephone and helps him to sit down.

'No, you don't need to pick up the receiver. We're not going to call anyone just yet. Put your index finger on the 1, your middle finger on the 2 and your ring finger on the 3 ...'

Victor sits, his hand hovering in the air. She can't tell whether he doesn't know which key is which or which finger. 'For God's sake,' Alicia thinks, 'he's a magician.' But she helps him. She takes his fingers and starts to position them over the keys. 'She has a very small hand,' Victor thinks. He realised yesterday that Alicia is not very tall. He only had to touch her elbow to know that. He had to bend down to whisper in her ear. Yet somehow he took it for granted that she was a big-boned woman with large hands – not fat, exactly, but thickset. He squeezes her fingers gently.

'What are you doing?'

'I'm sorry ... I didn't think ... It's just ... I realised, I don't know what you look like.'

It's classic. She has heard other technicians talk about it. Now it's time to go through the details – height, hair colour, the colour of her eyes ... Things that are useless to a blind person. Or perhaps they are useful. Alicia would prefer to go on working. She wants to push Victor to make a little more progress, to realise he is making progress. Perceived self-efficacy. Rhythm. But it's fine. It won't hurt to stop for a few minutes, to bond. After all, they will be spending a lot of time together. They have to talk about something.

'What do you think I look like?'

'Um, well, I know now that you have small hands. But the rest ...'

Alicia looks at her hands. She wouldn't say they were small.

'Tall or short?' she asks.

'Middling height. Five foot seven?'

269

'Nearly. Five foot three and a half. Hair?'

'Hmmm ... I'd say auburn.'

'Black.'

'Black black?'

'Absolutely. Black as a piece of coal.'

'And curly.'

'Well, sort of. Let's say it's wavy.'

'Short?'

'Very short. It's more practical. What else?'

'I don't know ...'

'I've got brown eyes.'

'Cinnamon brown? Honey brown?'

'I don't know, brown ...'

'And you're thirty, give or take.'

'Thirty-four.' Liar. She has just asked time to lend her five years in order to give herself an air of authority. It's ridiculous. 'Anything else you want to know?'

'Not at the moment.'

What else could he possibly ask? Do you bite your lip when you're running? Do you tilt your head when you're wandering around thinking about things? Do you ever fart in bed and stick your head under the sheet? Do you have a hidden freckle he might lick some day? What does your breath smell like when you've stuffed your face with peanuts? Because this is getting to know someone; the rest is just foolishness.

'OK. I'm going to take your fingers in my tiny little hands,' Alicia announces, 'and without lifting the receiver, we're going to put the index finger on the 1, the middle finger on the 2 ...'

Víctor lets her do the work, pretending to pay attention. Alicia touching him like this unsettles him. It's barely a touch, but his fingers feel especially sensitive, as though he has a fever or has burned himself. The skin of the fingertips is a frontier. It is where 'here' ends. *Finis terrae.*

'Come on, Víctor. One, two, three. Honestly, it's not that difficult.'

'Sorry, I wasn't listening.'

'I want you to press one, two, three.'

Víctor moves the three fingers in succession, barely lifting them from the keys.

'OK, from now on, I want you to say out loud the numbers you are pressing. One, two, three.'

'One, two, three.'

He's back. Víctor is back, he has reappeared after his sudden absence. And Alicia notes this. Rhythm.

'Move your fingers down a row: four, five, six.'

'Four, five, six.'

They go over the three rows of numbers several times. After that, they work from right to left: three, two, one. Then vertically: one, four, seven; two five, eight; three, six, nine. With no mistakes. 'He's really good at this,' Alicia thinks. 'Great, I've slipped even farther down the scale,' Víctor thinks. 'From magician to telephone operator. From pianist to typist.' But he is enjoying it. He likes being given instructions, complying with them.

'You've got it. Let's test you. You're going to dial my house. You don't need to pick up the receiver, obviously. It's just a test. I don't want any more surprises on my answering machine.'

She smiles as she says this. Víctor behaves as though he hasn't heard her, his fingers in the starting position. Alicia dictates her number and he dials it correctly. Three times. She goes on, making up numbers now. Adds international dialling codes. Víctor keys in the numbers. He doesn't want to do anything else.

'I couldn't ask for better, Víctor. Congratulations again. Not because it's difficult, but with your attitude you could learn any-thing you want.'

This is enough for today. Just as she is about to set aside the phone, Alicia notices the memory key.

'Well, there is one more thing. Do you want me to add any other numbers to your speed dial apart from mine?'

'No.'

'There's no one else you call regularly? Someone in your family? The supermarket? A friend?'

'No.'

'No' means 'No Entry'. But Alicia is not about to release her prey so easily. No man is an island. No one could be so alone. She remembers the social worker's report mentioned a teacher or

271

something. Someone who got in touch with ONCE to ask for help. Another person, another island. An archipelago.

'There has to be someone,' she insists. 'A former teacher, maybe?'

'I told you, no.'

Before he says this, he turns to face her. A year ago, he could have silenced her with a single look.

'Eight, zero, three . . .' Víctor says finally.

'Eight, zero . . .? What type of area code is that? Where did you get the number?'

'From a girl I know,' Víctor says, and goes on dictating, 'Zero, seven . . .'

Alicia keys the number into the speed dial.

'Right, it's speed dial two. Now, I really have to get going. Same time tomorrow?'

'Whatever suits you. I don't have any plans.'

'You don't have to walk me to the door. I'm happy today, Víctor. Take care.' She presses a hand against his cheek and cannot resist tugging his beard. Then she clicks her tongue and suggests: 'One of these days, we need to sort that out.'

Then she stands on tiptoe and he bends down a little to kiss her cheek. Just before they make contact, Víctor tilts his head to one side an inch or two. Their cheekbones brush against each other. Alicia's breath makes the hairs of Víctor's moustache quiver.

Light is God

He can see everything down to the last detail, note the gradual dilation of the lips, wonder at the colour of the tunnel of flesh opening before his eyes, at once strangely dark and brilliant. When he finally sticks out his tongue to lick it, he notices a slight increase in the pressure of Alicia's thighs against his ears, even feels the temperature rise slightly, thinks he can hear a whimper as he breathes in the sour-sweet emanations from her vagina.

He watches her belly, drawn in tight, tensed, ignoring Alicia's pleas for a few seconds, a spell, a word, come, come, come, seconded by the fingers buried in his hair, pulling him upward, a clear signal which in reality means come inside me, come in, come in me. And if Víctor is resisting, it is not through lack of desire, nor through a commendable wish to prolong the pleasure by waiting, but because he is fascinated by the way the downy hair stretches upward, like sunflowers at midday. Everything is so real that it cannot be true.

If Alicia can hold out a little longer, Víctor will linger over her collarbone, resist the urge to bite it, rub his beard against it and then, astonished by the lunar landscape of her nipples, will want to change position, find a way to free his hands. Perhaps he decides to sit. As he nibbles, as he strokes and kneads, as he presses, envelops, his face is pressed against Alicia's skin, eyes open, his microscopic vision attentive to the stirring of every cell, the frenetic exhalation of life through the pores. He wants her to cry, to moan, to thrust, to stretch. To swallow him whole. This is why, before he penetrates her, he hesitates, allows his penis to brush against Alicia's maddened flesh for a few seconds, as though he were preparing to bring a lamp into a grotto. To illuminate it.

Finally, he enters her. In a single thrust, sharp and slow. He enters her and then stays motionless. Only then does he draw his face away a little, just far enough so he can contemplate the weakened body of this woman, for it must be she and no other, this woman who smiles and moans, this woman who does not know what to do with her hands until she decides to bring them up to her mouth, this woman who arches her hips so she can possess him, lift him up, suspend him in the air. From here, Víctor can finally see how the light explodes, Alicia's whole body is lit from within and from that point it is not she who is the object of his onslaught, but the light itself. She understands and stops struggling, agrees to float with him, both motionless in a chemical eternity until the brightness erupts and both bodies dawn.

You can laugh now, Víctor. While you are not lingering, while you are clearing a path to the hidden sun you are about to find inside this woman, while this wild burst of laughter does not distract you from your duty, laugh all you like. If only you could see yourself. You have just found your new place in the world, your mission as an archangel. You will not drive anyone out of heaven with your bright sword. Quite the reverse, you will use it to open the gates to Eden. See how she surrenders herself? Possess her, convert her.

The light is God, Víctor. The book of Genesis is a fraud. Whoever wrote it was in too much of a hurry. That is the only possible way to explain the implausible order of the story in which a creator would fashion the earth, without form and void, as darkness was upon on the face of the deep, his spirit moving upon the face of the waters. Only afterwards did he utter the accursed phrase 'Let there be light.' Four words! Articulate, pretentious sounds condemned for all eternity to the menial task of indicating what already existed. And the narrator, not content with attributing an unfeasible power to these words, goes on to say that the light was good. Those are his exact words: 'And God saw the light, that it was good: and God divided the light from the darkness.' How? Did he test it? What kind of omnipotent God is this? The same God that later amuses himself by populating his creation, mapping out its surface over a period of six days, with rivers, mountains and deserts, with men and animals of every kind, cattle, snakes and vermin. The way your father did when he set out the train set, Víctor: tinfoil to create the river, mountains made of cork, cotton wool for the snow and a little stationmaster with a flag and a tiny whistle.

There were no pompous words. Nor even a buzzing sound. It is much simpler: the light is God and created the world because it was bored with seeing nothing. Be its apostle. Baptise this body. And cry when you awaken. Not for the dampness you feel, the wasted seed spilled on the sheets, not for the loneliness and the frustration. Not because a single goodbye kiss was enough to kindle this dream. Nor even because Alicia is not and never will be in this bed. Cry for the light you thought you saw. Wish with all your heart that you had been born blind. Those who are born blind don't dream in pictures. Shower, change the sheets, the ants are still hungry. And call Irina.

Behind the Mirror

When he wants to listen to 'If', it's easy. The CD has been in the machine for months now. His fingers have memorised the movements to press *Play* and skip forward six tracks. But, at the last moment, he decides to put on the cassette instead. He would rather listen to Saint-Saëns' Sonata for Clarinet and Piano, even though this means having to put up with all the other sounds on the tape, the soundtrack to the last minutes of Martín Losa's life. It doesn't matter. He has listened to it so often recently that his ears have grown accustomed to focusing on the music and filtering out everything else. The sound of the tweezers falling or the distant gasp of the death rattle are no more intrusive than the sound of the audience in a live performance. He has become obsessively fond of the sonata, especially the third movement, marked *Lento*. It is haunting, fluid, harmonious, strewn with pauses so timely that each note seems to herald the arrival of the next such that one need only whistle the first note and all the others fall into place. Every time he listens to it, he rewinds the tape so it will be ready the next time. Sometimes, during the day, he catches himself humming the melody, though perhaps he does not realise that these notes have taken over that place in his throat which, years ago, was occupied by 'If'. It is hardly surprising that time has replaced a lullaby with a funeral march.

He has other reasons for choosing the sonata just now. Víctor turns the volume all the way up and is grateful that the music, above the hiss and crackle of the old cassette, drowns out the screams of Alicia, who seems to have little imagination when it comes to insults, given that she has repeated 'son of a bitch', 'bastard' and 'get me out of here' seven times already. From time to time she attempts to formulate a threat: I'm going to ... I'm going to ... but she never actually completes it. Get me out of here right now. Time is another reason for choosing the sonata, because 'If' barely lasts three minutes while the various movements of the sonata run to more than twenty minutes. It's not much, but it will teach her a little lesson.

Alicia arrived this morning in a sunny mood, happy because yesterday everything went perfectly. Víctor doesn't like her displays of joy. He knows it is simply her way of seeming feisty, a means of trying to cheer him up, but it annoys him. Like her preposterous habit of speaking in the first person plural: let's do this, we have to get that, it's important that we understand I don't know what. It's an old-fashioned trick. Doctors do it, bankers and mechanics do it to try to gain their client's trust: we'll do an MRI scan; we're going to need to change this cylinder head. And he can't stand the exaggerated praise she heaps on his every achievement, however trivial, absurd and useless it might be: oh, you recognised the square; wow, you know the door is still there; bravo, you've managed to take three whole steps. He's not a fucking child. He's a blind man. All he needs is for someone to show him how to cope better. Even that's not really true; he was perfectly fine the way he was. But whatever he needs, what he doesn't need is someone giving him moral lectures.

Everything was going fine until Alicia started opening doors. They were in the hall doing echolocation exercises. That's what she called them. Apparently when objects block a sound they reflect sound waves which can be interpreted by the ear and are consequently useful to the blind. There are three doors in the hall: to the kitchen, the linen cupboard and the studio. The exercise involved trying to work out whether the doors were open or closed without touching them, from the echoes made by Alicia clapping. Until the fifth attempt, Víctor didn't notice even the slightest difference, but he forced himself to carry on trying. On the sixth attempt, he could tell that the kitchen door was open. A minor achievement which hardly warranted Alicia's effusive congratulations: Bravo, Víctor, perfect, you're getting the hang of this. Next, all the doors closed. And then Alicia opened the studio. Ever since they started the exercise, Víctor had been waiting for this moment, was dying to see how she would react when she stumbled on the little museum of wonders. He was slightly scared too, because he was beginning to get to know her and he knew that she would make the most of any excuse to talk about magic, to imply that some day he would be able to work again, that all he had to do was apply himself. That kind of bullshit.

But all Alicia said was:

'That's weird, the light is on.'

The light is on. In a blind man's house. Weird?

'Well, turn it off, then,' Víctor said.

He was starting to enjoy the exercise. He wanted to carry on working.

'No, you need to learn to do it yourself.' The same old story. 'It's easy. There are lots of ways of knowing whether a light is on or off. If there's only one switch, all you have to do is remember what position it should be in. If there's more than one, you need to get close to the bulb to see if it is giving off heat. Without touching it, obviously.'

'Maybe, but the thing is, I don't give a damn one way or the other.'

'That's what you think.'

This was the point when things started to turn sour, because what Víctor found particularly infuriating was Alicia's insistence that she knew what was best for him, what should interest him, what was important, better than he did.

'You're telling me that knowing whether the light is on or off will change my life?'

'For a start, it's wasteful.'

'Oh.'

'That drawerful of money isn't going to last for ever, Víctor. I don't know how much money you've got in there, but one day it's going to run out.'

'There's a lot more where . . .'

'I'd like to know when you last went into this room. I'm sure this light has been on for days.'

'Or months. Maybe a whole year.'

'Víctor, you could trigger a short circuit.'

'That would be tragic.'

'Enough of the sarcasm. Anyway, it's a matter of discipline. Doing things properly is a matter of discipline. And when training the visually impaired ...'

She had the nerve to talk to him about discipline. *To him*. He had spent the best years of his life on an island that floated in time, this is a deck of cards, this is how you hold the deck of cards, with your thumb you shift the top card two millimetres to the left, precisely two millimetres, bring your hand up like this, let the deck fall, this is a deck of cards, this is how you hold the deck of cards, with your thumb you ... Discipline? Give me good instructions, give me something useful, instructions that will illuminate the island that is my life, and then you'll see.

As Alicia held forth about the important points when training the visually impaired, Víctor crept up behind her and whispered in her ear. He knew she didn't like him pressing against her, but he did it anyway.

'Aren't you going to ask me what all this stuff is?'

And, just like that, Alicia's tone changed.

'I have no idea, but it's bound to be something to do with magic.'

'Bingo!'

Alicia detached herself from him so she could inspect the room, nose around a little.

'What about this?' she asked, standing next to the Proteus Cabinet.

'What?'

'This wardrobe.'

'It's a wardrobe, obviously.'

'I know that, but what do you use it for?'

'To disappear. Want to try it?'

'I'd love to.'

'Come on, then, step inside, and stand there.'

Víctor's voice took on a sombre tone as he began to explain the workings of the cabinet. It took some time before Alicia noticed. She was too busy watching the confidence with which he manipulated the locks and the hinges and thinking that his return to the stage was only a matter of time.

'The best thing would be to be able to see how it works from the inside and outside simultaneously,' Víctor said, 'but that's not possible. It's a pity: you can't be a spirit and a body at the same time. You have to choose. That's life. Go right in to the back. I'm going to close this.'

Alicia stood in the triangular space formed when the mirror was slid back against the rear of the cabinet.

'If this were a magic show, you'd hide in there before the start. I'd open the doors of the cabinet and the audience would think it was empty. Then I'd close the doors and make a little speech about a war between the spirits of the period.'

'Sorry, what period?'

'Eighteen eighty or thereabouts. It's a long story, so we'll skip over it. Anyway, I would explain to the audience that everything they saw was the product of science, that there were people capable of reorganising the molecules in the body to such an extent that they could appear and disappear at will. OK, that's a bit of an anachronism. These days, I couldn't talk about rearranging molecules, but I would use some pseudo-scientific jargon. And while I was telling them this, you would push the mirror back against the side. And then I would open the cabinet, except ... I can't seem to find the key ...'

'Víctor ...'

Alicia was suspicious. For some time now, she had thought that Víctor's voice was getting farther away, as though he were no longer standing beside the cabinet.

'I know it's around here somewhere. But obviously, since I can't see ... Even though the light is on in this room. What a waste, leaving a light on in a blind man's apartment.'

'Víctor,' Alicia forced herself to remain calm, 'that's enough now, I can't breathe.'

'Oh, no. With the amount of air in that cabinet you can breathe for hours and hours. Besides, you should be happy ...'

'Víctor ...'

'I'm performing magic. Isn't that what you wanted? Think about it, you've disappeared. I told you the cabinet was good for something. Oh, incidentally, I found out something about you. And I don't think you'll disagree.'

'What?'

Indignation was beginning to rise in Alicia's throat, but she still thought that Víctor was about to put an end to this prank.

'You're a little naive. Oh, and if you do manage to get out,' he added, 'don't forget to turn off the light.'

Alicia had beaten on the doors, but had been unable to open them. She had waited a short time before kicking, though it was barely a tap with the toe of her shoe. She was a good person and was afraid she might break the mirror.

'Hang on, woman. A little bit of discipline, please.'

Víctor had run his palms over the doors, as though saying goodbye. Then he had gone into the living room and turned on the music, loud. When she heard it, Alicia realised that he was no longer in the room and began to scream. A pity the third movement lasted only six and a half minutes, even though Stoltzman's clarinet revelled in its slowness. The fourth movement began, *allegro*. It sounds like a machine gun. Another six minutes. Actually, a little less.

He is thinking about rewinding when he gets to the end and playing it straight through again. Forty-one minutes of music. It's not much. He has been imprisoned in this blindness for a year and he hasn't insulted anyone. Alicia wants to put herself in his place: so let her. It's a question of discipline.

Turn down the music, Víctor. Don't be a shit. Go to the studio and take care of that poor girl. Let her out of the cabinet, there are no such things as spirits. She won't hit you when you set her free. You know a bit about her now; she'll be offended, but she has too much dignity. She is not going to reward you with a hysterical fit. Besides, her need to redeem you is too strong. Anyone else would leave your apartment intent on revenge. Not her. She'll go back to her place and go over the whole thing in her head, trying to work out how to turn off the wellspring of your pain once and for all. This battle is not between you and her, it is between the two of you and your blindness. She knows that the only way she can win is if you win. But you should prepare yourself for tomorrow. Because tomorrow she will make you sweat like the bastard you are.

Free Bar

Viviana hands her a checklist of Bach Flower Remedies and a felt-tip pen, offers her a seat and, before withdrawing, advises her to be led by her intuition. Alicia immediately crosses out the first five symptoms grouped under the heading 'Fear', and moves on. The first symptom under the category 'Uncertainty' does not seem appropriate either. The opposite would be more likely. 'Seeks advice and confirmation in others' does not describe Víctor's attitude as he seems to have decided that since he cannot see them, other people have ceased to exist. Or are simply an annoyance. She does, however, tick the box by the next four symptoms listed in this group: 'inability to choose between alternatives', 'hopelessness and despair', 'easily discouraged after a setback' and 'uncertainty over one's direction in life'. The third category, 'Lack of Interest in Present Circumstances', is the one that really forces her to think, because the answers seem ambiguous, even contradictory. She rules out the olive flower because it is prescribed for lack of energy. Víctor does not need energy. He needs to have his energy channelled towards an appropriate goal. Channelled – she's starting to talk like Vivi.

Clematis is no use either, because although it is used to treat 'retreating into one's own world', a symptom that clearly afflicts Víctor, it is also used for those who are 'waiting for better times'. Víctor is not waiting; he refuses to see or admit that better times might exist. She does, however, put an X in the box next to honeysuckle: 'living in the past', although she would have rephrased it 'refusing to accept the present'. She draws a circle around the X, then underlines it. White chestnut gets an X too: 'persistent thoughts one can't get out of one's mind'. She crosses out mustard, because it would be unfair to say he was suffering from 'deep depression with no known cause'. She has to concede that the cause of his depression is obvious.

When she reads the heading for the next category, 'Solitude', she suspects she will have to tick all the options. But, having read the list several times, she eventually draws a line through the whole category for the simple reason that the symptoms are too abstract. The following group is called 'Hypersensitivity to the Influence of External Ideas'. Alicia looks up from the checklist and is about to comment to Viviana that this Dr Bach must have been imagining Víctor when he compiled the list, but she doesn't want to break her concentration. Instead she marks a large X next to the first symptom in the group, 'resistant to change and outside influences'. According to the checklist, this can be treated with flower of walnut. Víctor would probably need to swallow the whole tree. She goes on reading, underlining all of the symptoms in the group headed: 'Discouragement or Despair'. She is not longer ticking the boxes because as she goes on it becomes increasingly difficult to concentrate. Besides, Viviana has already explained to her that she should whittle the list down to two or three basic symptoms. Two or three? That's going to be difficult. Luckily, the last category is called 'Over-Concern for the Welfare of Others'. She doesn't even bother crossing it out.

She heaves a sigh and rearranges the three pages as though she has no choice but to shuffle them and trust to chance. Viviana glances over her shoulder.

'That bad, is it?'

Alicia shrugs.

'There're too many there. You'd need a cocktail shaker.'

'It's just that . . .'

Alicia rereads the list quickly. Not only is she confident of every X, she almost feels inclined to include a couple of the symptoms she dismissed earlier. Viviana, standing behind her, massages her shoulders gently.

'Hey . . . Why don't we just give him a dose of arsenic?' But Alicia is in no mood for jokes.

'OK, don't worry. Let's start by trying to cut the list in half, then in half again, until we're left with three symptoms. I'll put on some music – you might find it helps.'

'I know this,' Alicia exclaims as soon as she hears the first notes of the violin, '"Forgetfulness", by Piazzolla.'

'"Oblivion", Ali, it's called "Oblivion".'

Viviana played it a year ago and Alicia had whirled and whirled around the floor so much that she even forgot about herself. To the extent that Vivi had had to come over and whisper that the session had finished five minutes ago and everyone else was waiting to do the relaxation exercises. Alicia had immediately gone out and bought the CD, and for months she did not listen to anything else.

Now she and Viviana score the symptoms she has ticked from one to ten and dismiss anything that scores less than eight. Then they divide the symptoms into three groups – A, B and C – according to importance. In the first group there are three flowers: honeysuckle for 'living in the past'; wild oat for 'uncertainty over one's direction in life' and walnut for 'resistant to change and outside influences'.

'Let's try these three for a couple of months and leave the rest till later,' Viviana says. She opens the drawer containing the thirty-eight bottles of flower essences neatly aligned, hunts for the three they have settled on and takes them over to Alicia. 'Who knows, you might find these three sort him out completely. Now, all you have to remember is the number three. Three symptoms, three drops, three times a day. Everything related to three has a beginning, a middle and an end.'

'Let's stick to the flowers, Vivi. Numerology is all very well but ...'

'It's pure science. Just like Aristotle. Or Pythagoras ...'

'What if he refuses to take them?'

'Can't help you there. Personally, I wouldn't rule out arsenic just yet.'

Or Valium, thinks Alicia.

'Vivi ...' Alicia has already slung her bag over her shoulder and is about to leave. She is a little embarrassed about what she is going to say, but she feels she can be open about her weaknesses in front of Vivi. 'Could I have something for myself?'

'Sure. Got a free bar going all day. What can I get our little miss?'

'Elm and oak.'

'What are you planning to do?' Viviana says, searching among the little bottles in the drawer. 'Put down roots?'

They hug goodbye. The last bars of 'Oblivion' are still playing. As she fixes her hair in front of the mirror in the lift, Alicia hears the little bottles clink against each other. They seem inadequate weapons for an attack on a fortress. Upstairs, Viviana looks up oak and elm on the list: 'overwhelmed by responsibility', and 'exhausted but does not give up hope'.

Light Years

He should hardly be surprised that her body is rigid and she seems reluctant to co-operate; after all, it is a strange position. They are both standing naked, strapped into Kellar's levitation harness. He had to swear to Irina that this was not some sadomasochistic experiment. Now he grabs her below the knees and, with a jerk, pulls her legs up around his hips as though he wants her to ride him. Then he tells her to hold on tight. Trust me, he says. She goes along with him, but shows little enthusiasm. Víctor reaches behind him, fumbling for the lever that starts the levitating mechanism. In the twelve seconds it takes for the board to reach the horizontal position, he hugs Irina even tighter. She holds her breath. There is a click, telling him the mechanism has reached its resting point. Kellar used to grease it with dubbin before every performance; there are eighty-five cables attached to the ceiling, and the slightest noise could ruin the illusion.

The most interesting thing about this position are its limitations. Irina does not dare move her arms because she needs them to cling to the board. He cannot do much either; the harness is strapped around his waist and the board extends only as far as his calves, giving him no support for his feet. If he is going to do more, it will have to be confined to his abdominal and lumbar muscles.

They hover for a long time without doing anything. Since they are about the same height, their bodies are pressed against each other, their faces together. They are not so much making love as breathing each other in. She can tell that he is ready. All too ready, between their bodies, is something warm and hard, something with its own pulse. What is more surprising is that he finds she too is ready, to judge by the dampness between her legs.

Irina is in no hurry to start, however. If it were up to her, they would stay like this for a long time. But she did not come here for a rest, still less for comfort or pleasure – she came to earn herself €230 euros. Plus tip. She knows Víctor is generous. Though she has not been in the profession for long, she has enough experience to recognise that, in this position, she has to take the lead. She lifts herself just enough to slide her hand between their bodies and reposition Víctor's penis. She wants to thrust her hips but can find no way of supporting her weight and is afraid she will fall. All she can do is press herself against Víctor's body. He places his hands on Irina's buttocks and squeezes.

These hands have spent one year tracing boundaries. This is me and here is where me ends. Everything else is there and there is not a place, but a whole world. Irina's buttocks are as round as the planet itself and he is inside her. Inside a floating world. They are eight feet off the ground, but they could just as well be light years away, in a galaxy barely discernible by its distant glow. His fingers exert only the slightest pressure, like someone testing a watermelon to see whether it is ripe. They both begin to breathe more deeply and their chests, as they expand and contract, generate just enough movement to make this much more than simply an embrace.

Irina breaks down and starts to cry. It would be pointless to try to explain the reasons why she is crying, since even she does not understand them. Perhaps it has something to do with anger, because she has just come. This is a slight problem since he came at the same moment and only then did Irina realise they had forgotten the condom, though this should not worry her too much: she never forgets to take the pill and, as for diseases, well, it doesn't seem likely she could catch anything from Víctor, except perhaps his loneliness. Could it be that she is crying out of sheer sorrow, because the end of this fuck means the end of an embrace? Come to think of it, are they going to stay like this much longer? Because he is crying too, and he hasn't taken his hands from her buttocks and doesn't seem in any hurry to activate the weird mechanism that will bring them back to the ground, back to the real world, the world of there, where men pay her, where she charges then leaves.

Eventually he moves. There comes a moment when the sweat cools, the scent changes, and the weight begins to bother him, at which point Víctor reaches for the lever. Once on the ground, he releases the harness and she feels the sticky, viscous fluid slide down the insides of her thighs, and asks him whether she can shower. When she emerges from the bathroom, her breathing finally back to normal, her eyes dry, she finds him lying on the bed. She goes over to him and cannot help but ask:

'Víctor, what is the matter with him?'

And without knowing nor asking why she is using the third person, whether she is trying to be polite or whether she simply hasn't learned how to conjugate verbs, Víctor answers:

'The matter with him is he's blind.'

'Much?'

It's absurd; the conversation is impossible. And yet Víctor is moved by her childlike way with words, the way she happens upon a single, inaccurate, ordinary word that nonetheless sums up everything.

'Completely, Irina,' he says. 'Completely.'

And he pats the mattress so she will come and sit next to him.

He is going to tell her his life story. He is going to go on talking for hours. Irina will interrupt him only once or twice to ask a question, and sometimes it will seem as though he is talking to himself. The torrent of words will sweep them both along. He will move from the darkness of today to the light of one year ago, from his loneliness now to the loneliness of his childhood, from the stubborn silence of the ants to the cockroach he could not wake up, from the hands that cupped her buttocks to those that once upon a time picked up a pack of cards for the first time.

When tiredness finally overcomes them, Irina will murmur, 'Darius'; she will try to fight off sleep only to give in, thinking it's just five minutes, only five minutes, before she gets up and goes home. And perhaps he tosses and turns as he falls asleep, goaded by some dark nostalgia, but at some point relief will cradle him. This is what words are for, Víctor. For laying down a burden.

Here is Your Shadow

At precisely 9 a.m., they are woken by the intercom, a buzz that is so loud and insistent that it cannot be the first. They both wake with a start and with a name on their lips: Alicia, thinks Víctor. 'Darius!' Irina shouts. Víctor hurries to the intercom and pushes the button that opens the door to the street.

'No, no,' he hears just as he is about to hang up. 'I'll wait for you down here.'

A breath of air moves along the hallway. It is Irina, rushing to the studio to pick up her clothes, which lie in a pile by the foot of the levitating table. Víctor asks her to fetch his too and put them in the laundry basket. Asks her to find him a pair of shoes and socks. A few short minutes later, she places the shoes in one hand and the socks in the other, then says goodbye with a caress. She smoothes his hair, runs her fingers across his chin. Something changed last night: they almost kiss each other on the cheek.

Víctor remembers that he hasn't paid her yet, and gestures to the dresser, suggesting that she get the money herself. Irina has never seen so much money together in one place, and seeing it, she suddenly feels Víctor's defencelessness, his life exposed in all its fragility, more than she did a few hours ago when he was pouring out his heart to her. She cannot even bring herself to put her hand in the drawer.

'You work out how much you want to charge,' Víctor says. 'That was a lot of hours.'

Irina says nothing for a few seconds.

'No. Two hundred and thirty,' she says eventually.

Nobody forced her to sleep there.

'There are no small notes,' he says. 'Take five fifties.'

Irina picks up the notes with the tips of her fingers and lays them out on top of the dresser one by one, her gestures exaggerated, as though he can see her count them out, so he will know she's not robbing him.

Downstairs, Alicia is wondering whether she should buzz again. It has been five minutes, but she's in no hurry. She is certainly not going to go upstairs. She is moving towards the staircase when she hears footsteps. Before she even sees Irina, Alicia knows it is not Víctor coming down. At that speed, he would kill himself. Besides, it sounds as if the person is wearing high heels. A neighbour, she thinks, when Irina finally appears. She could say something, ask this woman whether she knows Víctor, find out whether she can rely on her in case of an emergency, but she decides to leave it for another time. To judge from her rumpled hair and the dark circles under her eyes, the woman is late for work.

It is ten minutes before Víctor comes down. Alicia hears the door upstairs, closes her eyes and counts the steps. She draws in her shoulders, barely breathing, as though she is waiting for him to stumble. She would almost swear she can hear Víctor's hand brushing the banister. She opens her eyes a second before he comes around the last corner. The first thing she sees is his shoes, black ankle boots that hardly seem suited to his casual outfit or the weather. But they're better than nothing. Much better. She checks the urge to congratulate him and simply says hello, then offers him her elbow. She already knows neither of them will mention what happened yesterday. It is a sort of protocol they seem to have established without discussing it. Clearly the lessons learned have not been forgotten, the insults and the incentives have not been erased, but they never talk about the days that have gone before. Perhaps he believes that, in this way, by starting afresh every day, he will remain, stock still, at the point of departure. She on the other hand believes that the race has almost been won and, consequently, keeps shortening the distance.

Forcing him to go outside feels like she is punishing him, but Alicia has not made the decision out of a desire for vengeance. Quite the reverse, she is determined to demonstrate the antithesis of his malice. You lock me in a wardrobe; I show you the world. You abandon me; I guide you. They are not going to talk much;

she has no intention of irritating him with a long-winded lecture or getting him to perform some test. In fact, although she realises that Víctor is prepared to walk unaided, at least to the first corner, she will not let him. Nor will she use any of the opportunities for a lesson the short distance provides. When, as they step outside, Víctor immediately brings his hand to his eyes as though to shield them, she doesn't tell him that there's no need, that the light cannot dazzle him, that he would be better off using that hand to protect himself from knocks and bumps. When there is a shift in the slope of the pavement, at the entrance to a car park, she does not recommend that he remember this so he can use it for future reference. Only when they pass a van parked against the kerb does she say:

'Aren't you the one who said shadows are so interesting? Well, here's one.'

'What shadow?' Víctor asks, confused, his hand still shielding his eyes.

When she turns to speak to him, Alicia notices that, although he appears to be following her meekly, silently, Víctor is tense, his head drawn in.

'We're going to take three steps back,' she warns him. 'Listen carefully to the noise of the traffic. OK, now forward again.' Alicia stops next to the van. 'Listen again. You can't hear it as clearly, can you? The noise is slightly muted. Stretch out your right arm a little. You're touching the side of a van. It's higher than most of the parked cars, that's why it blocks more of the sound. It does exactly the same with sound as it does with light; it casts a shadow.'

'And that's useful how?'

'Well, in this case, I'd suggest you move slightly farther away, or at least protect your head.'

'Why?'

'Because it's likely that a van will have a wing mirror at just the right height to hit you in the forehead. It won't kill you, but it will hurt. And make you angry . . .'

They come to the first corner. Techniques for crossing the road take up several pages in Alicia's notes. However, this time she simply checks to see that there are no cars coming and tells Víctor he can cross. When they come to the next corner, they turn right.

'Calle Asturias,' Víctor announces.

His tone is so neutral that she cannot tell whether he is proud or indifferent to the fact that he knows where he is. They walk one block and come to Plaza del Diamante. It is 9.30 a.m. A waiter is setting out metal tables and chairs outside the only café on the square. Alicia notices the grating shriek of metal and, glancing at Víctor, can see that it is setting his teeth on edge. They sit at one end of a long stone bench that runs along the north side of the square. Although autumn is still a month away, there are already a few dead leaves on the ground. Two drunks are sleeping off their hangovers at the far end of the bench. A mother opens the gate to the children's playground so she can push her buggy through. It is like a small sheep pen, about sixty metres square, containing a slide, some swings, three rockers and three trees. The rockers are in the shape of a dragon, an elephant and a horse. Alicia notes all these details, but it does not even occur to her to describe them to Víctor. She is sure he has seen them a thousand times. They both sit in silence. Anyone looking at them would think they were old friends, a brother and sister, colleagues or lovers with nothing new to say to each other; people close enough to share the morning sunlight in silence. He has his eyes closed and seems to be enjoying the sun's warmth on his face. Pedestrians wander by. Víctor notices this only when he hears the leaves crackle. The only constant sound comes from the playground, where every now and then mothers shout at their children if they look as if they're about to fight, or attempt something too acrobatic on the swings.

'I need to ask you to take these,' Alicia says suddenly.

She puts her hand in her bag, takes out the three small bottles and puts them in his lap.

'What are they?'

'Bach's Flower Remedies.'

'Bach? The composer?'

'A different Bach. Though the composer was blind, or at least he was in his final years.'

'You don't say.'

'I'll tell you about it some day. This Bach was Welsh. He discovered that flowers have healing properties ...'

'A quack.'

293

'No. He was a doctor. But when he was young, he was found to have tumours and was given three months to live.'

'You're going to tell me that he miraculously cured himself using flowers and then had the munificence to share his discovery with the world.'

'More or less, yes.'

'And he's still alive?'

'Not exactly. He was born in 1886.'

'That was a good year. There was a lot of magic in the air. When did he die?'

'I don't know exactly. He was fifty-something.'

'Aha! So the miracle didn't last long . . .' Víctor takes the top off one of the bottles. 'And this is supposed to cure blindness?'

'No, you idiot. They are used for overcoming emotional problems. That one . . .' Alicia looks at the bottle Víctor is holding '. . . is wild oat, for periods of uncertainty.'

'Well, that's useful, then . . .'

Víctor brings the bottle to his lips.

'Hang on. There's a dropper in the top. All you have to remember is the number three. Three bottles, three drops, three times a day.'

'And how will I know . . .?'

'You'll feel it on your tongue.'

Víctor squeezes the bulb to fill the dropper. Then he turns his face to heaven, opens his mouth theatrically, sticks out his tongue, raises his arm and squeezes again. Five drops come out.

'OK, that's not going to do you any harm, but try to count the drops. That one is walnut, it's good for opening you up to change.'

She prefers not to mention 'outside influences'. Better not to tempt fate. Víctor screws the top back on the first bottle, puts it in his left trouser pocket, then opens the walnut flower essence and takes three drops.

'Perfect. And this last one will help you to break with the past.'

'That's useful, given my circumstances.'

He squeezes the bulb of the dropper forcefully, emptying the contents on to his tongue.

'Don't be stupid, Víctor,' Alicia chides him, but she is smiling. Even in her wildest dreams, she could not have imagined he would comply this easily. Although she doesn't believe in miracles, she's not that naive. She suspects Víctor has not baulked at taking the drops precisely because he doesn't believe in them. But at least he took them.

They walk back to his apartment in silence. When they get to the front door of the building, Víctor takes out his key but cannot seem to find the lock. Alicia rushes to explain how he should go about it, but he interrupts her.

'I'm blind, Alicia, not useless. I still possess a little imagination of my own. Place the left hand on the door and feel for the lock, then bring my right hand in towards my left ...' He does this as he talks. 'Try the key, start cursing because this one is the upstairs key, ignore the puny little one because it's the key to the postbox, try again ...'

His voice is becoming clouded by rage. Alicia knows this is one of the most delicate moments in the process. Blind people tackle the most demanding tasks with the courage of those who have everything to gain. But they deal with the impossibility of being forced to repeat small, simple tasks with the fear of those who have lost everything. She touches Víctor's hand, takes the keys from him.

'There are ways to mark the keys so you can recognise them by touch,' she says as she opens the door.

'Marked cards.' Víctor spits out the words, his face contorted in disgust.

'Exactly, marked cards. You'd know a lot about that.'

'I don't do ... never mind ...'

'Here.' Alicia hands him the keys. 'Keep them in your right-hand pocket. And since you mentioned the postbox ...'

'No, darling. Maybe some day you'll teach me to cook some fabulous delicacy, but don't ask me to collect letters I can't even read. And don't you even mention the word discipline ...'

'I suppose you won't need me to help you up the stairs,' she interrupts.

'Are we done for today?'

'For today, yes.'

'I think I can manage. Though I might have some trouble finding the key to the apartment. Since I won't work with marked cards ...'

Bitter though he sounds, he is trying to be funny. And Alicia is grateful.

'I'll wait here until you get upstairs. If you need me ...'

'I'll just put my lips together and ... blow.'

'I don't get it.'

'Because you don't listen to my advice. You haven't watched *To Have and Have Not*.'

'I promise you I'll see it one of these days.'

'We could watch it together.'

'I'll take your word for that.'

'It's just a manner of speaking.'

'Bye, Víctor.'

She puts her hand on his shoulder and pushes him gently. He walks off with a smile on his lips and effortlessly negotiates the first flight of stairs. Alicia listens to his footsteps as she manoeuvres her bicycle out the front door.

'Alicia!' he calls down from the third flight. 'What's that noise?'

'My bike.'

'Oh, so that's why you arrive all sweaty.'

But he says it as though talking to himself. Alicia holds the front door open with one hand, the bicycle with the other, until Víctor's footsteps stop and, after some muttering, she hears a door opening. She goes out into the street, shaking her head.

The Gallery of Famous Blind People: II

Bach was not the first person to be admitted to the gallery, nor is his case the most interesting, but he struts around the place with the arrogance that only hierarchy can give. He began to lose his sight in 1740 and, though he never stopped composing, he gradually withdrew from public life. A number of biographers claim he spent his last years shut up in his room, but as we know, darkness fuels too many legends. Whatever the case, in 1749 he decided to entrust himself to the hands of one John Taylor, a surgeon by profession. Our concept of surgery bears little relation to the practice of the time, so let's just say that Dr Taylor wielded a scalpel and he used it to operate on Bach's eyes. Aside from completely destroying his sight, he ruined his health and thereafter the maestro was plagued by various infections. On 18 July 1750, less than a year after the operation, Bach spontaneously recovered his sight. It is unavoidable, though useless, to speculate about the possibility that by this time Bach was aware that he would soon be dead and consequently he devoted what little time he had left to the contemplation of beautiful objects and beings. (Alicia invariably does so when she tells this story.) The fact is that Bach died ten days later and there were many things the ageing maestro did not see. With his dying breath (although nobody knows exactly whether this was hours or days before his death), he composed his last piece, but was unable to note it down himself so, according to expert graphologists, he dictated it to Altnikol, an outstanding pupil who was also his son-in-law. It is a chorale prelude still studied today as one of the supreme examples of counterpoint and harmony in G major. Alicia always makes reference to the fact that the composition is based on an earlier melody by Bach entitled 'When in the hour of utmost need', but for reasons unknown, he gave it the title (or rather asked Altnikol to give it the title) 'Before thy throne I now appear'.

Though he is not exactly famous, the surgeon John Taylor also strolls about the gallery without talking much to anyone and turning a deaf ear to the remarks made about him by Bach and Handel. Because Handel, too, went under Taylor's knife in 1751, two years after Bach's operation and barely a year after his death, with similar results. Of course, as we have already said, there is no place for bitterness or resentment in the gallery. Besides, poor Taylor received his punishment in life, since he too eventually went blind. But it is hardly surprising that the two composers should look at him askance and wonder whether his ear for music was as dull witted as his hands. Although they pay him little heed – they are too busy playing the vast grand piano in the middle of the gallery, attempting to decide whether its benefits truly outweigh those of the harpsichord. In any case, the composers are delighted to have been admitted to the gallery for it is here that they meet for the first time. It may sound strange but although they were contemporaries, and even exchanged jobs, sharing the task of dragging music out of medieval obscurity while protecting it from the banality of the Renaissance, they never laid eyes on each other during their lifetimes. Alicia loves to conclude the story like this, with the words 'never laid eyes on each other'.

As she hauls her bicycle through the door, she thinks that perhaps she should have told Víctor this story today. Some other day. It doesn't matter. They're just stories to pass the time, to raise a smile. Stories on Alicia's mind, now that she is happy.

A Trail of Ants

I am completely calm. My right arm feels heavy. My right arm feels heavy. My right arm ... this isn't working. This isn't working because Alicia hasn't mastered the first step in the Schultz relaxation techniques: 'Cancel out the outside world.' It's one thing to practise after dancing for forty minutes, with Viviana's deep voice whispering the formula; a very different thing to try it here, lying on the floor of her apartment. Rather than feeling completely calm, she feels increasingly hysterical. She closes her eyes and starts again. I am completely calm. My right arm feels heavy. She's not supposed to open her eyes. Anyway, the phone isn't going to ring, no matter how much she stares at it. My right arm is ... Urgent. Maybe she should have told him it was urgent. Maybe she should call again. Maybe he'll answer this time. I am complete. She could leave him another message, ask him to call back as soon as he can.

Alicia sits up quickly as though someone has pinched her, takes her mobile out of her pocket and, for the fifteenth time, checks she has not put it on silent, that it is set to vibrate. She abandons any attempt at feeling calm. She is going to be hysterical until the phone rings and she hears Mario Galván's voice on the other end of the line. For days now, she has been thinking she needs to talk to someone about this. If she doesn't, she'll explode. She has mentioned some of the problems at ONCE to her boss and in the group meetings with the psychologists, but she has kept most of the details to herself. The thing about the cabinet, for example. If she tells them that, they'll take the case away from her. That's what she would do in their place.

She has thought about telling Viviana and maybe she still will. It wouldn't be the first time she has gone to Vivi for advice, but right now she needs concrete instructions. Viviana would tell her to find her inner strength, to synchronise her outlook to Víctor's; wise counsel, but she needs something more practical, preferably from someone who knows him well. This morning, after making sure that Víctor could make it up the stairs unaided, she went for a long bike ride before heading back to ONCE. She enjoyed cycling around, feeling the breeze on her face. As she pedalled, she thought, I am not angry, I am just baffled. This man refuses to open his postbox, but he won't give up his keys; he's spent a year holed up in his apartment but when I tell him I'll wait for him downstairs he doesn't bat an eyelid; he has a perfect sense of direction but won't let go of my elbow.

As soon as she reached the office, she went to fetch Víctor's file so she could find the details of the man who had first got in touch with ONCE more than a year ago. She shares her office with several other technicians and she didn't want anyone to overhear. So she jotted down the number and phoned him from home at lunchtime and was surprised to hear a female voice: 'The King of Magic. Our opening hours are ten a.m. to two p.m. and from five p.m. to eight thirty p.m. If you would like to leave a message, please do so after the tone.' The first time, she hung up. She needed to find the right words. She called again: 'This is a message for Mario Galván. I'm calling from ONCE. I need to speak to you. It's about Víctor Losa. You can get me at any time on this number.' Stupid. She didn't even say the phone number.

She could call back, but it's only 4 p.m. Maybe ten minutes to. In the meantime, all she can do is wait. She hasn't eaten, and she's not going to eat. She could make herself some tea. No, she'll make herself a herbal tea. Where's the valerian? The telephone rings; it's Galván. She had imagined him to be an older man, but is surprised by how old he sounds. Ancient. A rumbling voice coming from the end of a long tunnel through which the wind whistles and wheezes like a bellows.

She introduces herself but doesn't give any details, says she would prefer to speak to him in person. She tells him she is responsible for Víctor Losa's rehabilitation and her duties involve assessing his environment. Since he has no family, she felt she had to call him. She does mention something about Víctor being secretive, adding, 'but I'm sure you know him better than anyone'. 'Secretive.' Galván repeats the word and allows it to hang in the air. It's true, he never really was one for talking. At no point does she use the word 'urgent', but she makes it clear how worried she is, hints that it would be perfect if she could meet with Galván today. She invites him to join her for something to eat, or for a coffee if he has already eaten, a walk, a glass of wine, even dinner. I'm free any time, she says, whenever suits. Galván replies that he's not really one for socialising. In fact he doesn't usually see anyone. But, if she is prepared to come to the shop . . .

It's downhill all the way. This is what she thinks as she writes down the address. She won't need to pedal at all. She imagines this is how everything will be from now on, like freewheeling downhill, and feels as though a great weight has been lifted.

An assistant pulls back the red velvet curtain and points the way to the stockroom, which smells of glue. Surprised to find that her footsteps are suddenly silent, Alicia glances down and notices that the floor is littered with sawdust and wood shavings. She cannot see anyone. 'Mario Galván?' she calls. 'Don Mario?' She goes over to a glass-fronted cabinet and peers at the spines of the books inside. They look old and valuable. Suddenly, she hears the rasp of a lighter, as though someone were lighting a cigarette. At that moment, from behind the cabinet, an old man in a wheelchair appears. He pushes himself slowly until he is next to her. The first thing Alicia notices is the two transparent tubes that lead from his nostrils into a kind of backpack which hangs on the rear of the chair. The second: how pale his face is. But this is not the pallor of someone like Víctor, who stays cooped up inside, but the ashen colour of a vampire in whom, as though forced to concentrate on his vital organs, the blood no longer flows to his face. The man picks up the lighter and the pack of cigarettes lying in his lap.

'Cigarette, young lady?'

'No, thank you.'

'Do me a favour, light yourself a cigarette. For me.'

She has never smoked in her life, but she is not about to refuse.

'Sit down.' Galván gestures vaguely to somewhere behind her, but when Alicia turns, she cannot see a chair.

'Here, right here, just move those papers.'

There is a trunk next to her, partly covered by huge sheets of paper on which are printed diagrams and instructions for building what seems to be some sort of cabinet. Alicia piles them up at one end of the trunk and sits down. She thanks Galván for agreeing to see her, and without further ado, begins to tell him about her problems with Víctor. This time, she leaves nothing out. In fact, she recounts all of their meetings in chronological order. And she doesn't just tell him about the problems, she is careful to tell him about Víctor's progress too. Galván listens without interrupting her, marking his agreement every now and then with a little jerk of his chin. It is as though even listening exhausts him. The story moves into the present, to what has happened over the past few days, and here Alicia hesitates. She finds it difficult to talk about the incident involving the cabinet. Partly because it shows just how lost she is, how ill equipped for this fight, but mostly because she is afraid that it will give the wrong impression about Víctor. He's not that bad. He can't be that bad.

'And he never talks about magic?' Galván asks.

'Never. And if I bring it up, he's furious. Well, he did mention it the other day, while he was locking me inside.'

'What did you say the cabinet looked like?'

'I don't know, just an ordinary wardrobe, I suppose, but there was a mirror inside it.'

'And you said he locked the door, then disappeared off to listen to some music?'

'Yes. I'm not sure what it was. That thing he's always humming.'

'Louis Armstrong, probably.'

'No. I wasn't really listening, but I think it was classical music. There's one part that was very slow and solemn. It goes something like this ...'

Alicia begins to hum, her voice shaky and uncertain, but by the third note she is surprised to realise that she knows the melody by heart, as though she has heard it a thousand times.

'Sounds like he's changed his tune,' Galván interrupts. 'That must mean something.'

'What? I don't understand.'

She doesn't understand anything. She doesn't understand why

she's wasting her time discussing music. She doesn't understand why she's sitting here humming. Come to think of it, she barely understands a word Galván says. She has to lean forward with her rear perched precariously on the edge of the trunk just to hear him.

'Smoke, please. Do it as a favour to me.'

Alicia brings the cigarette to her lips and draws on it briefly. Barely a sparrow's breath. Though she does her best not to inhale, some of the smoke inevitably seeps out through her nose. She coughs violently and suddenly hears a woman's voice.

'Are you at it again?' It is the assistant who met her when she arrived. She has popped her head through the door and is sniffing the air. 'Stub that cigarette out right now.'

'Don't worry, I'm not smoking. It's the girl. She's a little nervous ...'

Galván shrugs as though apologising to Alicia. Shaking her head, the assistant disappears behind the curtain.

'Where were we?' Galván picks up the conversation. 'Ah, yes, music ...' He gives the wheels of his chair a gentle push and brings himself closer to Alicia, as though he is about to tell her a secret. 'Listen, nothing I can tell you has any real value. I did everything I could for Víctor, but now he wouldn't open up to me, and that's exactly what you're asking me for, in a manner of speaking: a way in.'

'That's it. Exactly.'

'Forgive me for being blunt, but it's just occurred to me that you have something I could never offer him. Sex.'

The comment surprises her so much that she inhales a thick plume of smoke. She starts to choke theatrically. The assistant pulls back the curtain, stares at them for a second or two and, having seen that Galván is all right, disappears again.

'My God, but ...' Alicia protests as soon as she has recovered.

'Don't worry. I realise it's beyond the call of duty. And I'm not trying to pry into your personal life. But if you want me to help you, there's something I need to know. Has he ever made a pass at you?'

'No.'

Alicia starts to think that perhaps she has answered too quickly.

She thinks back over her encounters with Víctor. No, even when he was whispering in her ear he didn't seem to have sex in mind.

'That doesn't surprise me either. No offence. I've seen Víctor with dozens of one-night stands, but the women were always ... I don't know, it's not that they were ugly, I suppose they were just ... missing something. I'd go so far as to say that they were a little unhappy, looking for something. And although he never talked about it, nor did I really want him to, I suspect that whatever it was, he gave it to them in bed. Anyway, I'm afraid that's not much use to you.'

'No, not really.'

'I've just thought of another possible way in. It worked once, years ago, but that doesn't mean it will work now.'

'Tell me.'

Galván explains what happened during his second lesson with Víctor, after he forced him to sing 'If' and then describe the death of his father in the third person.

'Martín. His name was Martín Losa.'

For a second, the maestro seems to be reliving the moment, as though it transports him back to a time he yearns for.

'I had no idea. He's only mentioned his father once, but it didn't sound like he wanted to talk about him.'

'Well, maybe that means I'm right. Look, I don't know the piece of music you're talking about but I'm almost certain it will have something to do with the death of his father. With Víctor, everything is related to his father. Something tells me that you'll never get close to him until you persuade him to tell you what happened.'

Alicia is listening so attentively that she has forgotten the cigarette, which has smouldered down to the butt and now suddenly burns her fingers. She yelps and throws it to the floor. She looks up at Galván and apologises.

'Don't worry about it. But stamp it out, there's a lot of wood lying around.' He immediately offers her another. Alicia turns and glances towards the curtain, like a teenager afraid of being caught by her parents.

'It's OK. You don't need to smoke it. Just make sure it stays lit, I want to be able to smell it.'

But just as Alicia lights the cigarette, the assistant appears and plants herself beside them.

'That's enough now, Dad,' she says. She places a hand on Alicia's shoulder and adds: 'I'm sorry, but the doctor has insisted he's not to smoke. He's not even allowed to smell smoke. Besides, he needs to rest.'

Alicia gets to her feet and rearranges the papers on the trunk as best she can. She asks Galván whether he would mind if she called him again, depending on how things go with Víctor. The maestro says he is at her disposal. As she turns to go, Galván adds:

'Oh, I forgot about the ants.'

'Sorry? The ants?'

'Don't tell me he hasn't mentioned the ants. Miss, you've got your work cut out for you. It's very difficult to march into the present of a troubled man unless you go via the past. And Víctor Losa's past is swarming with ants. Follow the trail. The next time you're at his place, find an excuse to go out on to the terrace.'

He gives her a wink and turns the wheelchair around. At the last moment he stops again and calls out:

'Señorita? You're forgetting something?'

Alicia comes back, picks up the cigarettes and the lighter, looks him in the eye and then kisses him on both cheeks.

On the way here, it was all downhill, but now she has to pedal. And it's hot. Sex, thinks Alicia. She doesn't feel that it was a perverse comment on Galván's part. He didn't come across as a dirty old man. Frijda. The name comes back to her. Hedonic asymmetry. Pain persists for as long as the cause exists. Víctor's pain comes from a wellspring that will run dry only when he is dead. Is there perhaps at least some way to add the fresh water of some new pleasure? Is sex the answer? Dozens of one-night stands, the old man said. Well, there's the photo on her fridge. He was very good looking. And everyone knows performers have a lot of opportunities ... But her? She wouldn't sleep with Víctor, not for all ... well, the Víctor she knows now obviously. What about the Víctor in the photo? Maybe if she had known him back then ... those dimples ...

She goes over the conversation with Galván in her head and still doesn't know which way to turn. She had hoped for more from

305

their encounter, for concrete instructions, a clear way forward. Discounting the whole idea of sex, she is left with the father, the story of the father's death. And the ants. A trail of ants, Galván said. It's not much, but it's all she has.

Manners Of Speaking

'I'm sorry, but I'm sick and tired of working in the dark.' From the loud swoosh that accompanies three brutal tugs on the cord, and the warm sunlight suddenly spilling on to his face, Víctor can tell Alicia is pulling up the blinds. 'Besides, it's a beautiful day. Come on, let's go outside.'

She throws open the door to the terrace. Though there is not a cloud in the sky, the morning is chilly. For the first time, Víctor is wearing a long-sleeved shirt, as though the temperature has alerted him to the approach of autumn. Alicia goes out on to the terrace and begins to impart her wisdom as he makes his way towards her.

'The sun is a useful ally. If you know where it is, you can work out what time it is. And vice versa. If you know what time it is, you know which direction the sun is coming from. This can help you to work out where you are. Assuming you're not hiding away in your apartment.'

Víctor stands in the doorway. He assumes that by now Alicia has seen the ant farm and is suspicious that she has not commented on it. He doesn't believe in her sudden sunny disposition, the casual tone, the affected spontaneity with which she recites her little lesson.

'Barcelona is a perfect city for this, because the cardinal points are obvious. The sea is down there, to the south. Well, more or less. Up there, to the north, are the mountains. On the streets that run north–south, the sun only shines on both sides at noon. On the streets running east–west, in mid-afternoon. With a little practice, and good weather, it's easy to tell which side of the street you're on and in which direction you're looking.'

'Looking, for fuck's sake. I won't be looking anywhere.'

'Don't be churlish, Víctor, it's just a manner of speaking. Come on, let's sit down.' She stands next to him, offers him her elbow, settles him in one of the two chairs and sits down in the other. 'This is nice. By the way,' she adds, with feigned surprise, 'the plants in your window box have died.'

'What window box?' Víctor asks.

He knows how to play dumb too.

'This one.' Alicia raps the glass wall with her knuckles. 'Though I can see you still water it.'

She has seen the water in the moat. Has seen two ants scuttling across the surface.

'Well, you never know.'

'Of course. How do you manage to water it?'

'I chuck water at it.'

Alicia takes a deep breath. This is not going to be easy.

'Yes, but you're watering it at the base and from what I can see, you must be spilling most of it because the soil is dry.'

'I take the jug in my left hand, put my right index finger into the moat. When I feel the water come up past the first knuckle, I stop pouring.'

'Did you say moat?'

She's got him. Nearly got him.

'Moat, base, what's the difference. It's just a manner of speaking ...'

In your case it's a manner of *not* speaking, thinks Alicia. The trail of ants is getting away from her. If she wants to get to the past, she will have to take another route.

'That's good. It's the same trick I was thinking of teaching you for filling a glass of water or a vase. In case you get tired of drinking from the tap. That's what I wanted to talk about today. I thought we might make a list. Or rather, two lists. On one, we can write down the progress you've made, on the other, things that are pending. Things you need to practise over the next few days. The thing is, I forgot to bring a pen with me. Do you mind if I use the one on the dresser?'

Víctor turns towards her and simply waves his hand in response. Alicia gets up, goes into the hall, takes the Parker pen and heads back out to the terrace, preceded by the sound of the spring: click, click, click, click.

'Now, let's see . . .' she says as she sits down. 'Walking with a guide you've mastered. And you were a very quick learner.' Click, click, click, click. 'Although you could do with more practice, it's clear that you have a very good sense of direction. And as for finding your way around the apartment . . .'

Click, click, click, click.

'Are you nervous?' Víctor interrupts. 'You're going to break the spring.'

'Sorry. You told me it was your father's, didn't you.'

'Yes.'

'It's beautiful. I suppose it has sentimental value?'

'Pff.'

'Can I ask how he died?'

'An accident.'

She can barely hear him. It is as though he is breathing in rather than out as he speaks. The clicking starts again, but this time she does not even realise she is pressing and releasing the button. Alicia stares at Víctor, feeling a mixture of shame and fear. Shame because she does not like ambushing him like this. Fear because every muscle in his body exudes a tension that could explode at any moment. Perhaps he is finally about to break down, though it seems just as likely that he might lash out and hit her.

'What was his name?'

'Whose name?'

'Your father.'

'Martín.'

'Martín Losa.'

'Yes.'

'What happened to Martín Losa?'

Suddenly, all the tension evaporates. Víctor's body relaxes, his shoulders seem to deflate, and a smile lights up his face. Even his eyes are suddenly alive.

'Aren't you going to tell me how Galván is?' he asks.

Disarmed, Alicia sets the pen on the floor and thinks for a few seconds. Her whole strategy has just gone south, but she takes one last reckless shot at it.

'He's old, Víctor. He's old, he's sick, and he's dying. He misses you.'

It is impossible to know whether she has touched a nerve. Víctor tugs at his shirt cuffs, raises his eyebrows twice, moving his eyes as though trying to follow the path of a bird above the terrace. Alicia decides to put her cards on the table.

'I talked to him because you need help, Víctor.'

'You mean you needed help. Not me, you.'

'No. If I fail with you, my life will go on much as before. At least we have that in common, because your life will go on as before too. The difference is that my life is OK, and yours is shit. Sorry to be blunt. The one who needs to change is you.'

'So let's get back to your lists, then.'

'No. The lists are useless. I can teach you a whole host of things and you're perfectly capable of learning them, but they won't mean a thing unless you change your ...'

'... my attitude?' Víctor offers.

'Call it what you like. And don't think you're unique. What's happening to you has happened to thousands of blind people. They remain stuck in the past. They can't imagine a future in which their life could be full again.'

'You have too much faith in the power of imagination.'

'And you've too much faith in memory. That's why you're the way you are.'

Alicia shifts her chair towards Víctor's. She puts a hand on his arm. Brings her other hand up to his face and, as delicately as possible, removes his glasses. Víctor jerks his head as though she has just slapped him.

'You still wear glasses. I can't think of a better example of what I'm saying.' She holds the glasses up and looks at them. 'You even clean them from time to time. What were they for?'

'I was short sighted,' Víctor answers, 'and slightly astigmatic.'

'And now you're completely blind, but you still wear them. Your apartment is full of books you can never read. You have a room crammed with magical props you're still capable of oper- ating, but it's all closed up. Or you use it as a torture chamber. You never go out, but you always keep your keys in your trouser pocket. A lot of blind people watch television. Or listen to it. It's usually a good sign. I'll bet you never even turn it on, but there it is just the same. Covered in dust, obviously. Because you think you get by fairly well at home, but if you don't learn how to clean you're going to end up eating shit. Your home is not that of a blind person. It's the typical home of a person who refuses to accept he's blind.'

'OK, well, write it down: learn to clean.'

'No. As I said, there's no point in making a list unless you change. You have to learn to relax. To accept that you need help. You have to promise me that really you're going to try. Otherwise, I'm not coming back tomorrow.'

'Oh.'

Alicia gets to her feet.

'I'm leaving now. And you're going to sit here and get a bit of sun. And you're going to think about what we talked about. And this afternoon, you're going to call me and tell me whether I should come tomorrow or whether you'd rather I stayed at home. If I come, we'll make that list.'

'For the future.'

'For the present. The present starts tomorrow.'

'If you come.'

'If I come.'

'Can you give me back my glasses before you go?'

Down Is Where You Fall

It's not fair to question the amount of effort he has put in, to deny that he is trying his best. And even if he is heading in the wrong direction, that's something for which it's difficult to criticise a blind person. Because in his situation, many people wait for years before taking the first step forward, upward, and some never take it at all. What is rare is his stubborn determination to sink lower, deeper, his longing to hit bottom. He is like a terrified diver who, realising he is almost out of air and with the surface so far away that any attempt to reach it will cause his heart to burst, decides instead to swim down in search of some imaginary way out, a magical opening, a passageway to a topsy-turvy world where hitting the bottom forces everything to rise. Is that what he is looking for? Or perhaps he is just letting himself fall. Perhaps it's simply a question of pride: not waging the diver's doomed battle, but allowing his corpse to drift to the surface and reach its destination, caught up in a tangle of seaweed. But nobody can say he isn't trying.

Moving

There are still some things that Alicia does not understand. The first is this nonsense about the past. No one can blame her, since she does not have the necessary information, but Víctor is not anchored in the past. If only. He is condemned to the insolence of the present, scarcely sustained by the moment on the step on that murky afternoon when he did not realise that time was slipping away. And in the shifting present there is no way to drop anchor. It's not that the present is fleeting; it doesn't even exist. You close your eyes in the past and find yourself looking at the future when you open them again.

Her other mistake is not to have understood that, in spite of his apparent reluctance, Víctor is the perfect student. He waits for instructions and follows them to the letter, especially when they are calculated to help him cross the line of fire. Perhaps Galván should have explained that to her. With Víctor, you can save yourself the predictions, the analyses, the lectures: just give him orders.

Pity Galván cannot see him now, he would be proud. In a few short minutes, with no help, he has managed to get the number of a removal company, reserved storage space, counted out the agreed sum and put it in his pocket, because trusting a Romanian prostitute is one thing, but trusting a bunch of movers he doesn't know is something else. He greets them at the door, fully dressed and wearing shoes as God intended, gives them the money and explains to them that he won't be much help because he is blind. He has just said the words aloud: because I'm blind. Could it be the Bach's Flower Remedies?

There are five men. Three immediately set to work putting his books into boxes. Víctor has made it clear that they are to take all of them. The other two follow him around the apartment, nodding as he points to things: 'that yes, that no'. In fact, almost everything is a yes. In the kitchen, for example, all that is left is the fridge. The washing machine and dishwasher, gone. The crockery, the pots and pans, the cutlery, all boxed up. There is no need to take away the oven, since it is built in. There is no need for them to go into the bathroom or the workshop. In the living room, everything goes except the sofa and a couple of chairs. The dining table? Gone, gone. He doesn't need it. He's blind. A blind man who eats standing up in the kitchen. The dresser in the hallways stays. No one is allowed to touch the pen. The paintings, the photos, the posters on the walls, everything goes. Except for Bacall. When one of the movers asks him about the television he hesitates for a minute. Eventually he tells the man to leave it and asks him to find the remote control. He sits on the sofa and turns it on. He quickly realises that Alicia is right: he can listen to the television perfectly well without having to see it. In fact, at this time of day, though he flicks through the channels, all he gets for the most part is noise. Almost without realising it, he gradually turns up the volume so that it drowns out the racket the movers are making. A man has killed his father with an iron bar and attempted to run over his mother as she runs away. The mother escapes, but a well-meaning woman from next door comes out – you'd spread your legs for anyone, you're nothing but a whore and a liar, because you said he was sleeping with you ... turn it off, Víctor, you need to turn off this shit ... I'm not a liar, you're the liar, what I told you was that I contracted AIDS from him ... turn it off ... he infected me and I can prove it, we'll be right back after this commercial break when we'll find out who is telling the truth ... a court ruling in Málaga has ordered the city council to pay three thousand euros to a bride who was late for her wedding as a result of the brown bear who builds up layers of fat thanks to the salmon it feeds on because I was a couple of yards in front and the assistant didn't raise the flag ... you're holding the remote control, Víctor, it's there in your hand, press the button, Víctor, all you've got to do is press the top left-hand button ... well that's not what you said when you were going round claiming you were my best friend, of course not you slut, that's because I didn't know you were fucking my husband you have fifteen seconds to give me an answer which could win you the jackpot which stands at €80,000 and we'll be right back thinking of buying a new car call us now and see how much you could borrow.

The world has flooded into his home and now there has become here, nothing is in its place, but if he can leave, if he can run away right now, if he is able to get as far as the Plaza del Diamante and replace the sound of planets whirling out of orbit with the babbling of the children in the playground, maybe he will be able to find some peace. All he has to do is hug the walls, pay attention to the shadows. Second corner, turn right. It's not hard. He suddenly gets to his feet and immediately trips over a box one of the men has left in the middle of the floor. Two of the men rush over and help him to his feet. One of them hands him his glasses, which went flying as he fell, but Víctor asks the man to put them on top of the dresser, then requests that they help him as far as the door. He needs to go out for a minute, he says. They lead Víctor out on to the landing, pushing aside boxes, and do not let go of him until he has assured them for the third time that he doesn't need any help, that he can make it downstairs on his own, that he's done it before. He reaches the front door and goes out into the street. He takes a first step, almost on tiptoe, as though he had just waded into some viscous liquid or thick foam. Nothing happens. There is very little traffic. He could stop right here, take a deep breath and consider himself satisfied, but he needs to get to the little square. The verb to need is a tricky one. What he really needs is to be able to see. He imagines Alicia is watching him. He remembers her voice yesterday as she said now take it slowly, this way, that way. Remembers that she helped him avoid a lamp-post a few steps from the door. He leans back a little, draws his neck in and frowns. Thanks to this position it is his foot and not his face which hits the lamp-post. He is not hurt. You can let go of the lamp-post now, Víctor.

He makes it to the first corner and stops for a moment. Though he cannot hear any cars, he stands there for three minutes before attempting to cross. He can hear a bicycle approaching from his left, but he is not afraid. On the contrary, he is grateful, it is like a message from his childhood. Besides, from the sound of it, the

315

cyclist doesn't seem to be moving very fast, doesn't even seem to be pedalling, seems to be coasting so that, when Víctor decides to stop, it is not because he is afraid for his own safety but for that of the man on the bike. The man or woman. In recent years, Barcelona has become full of women on bicycles. Not one of them ugly. He remembers how he liked to watch them pedal, imagining whole lives for them in the few seconds as they cycled past, sniffing the breeze they left in their wake and, yes, sometimes thinking about their pussies, about the folds of their groin pressed against the seat. He knows it is an infantile fantasy, but it is one that he always allowed himself and he is not about to give it up now. Certainly not now that he can see a pussy only in his dreams. He twists his lips a little. He is thinking about Alicia. Alicia and her bicycle. He is astonished to find that he can walk and think about something else simultaneously. For the first time since he lost his sight, he can imagine a future in which his brain might not be condemned merely to survival – to I am blind and this is my left leg; blind, and this is my right leg. I'm blind and the wall is there in front of me, the bicycle is on my left. I'm blind and I am standing in the middle of the road. I'm blind and I am risking my life.

He suddenly feels a sense of urgency. He is never going to get to the square like this. He lifts his right heel and is about to take a step forward when he hears another sound. He has a last thought that hearing and seeing are very similar, that this sudden eruption is just like someone blocking his view of something beautiful or necessary. He is about to say as much, go away, let me listen to the bicycle, and he would say it if he were not so preoccupied with his dance with death, because that is what it looks like now as he takes a step forward, a step back, turns to face the source of this new sound and waits, suddenly paralysed, for the sound of the motorcycle changes, all too late, into a shriek of brakes. Don't stop moving, Viviana would say. Today we are going to work on the passage of time. Imagine you are dancing with death. The most important thing is not to stop moving, not even for an instant, or it will carry you off. Especially you, Víctor. And to illustrate her point, she would probably play Michel Petrucciani's demented version of 'Caravan', that *danse macabre*.

And Alicia … Alicia would not be quite so proud right now,

although if she could see him, if she could bend down beside him, perhaps cradle him, help him bear the pain until the ambulance arrives, she would say it doesn't matter, everything's fine, what matters is that you tried. In fact, even Víctor, despite the searing pain shooting through his hip, feels a certain sense of triumph. He did not make it to the square and he won't be able to go home, but right up to the end he has been able to interpret every sound, the skidding tyres, the choked screams of the other pedestrians and the crack of bones as he was knocked to the ground, the dull thud of his shoulder against the asphalt, the shouted apologies of the motorcyclist; he can even make out, over the noisy chatter of the crowd attracted by the accident, the distant sound of the ambulance siren coming to get him.

If you weren't so crazy

Alicia locates room 224 and walks quickly towards it, but before turning the handle, she takes a deep breath and tries to calm herself. It is not Víctor's fault that she hasn't slept a wink all night. And even if it is, now is probably not the best time to take it out on him.

Yesterday her boss phoned her around dinner time to say that someone from the hospital had phoned ONCE asking them for help with a blind man who had been brought in after an accident and had no listed next of kin. After making sure that he was not in immediate danger, Alicia had decided not to visit him straight away. Instead she spent the night going over things in her mind, trying for the umpteenth time to work out where she had gone wrong. She also hoped that Víctor would have spent those long hours learning valuable lessons: if he weren't so stubborn, if he weren't determined to isolate himself from the rest of the world . . . if he weren't so crazy. Because that is the first thing she would like to say to him right now as she opens the door and hears a television playing too loudly: if you weren't so crazy, everything would be much easier.

On the other hand, although Víctor took his life in his hands, and although his actions meant that she had to give a more detailed explanation to the office than she would have liked, it is undeniable that, in daring to go outside on his own, he has taken a large step forward. A reckless, foolish step towards a cliff, but a step nonetheless.

The first thing she sees as she opens the door is a television mounted on the wall. It is on. She has to step inside to be able to see the bed. If she didn't know that Víctor was blind, she would think he was watching TV. The bed is slightly raised, he is holding

318

the remote control in his right hand and his face is turned towards the screen. It is 9 a.m. A panel of journalists is discussing the measures needed to tackle the economic crisis. Alicia is worried that she might startle Víctor if she says hello – he may not have heard her come in – so she retraces her steps to the door and, without closing it, knocks gently.

'Come in,' Víctor says, not turning his head.

'It's Alicia.'

'Oh.'

'Oh what, Víctor?'

'Oh, Alicia. Hello. Come in.'

'You mean, oh, what a surprise? Oh, how did you find out?'

'That too.'

'ONCE called me.'

'OK.'

'No, it's not OK. You could have called me.'

'Yes, but I don't know your number off by heart. Besides, I'm not used to this phone.'

'Would you mind turning off the TV for a minute?'

'I thought you'd be happy I was watching TV.'

'Víctor . . .'

Víctor turns off the television, but goes on staring at the screen.

'Víctor, look at me.'

'Don't ask me to perform miracles.'

'I'm not asking you to perform miracles. I'm asking you to look at me when you're talking to me.' Alicia reaches out and, taking Víctor's chin, turns his face towards her. 'Let's start as we mean to go on. I'm glad it wasn't serious. I'm delighted you were brave enough to go out by yourself, although I would have preferred it if you'd warned me.'

'Well, next time I will. Thanks for coming.'

'No problem, it's my job. What did the doctor say?'

'Contusions to the hip, dislocation of the collarbone, fracture of I don't remember which metatarsal.'

'You're not in plaster.'

'No, but I have this.' Víctor puts down the remote control and lifts the sheet slightly to reveal his left arm in a sling. 'And

319

apparently, I'm not allowed to put any weight on this foot for a couple of days.'

'Does it hurt?'

'Not much. They've got me sedated.'

'Are you going to tell me what happened?'

'I was run over by a motorbike.'

'I know that much. In fact that's all I know. I mean before that, what happened. Why did you go out? Where were you headed?'

'It must have something to do with that flower potion you gave me ... I suddenly felt the need to break with the past, open myself to change and ... What was the other thing? Oh yes, put an end to uncertainty. Is there one for alleviating pain? Opium drops, perhaps ...' Someone knocks at the door. Victor is silent for a second or two, his face turned towards Alicia as though holding her gaze, then he says, 'Come in.'

The door opens and there is the sound of quick, dainty footsteps, as though a cat has entered the room. Alicia turns and sees a child toddling towards her with a shy smile. He must be about two; it's difficult to tell. The little boy stops next to her, opens his mouth as though to say something, hesitates, then turns back towards the door. Crouched in the doorway is a woman: she nods quickly three times, urging the child on. The boy turns and looks at Victor again and finally says:

'Hi, Victar.'

'Hey!' Victor says, his face suddenly lit up by a smile. 'That must be Darius.'

The woman comes over to the foot of the bed, takes the child in her arms, whispers something to him and ruffles his hair gently. Then she looks at Victor and says:

'I bring Darius because in morning I look after him.' She glances shyly at Alicia. Still holding the child in her arms, she comes to the head of the bed, and, lowering her voice, she adds: 'It is best not to telephone agency in morning. They not like.'

'I'm sorry. You'll have to give me your mobile number. Alicia will help me write it down. Oh, sorry, I didn't introduce you. Alicia is the light of my life. Irina ... a friend.'

They exchange a nod and Alicia remembers the woman she saw leaving the other day while she was waiting downstairs for Victor.

A neighbour. She has never seen Víctor so happy; neighbours and friends, neighbours and lovers. There are many possible combinations. Irina whispers something in Darius's ear. Alicia cannot tell what language she is speaking, but she can see that Irina is encouraging the boy to give Víctor a kiss. At first the child resists, smiles, then laughs to himself, and eventually brings his face up to Víctor's. He hugs him and sits in his lap.

'So, you must be Darius,' he says. 'Does Darius have tickles?'

Watching them play together, Alicia feels uncomfortable, out of place, as though she has no business watching this domestic scene. She thinks perhaps she should leave, but she cannot take her eyes off Víctor: she has seen him smile many times, but always with a trace of cynicism, which has now vanished completely. He has just asked Alicia for a coin and it is now dancing across his knuckles. Then he runs through the classic tricks: the coin appears and disappears, shifts from one hand to the other, appears out of Darius's ear, becomes two coins. The child watches, mesmerised. After every trick, he shouts:

'*Maimult.*'

'*Maimult* is "more" in Romanian,' Irina explains the fourth time.

'Víctor,' Alicia interrupts after a while, 'I was going to suggest we work for a while, but I can see you're in good hands.'

Did she sound too brusque? Why does it bother her to see him so happy? And that business with the phone number. She doesn't know which agency they're talking about, but it seems clear that Irina is here because Víctor called her. Is that the only number he knows by heart? Was it easier to dial than hers? Is she jealous?

'Are you coming tomorrow?' Víctor asks, not even turning his face towards her.

Irina keeps a hand on the small of Darius's back to make sure that as he bounces happily he doesn't end up on the floor. A family, thinks Alicia, they look like a family.

'Sure. I don't know what we can practise while you're not able to walk, but I'll think of something.'

'Can I ask you a favour?'

'Of course.'

'I left the drops you gave me at home ... The keys are in ...'

'Your right-hand trouser pocket.'

'And I think my trousers are in the wardrobe.' As Alicia is rummaging for the keys, she hears Víctor's voice again. 'And since you're going to the apartment anyway, I need you to bring me some money from the dresser drawer so I can pay Irina.'

Irina and Víctor begin to bicker. She refuses to take his money and he insists that that is what money is for. If you weren't so crazy, Alicia thinks as she closes the door to the room as quietly as possible, I might be able to work out what's going on in your life.

A neighbour who charges? What kind of arrangement is that? Barcelona is full of Romanian women who do all sorts of domestic work, looking after children and pensioners. Why not a blind person? Alicia knows what Víctor is like with money and she is sure that Irina is being paid handsomely. She remembers they mentioned an agency. He has rented an arm, thinks Alicia, Víctor has rented an arm and a pair of eyes. Give him a while and he'll tell me that he doesn't need to learn how to cook, or how to walk on his own. That he doesn't need anything. That Irina takes care of everything.

The Light of Your Life

So, I'm the light of your life, she thinks as she slots the key into the lock. She opens the door and, even before she turns on the light, she is overcome by the strange sensation of emptiness. The bare shelves in the hallway rise up like skeletons, but Alicia does not realise the scale of the looting until she comes to the living room and finds it empty. Worse than empty: the sofa and the television stand like two corpses pushed back into a corner. Two chairs face each other in the middle of the room, as though a pair of ghosts are engaged in an intimate tête-à-tête. It looks like a combat zone after the battle, but from the orderly position of the few things that remain, it was a battle never waged, a surrender. She goes into every room. Spends fruitless minutes trying to understand why the studio has been spared this carnage.

Back in the hallway, she sees a folded piece of paper on the dresser under the Parker pen. She picks up the pen, unfolds the page. It is an invoice from a removal firm. On the back, someone has written: 'Sorry, couldn't wait any longer. Since you haven't come back, we'll just close the door behind us. We'll take everything to the warehouse for storage. If you need any further information, you'll find our phone number on the invoice.' Beneath the illegible signature, someone else has added: 'We've swept the floors.' Alicia puts down the piece of paper. She stares at the telephone. Eight, zero, three, she thinks. Click, click. The agency. With her little finger, she presses and holds the number two. On the fourth ring, someone answers. As soon as she hears the greeting, Alicia hangs up as though the receiver has burned her fingers. A massage parlour. Víctor hasn't rented himself an arm, he's rented himself a pussy. She would never have guessed –

the woman looks like a housewife. And then there's the kid. It's difficult to put a kid in the scene that she is imagining. Or Víctor. She's not about to judge him. Click, click. He has every right, granted. Besides, who is she to interfere in other people's lives. But ... A prostitute? Congratulations, Víctor, she thinks suddenly. In spite of herself, she feels the corners of her mouth curve into a smile. Congratulations: you can eat, dress, fuck. You've dealt with every need. Now I really don't understand why you went outside. I mean, you have everything here. The only thing left is for Irina to shave you once in a while. Remember to ask her to cut your toenails. I hope the money in the drawer lasts. How much does a prostitute charge? And how do they charge? By the hour? By the fuck? Depending on the task? This much for a blowjob, that much for helping you to the bathroom?

She walks slowly to the bedroom. The bed, as always, is unmade and there are orderly piles of clothes on the chest of drawers. Only the grey outline where the picture frames hung attest to the presence of the removal men. Alicia sits down on the bed. She looks at Lauren Bacall. What you must have seen, hanging there, she thinks. She has to get round to watching that film. Without knowing why, she imagines Víctor to be somewhat passive. Irina, the consummate professional, devotes herself to giving him the pleasure agreed upon. Irina dressed, undressed, sucking, stroking. Irina listening. Alicia imagines Irina listening, after sex probably, relaxed, all defences stripped away, to stories from inside the fortress. Click, click. She is still holding the Parker pen. She lies back on the bed. Closes her eyes. Jealousy spurs her imagination: Víctor is whispering things in her ear. Nothing to do with his blindness. He is telling her about his childhood, about his father, telling her how he came to learn magic. Then she imagines Víctor's weightless body on top of her. She has never made love to a man as skinny as he is. She imagines she can feel his bones. She sits up suddenly, as though she has just woken from some unfathomable dream. She has work to do. She is paid to work, just like Irina, and they share a similar objective: Víctor's well-being. The light of your life.

She picks up a clean change of clothes, making sure not to

disturb the order of the piles. Before leaving the apartment, she goes into the bathroom and puts into her bag the three small bottles of Bach's Flower Remedies.

And Have Not

'**I** 've brought you a couple of things to keep you occupied,'
Alicia announces as she comes into the room. 'One is your
favourite film.' She places a portable DVD player in Víctor's
lap and rummages in her bag. 'I thought we might watch it
together.'

While she busies herself, plugging in the machine and putting in
the DVD, Víctor cannot hide his excitement and starts telling her
everything he knows about the film, what happened before, during
and after the filming, but Alicia puts a hand on his shoulder and
asks him to wait, to save all the details for the end, to let her watch
it without knowing anything.

Next come the practical issues. The player is set on Víctor's
lap with the screen turned to face Alicia, who is standing next
to him. They each take one earpiece, which forces Alicia to
bend down because the cable is too short for her to stand
upright. It is not very comfortable. She pulls a chair next to the
bed and sits down. This is better, though now she has to crane
her neck because the seat is lower than the bed. The Warner
Brothers' logo appears, a voice announcing the title in Spanish,
and Víctor immediately whips out his headphones. He refuses
to listen to a dubbed version of the film. Alicia presses various
buttons to get back to the menu and changes the set-up. They
start again.

'Here comes Humphrey,' she says. 'He's wearing trousers so
short you can see his ankles.'

'... a sailor's cap cocked to the right,' Víctor chimes in, 'black
shoes, dark socks, a white shirt, a scarf knotted round his throat,
his jacket slung over his shoulder. He's walking through a crowd
of people, goes up to a booth and buys a one-day fishing licence.

It costs him five francs, the official folds it in three, hands it to Bogart and tells him ... Want me to go on?'

'OK, I get the message, you don't need a running commentary.'

'Thanks. I'd like to imagine I'm in a cinema.'

'All right ... wait there a minute.'

Alicia pauses the film, walks over to the window, rolls down the blind then makes her way back to the chair. She is about to sit down, but changes her mind.

'Shift over a bit,' she says, nudging Víctor's elbow.

She takes off her shoes, lies down next to him on the bed and presses play. He is under the sheet; she on top. Their shoulders touch, their heads are almost pressed together. For what feels like an age, Alicia has to bite her lip to stop commenting on how strange it is that all the actors are shorter than Bogart, how unconvincing she finds the fishing scenes, her feeling that the plot and the atmosphere have been lifted wholesale from *Casablanca*.

'The music's not bad,' she concedes.

Víctor doesn't answer. Perhaps, with the earpiece in, he didn't hear her. Or maybe he's just concentrating. Alicia finds it difficult to understand why it's so important to him, this film about a bad-tempered fisherman and an old drunk ripping off an irritating Yank on a fishing trip. It is precisely thirteen minutes before Bacall shows up. Or, more precisely, her voice. 'Anybody got a match?' She could have said 'It's seven o'clock.' It doesn't matter. It is her voice, rather than the words she says, which exudes sex. Alicia hears the words in stereo, because a split second before she speaks, Víctor says the line aloud: '*Anybody got a match?*' Alicia looks at Víctor. The light from the screen casts shadows on his face. He turns towards her for a moment, as though he wants to share with her a complicity he has cherished for years: now you'll see; this is the good bit. Alicia envies Bacall's long, slender fingers in the few glorious seconds while she opens the matchbook, strikes a match and brings it up to her face to make sure that the camera catches the fire in her eyes.

If these people were real, it would be impossible to fall in love with them. He would stink of petrol and raw fish. She is a petty thief on the run from God knows what. It is the light which transforms them into gods. Alicia does not want to miss anything that happens on the screen, but she gives Víctor a sidelong glance, watches as his lips mouth every line of dialogue, even sing along with Bacall. Slightly out of tune, because the earphone means he can't hear his own voice. But he is happy. It is a blessed memory. They kiss for the first time. She initiates everything. She sits on his lap and kisses him. A real kiss. Not just lips pressed together, eyes closed, camera trained on the backs of their heads as in most of the films back then. He speaks, she speaks, then she kisses him again. The kisses are short, but passionate, intense. Alicia does not dare to look at Víctor now. He can tell they are kissing only by the silence that interrupts the dialogue. And because he knows the film by heart. Silence is the sound of the light. Sharing it like this feels almost indecent.

The end comes. Bacall goes over to the pianist to say goodbye. He interrupts the song he's playing and asks her: 'Hey, Slim, are you still happy?' and, as one, Bacall and Víctor reply, 'What do you think?' She turns towards the camera and walks away. The pianist plays a cheery phrase. She responds by swinging her hips gently, clearing a path through the crowded bar. For three seconds, the whole world sways with her hips. Today, we're going to work on the impossible. Imagine you are happy and move. Float, damn it. The camera closes on the pianist; roll the credits. Alicia reaches out and turns off the DVD. They sit there in complete darkness. If she leans her head a little it would be resting on his shoulder. Víctor's beard would tickle her forehead. It is several minutes before she breaks the silence.

'I'm not sure I understand the title,' she says, eventually.

'It's about a chance.'

'Sorry? What?'

'About having or not having a chance. It's explained in the book. They changed a lot of things in the film. In fact the two are completely different. She doesn't even appear in the book. And he dies at the end. He's shot in the belly and bleeds to death on the deck of the boat. Two men show up to help him and ask what happened. He starts to say something, but he's too weak. A man. He says those words several times: a man. The two guys think he's about to describe his killer, until he finally manages to say, "A man alone ain't got no . . . chance." They dropped the scene in the film, but I suppose they wouldn't have dared change the title.'

'No chance of what?'

'How do I know? That's all he says. Of salvation, I suppose, of surviving.'

'Oh.'

'You said you've brought me two things?'

As though this sudden change of subject puts an end to the reason they're here, alone in the dark, Alicia sits up and puts her feet on the floor.

'I'm afraid you're not going to like the other thing as much.'

'Try me, Slim.'

'Don't call me Slim.'

Walking blindly towards the window should prove no problem for Alicia, but she is barefoot and stubs her little toe against one of the wheels of the bed. Víctor hears her swear, then the sound of the blind being yanked up. Alicia comes back to the bed, searches through her bag for a minute then says:

'Here, take this. Use both hands.'

She puts a small block of wood in his right hand and a sheet of sandpaper in his left. Víctor strokes the paper, can feel the different texture of each side.

'What do I need sandpaper for?'

'Who knows. If you still refuse to do magic, you could be a carpenter. No, but seriously . . .' Alicia swallows before going on. 'It's an important exercise. The way your hand moves when you're sanding is very similar to the way it moves when you're using a cane.'

'A cane,' Víctor echoes. 'The white cane.'

'Yes. In theory you should do it on a table, but you can practise in bed. The idea is to turn the block of wood into a dice. In the workshops at ONCE, we even ask people to put tacks in it to represent the numbers on each side, but I'll be happy if you just sand the edges.'

'But you already know I'm not going to do it.'

Alicia pretends she hasn't heard. She leans down and presses the button that raises the head of the bed.

'You'll be more comfortable like that. Hold the wood in your left hand and move the sandpaper with your right. The most important thing is that your shoulder and your arm shouldn't move. You just move your wrist. That way you'll learn ...'

'Alicia.'

'What?'

'I've just told you, I'm not doing it.'

'It's not hard. It's just an exercise. And it's not as if you've much else to do.'

'Not this. Not the cane.'

'It's important. Very important. In fact, if you'd learned to use it earlier, you wouldn't be in this situation.'

'Really? You think I could have fought off the motorbike with my cane? What are you going to do, attach a bayonet to the end of it so I can stab the first bastard who comes too close? Why don't you just hang a bell around my neck. Like they used to do with lepers.'

'Victor ...'

Alicia doesn't want to continue this discussion. She's getting to know Victor. There are a dozen arguments she could recite, all intended to overcome the initial reluctance all blind people feel about using a cane, but she knows it would be futile.

'I went to your apartment yesterday.'

'Oh. Did you bring me the flower remedies?'

She takes the bottles out of her bag and hands them to him. He opens one and empties the entire contents of the dropper on to his tongue.

'There's not even a table any more, Victor.'

'I know,' he says, then adds, 'I like this one. It must be the walnut.'

'But you didn't empty out the studio.'

'I forgot. Since I never go in there ... I hope you left the light on.'

'Victor, I'm being serious here. Please tell me the reason you didn't have it cleared out is because you're thinking about the possibility of working again some day. Working. Performing magic. Earning a living like everyone else. And if you have too much money, then give some to charity. Because you have to do something.'

'A man.'

330

'What? Víctor!'

'A man alone ain't got no chance.'

'Enough of the movies. Tell me if . . .'

'All the things in the workshop were for Galván, Alicia. We spent two years together, recreating those relics of the nineteenth century with our bare hands for a magic show. He wanted to set up a museum and I decided to hang on to them so I could give them to him. But the nineteenth century is the past. Galván is the past. My hands are the past. And a little bird told me I'm supposed to break with the past. Isn't there a flower remedy for that?'

He opens another phial, opens his mouth and theatrically sticks out his tongue. Alicia grabs his wrist to stop him.

'No.'

'You're hurting me.'

Alicia relaxes her grip but does not let go.

'It's no use, the flower remedies, the sandpaper, even me, none of it is any use unless you're prepared to sacrifice something . . .'

'The thing is, I've already sacrificed a great deal. I've sacrificed my eyes.'

'I'm going, Víctor.'

Alicia opens her hand and Víctor's arm falls. The liquid in the dropper spills on to the sheets.

'But you'll be back tomorrow.'

'Don't count on it.'

'OK. Well, I'll be here . . .'

Alicia picks up her bag and leaves, not even stopping to take the DVD player, the phials, the headphones, the cables. Let him sort them out. Let him ask a nurse. A man. A man alone . . .

The Gallery of Famous Blind People: III

Learn these lines by heart, Víctor: '*Come husbands all attend my tale, come wives and widows in your glory, come children all, and hush your wails, and harken while I tell my story.*' Or make something up. It's not difficult. All you need is one verse to attract attention, after that just come up with a list of easy rhymes. Here's a few suggestions: wander rhymes with squander, dark with stark, and blindness rhymes with kindness, the word 'more' is useful because it rhymes with whore and door and also more or less with drawer – the rhymes don't have to be exact. According to tradition, you need a stanza apologising for any error, which, obviously, rhymes with terror, and likewise spoon with moon and June, repentance and sentence. Make a mental note that the last verse of the ballad should be: '*This ballad that you've heard me tell is in this chapbook here set down, which for tuppence I do sell that you may give it to any man and call him blessed.*' You're allowed to raise the price to account for inflation. Tales of crime and passion sell for a lot more these days. But at least you'll be able to make a living.

They're called Blindman's Ballads, because the blind recited them in the streets, the markets, in the squares. That was how they earned their living in the Golden Age. It's a lot less boring than selling lottery tickets. And easier than performing magic. All it requires is a good memory, something you have in spades. And it pays well. The last line mentions the price because, after the performance, they sold copies of the ballad accompanied by crude drawings. A handful of pages tied with cord. The study of these ballads is called *literatura de cordel*. The ballads tell of ghastly crimes, terrible vengeance, anguished repentance. Very up to date.

It's the sort of thing you might see on TV. And there's a guaranteed audience.

There was a lot of controversy in the Gallery of Famous Blind People when the balladeers were allowed in. Technically none of them, taken individually, was famous. But it is impossible to deny that, taken together, they represent something important, a literary genre some might dismiss as vulgar or even as a precursor to the tabloid journalism of today but one to which whole chapters are devoted in academic studies and in any encyclopaedia worthy of the name. When the dispute was at its height, Homer intervened and said: 'I don't see why we're arguing. These men invented a whole genre, for God's sake. Just as I did. It's not their fault if later writers abused it.' Some suspect that Homer just liked the fact that the gallery was heaving with people because that way he could go round hoovering up any gossip he overhead and then circulate it later as if it were his own.

In the end, the balladeers were admitted but, given that they were famous only as a group, it was on condition that they spoke in unison. Nor were they allowed to recite the last verse, since there was no such thing as money in the gallery. They proved popular for a couple of centuries: they made a lot of noise and the stories they told were fascinating. But after a while, everyone stopped listening. However much they dressed them up with extravagant words and rhymes, the stories they told always involved the same crimes. Worse still, there was no way for them to add to their repertoire since crime did not exist in the gallery. Not, it must be said, because its inhabitants were of superior moral fibre compared to the rest of humanity; it's just that there is very little point killing or robbing when you're immortal. You stab someone and the next minute he's alive again.

Leave her alone, Victor

It was her when it was simply a matter of speaking. Warm, honeyed words that carried something like a promise in every phrase, but that was only words. She was the one who took the initiative in those first kisses, and goes on doing so now that you have ripped off her clothes; or rather now that you have made them vanish, since that is how dreams work, the clothes suddenly disappear and suddenly your fingers are toying with the mole they've discovered on the small of her back, like someone glancing through a foreword, deliberately postponing the excitement because the best is yet to come, the moment when your hand slips down between her buttocks, when she tenses her stomach slightly and your fingers begin to discover flesh, fluid, skin, and perhaps you will hear her voice murmur in your ear, closer now, because only her voice proves that it is truly her rather than one of the thousands of women who could be in her place right now. If this happens, if she whispers a single word, you will want to enter her because her voice is a promise of paradise regained, and though she is tall and strong willed, you will turn her body to your every whim, perhaps you will direct her, lie back, part your legs a little more, move up, move back, tighter, harder; or perhaps you will simply grab her hips and go for the shortest, quickest route. But it's not possible for you to have sex with Bacall, you might as well know that before you even try. She is made of light, remember? You can't fuck a ghost. She will cease to be whoever she is the moment you slip inside her. It's a rule. Even touching her feels like insolence, and if you carry on, if you stubbornly persist in trying to find a sensitive spot, if you dare to brush your body against hers, the dream will probably evaporate. Pretend it is Irina, lick or nibble the collarbone you know so well, taste Irina, or if it's the unknown that turns you on, convince yourself that it's Alicia, cradle her slender limbs in your hands and do what you will with her. Or give in to the banal fantasy of imagining it's a nurse, any of the nurses who traipse through your room giving you more painkillers, the nurse who was here the day before yesterday who showed you how to find the play button on the DVD player, the nurse who knows you have not taken off your headphones since, not even when you go to sleep, the one who opens the door from time to time and finds you still muttering those lines in English at all hours of the day and night, the one who asked you this morning whether the girl from ONCE was coming back and, when you didn't answer, wanted to know whether you were all right, whether you needed anything. Be vulgar, tell her that there is something she can do, put her in a short skirt with too much lipstick and fuck her hard and fast, but leave Bacall in peace because you're going to wake up in a hospital bed, your shoulder will ache, you'll feel like someone ripped your hip out with their teeth, you'll be alone and the long fall from this towering paradise to the dank basement of reality might prove fatal. You should dream to order, Víctor. Lots of people do it. Before you close your eyes, tell yourself, 'I'm going to dream about this.' Something that is not painful. Something beautiful but inconsequential, something that you won't yearn for when you wake. A poppy field. Wet sand. You'll know. And phone Irina.

Without Edges

T he piece of wood is already a cube, so the only difference with a dice is the edges. They have to be carefully sanded, the edges rounded so that chance can glide across them and show its capricious face. Though he does not always manage to do so, Víctor tries to keep his shoulder and his arm still, as Alicia instructed. He feels like a washerwoman desperately scrubbing a shirtsleeve. When he gets bored, or when he realises that he is holding the piece of wood awkwardly and is about to sand his knuckles, he takes a break.

Darius assumed the cube was a toy and rolled it under the chairs a couple of times. After that he became obsessed with running his tongue over the sandpaper. Now he's tottering around the visitors' room, pointing at objects and naming them: chair, shoe, more shoe. Paper, he says just before pushing all the magazines off the coffee table on to the floor.

'He speak more good Spanish than me,' Irina says as she gathers them up.

Víctor reaches his hand out and offers Darius the cube. There is the sound of a wooden block rolling across the floor.

'Tomorrow I'll be able to pay you for the last few days,' he says. 'They're finally letting me go home.'

'This no is work,' Irina says.

'Of course it is,' Víctor replies. 'You wash me, you dress me, you help me find my way through these corridors. It's work.'

'Greek-style is work. French-style is work.'

'Someone really should invent the Romanian.'

'Sorry?'

'Nothing. Are you going to shave me?'

'Of course. All-inclusive price.'

336

Yesterday, he asked her to bring shaving foam and two or three razor blades. They get up, and Víctor takes her elbow. Irina did not need any instructions to be able to guide him. They start to walk, but Darius is still dawdling behind. She has to let Víctor go, pick up the boy, then offer him her elbow again. They ask a nurse for a washbowl and then head back to his bathroom. Víctor sits on the toilet. Irina drapes a towel across his chest, wets his beard then lathers it with lots of shaving foam. From time to time, she stop to glance at Darius, who has his hands in the washbowl. She starts to shave Víctor, but quickly stops. By the third pass, the blade is already clogged with hair. Víctor tells her to keep going, tells her not to worry if it snags, that it doesn't hurt, but Irina goes out and asks a nurse for a pair of scissors.

'Come over here, Darius,' Víctor says when Irina leaves. 'Give me a hug.'

They both open their arms. Since the boy is silent, it takes Víctor a second or two to find him. He picks him up, sits him on his lap and says:

'How much does Víctor love you?'

'Much!'

'How much?'

'Thiiiiiiiiiiis much!' Darius flings his arms wide, then starts clapping. It's something he learned today.

What would life have been like if I'd had children? Víctor thinks. I'm forty years old, I could have children in their teens by now. Would they look after him? Would they think he was a pain in the neck? Would they treat him with infuriating pity? Irina appears with the scissors and starts to cut his beard. Víctor likes the click of the blades next to his face. There are a few sounds that perfectly emit the light of the immutable world: the tinkling that slips in through his kitchen window in the late afternoon as mothers start to make tortillas; the rumble of the bin lorry that sometimes finds him lying awake in the middle of the night; the clicking of scissors; the muffled sound of Darius's footsteps. The sounds reassure him that the world is still there, that the cruel disappearance is not yet complete.

Twenty minutes later, Irina has reduced his beard to something closer to three-day stubble and both the towel draped over Víctor's

337

chest and the floor are covered in hair. Darius is sitting on the bed watching television.

'Wait,' Victor says. 'Start up here.' He points to his left cheek just below the sideburn. 'And just shave down as far as here. I want to see what a goatee feels like.'

'You are crazy man,' Irina says.

But she does what he asks. When she has finished, he asks her to shave off everything except the moustache. Irina tells him it looks horrible. Making the most of the fact that their faces are close together, Victor steals a kiss. A peck on the lips.

'Prickles.'

When, finally, there is not a hair left, she lathers his face and, dipping the last blade in the washbowl, shaves him again. It feels like the sandpaper rubbing against wood. When she has finished, she runs her fingers over his cheeks to make sure it is perfect. She straddles Victor's legs, presses herself against him, his groin, his chest, his face, especially his face. They move their heads, rubbing their cheeks together. They do not kiss; she breathes softly into his ear.

'Irina ...' Victor says as he feels a hand slip under his dressing gown, 'Irina ... Darius.'

She reaches out her other hand and gently pushes the bathroom door shut.

'One minute.'

She kneels down, pushes her hair away from her face, and takes the base of Victor's cock in her hand. She does not take it in her mouth, but she licks it. There are no edges to sand away. It takes longer than a minute. But not much. And he does not make a sound.

'Now you *have* to let me pay ...' Victor says when it is over. 'Because that ... That is work, yes?'

Irina does not answer.

Cliffwood Beach

Sitting on the floor next to the wardrobe in his bedroom, he cradles his father's box in his lap. He has not opened it yet. From time to time, he leans his body slightly, bringing his left ear close to the wardrobe. He holds this position for a few seconds then goes back to how he was. Yesterday, as the ambulance was bringing him home, he had the fleeting impression that he could distinguish the slightest movements in the air. Now he has just discovered that he can tell the precise moment when he is about to touch the wardrobe door. He tries it again, to make sure the effect is not temporary or simply a matter of chance. It is progress. A spontaneous development. Not something he has been practising. He feels more surprised than happy. Alicia has often talked to him about how the other senses become refined to compensate for lack of vision, but this is different. It is not that his hearing has become more acute. There is nothing to hear, neither the wardrobe nor his body is making a sound, there is just a slight shifting of the air, a subtle increase in pressure on his eardrum as he brings his head closer to the door. This progress is something offered him by time: a spontaneous increase in sensitivity, something that clearly also involves his skin, because he has just begun to notice a slight breeze on his wrists, his ankles, around his neck. No windows are open. It is simply the shifting of cold air slipping under the front door, tiptoeing along the hallway and coming into his bedroom to greet him. If Víctor believed in such things, he would call it a spirit or, to be more precise, the faint tremor spirits produce as they move. He knows exactly what Alicia would say, if he told her. Congratulations.

He is not going to say anything. He doesn't want to talk about the progress he is making. On the contrary, the reason he has taken out his father's box is because he wants to show her something that negates the very possibility of progress in the hope that he can get her to stop congratulating him on every little improvement. When the intercom buzzes, Víctor will open the box, rummage around and find the piece of amber then put the box back where it was, or maybe just toss it on the floor since none of the other objects inside interests him any more. He will wait impatiently for Alicia by the front door as she stows her bike in the hall and starts up the stairs, or maybe he'll use those minutes to go over what he wants to say, to find the right words, the right order: look, I want to show you something. And if she just stands there in silence, holding the lump of amber, not knowing what to do, or she just tells him it's lovely, Víctor will ask her to focus on the insect trapped inside. Nineteen sixty-six, he will say. Until 1966, myrmecologists dated the earliest fossil traces of ants to between forty and sixty million years. Everyone took it for granted that they had existed before that, but no one could find proof. The discovery came by chance. And it wasn't some adventure, some expedition, nothing to do with Amazonian rainforests, caves, jungles, insect bites or disease. An elderly couple were walking on Cliffwood Beach in New Jersey. A storm had broken up the clay embankments by the beach. As they wandered, they picked up a number of pieces of amber and, inside one pristine nugget, they saw what seemed to be the shadow of an ant. They then sent it to a university. His father told him all this years ago. He is not even sure which university it was: Harvard, Yale, one of those. Initial investigations dated the amber to ninety million years, something spectacular in itself, but the real commotion in the scientific community came when it was studied under a microscope. The insect – or what was left of it – had only two teeth, like a wasp, but had a gland specific to ants; the thorax of a wasp and the trunk of an ant. It was the missing link. Obviously what he is holding now is not the original piece of amber, but a scientifically accurate reproduction. A curiosity his father used to take pride in showing him.

Ninety million years, he will say, can you imagine? Ninety million, Alicia. Some wasp had to stop flying, learn to build nests by burrowing into the ground instead of the bark of trees; it needed to transform itself into an ant, and it did. Well, not that ant but her daughter, her niece, her grand-niece. A bug took a sideways step as it was born, before it was born, and wound up being something completely different. He will tell her about the importance of the discovery, because until then ants were popular with those determined to refute the theory of evolution. Man might be descended from apes, they used to say, but ants have no antecedents, they're not part of any chain. They're an example of the mysterious ways of God. This little piece of amber shut them up.

If he truly is as calm as he appears, perhaps Víctor may digress on the subject of chance, the enormous statistical odds, the endless possibilities, the tide that could have carried the discovery out to sea that day, the elderly couple who could have given this lump of frozen time to their grandchildren to play with, might have had it set into a necklace or, if they didn't have the means, might have sold it for a couple of dollars so that it would end up in a glass case somewhere, its significance forever hidden from the eyes of science. And Alicia will take this opportunity to say that it's beautiful, really pretty, interesting, but why are they still standing out here in the hall when she hasn't even had a chance to put down her bag, they have work to do and she doesn't see where this conversation is going. All this, she'll say. And though he will not be able to see her, she'll fling her arms wide to encompass the hallway, the apartment, the world and the curious motionless mass they form as they stand here.

'You don't see?' Víctor will say. 'You really don't see? Jesus …' He will sound almost indignant, though he will not raise his voice. 'Use your imagination, Alicia. This little creature, this chain of genetic information, this aberration, was once crawling up a tree and it stopped for a moment. And a droplet of resin oozed out of the tree. The insect didn't move. Wasps and ants don't usually stop moving for very long so the whole thing must have happened in a few seconds. Maybe it felt an atavistic urge to fly but didn't know how. It didn't know who it was. Worse, didn't know what it was. And the resin trickled down the branch and engulfed it, the way lava engulfs everything in its path. And before the insect realised it, it wasn't a wasp, or an ant, or an insect: it simply wasn't.

At that point, Alicia will begin to see where the conversation is leading, will realise that Víctor's thoughts are hurtling off course and will try to derail them with the first thing that comes into her mind. Hang on a minute, she'll say, there's something I don't get. Because unless I'm mistaken, wasps still exist. Not these ones, he'll say, these are extinct. It's a completely different species to those that exist now. They were solitary wasps. They laid eggs in the bark of trees. As a species, they didn't have much chance of surviving. And she'll say, but in that case, what you're telling me is fantastic. It means that at some point in time these wasps were able to evolve, to progress, to make a change that was essential to their survival. They lost their wings, but they learned to burrow into the ground, to create a social hierarchy and transform themselves into an almost perfect creature. How many years did you say? Ninety million? And they're still here. Ninety million years thanks to a sacrifice. They learned to walk, Víctor, because that's what we're talking about, isn't it, learning to walk when you can't fly any more? But though Víctor might be a bit obsessed, he's nobody's fool, and he'll say: no, no, that's not what we're talking about, don't try to use this as an excuse to give me another of your lectures. We're talking about the amber. And about me. We're not talking about the species, we're talking about the individual. And that's me, Alicia. Look at me. Can't you see I'm trapped in amber? It's inside my head, in my optical nerves, it has completely engulfed me.

When the day's work is done, when they finally say goodbye, their mouths will be dry from having talked so much, because they won't be practising anything today, they will just talk and talk for hours about the significance of this piece of amber without reaching any agreement. She will leave, feeling that she is missing something, that in spite of everything that has been said, in spite of the fact that she marshalled all her weaponry in an attempt to change Víctor's outlook, she still has to find an argument, a weapon which, properly used, could shatter the wall of amber in which he encases himself.

And Víctor ... Víctor will be left with the nagging feeling that he has lied, if only by omission. Because even if he is convinced of what he says, he cannot deny that right now, in spite of the year he has spent trapped inside his stubbornness, a year which feels like ninety million years encased in amber, inside the resin he has felt a quaver in the air. The tremor of a minuscule evolution, however much he refuses to call it that.

The Auzinger Toy

t looks like a badly choreographed ballet. On one side of the street is Alicia, a reluctant Víctor clinging to her arm and complaining about all the pushing and shoving he had to suffer on the metro. What's more, he is still limping slightly from his accident. Coming towards them is Galván's daughter, pushing her father's wheelchair, her face like thunder.

Alicia had to do a lot of work to arrange this meeting. This week, she has been to see Galván three times: the first time to suggest the meeting; the other two to make arrangements and to overcome his daughter's reservations. At first the daughter refused to take her father out of the shop on the pretext that, given the state of his health, a stiff breeze could easily kill him. Alicia took it for granted that Víctor would not agree to visit The King of Magic. In fact, Víctor is the only person who has been tricked into this, he does not even know that he is meeting Galván. It was difficult enough to convince him to agree to what she told him were exercises to help him get around on public transport. This is the crucial moment. She has to pretend that the meeting is coincidental.

'Hey, isn't that your old teacher?'

That was awkward.

'How the hell should I know?'

'It's Galván, Víctor.' Alicia turns and takes his shoulders. 'I've only met him once, but I'm sure it's him. He's in a wheelchair. He doesn't look well. You can't just ignore him.'

There is a café on the corner. This, too, is not a coincidence. The only neutral ground Galván's daughter would agree to is a hundred yards from his shop. They greet each other at the door. Víctor kisses the daughter on both cheeks but Alicia hurries them inside. When it comes to sitting down, the choreography becomes complicated. They have to move some chairs to get Galván's wheelchair to a table and in the process almost buffet Víctor, who stands there stupefied, awkward, silent.

'What's that noise?' he asks as Alicia sits him down next to the maestro.

'It's a bit crowded,' Galván's daughter answers, 'and the waiters are quite noisy.'

'No, not that ...' Víctor says. 'It's closer, like a hissing. It's coming from here.' He reaches out towards Galván's chair and touches the back of it.

'Oxygen,' the maestro explains, his voice barely audible. He is surprised, although he has the tank next to him twenty-four hours a day, or perhaps because of that, he cannot hear the hiss of air.

Víctor does not react. Galván puts a hand on Víctor's neck, forcing him to bend his head closer.

'I said it's the oxygen. Don't make me repeat myself, talking wears me out. Look, here, feel this.' He takes Víctor's hand and forces him to touch the tubes coming out of his nostrils. 'I have an oxygen tank to help me breathe.'

Alicia is nervous and cannot seem to stop her hands fluttering; she has already moved the ashtray and the napkin holder three times and shifted the position of her chair. She clears her throat. She has spent all week rehearsing this moment. She expects to start off with small talk so everyone is relaxed and then steer the conversation to the subject she wants them to discuss. Víctor and Galván will talk about the weather or something like that. Then Galván will scold Víctor for not introducing his friend. Víctor will have no choice but to explain that she is his technician from ONCE. The maestro will be surprised by the news, will congratulate Víctor and ask her about the progress he's making. She will talk about his achievements but then go on to say that there is one small problem and explain Víctor's reservations about using a cane. At that point, Galván knows what he needs to do. This is how they agreed things should go.

But it seems that the maestro is about to throw away the script. He is still holding Víctor by the neck and talking so quietly that his daughter and Alicia have to lean in closer to catch what he is saying.

'If I were thirty years younger, if I wasn't in the state I'm in, I'd kill you with my bare hands. I don't know if you'll ever perform again, but you could be the best blind person in the world. You have the best teacher. Alicia is an angel.'

Alicia frowns and bites her lip. This isn't how it was supposed to go.

'A guardian angel,' the old man continues. 'She knows everything there is to know. And she needs you to pay attention, because a student who doesn't want to learn is an insult. A waste of talent. I know that better than anyone.'

Rather than being angry at this ambush, Víctor seems bewildered. The hand with which Galván had forced him to feel the oxygen tubes now rests on the maestro's chest and registers the strenuous rise and fall of lungs desperate for air. Now and then he turns to where he thinks Alicia and Galván's daughter are sitting, as though hoping one of them might intervene. But Alicia has resigned herself to the fact that the old man is now in charge of this encounter and the daughter seems happy simply to wave her hands around, attempting to stop the cigarette smoke drifting over from the bar from reaching her father.

'Mario . . .'

'Don't interrupt me. I'd be only too happy to have a nice long chat, to talk about old times, for you to tell me what you've been doing this past year. Or what you haven't been doing. But I don't have the time.'

'Don't give me that old speech about how you're dying. You've been telling me you're dying for twenty years.'

'Exactly. I've been dying for twenty years, so now I'm ready. In fact, it's long overdue. I can barely eat, it's difficult to breathe, and it's clear I find it hard to talk. If I could magically disappear, I wouldn't hesitate for a second. I've had a good life, Víctor. This is my daughter. My daughter is already a grandmother. I'm a great-grandfather, can you imagine that? Until last week, I thought there was nothing left for me to do on this earth, but then this girl, Alicia here, your guardian angel, persuaded me there is still something I can do. She gave me one last mission.'

Galván fumbles in a bag hanging from the arm of the wheelchair. He takes out his hand, fist closed, and gropes for Víctor's hand.

'Take this.'

Víctor opens his hand and is immediately struck by the weight and feel of the metal cylinder.

'Auzinger.'

He squeezes his hand and the telescopic cane shoots out across the table, knocking the ashtray to the floor.

'I'll get it,' Alicia says, resigned to her role as an observer.

Víctor squeezes the handle again and retracts the cane. He brings it to his face and sniffs it.

'Smells of paint,' he says, as though he can't quite understand. Then a flash of understanding lights up his face. 'You've painted it white, you bastard!' He shrugs off Galván's hand and turns to Alicia. 'That goes for you too. Bastards, the pair of you.'

With surprising speed, given how weak he is, Galván's arm shoots out again and he grabs Víctor's lapel.

'More than twenty years ago I made a prediction which, thanks to you, came true. You became one hell of a magician, and you're still a little wretch. Now, I'm going to make another prediction: you will walk. You might never be a magician again. Nobody cares about that any more. And maybe you'll always be a little wretch. But you'll walk. You will use this cane and you'll learn to walk down the street even if it's only to come and visit my grave once a year.

'You want me to put flowers in the tip of the cane? Or would you prefer a silk handkerchief?'

Galván strokes his chin. Víctor crouches down, takes the maestro's face in his hands. He wants to hug him but the wheelchair is in the way.

'You're the best,' he says.

'Was, Víctor, I was. Now I'm nothing.'

'I'll walk. I don't have anywhere to go, but I'll learn to walk.'

'To my grave.'

'*Papá!*' the daughter intervenes. 'That's enough now. Besides ...'

'Yes, you're right. I shouldn't tire myself. I've said all I came to say. Let's go.'

347

The goodbyes take a long time. And not because of the words that no one says, but the hands that grip, that thank, that say goodbye for ever. Standing by the door, Alicia and Víctor watch as the maestro leaves, and hear his last words, almost drowned out by the roar of traffic.

'Shit, I love the smell of cigarette smoke.'

There is a sudden metallic sound. Startled, Alicia turns and sees that the cane has been extended.

'Right, then, over to you,' Víctor says. 'How the fuck do you use this thing?'

He is waiting for instructions.

The Gallery of Famous Blind People: IV

Milton, John Milton, the poet. Ring a bell? The one who wrote *Paradise Lost*. He has a place of honour in the gallery, but I need to tell you about it seriously. You don't joke around with Milton. As if being a poet while Shakespeare was alive were not punishment enough, fate visited him with a terrible blindness, with operations that were more like torture and a unbearable moral obligation because he believed that losing his sight had to be a punishment from God, something that he deserved, though he could never determine what his sin had been. He was very religious, was Milton. He had studied to be an Anglican priest, though he never practised, and he spent his whole life writing sermons. He made translations of the Psalms, and went so far as to add to the line 'Mine eye is consumed because of grief; it waxeth old because of all mine enemies' the words 'and dark'. Waxen old *and dark*. There is no reason in terms of rhyme or scansion for adding this; he did so because he wanted to. Because he was obsessed.

These days he could have avoided all that guilt; from the symptoms he describes so well it is possible to infer that he suffered from opto-chiasmatic arachnoiditis, the result of a tumour on the pituitary gland. His blindness, like yours, Víctor, was white, something he found astonishing. I don't know why everyone always assumes the blind see nothing but blackness. White is just as blinding. The tumour would also account for his vitriolic temperament, the spitefulness attributed to him.

He was treated by a quack in Paris. The cure, if it can be called that, was to be achieved through a superficial but excruciatingly painful operation, involving cauterising the skin on his temples and on his forehead just above the eyebrows. Cauterising at that time was an exact synonym for burning. Afterwards, threads dipped in egg white were inserted under the skin. I hardly need tell you the treatment was utterly useless.

Blindness conditioned Milton's life so completely that it even changed the way he dreamed. Milton was already blind by the time he met his second wife, Katherine, something which did not prevent her from quickly falling pregnant. It was a difficult labour and Katherine died soon after. The poet insisted that her coffin should be closed 'with twelve several locks, that had twelve several keys', which he distributed among his friends on the day of her funeral. This had nothing to do with his blindness but arose from the fact that Milton, in spite of his quarrels with the Almighty, still believed in eternal life. It is possible that he was surprised when he arrived in the gallery, since he must have imagined her very differently. The fact is, when Katherine died, scarcely more than a year after they met, he had never seen her face. Shortly before the funeral, he wrote his most important sonnet, which begins 'Methought I saw my late espousèd saint'. He goes on to say that she appeared to him 'Rescu'd from death by force, though pale and faint'. But the true miracle of the dream is not this, but that he can finally see her 'vested all in white, pure as her mind'. Poor Milton, if that was the only time he ever saw her, you'd think she might have appeared nude. Or at least dressed in a different colour. In the dream he does not even see her face, as it is hidden by a veil. This does not prevent him from detecting the sweetness and the goodness she radiates. He ends the sonnet: 'But Oh! as to embrace me she inclin'd, I wak'd, she fled, and day brought back my night.'

Incredible, isn't it? I don't really know what it means, so don't expect me to draw some moral from it. But it does seem cruel to me that he couldn't see her face. I don't know, if perhaps the dream left him with hope, a yearning to see her again, a feeling that on some other night, in some other dream, he might finally see her face. Or perhaps the meaning is more subtle. The dream could imply that it's not really her, because back then a person's identity was inextricably linked to their face, to their eyes in particular. Or worse still, perhaps it means that dreams are capricious; imagine that he lifts the veil and finds a monstrous nose, or skin scarred by the pox. In not seeing her face, he is spared all this. Of course, it's possible to go for his favourite explanation for everything: divine punishment.

Milton was buried in a place which was, back then, on the outskirts of London, but even in death he got no rest because, a hundred years later, a bunch of savages desecrated the grave and didn't even leave his bones. Apparently it was a mob of hoodlums on a drinking binge, though it could just as easily have been relic hunters. In the gallery, he doesn't need his bones. What is most surprising is that Milton hardly ever complains: he likes to eat well, and as long as he can do that, he doesn't care about anything else.

Sorry, I'm going off on a tangent. I started telling you about this so you'd forget about the meeting with Galván. Obviously, I set it up, you know that now. But it doesn't matter. There's no such thing as a chance encounter. If they're not engineered by a third person, then life contrives to arrange them. Who cares? History is fully of brief, dazzling, unrepeatable meetings, moments when fate or self-interest or connivance brings together two minds destined to meet for some reason. My favourite such incident is Milton's encounter with Galileo. They met in Italy under difficult circumstances. The astronomer was a very old man by then, and had only five or six years left to live. The Inquisition had turned a deaf ear to his pronouncement *Eppur si muove* and spared his life but kept him under house arrest in Arcetri. He was a broken man: they had refused him treatment for a painful hernia, his daughter had died three years earlier and he could no longer even take comfort in playing the lute because his fingers were gnarled with arthritis. Milton noticed the dusty instrument lying abandoned in a corner. The most interesting thing about the meeting, from our point of view, is that Galileo was blind. The myth that Galileo lost his sight from staring at the sun through his telescope is rubbish. He suffered from cataracts and glaucoma which, by 1637, had left him completely without sight. We know it happened then because there is a letter written by a Father Castelli, one of his favourite pupils, which confirms the fact: 'The noblest eye is darkened which nature ever made, an eye so privileged and so gifted with rare qualities that it may with truth be said to have seen more than the

351

eyes of all those who are gone, and to have opened the eyes of all those who are to come.' Just like Galván, don't you think? A noble eye that opens other eyes. It's like some cruel joke. Milton was so moved by the encounter, so incensed by the conditions in which the scientist was forced to live, that he made freedom of belief the central tenet of his life. Despite the fact that his writings are filled with religious dogma, he was distressed at the very idea that anyone could be imprisoned because of his ideas. We don't know what they talked about. We don't know whether anyone made any predictions. But Milton never forgot the encounter.

The Last Step before the Last Step

I don't want you to go all melodramatic on me, Viviana warns them. It is a happy moment and a sad one, but it's not a tragedy. I have asked you to take the last step, but none of you is going to die in the process. I want you to imagine that you've spent your whole life walking towards a goal, OK? Walk, that's all I'm asking, I don't want you dancing. And make sure every step you take is the last. Then take another step. Do you know why? Because your goal walks with you. Every step we take moves the world. Do you understand? OK, start moving. What are you waiting for? Music? There's no music today. You move towards a goal in silence.

Alicia finds it difficult to start. She chatted a little to Vivi the other day, told her that Víctor is taking his drops, that he's even started using the cane, but he's not really making any progress. Or rather, he is progressing, but he doesn't know where. Viviana didn't have any magic advice to give her. Just a little comfort, a hug. And now she is devoting the class, the session, whatever this is called, to her. The others have no reason to know this, but it seems obvious that today's theme was chosen for her, it has her name on it.

She puts one foot forward. Then the other. Not like that, Alicia. She stops. She feels she is going to disappoint Vivi, that she won't be able to make the most of this gift. Five years of biodance, and this is the best you can come up with? You know from experience that the trick is *not* to think. Viviana says it every Tuesday: you don't come here to think, you come here to move. Don't think about what you're going to do; just do it. Try to make your mind a blank, an empty space that can only be filled with movement, where day-to-day thoughts slip away. There is a noise in her brain. An unbearable noise, like the sound when you turn the radio dial looking for a song to listen to. She tries to imagine a moving goal, an end that is a starting point, because unless she misunderstood, that's what this is all about, about taking a step that is not only the last, but the first. Maybe if she moves in circles, if she revolves without moving forward ... A circle is eternal, infinite, a step that spins the whole body, a single step that leaves her exactly as she was before, yet she is utterly transformed by the mere fact of having taken it. Víctor, ants, amber, amber, Víctor, wasps. Get out of my head, Víctor, you're getting tangled up in here.

If only Vivi would come over and give her a push. But Vivi is not even looking at her. Or is pretending not to see her. Alicia watches everyone else, trying to see whether anyone has come up with a pattern worth copying, a movement, a trend, an evolution; that's it, that's why they talk about a dancer evolving onstage, because they move here and there and with every step they change. One of the other dancers moves past her, eyes closed, and Alicia reaches out her arm, places a hand on her shoulder so that they don't collide. She begins to walk behind her, with her, adapts to her rhythm, becomes her shadow, confining herself to following the woman's steps, the mute instructions of her movements, finally free of the need to think. They walk slowly until they reach the far wall and then, when they turn, it is her fellow dancer who leans against her, not with her hand but with her whole body, so that Alicia has no choice but to walk, to go on walking, otherwise they would both fall. She speeds up and now she is not thinking, guiding and being guided, it's impossible to tell who is pushing who, but Alicia does not stop moving, she is in a hurry to walk, to get somewhere. To the other end of the room, to the end of the lesson, to the goal that moves with her. She smiles and glances over at Viviana, who is looking at her now, almost nodding in approval. She puts her arms round her companion, lifts her off the ground and begins to run. She crosses the room, once, twice, a third time, although she knows she does not have the strength, that soon she will have to stop, to set her partner down and rest her arms, and perhaps when that happens the spell will be broken and her mind will go back to the amber, the insect, but that doesn't matter now because she has a plan. I have a plan, she thinks as she catches her breath, her heart hammering in her chest. I have a plan for you, Victor. I've finally found the Trojan Horse that will infiltrate your fortress. Because a man alone ain't got no chance, remember?

Your First Egg

I t's a good thing he's blind, Alicia thinks with a laconic smile. If he could see me here he'd have a heart attack. She is standing in a doorway opposite Víctor's building. It is five o'clock on a cold November morning. She feels stupid playing detective, but this is the only way she can think of to approach Irina. Yesterday, taking advantage of a moment when Víctor was in the bathroom, her fingers trembling, she pressed the speed dial number for the agency. The girl on the other end politely, though a little warily, informed her that Irina did not offer lesbian services. While Alicia hesitated, wondering whether it might not be easier just to tell the truth, she heard the toilet flush and had to hang up. Since she doesn't know where Irina lives, she has no choice but to wait for her here. In fact, she knows nothing about her other than the fact that she is a Romanian prostitute with a sweet face and a two-year-old son. She asked Víctor about Irina only once and he simply told her that they usually spent Saturday afternoons together. Irina would drop by with Darius to pick Víctor up and they'd go down to the park for a while. Nobody mentions sex. Alicia doesn't pry into other people's personal lives, but she has eyes. And a nose. More than anything she can smell it. She reckons that Irina comes over about twice a week.

She can't even be sure that Irina is in Víctor's apartment right now. There is a light on in one of the rooms on the top floor, but that doesn't mean anything. But if it doesn't happen today, it'll happen tomorrow. Or the day after. She's in no hurry. Well, she is, but she's patient. She makes the most of the time by going over her plan. She needs to take every possible precaution because the stakes are high. She has decided not to ask her superiors at ONCE for permission, because they would only say no, it's too risky. How is she going to gain Irina's trust? Money? If only it were that easy. She would happily spend her life savings if she thought it would convince her. But how could she possibly even suggest such a thing: I have a plan and I need you to rent me out your son for a couple of hours. No, all she can do is appeal to her good nature, to her compassion. And minimise the risks. Although, thinking about it, what is the worst that could happen? Darius throws a tantrum? He needs his nappy changed and Víctor can't work out how to do it? He falls and bumps his head? Kids bounce back, they're like rubber.

It is after six by the time the light in the stairwell comes on. Alicia crosses the street, stands in the doorway, mentally counting the steps, come on, Irina, it's not like you're blind, get a move on. She sees her as she starts down the last flight of stairs, prepares her best smile and realises that although she has memorised everything she is going to say, she hasn't thought about her first line, the most important one, something that will win her over immediately. Irina opens the door and Alicia rattles out words like a machine gun.

'I need to talk to you. It's about Víctor. I need your help.'

Irina folds her arms across her chest, adopting a defensive posture when she hears the first sentence, frowns at the second, and opens her arms at the third.

'OK. But I need hurry for my son.'

She is still standing in the doorway. Still holding the door open. Not like this, Alicia thinks.

'I'll walk with you so we can talk,' she suggests. 'Where do you live?'

'Near to zoo,' Irina says somewhat ambiguously.

'Do you fancy some breakfast?' Alicia says, 'There's a kiosk near the zoo, in the park. Doughnuts and hot chocolate? My treat,' she hastens to add. 'I'll be quick, Irina, I promise.'

She stops the first taxi they see. During the ride they talk about the weather, the cold, about the fact the sun will be up soon. Sometimes they sink into silences so long that Alicia tenses her toes in sheer dread. When they get to the Parque de la Ciudadela, she sees the lights are on in the kiosk and heaves a sigh of relief. It was a blind guess. When she was at university, she used to come here when she'd studied all night, but she hasn't been back since.

Irina does not talk much. Alicia cannot stop. She struggles to find examples to explain her case, Víctor's mental block, his unwillingness to change, his enormous potential wasted. Knowing that Irina's Spanish is limited, she avoids metaphorical lumps of amber, complicated theories and images, and tries to find concrete examples of what she means. When breakfast arrives, Alicia says nothing for a minute or two. She notices Irina can stuff herself with doughnuts and still look elegant – no mean feat. Perhaps it is this, her innate poise, this artlessness so like elegance, which means she does not have to work the streets as most of her compatriots do. She wants to ask her what she did before, before she came to Spain, but decides not to. This is where you come in, she says finally. Or rather not you, but Darius. Irina drops her doughnut when she hears her son's name, but she does not object, does not end the conversation. There is no anger on her face, just an almost comic astonishment which Alicia quickly attempts to assuage with promises: it won't be for long, she'll be right there ready to intervene if necessary, nothing is going to happen. Well, she concedes, nothing much. Irina is a pragmatic woman. She does not question the possible outcome of the plan or ask Alicia to explain its theoretical basis, she asks only for specific details: what day, what time, for how long, what's her own excuse. Alicia begins to see light at the end of the tunnel, because she has rehearsed this part a thousand times. Perhaps it is the convincing way she explains every detail, her confidence, which persuades Irina to accept with only one condition: she has to be present too. If not, there's nothing more to discuss. I am there too, she says again before finishing her hot chocolate and setting down her cup. I am there too.

The first twittering of the birds in the park announces the imminent arrival of sunrise. They hug as they say goodbye, an embrace in which there is a space left for Víctor, because he is the one they are protecting as their cheeks brush against each other. Alicia takes a taxi home, has a quick shower, and, utterly exhausted, sets off on her bicycle to Víctor's place. Fortunately, he won't be able to see the bags under her eyes, but his hearing is keen enough to detect the slightest stress or tiredness in her voice. So the first thing she does, as casually as she can, is ask him for his keys so she can have copies made. She is about to tell him that she needs a key only to the door downstairs, that she was in the area last night and couldn't find a safe place to park her bike, but didn't want to disturb him because it was late. But before she can say a word, Víctor puts his hand in his trouser pocket, takes out his keys and hands them over. He doesn't give a damn that she has keys to his apartment, that she knows where he keeps his money. He doesn't give a damn about anything. Alicia puts the keys in her bag and tells him she will bring them back later today as soon as she's made a copy.

This is the final piece she needs in order to set her plan in motion. If it were up to her, she would go home straight away, sleep all morning and spend the rest of the day preparing for Saturday. But she is going to stay and act as though this were a day like any other. Which is to say that, although she cannot look at Víctor without the tender pity reserved for victims of a well-intentioned con, she will be stern with him, push him, refuse to be swayed by his lack of enthusiasm, force him to do things. Practical things.

I'd like a hard-boiled egg, she says to him, and I want you to cook it for me. Víctor agrees with a resignation that Alicia recognises all too well after weeks, perhaps months, of practice. OK, if you insist, I will boil an egg. Just one. But don't think that means I have the slightest intention, etc. ...

Alicia has brought everything he will need in her bag. The egg, obviously, wrapped in several layers of newspaper. A small bottle of vegetable oil, a small quantity of salt in a plastic container, a long-handled saucepan, a plate, a knife, two forks, even a lighter specially adapted for the blind. With a long wand. She has everything covered. They go to the kitchen and both do what they are best at: Alicia gives precise instructions and Víctor carries them out.

Hold the saucepan in your right hand, put your index finger inside. Find the mixer tap with your left and hold the pan underneath. Run your hand down to the bottom of the mixer tap and turn it on. As soon as the water comes up to your finger, turn off the tap. Set the saucepan down on the counter, but keep your hand on it so you always know where it is. Take the egg in your other hand. It's right in front of you. At eleven o'clock. They have been talking like this for some time now, referring to the position of things as numbers on an imaginary clock. You're going to put the egg in the pan, carefully, so it doesn't break. Add a pinch of salt. It will raise the boiling point and also stop the shell from cracking. Take a step to your right. Find the burner you're going to use on the stove. Take the pan and put it on the burner. Don't centre it completely. Move it a little more towards twelve. Not quite so much, you just need enough space for the tip of the lighter. Since you haven't turned it on yet, you can touch anything you want. When you've got this down to a fine art, you'll always keep the lighter in the same place, but since it's your first time, I'll hand it to you. No, take it with your right hand. That's it. Bring it closer to the burner. With your left hand, turn the knob to low. Hear the gas? Ignite it. Put down the lighter. Bring your hand up to your chest. Can you feel the heat? This part is important – if you can't feel any heat, that means you didn't light the burner and gas is escaping. In that case, you need to turn off the burner immediately and start again.

Since this is going to be the only time, Víctor is determined to do it properly. He concentrates as though she were teaching him the most spectacular magic trick in the world. Which is what it feels like. To the observer, filling a saucepan, putting in the egg, the salt, setting it on a burner and lighting the gas looks like one single, continuous action. To do it blind is an exhausting sequence of tiny actions which work only if each is accomplished with absolute order and precision. You need to know what it is you want to do before you start, and afterwards check you have done it. Jesus Christ, he thinks, all this just to boil an egg? And we've only just started.

Feel the heat? Good. Move the pan so it's centred on the burner. Remember, you need to move a fraction towards six. That's it. Now, you need to shut up and listen. There are people who put a teaspoon in the bottom of the pan so that when it moves they know the water is boiling, but I don't like that. It's too messy. If you listen closely you'll hear when the water starts to boil. You'll have to practise a couple of times a day for a while. Imagine you want spaghetti, for example. You can't put the pasta in until the water starts boiling.

A few bubbles are beginning to rise from the bottom of the pan, but Víctor does not react until the water is boiling steadily. Is that it? Yes. Now, the easiest thing would be to use a specially adapted timer, but I didn't have time to swing by ONCE this morning and pick one up. It takes eight minutes so I'll let you know when. While they're waiting, Alicia tells Víctor that one of the blind people she worked with had a selection of operatic arias chosen specially because of their length. The person in question used them to time things they were cooking. Some older women say specific prayers. For a casserole or a roast, they might say a whole rosary. OK, that's eight minutes. Turn off the gas. Remember the position of the saucepan handle? It's at three o'clock. Pick it up and carry it over to the sink. Turn on the cold water. With a bit of practice, you'll learn to take the egg out with a small strainer. In the meantime, let the cold water run and count to a hundred. Now it's safe to put your hand in. Take out the egg. Open the bin. Peel the egg. You already know how to do that. Run your fingers over it to make sure there aren't any pieces of shell left. Remember where you put the plate? Perfect. Put the egg on it. Take this knife. You're not going to cut it into slices. Perfectionism is all very well, but sometimes you can go too far. Find the two ends of the egg and cut it in half. One for you, one for me. Excellent, Víctor, you've just boiled your first egg. All you need now is a little drizzle of oil. I'll do that if you like. Here, I brought a couple of forks.

But Víctor doesn't wait. He launches himself at the plate, grabs his half and stuffs it in his mouth, chews four times, presses the mass against the roof of his mouth with his tongue, screws up his face, makes a low purring noise and when he turns his vacant eyes to Alicia, she sees that they are shining with tears and she cannot understand that it is not because of his hunger, because he likes the taste, that it's not the salt, the oil or the egg, but the temperature, the unexpected contact of something warm against his taste buds which for more than a year now have been condemned to a merciless regime of cold.

I'll Wait Here For You

She feels a little ashamed when she realises that a number of passers-by, surprised to see her holding a camera, stop and glance up the street to see what she is filming. The camera offers her a false pretext: she is about to film an important event and perhaps the resulting footage will one day be used to train future technicians. But if that were true, she would have told Víctor that she was thinking of filming him. Since she hasn't done so, the only possible conclusion is that she is spying on him and that her very presence, with or without a camera, is a sign she doesn't trust him. Because until just now, she suspected Víctor would not fulfil his promise and come alone, she was convinced that at the last minute he would be afraid and would call Irina.

All this changed the moment she saw him approaching the bus stop, his body tense, his face grim, but walking with confident strides. And by himself. That is the important part: by himself. Using the cane. Since that moment, Alicia has been standing almost on tiptoe, holding the camera as high as she can, her right arm out to stop anyone else from wandering into shot. She is nervous: now and then she brings her hand to her mouth, bites her nails, curses the fact the bus is late. If she had to award points, she would give Víctor a 10 so far. He arrived on time and, from what Alicia can tell, he has done everything he should: he's standing at the back of the bus shelter, well away from the road in order to avoid an accident, has asked whether there is anyone else waiting, explained that he wants to take the number 39 so can they let him know when it arrives. An elderly woman with a kindly face replied. Unfortunately, Alicia couldn't record their conversation, but the images spoke volumes. She followed the exchange so enthusiastically that her lips began to mouth silent words of encouragement: that's good, Víctor, you're doing well. There he is, standing still, cane retracted, hands in his pockets. Actually, were it not for the fact that this stop is served by several bus lines he wouldn't even have needed help. He's perfectly capable of telling when the bus has arrived from the sound; all he needs is for someone to confirm that this one's a 39. They went over these details only yesterday.

The longer Víctor has to stand at the bus stop, the more anxious he will feel. Just as Alicia is beginning to curse the council and the bus drivers' union, she sees the bus appear at the end of the street. The elderly woman goes over to Víctor, whispers something in his ear and takes his forearm. Alicia zooms in with the camera as close as she can, though she does not need to see Víctor's face to know that he will be bothered by the woman touching him. Víctor's lips move, he is clearly making a cutting remark. The woman lets go of his arm and takes a step back. How rude.

Tense, concentrating, Víctor recognises the sound of the engine when the bus is still some thirty yards away. With a speed that perhaps even the camera will not capture, he extends the cane. Perfect. The bus comes to a halt and opens its doors a couple of yards away from the stop. Alicia curses the driver. Víctor steps forward, holding the cane out in front of him, stands in front of the door, finds the first step with the tip of the cane, brings his hands up and fumbles for the handrail, climbs aboard and immediately puts the cane in the diagonal position to make sure he does not trip over anything. The woman is behind him, ready to offer help should he need it, but she makes no attempt to intervene. Alicia is thankful for her patience. Usually, there's some arsehole in a hurry. She switches off the camera and tiptoes to the door of the bus. She is barely breathing. If Víctor finds out she's spying on him, he will kill her. Through the windows, she sees Víctor take out the ticket she gave him, printed in raised ink so he knows which way it needs to go into the machine. Then he brings his hand up to the top rail, still holding the cane in front of him with the other, and moves towards the middle doors, where he stands next to a pole. Yesterday, she tried to show him how to find an empty seat but Víctor finally yelled, 'I'm not an old man, Alicia, I'm blind. I'm capable of standing up.' The bus moves off. Bye-bye, little old man, she thinks as she watches it move way. She feels like waving, like blowing him a kiss.

She hails a taxi, gives the driver directions and tells him she's in a bit of a hurry. She can't afford to get there after Víctor. For the first few minutes of the journey, she watches what she has filmed on the monitor. She has to congratulate Víctor, he didn't make a single mistake. When the traffic begins to clear and the taxi over-takes the bus, Alicia leans her head back, closes her eyes and takes a deep breath. That really took it out of her. They made the same journey together two days ago. Without the cane, with Víctor still clinging to her elbow like a limpet. She talked the whole way. Stand like this, listen to that, pay attention to this, ask for that, walk up to here, grab the rail with this hand, no, higher up, get on board, put the cane here. Instructions. Víctor said nothing but complied. It was like carrying a heavy rucksack.

The following day, they did the same journey again, but with one difference: Víctor still stuck to her but this time he was the one who didn't shut up. When he wasn't arguing loudly, he was muttering under his breath: Christ, it would be so much easier to take a taxi, for fuck's sake, it's not like we even need to go anywhere ... He tripped over everything in his path, elbowed people aside and at one point Alicia was afraid that he was going to hit her with his cane.

The third time, he did not make a single mistake, but Alicia was reluctant to set too much store by this. She knows what he is like now. All he really wants is for her to leave him in peace. Some days he will pretend to be unbelievably clumsy, hoping that maybe she will take pity on him, or at least give him a break. If that doesn't work, he does the exact opposite: he will demonstrate a skill which, far from being encouraging, is all about contempt. It might mean that he is ready to take the bus by himself, that he doesn't need any more lessons, but it also means he has no intention of ever taking the bus again. There is only one flaw in this strategy: it's impossible to fake a skill. So whenever Víctor insists on proving he can do something in order to get her to stop showing him how, Alicia chalks up a little victory. Her mission is simply to teach him how to take the bus; whether or not he ever takes it again has nothing to do with her.

Since he refused even to discuss the possibility of doing the same journey without a guide, they came to an agreement. She would go with him, but she would simply follow and be ready to intervene if necessary. They decided to try the strategy out the same day on the bus back, and everything seemed to be going well until, as he was boarding the bus, Víctor dropped his cane. Instead of bending down and feeling around using the techniques which he had mastered perfectly in their first week, he started waving his arms around wildly to stop himself being trampled. One person did yell at him, but the real problem was the two girls who immediately bent down to help him find it. Víctor felt something brush against his leg and lashed out with his feet as though he were being attacked by a wild boar. Alicia had had to put her arms around him and forcibly move him away from the door. Only after she had had to listen to his hysterical ranting about how she should have intervened earlier did she manage to calm him.

As she leans back in the taxi, it occurs to her that the real miracle was that he was prepared to try again the following day. She congratulates herself on her powers of persuasion, although it wasn't easy. If everything is going to plan, Víctor is now standing next to the middle doors, holding on to the rail and counting the stops. In fact, all he needs to do is ask someone to let him know when they get to his stop. People are usually happy to help the blind. It's not unusual to find those who will go out of their way to help. But Víctor refuses to ask for help. Alicia does not know whether this is out of pride, shyness or insecurity, but she tries to take advantage of the fact – for as long as Víctor refuses to ask other people for help, he has no choice but to learn to take care of himself. At this rate, he will turn out to be the perfect blind person. A little rude, a little lonely, but perfect.

She pays the driver, gets out and stands inside the bus shelter, camera at the ready. Everything went so well yesterday that, as soon as they arrived, Alicia said:

'Tomorrow you'll do it by yourself. I'll wait for you here. Eleven o'clock.'

'You might end up waiting all day,' he said.

'Fine, I'll take that risk . . .'

The bus is approaching. Alicia gets the camera ready. The doors open and the first thing she sees on the monitor is the white cane, perfectly perpendicular to the ground. He finds the step, then moves the cane forward to make sure there are no obstacles in front of him. Next his feet appear on the screen. Ten out of ten, Víctor. The doors close, the bus moves off and Víctor stands, motionless, on the road. Alerted by the noise of traffic, Alicia looks up from the camera and is about to shout to him to get off the road when he taps the cane to find the kerb, steps up on to the pavement and, shrugging his shoulders, says:

'Right. Well, now I've learned to get around by bus.'

Which means: if you like, we can move on to something equally pointless.

There are three steps between them. She stands, staring at him. She could kill him. She could kiss him.

For an instant, Víctor thinks that Alicia is not at the bus stop. Only for a fraction of a second, but in that moment she can see the fear in his eyes. She calls to him even before she turns off the camera.

'I'm right here, Víctor.'

'I was saying, now that I've learned . . .'

'No, Víctor. You've learned how to get on and off a bus, that's not the same as being able to travel. Nobody takes a bus just to take the same one back. You take the bus because there's somewhere you want to go. Remember the café where we had a drink with Galván?'

'Of course. It's on this street, same side, two blocks farther along.'

'Tomorrow, I'll wait for you there.'

'Aren't you going to congratulate me?'

'Tomorrow, tomorrow . . .'

'Will it always be like this?'

'What?'

'Is there always something left to be learned tomorrow?'

He is speaking in a low voice, but the words are like a scream: is this hell going to go on for ever?

'No, Víctor. There will come a day when it's complete.'

And that day is not far off, though neither of them says this. They stand in silence. To reach that goal will be a triumph, but even to think about it is sad. For both of them.

Tickles

They both spent the first half-hour with their ears pressed to the door, listening for the slightest whisper, but some time ago, feeling a little calmer, they decided to sit on the landing outside the door. From time to time, Alicia reaches up and hits the timer switch on the light. Everything is fine. The silence is tense, but they have relaxed their vigil somewhat because Víctor, like anyone else when they're talking to a child of that age, is speaking about an octave higher than usual, in a sing-song voice which means they can work out what is going on inside the apartment as easily as if they were watching it happen. Alicia clings to the copies she had made of the keys and the knowledge that they can let themselves in if they need to is reassuring.

Inside, they seem to be drawing. That's lovely, Víctor exclaims from time to time. Draw a circle for me. Irina stares at the door. Alicia closes her eyes so she can translate what she is hearing into pictures. They must be sitting on the floor, since there's no table. She visualises Darius holding the Parker pen. Where did they get the paper from? Maybe they're drawing on the sofa. It doesn't matter. What's that? She hears, Mickey? Oh, Mickey Mouse. Silly me, I should have recognised him. Can you draw Pluto for me? You know who Pluto is? When they hear Darius's whispered replies, Alicia opens her eyes and looks at Irina to make sure everything is OK. The boy uses one Spanish word for every two or three in Romanian. He has just said something. What? What do you want, Darius?

Alicia would like to be able to make the most of this silence to talk to Irina. She wants to thank her, obviously. She could never have pulled off her plan without her help. Irina had arrived at twelve on the dot as they had arranged, and performed her role with the skill of an accomplished actress. I need leave Darius with you, she said as soon as Víctor said hello, as though she were in a desperate hurry. Neighbour she go holiday. No have no one to babysit. I be quick. Come straight back. Then, following Alicia's instructions to the letter, she pre-empted any misgivings Víctor might have had by rattling off a list of instructions: in this bag is nappies and baby wipes, cookies here. Here, touch. Alicia had insisted that Irina get Víctor to touch everything so he would feel more confident. Irina had to leave immediately, thank you, Víctor, thank you, and having thrust Darius into his arms, whispering something reassuring to him in Romanian, she had rushed out. Alicia heard everything from her position on the landing. When the door opened, she held her breath, careful not to make the slightest sound, nothing that might reveal her presence. Trying to be a spirit. But she had her eyes open. And, seeing the expression of puzzled gentleness with which Víctor cradled Darius in his arms, she swallowed hard and thought that everything was going to be fine.

'Water?' She hears Víctor's voice. 'Come on ... What do you say? Something to ...? Something to ...?'

'Dink!' She hears the boy's voice.

'That's right. Here you go, drink. What do you say, Darius? Thank you, you say thaaaaank you.' It's magnificent. He's not only keeping the boy amused, he's trying to teach him. An altruistic act. More than she could have hoped for. Irina cannot possibly understand how much this means, but Alicia can. She is not about to tell her about ants and solitary wasps, but she can imagine the cracking sound as the amber shatters. The plan is working.

There is a burst of laughter from Darius, followed by a silence, then a louder laugh. And another. Tickles, thinks Alicia. The two women smile. Then they hear footsteps coming closer. They must be in the hallway. Darius is running up and down. Víctor chases him, catches him and covers him with noisy kisses then lets him go again. Until Darius starts to cry. 'It's all right, it's OK,' Víctor's voice reassures him. 'You fell down, but you're not hurt.' 'Yes, hurts,' the boy whimpers. The two women quickly get to their feet. Irina gestures for Alicia to give her the keys but Alicia clasps her hands together: please, let's just wait for a moment, it's nothing serious. Víctor's voice says the words 'It's nothing serious, Darius. Show me . . . Where did you hurt yourself? Here? All right, Víctor will kiss it better. There you are, you're OK now.' Darius has stopped crying and whimpers, 'Me hungry.' The voices move away but a minute later comes the sound of Darius laughing. Irina and Alicia sit down again.

Perhaps now is the moment to bring the experiment to a close. Irina can go downstairs and press the buzzer on the intercom as though she has just arrived. The idea was that, for the first time in a long while, Víctor would have no one to look after him, but he would have to look after someone else. A moral obligation to attend to someone else's needs. Has it been enough? How long does one have to be exposed to other people to forget oneself? Does she need to repeat the experiment? Would Irina be prepared to let her?

Put your hand here. Víctor's voice sounds as though it is extremely close, just on the other side of the door. The bastard, Alicia thinks, the arrogant bastard. They both get to their feet. 'Over here, Darius, I can't put your coat on if you don't help me. Come on, we're going to go out.' Alicia is the first to react. She grabs Irina's elbow, presses a finger to her lips asking her to remain quiet and pulls her away from the door. They barely have time to make it up to the next landing before the door opens. They lean over the banister carefully so Darius will not see them. Víctor is carrying Darius with one arm. He is holding a cheese and ham sandwich in his teeth, like a hunting dog reluctant to give up its prey. With his free hand, he closes the door, then he pats his trouser pocket to make sure he has his keys. Other way round, Alicia thinks, and cannot help shaking her head. The other way round, Víctor, first you check to make sure you have your keys, then you close the door. There's no point otherwise. She's told him a hundred times.

'Here, take this. It's bread, honey. Bread and ham. You like ham?' Darius accepts the sandwich and takes a bite. Although his feet seem to know the precise distance of every step, Víctor keeps his left hand on the banister at all times, and brushes his right shoulder against the wall. They leave a trail of breadcrumbs as they go, all the way down to the entrance.

Irina is about to push Alicia out of the way, but there's no need. They both dash down the stairs, two at a time, and when they get out on to the street, they stop dead. About five yards away, Víctor is walking with long, slow strides as though he needs to steel himself at every step. He manoeuvres the cane with his left hand, his right holding on tightly to Darius, who trots along beside him – or rather, one pace ahead, as though trying to guide him. The child's steps – four little hops for each of Víctor's strides – follow the strict, steady rhythm of the tapping of the cane. Regular as a metronome set to *andante*. Rather than looking at them, Alicia, ever the professional, runs her gaze quickly along the pavement to the first corner. There is no imminent danger, no scaffolding, no dogs, no motorbikes parked on the pavement, no group coming the other way, and what few pedestrians there are, alerted by the white cane, step to one side even before they reach Víctor.

They are so close that Alicia does not dare speak. She gestures to Irina to move back a few steps, whispers in her ear: 'I'll go after them, Irina. I promise you everything is going to be fine. I just don't want Darius to see you.' By the time Víctor gets to the corner, Alicia is on his left, walking one step behind, focused on the impossible task of mentally controlling his every step. She counts the sounds: tap, tap, step, tap. When she comes to the crossing, having checked that there are no cars coming, she crosses in front of them, tapping her heels hard against the road surface to let Víctor know it is safe to cross. She turns and watches him, lets him walk past her and waits for Irina. She is not worried now. The little square is a pedestrian zone and Alicia, who knew at once where Víctor was heading, takes a deep breath.

Víctor does not let go of Darius's hand until they are inside the playground. Alicia and Irina remain outside, leaning against the wooden fence. The boy rushes off to the slide. Víctor stands in the middle of the playground and raises the hand holding the cane.

'Is there anyone else in the park?' He is almost shouting. 'I need help.'

A young blonde woman goes over to him. She is carrying a small black child about a year older than Darius.

'What's the matter?' she asks.

'I'm blind. The boy isn't my son. I was minding him at home but he was determined to go out ...'

'That's fine,' the blonde woman says. 'What's his name?'

'Darius.'

'Darius, come here.' The blonde woman crouches down and draws the two children together. 'Would you like to play with Yedne?'

'Sorry?' Víctor says. 'Yedne?'

'He's from Ethiopia,' the woman replies. 'He's adopted. Come on.' She turns to the children. 'Who wants a go on the slide?'

A great weight lifted from his shoulders, Víctor feels his legs give way. He sits on the ground at the foot of the slide. From the top, Darius counts to three in Romanian and slides down. Yedne follows him. As soon as they get to the bottom, they stand up and both of them rush into Víctor's arms, convinced that that is why he's sitting there. They fall backwards. Víctor lies still for a second or two, then roars, grabs for them and tickles them, rolling around with them, laughing wildly.

After ten minutes, they are all sitting around him. Everyone, including the blonde, two other women and their children. Víctor has taken three small rubber balls from his pocket and magically transformed them into one, then they multiply again, disappear up one sleeve and reappear out of the other. He puts one ball in his mouth, then takes it out, but then takes out another, and another, and another. There are five balls now, all different colours. The mothers clap and the children, who are too young to realise what is happening, laugh and wave. The excitement is contagious. Darius lets his mind wander for a minute, looking vaguely across the square, then shouts:

'Mum!'

Without even looking at Alicia, Irina reacts immediately. She goes into the playground and sits on the ground next to her son and, as she hugs him, and kisses him, she puts her free hand on Víctor's shoulder, apologises for being late and in her clumsy Spanish explains that she was rushing back to his place when she saw them here. Now she's asking whether Darius has had anything to eat. Alicia moves away, walking backwards so as not to take her eyes off them. She clasps her hands together at chest height and makes a little bow: thank you, Irina, thank you. She blows a kiss, turns and leaves, happy that the plan has worked, although she does not want to claim all the credit because it is time which causes amber to wear away, the same time that dictates that children in playgrounds all over Spain are no longer called Pedro and Antonio, but Darius and Yedne, the same wretched, obdurate time that one day forced Irina to take a train and cross the border with a baby in her arms, the time that now urges Alicia, demands, that she say goodbye to Víctor, because the day has come when her presence in the life of this bastard, this intractable genius who has made her life as difficult as he could, is no longer necessary.

A Double Grief

Sometimes it is better to say nothing and just watch. Even though she wants to ask him how he is feeling, even though she cannot help speculating about the effect Galván's death will have on Víctor's fragile spirit, Alicia realises that now is not the time to pester him with questions. But his apparent calm makes her suspicious, the stoicism with which he took the news. And especially his silence. She is still waiting for him to say something. His only reaction when he first heard was to ask her to help him find the leather case in the studio. Then, as he wiped off the dust, he said:

'Right, let's go . . .'

'Go where?'

'Where do you think? To the morgue, to his house, to wherever the vigil is. The daughter did tell you, didn't she?'

'What's the case for?'

'It was his. I want it to be buried with him. Or burned. Whatever.'

After that point he spoke only once, when they reached the street. He said he wanted to go by taxi. The driver, perhaps alerted by their silence or as a mark of respect because they were going to the morgue, made no attempt to engage them in conversation. In fact, he even turned off the radio. Víctor now pays him with a fifty-euro note and gets out without waiting for the change.

They check which room they need to go to, take the single flight of stairs that leads to the basement, convinced they are going to be met by a crowd, because in spite of the silence imposed by the surroundings, they can hear an almost solid murmur that must be hundreds of voices. This is not the time for demonstrations of independence. Víctor folds his cane. Alicia offers him her elbow and walks on ahead, clearing a path through the crowd. Each

374

group of mourners falls silent as they pass; someone breaks away from the group, comes over to Víctor and whispers in his ear words that Alicia can barely hear, but which she imagines are words of condolence over Galván's death and happiness or surprise at Víctor's presence at the vigil. Others simply hug him. Víctor responds to each of them with a polite smile, nodding constantly as though his head were on a spring, offering the occasional monosyllable. Then, when he decides it is time to move on, he gently squeezes Alicia's elbow.

'Thank you, Víctor,' Galván's daughter says when they finally reach the room. 'Dad would have been happy that you came. He always felt you were like a ...'

Víctor lets go of Alicia's elbow and fumbles until he finds the woman's cheek. He strokes it awkwardly.

'What would have made your father happy,' he interrupts her, 'would be knowing that his prediction has come true.'

'He never doubted that it would. Besides, Alicia has been keeping us up to date with your progress.'

'I have a favour to ask you.'

'Of course, what is it?'

'I'd like you to bury this with him.'

He holds up the leather case and waits for her to take it.

'What is it?'

Víctor raises his eyebrows, pulls at his shirt cuffs and clears his throat.

'Well ... it was his. Or rather, it belonged to Peter Grouse, but Mario gave it to me as a present, it must be ...'

'Peter who?'

'Grouse, Peter Grouse.'

'I don't know who you mean. Anyway, it's not important. If you think it had a particular value for *Papá*, I've no objection ...'

'I don't know. I'm having second thoughts now. Maybe I should keep it to remind me of him.'

'Whatever you think best. I have a favour to ask you too. I was thinking of organising a tribute to my father. In a couple of weeks, when things have calmed down a little. I'd like you all to come. His students, I mean, the magicians of Barcelona, the people who really mattered to him. And I'd like someone to perform an illusion in his honour. Something simple. I thought maybe you ...'

'Where?'

'At the museum.' She takes a deep breath and smiles. 'Well, I don't suppose there will ever be a museum now. You know where I mean, where he used to give lessons.'

'I'll be there.'

Alicia all but jumps for joy, but Víctor immediately feels for her elbow and squeezes it several times as though trying to tell her something in Morse code. Now he does look nervous, or sad, or confused. She does not know what to call it. She decides to get him out of there.

'I didn't really know your father,' she says by way of goodbye, 'but I do know he was a good man.'

They make their way out, Víctor giving Alicia a little push, urging her not to stop every time someone tries to talk to him. They come to the foot of the steps. Alicia would like to stop here, ask him why he was suddenly so agitated, but Víctor immediately opens up his cane and starts up the stairs.

'Stop, wait for me,' she mutters. 'Don't you want to stay for the funeral?'

Víctor waits for no one. With a confidence that Alicia cannot allow herself to admire just now, he heads to the exit and walks towards the taxi rank. In the back of the taxi he sits next to her, the leather case at his feet, not uttering a word. Alicia respects his silence just as she did on the way there. What she cannot know is that Víctor is dealing with a double mourning. He is grieving for Galván, obviously. But also for Peter Grouse. Peter Grouse doesn't exist. He has never existed. This is something Víctor has just realised in a painful flash. Peter Grouse was someone invented by Galván, a tool with which the maestro made his best students a prisoner of his plans. As always when we suddenly become aware of a lie, what most bothers Víctor is the fact that he did not realise it earlier. In his mind he goes through all of Galván's lessons, their long chats, berates himself for his own foolishness. It was all a story. A fable filled with moral lessons. Every part of the story was an imaginary finger pointing out the path he should take, the scope of his ambition, the line of fire and how to cross it. But it was more than that: Grouse was a model even in trivial matters, supposing of course that Galván believed that anything could be considered trivial when it came to magic. Curiosity. The way a magician should dress. Punctuality. Vigilance. Obsessive planning. Tenacity. Daring. The ability to improvise.

You're an imbecile! A dupe! A blind man before he went blind. A deluded seer. Because not only did Víctor believe everything Galván told him. He saw it. He has spent his whole life seeing it. He has a perfect portrait of Grouse in his mind, can hear his voice, knows his tics, his habits, his every gesture. But it is not simply that he has been gullible – he gave Galván his imagination, his collusion, because Víctor had invested more effort and more care in developing the myth than the maestro did himself. Unquestioningly, without ever wondering how such an important figure in the history of magic could have left no written record, how it could be that, even in a library as comprehensive as that of Galván, there was not a single word written by or about him, not a document, not one miserable photocopied patent. Nothing.

He squeezes the handle of the leather case. I'd like you to have this, Galván's voice whispers in his ear. This is so you can tie it to your wrist. If you lose it, I'll cut your hands off. Who is Peter Grouse? A magician. I'll tell you about him some time. You only had to feel the touch of cracked leather to believe, Víctor. A fabrication, a spirit conjured out of the cabinet of time. Are you going to get angry with Galván? Are you going to get annoyed because, like any good teacher, he gave you the exact tool you needed so you could decide who you wanted to be? Does that seem fair? You can hear his voice. This is a deck of cards. This is how you hold a deck of cards. This is you. This is you? That is something he never said. He didn't have to say it, it was enough for him to create a model, a mirror in which you could see yourself and say: this is who I am, I am Peter Grouse, I am going to be the finest magician in the world, the finest in the history of magic. No one understands better than you that spirits do not hide behind mirrors, but appear on their surface.

You can't say you weren't warned from the very first day, when Galván put the copy of Hoffmann's manual into your hands and asked you to read, and you read excitedly, until finally you stumbled over the Latin: *Populus vult decipi*, remember? People want to be deceived. A good motto for a magician, he told you. *Deci-piatur*. Then let us deceive them. And now you are more alone than ever. Galván is dead, Grouse is dead, and here you are. Mourning both of them. Walk, Víctor. Fulfil the predictions. Walk to your own grave. And let go of the leather case. Alicia is trying to take it so you can get out of the taxi. Next she will ask you who Peter Grouse is. It's inevitable. She heard you talking to Galván's daughter. Besides, the name is stamped into the leather. A magician, you'll say. I'll tell you about him some time. But Alicia will insist, you already know that. You will have no choice but to whisk her away to a chilly London afternoon and paint the picture of a modest, elegant pickpocket standing on a corner about to bump deliberately into a mysterious stranger who is carrying this same leather case. You will go through every incident, and when memory is not enough, or when Alicia raises doubts, you'll invent some-thing, you will do whatever is necessary to make sure Grouse does not cease to exist, because, now that you have been robbed of the blessing of innocence, it is time for someone else to take up the baton and go on believing in him. That's only fair, Víctor. Do it well, it must be convincing. Perhaps you think that Maskelyne, with his falsetto voice and his pseudo-scientific pretensions, has more right to be remembered than Grouse? What about Kellar? Does the brutish Kellar deserve more faith simply because he left a record of his travels? Which is more real, the image of your father as a cockroach or the face of Peter Grouse, appearing on the poop deck of a ship heading for America? Are you really thinking of obliterating him? Is he not as real as that wasted light with which Bacall smiles down on you each morning?

Take Alicia by the hand, lead her through as many doors and mirrors as it takes, light a candle in a garret room in London so she can see the diagrams, the screws, the tools strewn everywhere, a pig's innards, a hand moving through the air. Let her see the air, Víctor. The invisible air. That is the miracle. Listen to her, she wants to know more, wants to know what happens next. Tell her how he invented the thumb. Better still, show her. Don't worry about revealing his secrets. Explain how it works. Tell her that this is where all the disappearing silk handkerchiefs go. Millions of thumbs that these days are not made of wood but of plastic.

She will say: it's not possible. She's seen it on television and she's never understood how it was done. Tell her that this is proof that Grouse existed. More than that: that he still exists. That he is reborn every time a magician, with an innocent smile, holds up his empty hands to the audience. Linger over the details as you describe the dimly lit room where, in his later years, he used to give lessons to neophytes, to teach them the possibilities of this thumb, rhapsodise about the importance of this moment in the history of magic. And tell her that, from that point on, he never invented anything else. That from the moment he disembarked in London on his return from America he knew he had come to the end of his career as an inventor, realised that all that remained for him was the honest task of showing others how much he had learned, and charging them an appropriate fee for the privilege. It is not a bad ending. The thief becomes maestro. In doing so, you will honour both your dead.

Fire

'I'm really grateful to Víctor,' Galván's daughter says.

'It's the least he could do,' says Alicia. 'After all, it was your father who taught him . . .'

'I wasn't talking about that. Yesterday, he came to the workshop to go over the preparations and asked me if I would rent the place to him.'

'I don't understand.'

'He wants to give lessons. He said he would like to give them here. And that, if we help him, he'll bring all the old contraptions he and my father built . . .'

'The museum.'

'Exactly. You don't know what a weight off my shoulders that is. I've spent a lot of time here this past week, in this empty hall . . . I don't know how to explain it . . .'

'Don't worry. I understand, honestly I do.'

They are at one end of the hall, by the green door. Downstairs, they can hear the murmuring voices of the first guests.

'Make sure you get a good seat,' the daughter says, squeezing Alicia's hand one last time. 'It's going to be a full house.'

As the people file in, Alicia rushes to take the seat in the middle of the front row. She doesn't want to miss a thing. She is curious. She has no idea what Víctor is going to do. Several times over the past few days she offered to help him, but he declined, saying that he was not organising a show, just one trick, a small homage that would be easy to prepare. Despite this, she knows that he has spent hours every day shut away in the workshop at The King of Magic. So it can't be that easy. She scans the stage, looking for some clue, but it is completely bare. The space is barely lit and the stage and the backcloth and the sides are all black.

There is a deafening knock on the green door, then another, as if someone has arrived with an urgent message. The audience, still standing in the aisles, laughing and chatting, immediately rushes to sit down. Alicia turns round in her seat. The door is flung open and Víctor stands on the threshold. His face is deathly serious, and he waits until there is complete silence. He is dressed in black from head to toe. Recently shaved. Impeccable. Alicia cannot help but glance at his shoes. She wishes she had X-ray vision so she could see his toenails.

Víctor wanders between the seats. He has no cane. Alicia holds her breath. All it would take is for someone to have left a bag, an umbrella, lying around ... Mentally she runs through their lessons as she watches him: counting steps, hand correctly positioned in front of him, the imperceptible glide of his foot on the carpet, testing to feel where the surface changes so he will know where to turn right.

As he passes Alicia on his way to the three steps that lead up to the stage, Víctor does not pause, but stretches out his arm towards her and drops something into her lap. It is a small, weightless object. She brings it up to her face and recognises the block of wood she gave him almost two months ago so he could practise sanding. Except it is no longer a block. She quickly takes her mobile phone out of her bag, presses a key so the screen will light up and brings it close to the piece of wood. She can make out the shape of a fingernail, the wrinkles round the knuckle. It is a hollow cover. She bites her lip, takes a deep breath. She has known for days that at some point this evening, what with the stress of the previous months and the excitement of seeing Víctor up on the stage, her mixed feelings of sadness and joy at finally having reached her goal ... Well, anyway, she knew that at some point she was going to cry. She is prepared, she almost wants to cry now. She has an unopened packet of tissues in her bag. But it's too soon.

'Mario Galván died when I was forty years old,' Víctor says suddenly, standing in the middle of the stage.

There is scattered applause followed by a tense *shh* demanding silence. For Galván. For Víctor's comeback.

'Everything I know, I owe to him,' he continues. 'Everything I am. Including this.'

He brings his hand up and extends the Auzinger cane. He comes to the front of the stage and begins to pace from one side to the other. Instead of using the cane to detect the edge of the stage, he brandishes it, like someone holding up a trophy. Alicia's gaze darts from his feet to his ramrod-straight torso, from peril to poise, from the floor to the hand holding the cane. For the first time she notices the slight tan on Víctor's face and realises its significance. Though it could be make-up.

'This,' Víctor repeats, waving the cane, 'is a prosthesis which does much more than help me walk. It is a reminder of who I am, of my limits and the resources I possess to help me overcome them. Or, at least, get close to doing so.'

Alicia remembers the reviews she read before she met Víctor, how they mentioned his mastery of drama, his charisma, the power of his voice.

'I climbed these steps for the first time more than twenty years ago, walked through that green door and stepped into this room. Mario was waiting for me.' As he speaks, he moves back to the centre of the stage. 'But I didn't know he was here until he welcomed me.'

There is the rasp of a lighter, and a flickering flame appears at the end of the cane. Víctor dips the cane, pointing it towards the stage, and slowly spins around, tracing a circle which immediately erupts into flame. This is not a symbol, an illusion. It is a fire. One that quickly surrounds him, the flames coming up to his knees, threatening to lick at his clothes. Snaking, crackling, giving off a plume of black smoke. Someone behind Alicia gasps. Her fists are clenched so tightly that, although she does not realise it, she is imprinting the outline of the wooden thumb on the palm of her hand. The spotlights have gone out; the only thing now illuminating Víctor's body is the flames.

'Mario taught me that time surrounds us with a line of fire.' Calmly, as though his blindness makes it possible to ignore the flames encircling him, he points with the cane, first behind him, then in front of him. 'And although I regularly struggle to cross that line, he knew that it is impossible.'

He takes a large pace to one side, as though to step out of the circle, but the fire follows him. He starts walking quickly towards the back of the stage. Nobody, not even the professional magicians in the audience, is wondering how the trick is done, what prop makes it possible for the flames to move like this, without ever breaking the perfect circle that surrounds Víctor. They are all worried about his safety, because the flames now rise above his hips and the smoke is getting thicker.

'The future and the past encircle us,' Víctor says, still pacing the stage. 'Only the stories we tell ourselves make possible the illusion of crossing the line. Only words, in the brief instant before they fade, can carry us, carry messages from the other side of the fire. Every word that is uttered is a memory or a prediction.' By now he is at the front of the stage and the circle has become a blazing wall of flame that reaches his chest. Víctor seems unruffled. He gestures along the front row with a sweeping movement of his head as though taking his leave of them. For ten unbearable seconds, he is silent. Then he begins walking backwards, talking all the while.

'And only the present can protect us. In exchange, it insists that we keep on walking. That we carry it with us all the way to the grave.' He has stopped in the exact centre of the stage. With one last surge, the flames rise until they envelop him completely. Now, the only indication that he is still there is the sound of his voice, calm, as though none of this is happening. 'Until we disappear, consumed by the fire.'

The flames are suddenly extinguished and the spotlights come on. The stage is completely bare. Alicia blinks, as though pretending to fight back the smoke which still hangs in the air rather than the tears she has been trying to suppress ever since she realised that the end was coming, the inevitable end, Víctor's disappearance. The audience is now applauding wildly while she, her face tense, her fist clutching a hollow block of wood, imagines him in the future, hiding in the darkness of this same room, scrutinising a newly arrived student before greeting him with an instantly recognisable sound; perhaps not the rasp of a lighter, perhaps the noise of a Parker pen, click, click, preparing to pass on the power of a few words which, he hopes, will resonate, beyond the tomb, beyond the flames, in the luminous gallery where he will discover that a Monet portrait has stopped time, where he will listen intently to the whispered exchanges between Milton and Galileo, entertain those present with some humble illusion when Bach tires of playing the piano, and perhaps smile if he should hear them say: it's not possible.

References

The late 19th century is the most fascinating period in the history of magic, not simply for the dazzling audacity, importance and enduring appeal of the illusions developed during the period, but for the immense wealth of anecdotes about the people who performed those illusions. The autobiographies of Houdini and of his hero, Jean Eugène Robert-Houdin, are well known. If you are interested in the treasures of the period but do not want to spend time and money at antiquarian book auctions, you can easily find facsimile editions of Harry Kellar's *A Magician's Tour* and Hoffmann's *Modern Magic* on the internet. But no one, not even in these original sources, succeeds in describing the people and the milieu in which they moved with the skill of Jim Steinmeyer. His books – *Hiding the Elephant* (Carroll & Graf, New York, 2003) and *The Glorious Deception* (idem, 2005) – are real treasures, not only for the entertaining, rigorous and detailed technical information they provide, but also for the glimpses they afford of Steinmeyer's profound understanding of the human condition, the compulsion to invent, and the nature of deception.

The magicians in this book existed in real life, and used many of the gadgets and contraptions I attribute to them here, but I should point out that I have treated them as fictional characters; attributed to them thoughts, words and actions which are not necessarily true. For example, though Harry Kellar had a famously explosive temper, it is unthinkable that he would have been capable of the act of calculated cruelty against my good guy, Peter Grouse.

The shop, El Rey de la Magia, really is on calle Princesa in Barcelona. Established in 1881, it is one of the oldest specialist magic shops in the world and delights in the impeccable management and unfathomable wisdom of Josep Maria Martínez, magician, sage and maestro. In recent years he has also managed a museum and a theatre dedicated to magic.

The Seybert Commission also existed. The excerpts from its preliminary report are quoted verbatim.

For decades, the Egyptian Hall was the venue for every conceivable kind of magical and pseudo-scientific performance. It was housed in 171 Piccadilly, now an office block.

Acknowledgements

A maestro from my own childhood, a man named Pepe Marín, taught us to tell stories. I have always known I owe him a great debt, but have never found a means to repay it.

The hands of Ignasi Hendersson as, blindly, he plays a Bach fugue, have taught me more than any book could.

Rosa Montero, Antonia González, Juan Gabriel Vásquez, Oscar López, Yolanda Cespedosa, Víctor Pinyol, José Ovejero, Santiago del Rey and Pere Sureda were generous in their comments on the first draft of the book. Their eyes see more clearly than mine.

An angel by the name of Pílar sparked the first flame that became this novel. La Peña Diamant filled the days with wonder. Juan Arenillas gave me the indispensible Doctor Leber. At the far end of the tunnel were dazzling lights: Kirsty, Angela, Cecilia and Joao, Patrice, Carmen Pinilla, all those publishers who lit up half the world with my lies. Thanks to the team at Edhasa in Buenos Aires, I know that in my next life I want to come back as a porteño. Emma Noble performed magic in Sydney: she pointed to the heavens and produced flashes of lightning.

My mother made the miracle of silence possible month after month. Daniel Fernández waited and hoped with grace. Gloria at Agencia Balcells understood from the very beginning. Miguel Oros liquefied nicotine. The Vásquez Montoya family (and Hernán, and Soco) practised the magic of hospitality. It was in their house in La Calera that I visualised Víctor's cane for the first time.

Berta taught me to read music. I owe Elena for many unforgettable lessons. For example that 2/4 time is for walking, and 3/4 for dancing. Then came Joan Pere with a blast of air that is still keenly felt.

Josep Maria Martínez was the greatest possible magic teacher; I probably his worst pupil.

And Yolanda brought the radiant light of life.